Heaven's Gain

The Final Adventure of Harry and Paul

Paul John Hausleben

The cover photograph and all other photographs by Paul John Hausleben
Cover design by Paul John Hausleben

Published by God Bless the Keg Publishing
Somewhere, U.S.A.

ISBN: 978-0-9906979-5-4

Dedication

To: Harry M. Redmond Junior, Paul John Henson, number twenty-seven, Pastor Paul John Henson, Binky Hobnobber Henson, Rose Redmond, Renee Gorman, Ronzo, Jeff Porter, dear Mum, the old man, Mr. Redmond, Mr. Porter, Dottie, Gramps, Cocoa, Pussface the cat, James T. O'Malley, Bishop Von Houten, Senator William T. Hobnobber, Rabbi Goldberg, Howard Pailet and many others. Amazingly, there now are too many to list. Thanks for riding with me on this journey through part of my life and allowing me to bring you to life. In many ways, you have all given me a refresh on my own life. It has been a journey of joy. My hope is that this has been a journey that has touched the hearts of others as much as all of you have touched mine.

Heaven's Gain

The Final Adventure of Harry and Paul

Paul John Hausleben

Contents

Acknowledgements

Thank you, as always, to Mr. Harry M. Rogers Junior and to my family and friends. Thank you to everyone who read these many adventures, told me how much they have enjoyed them, and how much they meant to each of you. I cannot individually thank you all, but please know that your kind words have touched my heart and been a wonderful part of my life.

"Our loss here on Earth is simply Heaven's gain."

Paul John Hausleben

01 October 2016

Preface from the Author

It is finally time to end the many adventures of Harry and Paul.

Therefore, here we are at the end of the line.

It is time to bring Harry and Paul to a conclusion.

I do so, not because I harbor any great animosity towards the characters, or the stories, or I am bored with them. I also do not want to hurl one of them or both of them to their grisly death, as did Sir Arthur Conan Doyle with Sherlock Holmes when he could no longer stand the character. Although, I must say that Paul John Henson can get on my nerves quite often.

No, instead, I have resisted that particular urge. I simply feel as if there has to be a beginning to the adventures as well as an end. Just as it is in life.

These many adventures and chronicles have been a joy to write, a journey of emotions, both happy and sad, and humor-filled too. I must say that Harry and Paul have been, and are, as if they are two old friends to me. Apparently, according to what many readers convey when they speak or write to me, many readers feel as if they are old friends to them too.

They have comforted me on long nights of writing, made me laugh at their wild antics, made me dream of the glorious times of old, made me jealous of their gorgeous women and forced me to admire their many adventures and amazing friendship. They have been companions to me in lonely hotel rooms, tapping away on my laptop during sleepless nights on the road. Harry, Paul, and the extensive cast of characters, kept me company on the cold, winter nights and during lonely holidays spent alone. Somehow, they all sat next to me and watched over my shoulder while I created their adventures during hot, sticky days alone in my writing command center with a fan whirling about in a futile effort to keep me cool. I guess that it is time to admit that the two characters are a part of me as I am a part of them too. There is little doubt that in some manner that I will profoundly miss them.

When I long ago, wrote the original, three novellas contained in *The Time Bomb in The Cupboard and Other Adventures of Harry and Paul,* and then resurrected them one day out of sheer boredom, (not out of inspiration of any means) I had no idea the journey that I was about to begin in my life. Initially, it was to be a spoof, a way to pass the time, a fun and unique idea. Miraculously, readers actually enjoyed the stories and connected with the two characters. Then, in a deep, dark, time in my life, when I felt a sudden urge to write in order to purge some pain from my soul, along came, *The Night Always Comes* and then *Reunion* and well, onward we typed and typed.

Now, with *Heaven's Gain,* we end it all.

Before all the fans of these two characters and the other characters, flood me with protests, I will admit that there remains in existence, many short stories and a number of draft novels of *The Adventures of Harry and Paul* that I wrote here and there, and they fill in many gaps of the timelines of their lives.

Therefore, hold on to your keyboards before you type because, I am not saying that these two pineapples and their supporting cast will not once again appear in pages of some collection somewhere, but with this novel, we now have a beginning and an end.

There also exists some material, which contains some solo adventures of the various incarnations of Paul John

Henson. Within the story vault, there are even some solo adventures of some of the other characters too.

Who knows what the future will bring?

Right now, there are some new ideas that I want to explore and some new characters that are itching to jump out of my eccentric mind and into some pages.

Here we are and I thank you the reader, as well as in a strange and profound manner, I thank Harry and Paul too. It has been a great ride, a wonderful time in my life and just as Harry M. Redmond Junior always tells us, once more, let's jump into the pages of this book, begin a final ride together and see where it all takes us. Who knows? As much as it pains me to admit, they are very cool guys to hang around with in life.

Thank you, dear reader, for taking the time out of your life to sit around the old kitchen table at 20 John Street and share a few beers and lots of laughs with Ronzo, Mr. Redmond, the old man, the Big Spike and the rest of the gang. In addition, thank you for sharing your own emotions and thoughts while taking the time to sit on the front steps of 182 Belmont Avenue with the endless dreamer, Paul John Henson. Together, we all sat and listened as he rambled on with his narratives of these adventures, and we delved into his own thoughts while we watched his world go by.

Thank you for standing fearlessly with number twenty-seven as he faced a blazing slap shot from the point and he made a last second save in the hockey goal. We all knew that all the time while he played, he actually was trying without success, to remain hidden from the world and escape his pain while hiding under his transparent disguise, known as his faithful, old, goalie mask.

Perhaps, best of all, thank you for laughing and celebrating, while enjoying music blaring from the eight-track tape deck, as we all jumped in Harry M. Redmond Junior's sports car and took a summer's evening cruise for "twigeons" and adventure.

I imagine hanging out with them has been quite a bit of fun. Together, we laughed, cried, loved, grieved, and in the end, we all rode the circle of life.

It is my hope and sincere wish that you enjoy this book and all the adventures as much as I have enjoyed the experience of writing them.

Paul John Hausleben

01 October 2016

Prologue

A long-haired boy of about ten years of age or thereabouts tore around the corner of Belmont Avenue and John Street in Haledon, New Jersey. He was running fast and hard—the boy could run fast and hard.

Even at this young age, it was easy to tell that he was a great athlete.

As he ran by an old house with the number 20 proudly mounted on the front door, another ten-year-old boy, who was sitting on the steps of the house with a football in his hands and with a small puppy that sat by his side, called out to the running boy, "Hey! Where ya goin'?"

The long-haired boy stopped in his tracks and pushed his longhair back from his face.

When he caught his breath, he smiled and answered, "Oh, hello, there. I am going over to my buddy, Jeff Porter's house. He just moved into the neighborhood here."

The boy on the steps smiled, nodded and stood up from the steps. He walked down the steps to meet the long-haired boy. The boy's puppy followed him and while he walked, he threw the football up and down in his hands and caught it.

"You live over on Belmont Avenue. Right? In the big house, next to the old, shitty restaurant. Right?"

"Yes. That is correct. I live at 182 Belmont Avenue. I am Paul John Henson. I have seen you around. Your name is Harry, right?"

The boy with the football nodded and tossed the football

to Paul John Henson, who caught it and threw it back to him.

"Yup, that's me! Harry M. Redmond Junior. I am world famous, ya know! Say, do you want to get Jeff and maybe hang out wid me today? Maybe we can be friends!"

"Sure, sure, sure, that would be cool. I would like that. Let's go get Jeff and we can toss the football around."

Harry smiled, opened the gate to his house and as the pup followed them, Harry put his arm around Paul and he said, "Man, ya really tall and strong too. Ya got real long hair and look kinda like a hippie kid. Are ya a hippie kid or maybe just an old lady of some kind? Ya awfully polite."

"I don't know. Maybe."

"Cool, I like you, Paul. Ya really cool and calm too. Man, ya can run fast! Ya, like some kinda deer. It's gonna be fun to hang out and to have a friend."

"Yes, it will be. Thank you. Say, what is your dog's name? He is very handsome." The little pup jumped up on Paul while Paul greeted the little dog.

"Handsome? Man, ya might be an old lady. Ya use such big and weird-ass words. Ah man, that's just, Cocoa. He is just a little pup, but already, he is the world's smartest dog. I just got him a few weeks ago, from some guy that my old man works with over in his shop. His dog had pups, and Cocoa is one of 'em. Let me tell you about him. . .."

As the two boys and the little pup walked to meet their other friend, the sun suddenly broke out of what had been until now, a cloudy, dark, and overcast sky. Rays of golden sunlight beamed down onto the old city neighborhood, and the urban grit and hardness of the old neighborhood suddenly glowed in a profound beauty, with golden rays sent straight down from Heaven to illuminate the old neighborhood.

In the backyard of the old house located at 20 John Street, it seemed as if there were soft whispers in the air as the sunlight beamed down everywhere. Whispers, which floated in and amongst the rays of sunlight, as the beams of sunlight danced upon the ground and chased into every corner of the yard. Were these the whispers of ghosts, or were these actually the whispers of angels from Heaven? Angels, which for some reason arrived on the golden rays that floated around the yard and the house.

If you listened carefully to the whispers, as the murmurs seemed to dance in the air, you could hear that they all told stories. Stories told upon a backdrop of their strummed harps while they sang their glorious songs in the air. Songs, which sounded as if they were gentle whispers in the wind, but in actuality, they all whispered tales of miraculous, old adventures.

Heaven's Gain

Chapter One

When All Your Diamonds Turn to Dust

Looking back on all of this, it almost seems as if it is all a blur. The best analogy that I can use is that of an old-fashioned movie newsreel, flipping frames quickly across the screen. You know the type of newsreels that I am trying to describe. The old type of films as they used to play in movie houses of long ago. The black and white images are of poor quality. They are somewhat hazy; there are lines that crisscross the images haphazardly across the screen. The frames quickly flip by and then suddenly, it ends, and you hear the sound of the film slapping along the reels of the projector. A blur which ends suddenly, abruptly and in the case of my newsreel, tragically.

A blur.

Dear reader, as has been the case with all the adventures and chronicles, of which I have shared with you over the years, I cannot relate this story, unless I begin where it started. During the writing of this narrative, it might be too painful or too complex, and I am not skilled enough as a writer to convey some of what happened with the proper words to capture the emotions. I might write those parts, or I might just skip over them. We shall see. . ..

Here is where it begins, a revolting ride of suffering and loss and a story of pain. Most of the horrid in-depth details, I will skate over the top of, because even now, they are too painful to detail or write.

I tried hard to prepare myself for the aftermath, the onslaught, the recovery time. At one time, after a night of incredible pain and gut-wrenching anguish, I proudly pronounced myself healed. Healed, as much as Harry was, on that hillside so long ago, when he collapsed in front of his wife's grave and poured his soul out to all of us and to Heaven too. The parallels in our lives now provide both Harry and me, with more than just pause. We have now both wept together while suffering a common pain while holding each other in our arms.

I was only fooling myself that I healed.

As I write this long story, you will see dear reader that the healing comes much later in my life and in the story. Healing from grief and pain is one of the circles of this life that we all will at one time start, must journey on, and then finally complete. Only then will the healing be complete. We do not heal within one night or a single event. It is a process. A long, long process.

While I sit here and try to begin to write this long story, then I must make it clear that when this adventure began, I was a depressed and devastated man. Dear reader, nothing great or wonderful can come out of this story, unless I make that point very clear. At the beginning of this tale, I harbored more pain and more animosities than I could ever convey. I was at that time, in addition to the depression and devastation, an angry man.

Now that I have conveyed that point, let me begin to unravel this story. . ..

Time and experience had taught me that trying to fool my own mind was indeed a hopeless endeavor. When you have diamonds in your hands and the diamonds all suddenly turn to dust, then you are at a loss for words. You are void of your emotions; it feels as if all of your energy and thoughts have left your mind and body. I now knew how Harry felt when Sky Blu passed away. I thought that at one time, I could understand and relate to his immense grief and pain, but I now realize that at that time, I could only imagine. It is a pain and emptiness, which is unimaginable. You cannot feel it, control it, or pretend to understand it, unless you experience it firsthand.

Even then, it is beyond words.

Yet, here I try a vain and somewhat hapless attempt to capture it with words.

Now, I knew it firsthand.

After all of this has now occurred, and eight months or thereabouts, passed on, I now have found the courage and strength to try to go back to my writing. I write in a desperate attempt to recover what remains of my soul and of my life, and to purge my soul of the pain. Writing also seems to assist me with self-examination of my faith.

Here I was, a man who made a part of his life's work to promote God, the Gospel, and to be an advocate for the belief and power of the Holy Trinity. I am a bishop in the Lutheran Church, a leader, and even though I never felt entirely comfortable in this position, I felt as if I did the best job that I could do. The popular opinion is that I do an outstanding job, but I am not so sure that is an accurate description of my performance. Before this current position, when I served as a pastor of a large congregation, I was very successful in guiding and leading my parishioners. Now, in contrast to the bishop position, I always felt as if I was comfortable in the role of a pastor and that I did do a fine job there. While beginning this story, I will utilize a very apathetic summary of my pastoral career with one word. Whatever! It is what it is, and in the big picture, it no longer matters to me.

For me, it is all a blur and a faint memory. Now, please do not misunderstand me. I retain my faith. I still, despite the anguish, for some reason, believe. In fact, my faith in God and the fact that there exists a plan for all of our lives is even stronger, and that fact bothers me more than any other fact. I still believe in God and all the rest of the associated beliefs, but I no longer *accept* his plan for me.

Pastor Paul John Henson officially rebelled. There, I said it and it made me feel well to do so!

I had no other choice, but to be angry at God's plan for my life. I still honor God in my heart, but much the same as Abraham did, I will obey and trust but not agree. I do not find anywhere in scripture or in my heart where I must agree with God. Perhaps, know the saving grace, worship it and hold it in my heart, thank him, for sending Jesus to cleanse my soul, but no damn way, do I agree with what he planned for my family and for me.

How the hell could I?

God called me to do my work, and I felt as if I held up my end of the bargain! Whatever the deal actually was. . ..

Yet, as this story unfolds, I will write it all down, in the complete range of emotions that I felt from the beginning to how I feel at the end.

In the beginning, it was pure torment that I felt.

When the police came to the front door of our house, then I knew it was not going to be good news. My wife, Binky, and I shared a profound connection, a connection that our souls were in touch with each other all the time. Even when we were apart, we felt it and shortly after she left for running some routine daily errands; I felt the strong power deep in my soul that something was seriously wrong. The police officers stood in our doorway. They told me the horrific news, and I held onto my soul. My soul tried to escape my body. It took all my strength to capture it as it lifted out of my body and tried hard to leave this world.

"Jesus wept."

I often feel as if those are the only two words that this sorry and very sad world ever requires. Those words reverberated in my mind when the officer tried to speak to me and tell me that my beloved wife had left this world, and my arms, to reside forever in the open arms of Jesus.

Jesus wept, therefore, so did Pastor Paul John Henson.

"Bishop Henson. There has been a terrible car accident, and it is with a profound and deep regret. . .."

The officer stumbled over the words. He choked on the blood of Jesus too. Honestly, so did Pastor Paul John Henson.

It was then that the wretched newsreels started flipping through my mind.

Endlessly.

I could not at this time stop them in my mind. Eventually, when the entire plan unfolded, they stopped. However, right at this moment, I swear to the fact that everything that Binky and I ever shared in our lives together, flipped through my mind. Every adventure, every kiss, every passionate night of making love, the touch of her hands on my chest, the taste of her lips, every word that we ever spoke. The smell of her hair, her smile, her voice, the sounds of her screaming out in anguish while giving birth to our children, every laugh, every cry and every smile.

I swear that I experienced it all. Then, and some more too. It was then that my anger with God and his plan surfaced.

"You will need to go to this address and claim and identify your wife's body. We are so deeply sorry, Bishop Henson. So . . . sorry."

Those words from the police officer plunged a hole into my heart and my mind. An echo of pain, which you cannot describe. I will try not to dwell, dear reader. I beg you to use your imagination and pray that you never have to experience any such thing.

I put my collar and black suit on for what I thought was the last time.

Harry accompanied me to the morgue to identify Binky's body. As I had stood with him, then he stood with me. He told me that I did not have to go in there. Harry told me that he would do it for me. I would never allow him to perform that mission alone. It was up to me, and one thing that Paul John Henson could easily say that he stood for in his sad example of a life, was that he was not afraid of jackshit. Harry held my hand when we walked into the room together. Our tears fell like rain and our bodies trembled, as we both collapsed together on the floor at the sight in front of our eyes.

At first, I held his soul and then we held each other's souls.

When I stood in front of and identified the body of the most precious and beautiful wife whoever walked this Earth, and I acknowledged the body to be that of Binky Henson, the world was not even dark, it was black. It was void of all life.

I heard the doctor in charge, mutter, "Bishop Henson, I must inform you that I have to perform a State of New Jersey, mandated autopsy to determine the cause of death. I will need you to sign this form."

It was then that I was most fortunate to have the immense power of Harry M. Redmond Junior with me. Dear reader, there was no other person on this Earth, no power on this planet, and no force, other than Harry M. Redmond Junior, who could have had the power to control me at this point. The Archangel Michael would have had his hands full trying to overpower Pastor Paul John Henson. I turned into a grief-stricken monster. When I heard his words, I picked the doctor up by reaching under the poor, shocked chap's armpits, carried him with his feet dangling in the air and ran him forcibly into the wall.

I screamed at him, "Do not dare touch her! If you desecrate her body with your scalpel, then I guarantee that I will unleash all the power of Heaven upon you. There will be no place on this Earth that you will be able to hide. The angels of God, all the Lutheran saints of Heaven and then some, will join me and we will seek you out and make you sorry that you ever existed. I will tear you and this office apart and curse you forever!"

A police officer rushed into the room, medical assistants ran in and they all begged me to release him. I remained locked on, shaking the poor doctor by his armpits, as I still held his feet a foot off the floor.

"My wife's body will be cremated tomorrow, and in a Lutheran service, her ashes scattered, as she wished, on the grounds of Reunion Lutheran Church. Damn well, agree with me now, or I will snap your neck like a twig and I gladly will die with my beloved wife."

The police officer rushed in and Harry intervened.

Harry held my arms and tried to pry me off the doctor.

"Paul, let him go. Please, Paul, let him go. No one will touch Binky. They will not touch her. Let him down, Paul. Please stop, I beg you, my brother, to let him go. You do not know, or ever have realized, how powerful you actually are. Heaven has heard your pleas and the saints all know of your suffering. Please, Paul. Do not invoke that power. No one here, other than me, truly understands the power, of which you can unleash. No one will touch her. I stand with you, Paul. We both will die first. We will die together."

I looked at Harry, recovered my senses, nodded to indicate that I understood and let the doctor free.

I swept my long hair out of my eyes and while letting the doctor go, I softly mumbled, "I am sorry, doctor. Very sorry."

The doctor nodded, placed his hand upon my shoulder and with tears running down his face he told me, "There will be no autopsy, Bishop Henson. I assure you. None. We all feel your intense grief, we certainly do. I feel as if I must reveal to you that your beloved wife felt nothing. As a medical doctor, please take comfort in that from my observations. Please, accept my deepest condolences and my apology at the suggestion of any such practice of an autopsy. We will release the body to the custody of the Lutheran Church, according to your wishes."

I bowed my head, my hands were trembling, sweat ran down my neck and my face, as Harry held me tightly. The doctor and the police officer both reached out their hands for me to shake them. I gradually regained control, reached out my hand, and gently shook their hands in acknowledgment of their forgiveness, kindness and understanding.

Finally, I gathered the strength that I needed to do my job as a husband as well as a man of God, "Thank you. Now, if you can all forgive me for my uncontrolled outburst, please let us gather in, hold hands and pray."

Everyone in the room did so, and as all of us rained tears down upon the cold, stark floor of the morgue, I somehow mustered enough strength to continue to speak. I bowed my head, apologized again and gathered everyone in the room around the table which held my wife's now cold, lifeless body.

"Lord, please, forgive me. I do not understand this, nor pretend to agree with your plan. I will retire from your service and unless you convince me otherwise, I will do my best to disagree with your plan for my life after this prayer. I will cry tears of never-ending loss at this wretched event, yet, I know that this all happened for a reason. I suspect that you felt as if you needed Binky in your kingdom. So be it. Jesus wept, and so do we. I despise and curse this moment more than any other moment in my life, yet, I know that our loss here on Earth is truly Heaven's gain. In Jesus' name, we pray. Amen."

When I left that wretched place, I tore the pastoral collar off my shirt, tossed it aside, and at that point, I swore that I would never wear it again.

The next day, I wrote, emailed, and mailed a follow-up letter to the Director of the Northeast District Governing

Board of our synod, immediately requesting a bereavement leave of absence. I also had the option of using my accumulated three months of vacation time. I had a lot of time accumulated, because for many years, I was a fool who worked endlessly and was too stupid to realize how short and precious life really is.

In a roundabout and unusual manner, I was so glad that all of our relatives and many of our friends had already left this world. They would not have to endure this horrid moment. They were all gone off to their rewards. Binky's parents, my parents, Ronzo, Linda, George, Patty, Mr. Redmond, and Bishop Von Houten. All of them gone to where Binky now joined them all in a joyous reunion.

We even lost Binky's brother early in his life. My beloved brother-in-law, Tinky Hobnobber, lost a hard-fought struggle with cancer. His wife, Betty Anne, and their two daughters were grief stricken, and they fled to start a new life on the west coast. It was very strange how so many of our friends and relatives left this Earth so early, all to be saints in Heaven. Now only my dear sister and her family, and Harry, Rose, Blue and our children, remained in our immediate family to endure this wretched pain.

It was our devastating loss, but it was Heaven's gain.

That brings me to explain our family. Life is always full of twists and turns. I always found that it was very ironic that our son, Paul William, had grown up with Harry and Rose's daughter, Blue Cloud, and they played together since they were small children, but as they grew older, they fell in love. Paul William is five years older than Blue Cloud is, but that is nothing in the timeline of romance. Age is just a measuring stick. In retrospect, I guess that it was inevitable for them to fall in love. Blue Cloud is a stunning woman and Paul William, is a tall, intelligent and handsome man. Blue Cloud shared much with the appearance of her gorgeous mother, dark hair, captivating dark eyes, perfect facial features, perfect figure, and a dazzling smile.

Blue Cloud is remarkable. . ..

Above all, Blue Cloud is intelligent, impeccable in her qualities; just the manner in which she carried herself captivated everyone. In addition, we did know her parents quite well.

They married, and an immeasurable bond joined our families, which in looking back, was more than just profound.

It was God's plan. That part of the plan, unlike other parts, I gladly accepted. They were deeply in love, and most likely had been in love forever. Given the history of Blue's birth, her illness as a baby, and all the miracles surrounding that incident, then I knew this was the culmination of their destiny together.

Our daughter, Heather Sarah, followed in her grandfather's example and she became an attorney in her own private practice. Along with a host of other clients, Heather Sarah handled all of our family's investments, legal and business matters, as well as that of Harry's extensive empire. While attending an undergrad university in Florida, Heather Sarah met a young man, who also became an attorney, they married, and they now lived in Florida. We had one grandchild. Heather Sarah and Ian had a precious little girl named Sarah. They too seemed to be happy. At least, appearance-wise, they seemed to be happy.

Both of our children were only just beginning in their young lives. It made a horrible situation even more tragic. They were forming their lives, striking out on their own, and now it all came crashing down. I wondered, hoped, and even prayed that the children would recover emotionally.

Perhaps they would or then again, perhaps. . ..

Reverend Charles T. Braun Junior, the Senior Pastor of Reunion Lutheran Church, performed the funeral service for my beloved Binky. Heather Sarah, Paul William and I held the vase, and together, we spread Binky's ashes out upon the rose shrubs that she had planted in the rear of the parsonage. We always loved that house, the grounds, the natural beauty of the setting of Reunion Lutheran Church, and I think that it was here that we were the happiest in our lives. All of us. Each of us kept some of Binky's ashes and we poured them into tiny golden urns, which I had made into necklaces. We could wear them if we wanted to wear them. The children chose to place the golden urns in a safe place, but I often wore my golden urn around my neck.

The day of the funeral was a beautiful day and the sunset that day was just as I expected that it would be, with magnificent hues of blues, reds, oranges and a touch of gold. A gold, which I could not ever begin to describe or begin to understand, but I knew that it was a ray of love sent down from Heaven. Love sent straight from Binky's heart to all of us. It represented joyful noises, which echoed all the way to Heaven and beyond.

Heaven's gain.

I read the police report amongst a drowning of tears. No one was to blame; it was a malfunction of a large truck's brakes. Just a terrible accident, and my wife was in the wrong place at the wrong time type of situation. It was little consolation, yet I held no human responsible. There would be no silly lawsuits; money means nothing to me. There is no compensation for the loss of a loved one's life. I will lay no blame here on Earth. Instead, my pain laid the blame squarely on Heaven.

Now, all my diamonds had turned to dust, and they left me with nothing. I should not say that because I did possess some things. Yes, in every corner of my life, misery, loneliness and despair followed me. All those words that I had preached over the years seemed as if they had no meaning and were the foolish, rambling words of an idiot. I felt stripped naked and exposed. My soul tore open, my heart was now empty of feeling, and I felt as if the compassion of Heaven and promises of God were empty and without fact.

When God took Sky Blu, so early in her life from Harry and the rest of the world, it changed me and I accepted it and understood. In fact, the explanation led me to where I became an advocate for the plan, for the Gospel, for the belief. This plan, to take my beloved wife from our children, from me, and from the rest of the world, well, I was not going to accept this one.

I felt no shame as I carefully packed away my clerical garb, my Bible, my volumes and pages and pages of religious writings, my sermons, all of it was now a fraud. It was a part of me that I happily packed away in dusty boxes and tucked away in dark corners of my life. I needed time to think, time away to decide if I would serve again and return to my position as a bishop or a pastor. During my grieving time, I felt as if by packing away the signs of my position, it would erase it from my mind and from my heart, until such a time, where I could decide where I now was within God's plan. Right now, in my mind, I felt if I never wore my collar again, then it would be too soon, if I ever read another Bible verse, then I would be surprised and if I ever thought of anything other than questioning God for my life, then I would be shocked.

I ignored the telephone calls and pleas from more people than I ever wanted to count, calling with their endless condolences. I did not want to speak to anyone right now and just wanted to be alone.

Right now, nothing was important, I did not care, did not agree, and felt as if life was worthless. All I knew was one thing: that my beloved wife was gone. Taken from my life in a flash, and my anger and our children's heartbreak, shook the ground and erupted in the Heavens. God could not provide a valid enough explanation, nor did I even care to listen hard enough to hear it. Harry, Rose, our children, my sister, my fellow pastors, no one, could console me. There were no words to convey the pain, and there was no longer any meaning to anything.

Now, dear reader, while I sit here at this desk, in my office and look back on it all, I know that in many ways; I was correct and in many ways; I was incorrect too. For me, the release of all of my emotions slowly evolved over a long period. It started in some manner when I was a young man. Reading and writing endlessly. Releasing my dreams, creating endless characters and detailing all of what I observed. Then when I realized the power of words and that my life was anything but ordinary, I felt as if someone had to detail and record some of the many adventures of Harry and Paul, and so I did. I wrote them down, laced with facts, embellished here and there, some humorous, some sad, some upbeat and some of it, very emotional, but I wrote them all down. Then, for some reason as a young man, I stopped writing. Life was in the way. My writing sputtered, and it stopped. However, the words and the characters remained inside of me.

Now that all I had was pain, it all returned to me in a rush, in a strong flow, and it allowed me to relive the happy times, and all we had experienced. Whenever I wrote, I felt Binky's warm touch on my arm; I heard her voice, her laugh, her gentle advice and her quirky, but loving ways. I felt her sweet kisses and the smell of her hair and her skin and her cries of passion on long nights that we shared. In some ways, it was torture to release it from my soul, but it allowed me to have her next to me, for her still to remain within me, and me with her. Binky will never leave me. . ..

I heard once again, the voices of Mr. Redmond, Mr. Porter, my dear Mum, and the old man. The laughter of the wonderful, and in many ways, immortal, Ronzo Boatmann and the golden singing and speaking voice of Linda. I heard the deep, strong voice of my grandfather as he lent me some more of his amazing wisdom on the front steps of 182 Belmont Avenue.

Gramps started a sentence with his usual smile and his gentle English-accent, "Paulie Boy. . .."

All of them returned and they will live forever more in these pages, in these words, and mostly in the memories of all of us. I would never allow them to escape. Not ever. I promise.

Yet, in and amongst the rubbles of which had become my life, one event rose above all of it. It was a faint memory of another difficult time in my life. A time, which until about ten or so years ago, I had buried, and then banished from my mind forever. When I recalled it, the memories caused me pain, and then ultimately, a wonderful rebirth, when I accepted my past. I regained parts of me, which I had lost along the way, and my beloved Binky stood by me, as she always did, while I struggled to regain my spirit and accept and understand parts of my past. Once I did so, then our marriage was never happier, and our lives were full of joy. Binky and I traveled and vacationed to all the places we always wished to visit, I worked less, we enjoyed nights out on the town, dinner, dancing, music concerts, art festivals and most of all—we regained all of our nights of long passion.

Out of that memory, out of that magnificent rebirth, some words that Harry told me, when I was feeling about as awful as I ever had in my life, now echoed in my head.

I heard Harry's voice telling me, "Just wanna say, she might have broken your heart, but ain't no one or nuthin' in this entire world, who can ever break number twenty-seven's spirit. Your spirit is still alive and above all, ya still are the world famous, number, twenty-seven. Powerful and fearless. Ya always will be. . .."

Yes, Harry, nothing will break my spirit. You are and were, correct. I promise, and above all, I owed that to

Binky. Those words, combined with Harry and my family's belief in me, allowed me to rise above all of this and heal.

In the aftermath of despair, I turned to the only solace of which I knew. No, that was not correct, because there were two things in my life that provided solace. Since I felt as if God abandoned me, I no longer agreed with God's plan for my life, and my beloved Binky was now gone, I knew that I had two things that provided me with some comfort.

One would be the words that I placed upon paper, and the other was a hockey game.

Chapter Two

You Have to Start Where You Began

Now that you know the beginning of this adventure and my deepest thoughts regarding the same, here we go, dear reader, together on this journey and I will try to relate to you how this all occurred. I will leave it all out here on these pages and I do so in hopes that I can then stop the newsreels in my mind. Once I do so, then I will leave you with one last vision.

"Dear Father . . . Blue, Harry and Rose and my sister, are now very worried about you. Dear Mother would not want this. She must be looking down at you and be rather surprised at your broken spirit. For years, you pulled people out of grief and despair with your words, power and inspiration, and now, here you sit, day-after-day, hour-after-hour at this desk."

Our son, Paul William Henson, had stopped by our house early in the evening to lecture me and to check on me. Harry had been by just a few days ago, and the big guy told me almost the same bullshit words. I suspected the two of them were comparing notes and teaming up on me now.

I looked up from my desk and put my hands on top of my head. I didn't really want to discuss this all over again. I reached down in a desk drawer, pulled out a hair tie, and tied my long hair behind my head. Once or twice, I almost grabbed a razor and shaved all this silly hair off my head. Somehow, Binky stopped me from doing so. I have no words or reason to explain why, other than she whispered in my ear not to do it. It was symbolic. As much as it all was a pain-in-the-ass to deal with all these long locks, and it was a look from a bygone era, it still felt good. I kept my beard and facial hair too, because once you are an old hippie, then you remain forever, an old hippie. Oh well.

"I am writing, Paul William. I told your father-in-law that yesterday and I will tell you the same thing today. In fact, it was what I told Heather Sarah last night when she called. I cannot write when people keep coming by to check on me every day. It interrupts my flow. You know how the flow is important to me. It always has been."

"Oh yeah? Now, that is pure bullshit. What are you writing? You have not put out any new material in forever and a little bit more. Mother passed away quite a bit ago, and all I ever see on your laptop is a file open to the first chapter of some story or some book that never progresses beyond that first page. You, long since, have had your contract voided with the publisher for not fulfilling the requirements for new material. Damn sure are tons of empty beer bottles in the recycling bucket though."

Now, I stood up, waved my hands at our son and walked over to the window of the office. I put my hands in my pockets and stared out the window. I could feel Paul William studying me from where he sat in the chair opposite the desk.

"So, now you go through my trash too, eh?" I asked him without having the courage to face him; instead, I kept my back to our son.

He did not answer me, and I turned around to look at him and gauge his reaction. Paul William stood up from the chair. He walked over to my desk, stood behind it and leaned in to read the screen of my laptop.

"Okay, now. Yes, indeed, chapter one. Some sparse words on a page. Eleven sentences, eh? Same bloody thing that was on the screen last week."

I now faced him and shrugged my shoulders. I did not

know exactly how to answer him, so I decided to answer him with the truth.

"Sometimes, it is not too easy to write. It is more difficult than what you think it is. Words just do not magically materialize in my head any longer. I have to work hard to find them."

"Not true, Dad. Remember that I write too."

"Different. You are a sports writer, Paul William. You do not write fiction, novels, or shorts. You write about facts and events. What I do now, it is not easy."

"Not for you. I would watch you pump out pages of material without blinking an eye. Look, please stop. You have to stop this, Dad."

"Why? Stop what?"

"Stop the slinging of bullshit. That is what you need to stop. You cannot fool us. Most of all, you cannot fool yourself. If you are going to write, then you will write. All we see is that you have abandoned God, we all see you drinking too much, and not eating, sleeping, or taking care of yourself. I see very little writing or recovery from your grieving occurring. You do not speak to anyone, return phone calls, you never leave this house unless you need more beer and you have become a recluse. Rose sobbed her eyes out yesterday. It took Blue Cloud, hours and hours to calm her down. Blue reported that her mother's entire body trembled in anguish. Rose said you would not return her calls. She said that she must have left you twenty phone messages, sent multiple texts, and that you would not return them. Rose said that she even came over here yesterday and banged on the door, begging you to open the door so she could check on you. You would not open the door, even for Rose! Is that true? Did you really do such a wretched thing to my wonderful mother-in-law? What the hell is with that? You love, Rose. You two, are closer than anyone else is in the entire world. I think even more than you are with your children and even with Harry. Shit!

You need to get it together! This is bullshit now."

I vaguely recalled the incident from within my drunken haze of a bender from yesterday, and now, I felt horrible about my behavior.

I admitted that it was true to our son, "Yes, it is true. What I recall of the day. Honestly, it was a rough day. I was in no condition to see Rose. I did not want her to see me as I was. I was drunk as hell. Blasted. Bad day. Very bad day and I feel horrible that I did that to Rose. She is amazing and I love her dearly. I will call and apologize. I apologize to you, to Blue, and to Harry too."

Paul William studied me for a few seconds and for the first time in my life, I saw our son appear as if he was disgusted with me. I could not blame him. Rose was a wonderful human being who was rare and precious. I was disgusted with myself for treating her as I did. Rose was very special to me, and she did not deserve such terrible treatment. I was ashamed beyond words for hurting her.

Paul William shook his head and his tone changed a little because it seemed that he sensed my sincerity in my sorrow over my behavior.

"Okay, well, I accept the apologies on their behalf, but you better call Rose soon and apologize. Never thought that I would see my powerful and wonderful father become a man who wallowed in his own self-sorrow. You always attacked adversity and never allowed it to defeat you."

"Okay, thank you for the acceptance of my apologies, Paul William. I will call Rose. However, let us go back a bit and clear something up, which you said before. Correction, I have not abandoned God. I have simply taken a three-month leave for bereavement while I sort this all out. After all of my years of hardly taking a bloody day off, then you would think I deserved it, and you would be happy to see me away from the office for a bit while I put my head back on straight."

"Well, yes, I understand that, but it is just the manner in which you are grieving that has us concerned. It is more as if you are shattered apart. We have never seen you like this."

I put my hands on my desk and tried hard not to lose my temper with our son. I folded my hands, looked him in the eye, and said, "Yes, I guess not. It is the first damn time that God took my wife from me and sent her to Heaven! Your mother! Do you think this is friggin' fun? What the hell? Right now, I am pissed. God abandoned me, and us, and changed the game plan too many times for me. I disagree with God's plan, and I have rebelled, to the point where I need to rethink if I even want to promote the plan or preach the Gospel . . . but I still love God. Why, I do not know, but I do. God exhausted me with all these wretched twists and turns."

"Okay, I get it, but you know what? I say, whatever and however, you want to sort it out in your mind, or justify all of this, then go ahead and frame it however, you please. All that I see is defeat, and that is not my father. He never gives up. Ever, even with something as disgusting and horrible as this. Even this."

I felt the need to focus upon my writing, or lack thereof, so I pointed at my laptop open and sitting idle on my desk and told Paul William, "By the way, I do not need to worry about deadlines, Paul William. We will self-publish material from now on and to hell with any deadlines. I write, when I want to, or have something to say, and will continue to write until I have nothing left to say. It is not as if we need money. I am not writing for money, so I couldn't give a damn about publishers dropping me. In fact, Harry told me a few weeks ago that he wanted to open his own publishing company with us. He wants all of us to be partners."

Our son did not react to my statement, and he stared at me. I felt as if another change of subject was in order, because he was correct and right now, my writing focus was poor and it was not very ambitious. Instead, I whipped up another excuse.

"Look around here. Bloody big house for one washed up old goalie, and broken-down pastor, slash shitty writer to live in."

"Then, let's sell the house. I agree, you do not need all of this room. It is a bloody mansion, and all you do is live in your office, drink beer and sleep in your chair. You need an apartment or a townhouse. Heather Sarah wanted you to sell it a week after Mother left us. You refused, and just managed to piss my sister off more with you trying to do everything on your own. Time to realize that you do not have to be alone. You are a goalie, with a team in front of you. Time to cut the pity party and strap on your old mask once more. Harry is correct, twenty-seven never quits, and I think that is really, why everyone is so worried. This is not the man we all know and love."

I walked over and slumped down in the same chair, of which our son had just abandoned. It was a special chair, given to me by a special person, a very long time ago. The chair felt good. I had not sat in this chair in a long time, and rather than remain slumped in it, I wiggled my ass deeper into the seat and I sat up straighter.

"My father-in-law was very upset last night, and I caught him sobbing when Blue and I stopped to take them out for dinner. He told me he heard about how it went down with Rose and that he never believed that anything could break twenty-seven's spirit. Ever. He told both of us that he felt even this horrible loss would not be able to break you. And he is afraid that it has. It was horrible, because when Rose spotted Harry so upset, she started crying once again. Off she went, sobbing uncontrollably, and she told me that you were not the same person. She is frightened and concerned for your mental health and your physical health too."

Paul William walked over and he placed his hand on my shoulder and squeezed it hard.

"My father-in-law told me last night that he told you once, many years ago, when you went through some tough times that . . . hmm . . . I am used to recalling athlete's words from interviews. I hope I get this correct, there ain't no one or nuthin' in this entire world, who can ever break number twenty-seven's spirit. He told me that your spirit is still alive and above all, ya still are the world famous, number, twenty-seven. Powerful and fearless. Ya always will be. . .."

The words resonated through me and I did recall them as well as why and when Harry spoke them to me. I slowly nodded my head in acknowledgement of the statement. For some reason, sitting in the old chair and listening to Paul William testify to the faith that Harry had in me, and always did have in me, hit me very hard. Extremely, hard.

"Did he tell you that, Dad?"

"He did. It was under different circumstances. Much different. Someday, I might share the details with you and Heather Sarah, but not now. But, yes he did."

"Then why can't you see that we all count upon you all the time. If you are broken down, then we are all broken down too. Mother is gone. We all feel it, but it is a terrible fact. She is gone. And Heather Sarah, and I do not want to lose both of our parents! This is what you do for a living. You assist in grief counseling! You know all about this! It is time to be number twenty-seven again, and not some broken down wreck of a man. We all believe in you, dear Father, and even if you do not want to accept it, God still believes in you too. Grandpa Henson would be pissed. He would tell you to get your sorry ass back in the game. I never met him, but I surely have read enough of your stories, to bloody well, damn sure know that my great-grandfather Alcott would be telling you the same thing. And what about Martha Wiggins? How long has Martha been your assistant? Forever, or maybe longer. Martha has been holding down the office all by herself, waiting for you to get it together. She does it because she loves you and because of her faith in you. Soon, Martha will be over here looking to kick your ass too."

"You are correct, Paul William. They all would kick my ass until it was red and very sore too. I spoke with Martha many weeks ago . . . shortly after your mother passed and never had the heart to speak with her again. She is a wonderful person, faithful, honest and loving. Martha has called a number of times this week and emailed me and once again, I am ashamed to say that I have not returned her attempts at contacting me. Martha is doing her best at holding the office down on her own. It is terrible for me not to support those efforts."

I looked up at our son and nodded my head to affirm my poor opinion of my own behavior while placing my hand over his as it rested upon my shoulder. Paul William had tears in his eyes and he tapped my hand and pulled away from me. He did not want me to see his pain and now, I felt ashamed that I had let him and everyone else down by not being stronger than what I presently was. He reached in his pocket, took out a small piece of paper and handed it to me.

"Has this chap been leaving messages for you?"

I glanced down at the paper, read the name and handed it back to Paul William.

"Yes, he has left a few messages. Sent a few emails too. Actually, quite a few. I delete them from the machine and from my in-box. Honestly, along with Martha and this chap, leaving and sending messages, so do a number of other people these days. I ignore them all. I am too upset and too busy to call them. Why do you ask?"

"Ha! Too, upset, yes! Not too busy. You are too busy doing shit all day and drinking all night. I ask because he is with the Boston Bears and he is asking about your availability for a possible meeting up in Boston. He heard about Mother and that you had taken some time off from your position. He thought you might want to come up and hang out with some old friends in the organization. I ran into him while covering a game in Toronto, and he told me that he was trying in vain to reach you. He also said that after all of these years, everyone still remembers how great you were. I corrected him and I told him, how great you still are."

I stared at Paul William and studied his eyes for a bit. It felt as if I should dismiss the testimony, but I was not sure exactly why.

"At one time, a solid goalie maybe, but that is all. Nothing special. I did not make it to the big league."

"Oh c'mon, Dad. More pity bullshit! You were, and most likely still are, a great goalie. Solid is not an accurate description."

"I appreciate the compliment, but you never saw me play in the pro leagues."

Paul William waved his hand in the air towards me to discount what I just said and he told me, "I am a sports writer and have access to film. I would hope that you are not so lost that you are still able to recall my profession. I have seen ya play. Besides, no one knows the game of hockey better than you do. When we played street hockey at the parsonage, you used to draw up power-play formations for Harry and me in the dirt next to the driveway. Shit, I was only eight years old. Harry and I did not understand a bloody word of what you were teaching us, we just nodded our heads and pretended that we did. While I never played on the same level as you did, I still played a ton of hockey, and I can honestly say that there were not any coaches that I ever ran into, or played for, with even a touch of your vast knowledge of the game. You are more than just a student of the game. You are a damn professor of hockey."

"The game has changed quite a bit since I was involved. They do not wear fiberglass masks any longer. I am almost fifty now, not twenty years old. What would they want to meet with me for? Honestly, I am not too keen on hanging with old hockey buddies. Can't imagine why they want to hang with me?"

Paul William now became a little intense and I could tell that he now grew frustrated. He pulled a wooden guest chair out from the front of my desk and slid over close to me and he sat in it.

Leaning forward in the chair, our son said, "Maybe they are friends, and they care about you, and want to give you something to take your mind off of things for a bit. Talk about the game. The game that you love and the game that was, and is, a huge part of who you are and what made you great in everything you do. The game has changed, but you still defend a net, try to possess the puck in the opposition zone longer than your opponent does, and try to blow a hole through the defending goalie and score more goals than they do. Simple game. Simple premise."

I leaned back and actually smiled. It had been a very long time since I had smiled, yet, I could not help to smile as our son recalled and spoke the exact words, which I taught him so long ago, when I taught him the basics of the game of hockey.

Paul William continued, "The only thing that has changed is that players such as James T. O'Malley, no longer exist. The insurance companies and police outlawed them. The game is a part of you, and you are, a part of it. Right now, it would be what you need. It will return the parts of you that you left so long ago on the ice and allow you to regain the one thing, of which you need the most right now."

"And what is that, dear Paul William?"

"Your purpose, Dad. Your purpose."

I did not answer him, mostly, because I had never given

returning to the game of hockey even a passing thought.

Until now.

"You know, dear Father, I think the one aspect of this entire tragedy that surprises me the most, is not your lack of motivation at writing, or you turning your back on the ministry and all the glorious things which you preached to all of us . . . I think that the biggest surprise is your lack of strength. I am not ashamed to say that. We all lost, dear Mother! It was not only you, who lost a dear and precious soul! It was all of us! Damn! Dear Father, can't you see? She was your wife . . . but she was our mother."

Paul William stood up and he was animated. As he pranced around preaching at me, I suddenly admired him. He was not only his mother's son, but also right at this moment, I saw my grandfather in his quiet power and his wisdom. He was a powerful and forceful speaker.

Perhaps I also saw a hint or two of the man that I used to be.

He stopped and pointed his finger at me and quietly told me, "Yet, you were always the rock. You used to carry around a rock in your vest pocket to remind you of that fact. Used to show my sister and me the rock all the time and tell us the stories behind it. You were the strength under and above all the chaos. The man with quiet explanations and with the power of the Gospel and all the saints in Heaven to back him up. A man of courage who stood tall in the net for years and has the scars on his ass to prove it. A versatile writer who has composed some awesome books, grand short stories, and powerful religious works. A voice of reason, in an unreasonable world. For you to tear off your collar, hand in your Bible, shelve the skates, box up your magical goalie mask with all of its power and glory and turn into a mad man, saying nothing, writing nothing and drinking yourself stupid every night, was to my sister and me, the biggest surprise of all. In fact, it was to my in-laws too. To everyone who knows you. Mourning yes, stupid no. Above all, you are not weak and you are not stupid. You are the smartest man that we have all ever met, and the strongest too. Truly, dear Father, I thought there was nothing on Earth, which could cause you ever to give up, on the ministry, hockey, or writing, or even more so, on all of us and on life. Even God taking, our dear Mother. Even that."

"Once again, I did not give up on the ministry, Paul William. I have just taken time off. Why does everyone think that I gave up? I never renounced my ordination or quit my job. I am on bereavement leave. The governing board granted me three months' leave and I still have my vacation time too. They understood. Why does my son and my family not get it too?"

Paul William jumped in and told me rather forcibly, "Because the governing board members do not see you acting as if you are a drunken madman. We do. That is why."

I nodded and admitted that he was correct.

"Yes, I need to stop that behavior and act like a clergyman. I have no defense for that because you are right on. I am still a pastor and the bishop. Right now, I need this time, I feel as if right now, until I control my emotions over this wretched event and our loss, that I have nothing of significance to say from the pulpit and the spirit of which to deliver it. That is not giving up. That is different from what giving up is."

"That my dear Father, with all due respect, is unadulterated bullshit in the finest form."

"Your mother would not approve of you cussing so much."

"Well, Mother would understand. You are not the only one who has been hardened by all of this. I swear that I am going to call my sister up tonight and tell her that latest horseshit excuse from you and if she does not catch a flight to come up here and kick your ass, then I will be surprised.

She is her mother's daughter, and she inherited Mother's superhuman strength."

I nodded in agreement with his statement.

Paul William waved his hands in disgust at me and continued to lecture to me loudly, "Besides, that is not true and you know it too. You always know what to say, Dad. You always have something to say and know exactly what words to speak and when to say them."

His words sent a shiver down my spine, because I recalled a very special person in my life, telling me the exact same thing. She told me the same thing, a long time ago, during another horrible period of mourning over the loss of a loved one in her life. I closed my eyes and felt my son studying me, but I needed to allow the ghosts of the past to haunt me. For some strange reason, the ghosts were always a comfort to my soul.

I heard their whispers in my ear.

I sat there, the visions returned, and I heard Renee's soft voice tell me, "Not true. I mean the part about you not knowing what to say. You always know what to say, Paul John Henson. That is part of your quiet magic. Thank you for you and all that you are."

The circle of life is amazing.

Opening my eyes, I looked at our son and nodded my head. Everything he had told me today was correct, I could accept his witness of me, and I did. My behavior had let many people down in their hour of need, and I had given up. Time to face up to it, number twenty-seven. Maybe it is time to get your ass back in the goal and in the game.

"I agree. I have lost my way. I am drinking too much and ignoring my loved ones in order to dull the pain. Grief can overpower you, Paul William. My wish is that you never feel what I feel right now. The strength is still there, yet, overpowered by grief. The rock exists, it is still strong, not damaged or crushed, just buried under soils of grief. No doubt, your assessment and criticisms of me are all valid. I lost so much more than my soul mate when your mother left this world, I lost a part of my spirit. I am not too sure that you can understand that fact. I hope you do. However, your comments are accurate. I cannot, and will not, dispute them."

Our son sat opposite me and he stared deeply into my eyes. Eyes full of tears and a mouth trembling with emotion faced me and stared me down.

We both remained silent for a long time.

Our son finally spoke, "What does Aunt Dottie say about all of this?"

"She told me last week that the power and the glory of the Lord will never leave me. Despite my anger, my sister told me that the plan will unfold in due time and that the Lord will guide me just as he always has. She told me to get it together and go back to God's work."

"She is brilliant. She is such a kind and gentle soul, who loves you more than you, can ever measure."

"No doubt, as I love her too."

"When was the last time that you skated, Dad?"

"About three years ago. Your mother and I went on one Saturday night to the local rink with Harry and Rose for a dance-on-ice-night. They served beer, wine and cheese and played throwback rock-and-roll. It was wonderful. It was, as an old friend used a specific phrase to describe a wonderful time; it was a magical evening. Your mother is an excellent ice skater. You know, she never took a single lesson, she just picked it up and off she went. She is amazing."

He ignored the tense of which I referred to his mother in, Paul William nodded and asked, "Ran or lifted weights?"

"Long time now. Around a day or so before your mother left us."

"You are heavier than I have ever seen you."

"It is the beer. I drink gallons of beer and do not eat

correctly." It was time to stop the bullshit and face the facts.

"Your cooking does suck, but you are always invited over to our house, or you know how much Rose loves you and would cook you up an Italian meal of wonder."

"Your mother was an amazing cook, Paul William."

He ignored my comment and moved on, "Blue and Rose love you with all of their hearts."

"I love them too. You know that. That is not in question, Paul William."

"I cannot believe that you would disappoint them and worry them so much. Time to get your ass in gear and take care of your body. My research last week, Dad, told me that even at your age, you could condition your body for playing shape within a month or thereabouts. You were a professional athlete and until a little while ago, kept your body in prime condition."

I almost smiled because he *was* his mother's son. Still researching every angle of life, just as she taught him to do. Instead of a smile, I only nodded, in a painful admittance that I had for the first time in my life, become lazy and complacent and allowed my physical condition to slide.

"Tell me again, when was the last time that you visited, Heather Sarah and your granddaughter?"

"I have not seen them since they left after the funeral. Looking at that fact, then I imagine that your sister has a right to be angry with me."

"Sure, as hell does. So, does little Sarah. She loves her grandpa with all her heart. You should see once again how her eyes light up when she sees you."

"I sent her a bunch of dough, a few toys and a nice card."

"Nice, but not the same as hugging her and kissing her and your daughter too. Sarah looks just like Mum. That is where you feel the pain. I know that, but get over it. Sarah honors Mum. It is another bloody awful, bullshit excuse."

Again, we both remained silent for a long time.

A very long time. Perhaps an hour or more passed us. It was as if I could not speak or move. We were now both void of emotions and void of words. Based upon our son's forceful visit and his factual and deep analysis of his father, I made a fateful decision.

Awakening from the long ponder, I reached my hand out and spoke, "Please, Paul William. Hand me the paper with this chap's number on it. Once again, what is his name? What does he want from me?"

Our son bounced up from his chair, his eyes lit up and a smile broke out on his face.

He anxiously reached for the paper, handed it to me and said, "Tommy Hayward. He is in some type of upper management position with the Bears. Not too sure exactly what he does. He knows you, or of you. Not too sure, which it is. All he said is they would love you to come up, hang out with old friends, and go to some practices and games. The season is almost over, so you had better get your ass in gear soon. That is all I know. But it would do you good to help clear your head and get out of this house."

I took the paper and glanced at it. I held it for a long time and a million memories came rushing back. I looked up and smiled.

While standing up, I said, "I do not recognize the name, but that does not mean anything. It has been a long time since I fell out of the hockey circles. I will call him tomorrow. I promise that I will."

Paul William rushed in and he warmly embraced me. He was almost as tall as I was. He was our son, and I loved him more right now than words could ever convey.

"Fantastic! I love you, Dad. Right now, Mother is smiling. I know she is."

"I love you too. I think you just might be correct. Perhaps, in this life, when you need to start over again, you have to start where you first began."

We hugged each other and held onto each other for a long time.

We shared some more emotional moments; I thanked him and we exchanged heartfelt goodbyes. When our son left, I climbed the long set of stairs to our bedroom. Opening a closet, I moved a number of boxes around and pushed them out of my way.

Since Binky left, I fell into a bit of disorganization.

In the rear of the closet, I found a very special box. Blowing the dust off the lid, I tore the top off and peered inside. I carefully lifted my old goalie skates from the box, held them in my hands and studied them. The blades were still straight, strong, and true. The steel blades were immaculate and even in the dim light of the room; they reflected an incredible shining power. The protective shells surrounding the skate boots had countless puck marks on them, and a brown discoloration from my old pads licking the tops of them for all of those years. Yet, they were still my skates.

None better.

Nowadays, you could never buy a pair of skates of outstanding quality such as these skates are.

Reaching inside of the box, I pulled my old goalie mask out and held it in my hands. It still had magical properties, and while holding it, I felt some type of healing within my soul.

It was all so strange.

Long ago, I had shelved this life; it was a forgotten dream and an old way of life. Never did I think that I would return here. Yet somehow, someway, I felt as if number twenty-seven was back. Back from despair, back from exile in a land of woe and anguish. It was then that the final piece of inspiration fell into place. From deep within the confines of my mind, a place tucked away for safekeeping, the ghosts returned, or more specifically, my grandfather's ghost appeared before me. While I knelt in front of the box, holding the magical mask in my hands, I could feel his powerful hand on my shoulder and could feel his grip on my soul.

Turning to look at him, he smiled, and his words were loud and clear in my mind's eye.

"Here, Paulie boy. What is it that you see?"

He held a rock in his hands, the rock, which he found in the dirt in front of 182 Belmont Avenue on a spring evening, while we were sitting on that blessed front porch together.

I once more, took the rock from his hands and just as I had so long ago, I studied the rock for a few moments, it had some dirt along the edges, was small but solid, not colorful, rather dull, it was nothing special. I turned it over repeatedly in my hands and then I smiled at my grandfather.

Finally, I spoke, "I see the spot on the ground in which you and my grandmother first stepped on when you came to America from England. Perhaps, this rock was part of the actual ground where your feet first landed. It was underfoot as you stepped off together, arm-in-arm, hand-in-hand, together into a journey of the unknown. The rock did not break or give way. Instead, it helped to lead you. It became a little smoother, but the rock remained solid and powerful. It was here before you arrived here, and it will be here long after we are gone. It is part of a new life, a symbol of hope, a part of the pathway to where we all are right now."

I looked up and Gramps once again, put his hand on my shoulder, and squeezed it tightly. I could feel the power in his hands. He was a powerfully strong man, both in emotion and in physical prowess. A man of unparalleled strength. His grip was strong and deep.

This was, however, not a grip of control; this was a grip of encouragement, a grip of love.

Gramps smiled widely as he told me, "Bloody amazing! You see how well, in which you can imagine, Paulie boy. Wonderful! Study for now. Then you can write when you decide the time is right. However, please, someday write. Most of what I have learned in life, I learned by reading. It is a gift that we all can take advantage of and share."

"I will, Gramps, I promise, someday."

Gramps looked at me, smiled a bit and said, "I do, however, think that is a stone you are holding here, Paulie boy . . . rocks are bigger."

I shook my head and replied, "Sorry, but with respect, you are wrong, Gramps. It symbolizes you. You are too powerful to be just a stone. I have to say, the least of all here in my hand that I see, is a bloody rock!"

I hung my head and with tears streaming down my face, I whispered, "But Gramps, I still expect her to come through the front door, with that incredible smile, with her blonde hair trailing behind her. . .."

I felt his power envelope me and clearly, in my mind, I heard him say, "Paulie boy, you already know this but your dear Binky, just as all of us, will never leave you. Never. We all are together forever. Just as I am here with you right now."

I wiped away the tears, closed my eyes, and when I opened them, my grandfather was gone. No, no, no, that is profoundly and unequivocally incorrect.

He never left me.

His ghost was gone. But Gramps remained here with me.

I jumped to my feet, ran into our bedroom, and opened the top drawer of my dresser. Fishing around in the drawer, I finally found it. There it was, hidden beneath a watch box and a collection of hockey awards. I picked it up and studied it while smiling. It still looked the same; I used to keep it in my vest pocket, to put my fingers upon, when I needed its strength and quiet power. When I required a reminder—it was there for me. This was one of those times, and my foolishness at banishing it under a box for a watch that I never wear and hockey awards were all too apparent. I squeezed my hand tightly around the rock in my hand. I opened my hand and studied it. Dull, colorless, yet full of power, solid, strong, and forever.

Am byth.

Yes, indeed, no way was this just some ordinary stone.

It is, was, and always will be, the rock.

I slipped the rock into my pants pocket. Later on, when I wore my vest, I would place it in the lower pocket, right where it was supposed to be. While in the drawer, I also grabbed the urn necklace and slipped it over my head.

That night, at my desk in my office, I sat in front of the computer, my usual mug of beer, now replaced by a hot cup of tea. Tea with melted organic honey. A healing drink for your soul and your body. I stared into the keys on the keyboard and went to type, then stopped, as the words of Harry resonated in my mind.

"There ain't no one or nuthin' in this entire world, who can ever break number twenty-seven's spirit. Your spirit is still alive and above all, ya still are the world famous, number, twenty-seven. Powerful and fearless. Ya always will be. . .."

I put my earbuds in my ears, dialed up, "Close to the Crevice" by No Way on my MP3 player, and began to type.

"Eleven Sentences. Chapter One. The Old Pub. I think that at one time or another, in all of our lives, certain unusual situations come along that at first glimpse, you just cannot understand. They seem at first glance to be normal, or a chance coincidence, and then upon further examination or study, we cannot explain them. Occasional instances occur during all of our lives that contain a mystery, an unexplained twist of fate, an encounter with strange or different people, or a bizarre or unexplained turn of events. It is something that I am very sure all of us have experienced, and when you take the time to look back upon it, you have sometimes wondered from where it all came.

I am no exception.

I had just finished an ice hockey game in Concord, New Hampshire. Concord was one of my favorite places on Earth, a clean New England city that most areas of the country would consider a town. I enjoyed it for the people, for the climate, and the general atmosphere. I may have been born and raised in northern New Jersey, but I really enjoyed visiting and playing professional ice hockey in New England quite a bit. While you could never remove my hard New Jersey accent, my poor grammar, street slang, and other elements of New Jersey from me, I think I was becoming an adopted New Englander."

I stopped typing, leaned back and smiled. It felt strange to smile. In fact, that was now two actual times today, in which I had smiled an actual heartfelt smile. It had been a long time since I actually smiled like this. I fingered the urn around my neck and tapped the rock in my vest pocket. I thought about how Binky and Gramps are now very proud of me. It was now time to place the urn in a place of honor and for me to wear the urn only on special occasions. I needed to wear it as a token of reverence and remembrance, not as a wound upon my heart.

It was time to be the rock. Binky would agree with me. I knew in my heart that she agreed.

Oh yeah, maybe I had returned to where I started and it felt wonderful. Really, really wonderful.

Chapter Three

Aduniad

The next day, I did call Mr. Hayward, and he seemed very excited to speak with me. He was a special assistant to Mr. Brian McClure, who was the new General Manager of the Boston Bears. I knew Brian McClure from my hockey circles a long time ago. When I knew Brian, he was the Director of Player Personnel with the Albany Flying Dutchman hockey club in Albany, New York. Brian was a good man. The two of us always got along quite well. It surely appeared as if Brian did very well for himself.

For me not to even know that he had risen all the way through the ranks to be the General Manager of the Bears, told me how out of touch with the hockey world that I now was. At one time, I called this man a friend; in fact, we were very close friends years ago. I could safely say that we were still friends. Out of touch. But we were still friends. We roomed together on the road; we went out, drank beer, and had dinner together almost every day during my stay in Albany. Shame on me for not staying in touch with people such as Brian. I bet it had been over a year since I looked at a hockey game on the television, or even glanced at hockey news in a newspaper or online. Even articles that our son wrote.

"Pastor, or is it bishop, or even Mr. Henson, Mr. McClure, wanted me to reach out. . .."

"Please, just call me, number twenty-seven. Even, I do not know who the hell I am right now. Too many identities, but I will always be the number, twenty-seven. No one ever calls me Mr. Henson, and only a handful of people, who know me well, tend to call me, Paul."

Mr. Hayward sounded very young. I wondered if he was an intern whom Brian recruited to groom for an executive position someday. Brian was an excellent and very sharp businessman, so I knew that this young man had talent and a purpose too.

"Oh, yes, indeed. I do apologize, you are correct. Mr. McClure warned me of that fact beforehand, and I slipped up. You are still a legend around these parts. Mr. McClure still tells everyone that you were the best goaltender that he ever saw. Number, twenty-seven, I have it correct now. Sorry."

"Please, there is no need to apologize. Thank you for the compliment. How is Brian? He is a good man. Actually, he is a dear old friend."

"He is doing quite well. Adjusting to his new position. Yes, he told me that you were old friends. If I do recall, you roomed together. Well, we ran into your son in Toronto while he was covering the game between Boston and Toronto a few weeks or so ago, and Paul William shared your number with us. I need to say that all of us here with the Boston Bears are deeply sorry to hear of the loss of your wife. Number twenty-seven will always be a part of this organization, and we send our condolences."

"Thank you. That is very kind of you and very much appreciated. Yes, I did actually receive a nice card and flowers from the hockey club and organization, when my wife passed."

"Yes, yes, yes, Brian would love to meet with you, twenty-seven. There is a need for your expertise within the organization. Brian wants to meet with you and see how you are doing, talk about the old times and see if you can assist us with a potential goaltending prospect."

I became immediately intrigued and interrupted Mr. Hayward, "Assist you? A potential goaltending prospect? I am not sure that I know too much about modern goaltending styles. Things have changed quite a bit since I played."

"That is exactly why Brian wants you to take a look at this young goaltending prospect. He feels you are the one goalie in the entire world who can correct his issues by teaching some old-time hockey to him."

I pondered his words for a bit of time and then asked, "Issues? What type of issues?"

"He is currently in Norfolk. Your old team and he suffered a terrible neck injury last year and now seems to be quite puck shy on certain shots. Brian wants to bring him up to the big league for the last few games of the season and see what he can do and if he will come around. He was quite a prospect before the injury and the Bears have invested quite a bit of time and money in him."

Mr. Hayward's words sounded very familiar to me. The story paralleled my own hockey career. Norfolk, injuries, trying to save my career. Remarkable. I thought how this might just be part of the plan starting to unfold a bit.

"I see, yes, I understand. I was there in the same spot once too. The Bears tried to save my career too."

"Yes, Brian told me all about number twenty-seven. After my briefing, I accessed your file and brushed up a bit. The Bears will pay all of your expenses, you still receive a pension check and we can draw a little contract and agree to add a few dollars to your check for consulting fees."

"A goalie consultant, eh? I still have bereavement leave available, as well as quite a bit of unused vacation time from my clergy position. Yes, I am intrigued and available. I owe the Bears and I owe Brian too."

Mr. Hayward grew quite enthusiastic on the telephone and the volume of his voice increased, "Wonderful! This is wonderful! In addition to the assistance in saving a marvelous young goalie's career, we all thought it might do you good to hang around a hockey rink with some old friends right now. Maybe help you with a diversion from the last few months. As I said, number twenty-seven will forever be a part of our organization. Brian cares about you, and he was quite upset to hear of your loss. We want to reach out to you and see how you are doing."

"That is very kind of Brian, the Bears, and you. They were, and always will be, a huge part of my life and are a topnotch organization."

"Thank you. So, twenty-seven, can you arrange your schedule to come to Boston within the next few weeks?"

I paused and a million thoughts ran through my head. To be honest, for some reason, all types of doubts suddenly filled my mind. I prayed to God to erase them, to steer me if this was part of the plan.

I remained silent and Mr. Hayward questioned the pause, "Twenty-seven, are you there?"

Still, the grief caused a million excuses to run through my head, as to why I was not available to meet with Brian. I felt the front pocket of my vest and tapped the rock. C'mon, Paul, get ya ass in gear. The only legitimate excuse was the vow that I made last evening to book a flight to Florida to see my daughter, granddaughter, and son-in-law. The rest were stupid smokescreens. Then the realization arrived loud and clear in my mind that right now, I was a physical wreck. No doubt that I was in the worst shape of my entire life. Soft, flabby, and weak, with no skating legs. Right now, I was a bum. Yet, it was time.

"I would love to meet with Brian. It is long overdue. I have a few things scheduled before I would be able to shake free, but I am anxious to meet and speak with Brian. How about we say, about two weeks from now? Will that leave enough time in this year's game schedule?"

"Perfect!" Mr. Hayward grew enthusiastic. I liked this chap's spirit. "We want to bring Vance up from Norfolk for the last few games, so a few weeks from now will be right at season's end and will work out quite well. We had a terrible year. Last place this year, so there are no playoffs for us this season."

"Yes, our son told me that the Bears had a difficult year. Poor goaltending will do that. Vance, eh? What is this chap's full name?"

"Vance Howard."

"Okay, I got it. I need to clear some things from my schedule and visit my daughter and granddaughter in Florida. Admittedly, I also have to whip my soft backside in some kind of shape. Not too sure that I can skate without tumbling down right now. If you want me to skate around a bit, then I need to get it together."

Mr. Howard quickly stated, "Yes, I do think that you might need to get on the ice to observe his issues. Sidelines and video will work, but right on the ice would be best."

Oh yeah, I had to get my ass in gear. Quickly! Good thing that I still have my beloved skates. I would hate to have to break a new pair in right now in such a short time.

"I agree. Okay, what day is best to meet? Let's say Tuesday to Friday, in two weeks from now. I never fly on Mondays unless it is for a game. Brian might recall that."

Mr. Hayward laughed, and his voice echoed quite loudly within the handset of the telephone.

"He did tell me and predict that. Yes, indeed, he did. It seems as if some years might have passed, but you have not changed much in your habits, twenty-seven. You might recall the office address here in Boston. I will email you the details. We will arrange for the call-up of Mr. Howard to coincide with your visit. Your son gave us your contact information. I will pencil it in for a lunch meeting, two weeks from now on Wednesday, the 27th and take care of all the arrangements."

Everything was a blur after Mr. Hayward told me the date. All I could think about was how I had to visit my lovely daughter, hold and kiss that precious daughter of ours, then hold and kiss that precious little baby girl. After some of that loving, I needed to return home and shake my ass. If I needed to hit the ice, then this body was not going to cut very much ice in a very impressive manner. Special goaltending consultant? Shit, I could not touch my toes. In fact, right now I could not even see my toes. I had this big, old belly in the way.

After hanging up with Mr. Hayward, the first call that I made was to our daughter. The second call was to the airline to purchase round-trip tickets to Florida and Boston, and finally, I made the calls to the three people that I knew I could count on to whip my sorry, old ass into shape in a very short amount of time. First, I dialed up Mr. Harry M. Redmond Junior and spoke to an elated, and very excited, number thirty-five.

After I told him how I needed his help, apologized for my outrageous behavior as of late, what my plans were, and where I was heading to, Harry proudly told me before we hung up, "I love this! Now, this is what I am talking 'bout! Been working on that son-in-law of mine, teaching him to stop babbling about sports records and statistics that he researches all of the time and to be more forceful. Looks as if I hit pay dirt. Words cannot tell you how glad I am that number twenty-seven is back. Rose, Blue, Paul William and number thirty-five were counting on ya! Geyer Street guys never quit. Ever. Buckle ya ass in there, Paul. I am gonna try to shoot a hole in ya."

"Thank you, Harry. That is what I am counting on. You are correct. Paul William does seem to speak his mind. He also cusses an awful lot when he is being forceful."

"Yeah, he does. Like I said, I've been working on 'em. Despite how great I am, it would be difficult for even my ego not to admit that I was not the only contributor to his personality. He is Binky's son and your old man taught him to cuss more than I did, ya know."

"No doubt, Harry."

"Seriously, twenty-seven, I will be thrilled to get out the

sticks and the skates and whip ya old ass into shape. Been too long, my brother, too long. Time for a reunion on the ice for all of us. Long overdue. I am thrilled."

My face broke into a wide smile, and I held the receiver of the telephone away for just a moment.

It felt as if I could break up emotionally for just a brief second, but I recovered with a whisper of a word, "Aduniad."

"Welsh bullshit, Paul. I don't speak it. Don't wanna. Only speak New Jersey on this end."

"Sorry, it means reunion. I am glad too, and I do agree that it is long overdue. Yes, we never quit. Thank you, thirty-five. From the bottom of my heart. Thank you."

After hanging up with Harry, I then called Paul William. Our conversation was exuberant. I explained to him that I needed some of his time, and for him to make sure his hockey skates were sharp and that his stick and other equipment was ready to go. After asking him for the dates he was in town, explaining that I was heading to Florida for a long overdue visit, I thanked him for all he is in my life and for having the courage to tell it, as he had to tell it. I also told him that his mother is very proud of him too.

The next number that I dialed was to now retired, Pastor James T. O'Malley.

With all the planning and the telephone calls behind me, it was now time to come to some kind of terms with all of this. It was long past the time for me to realize where I am at in my life and to have the courage to acknowledge what had happened to all of us.

That dear reader, in the countless adventures of Harry and Paul, both written and unwritten, was undoubtedly the most difficult thing that I ever had to do.

Once again, dragging my sorrow with me, I climbed the staircase to the second floor of our home. An empty home, a home that was much too large for me now, and a home filled with ghosts and echoes of the past and voices from beyond, calling out to me from every corner of every room.

I am listening and watching and I hear and see them all!

Our daughter was correct; it was well past the time to sell this home. I had no need for all of this room now. It was just a reminder of my past and in some ways our dreams of unfilled destiny. Right at this moment on this Earth, material things meant nothing to me.

Reaching our bedroom, I sat upon the edge of the bed, reached into the drawer of the end table next to our bed and pulled out my Bible.

Well-thumbed it was. . ..

I used this same Bible every Sunday when I was in the pulpit at Reunion Lutheran Church. What a wonderful and enlightened time that was in our lives. A time in our lives, when we had the rays of Heaven shining down upon us, and our mutual joy filled the entire Earth. Grasping the Bible, I knew quickly and rather instinctively of where to open the pages to. My fingers flipped and maneuvered the pages quickly. I might have taken my bereavement leave, but as I will always be a hockey goaltender, I also now came to realize that I would soon return to the bishop's office, because I always will be a pastor.

I spoke the words aloud as I read them, "Precious in the sight of the Lord is the death of his saints."

My Bible was not actually required for me to recall this verse, since it was in my mind and in my heart forever. Rather, it was as if the printed words were a reinforcement of the immense power and glory of them. Bowing my head, pulling my hair behind my head and tugging it in anger and rage, there was only one thing left for me to do. I needed to grieve as I had not yet grieved. Pastor Paul John Henson needed to cry and fall on his knees and ask God the one question of which, until now, he was too afraid to ask.

"Why?"

That is exactly what Pastor Paul John Henson did.

I fell upon my knees, cried a rain of tears, and suffered through a series of uncontrollable, sobbing sorrows, which wracked my body with pain and force as the grief left me. It was a forceful destroyer of my soul, of which I purged from deep within me. While I mourned, I felt my anger at God subside. Healing blessings poured into me, sent from my beloved wife in Heaven and from all the saints who now joined her. I came to sense a hope and joy of the plan of which Heaven sent to me. A plan that was now up to me to continue to follow, and to use stumbling, yet blind faith, to enact it.

Not to understand it, nor ever pretend to agree with it, but to follow it. It was part of my vow, part of my job and part of my essence.

Sky Blu's words from so long ago echoed in my mind. The words echoed as if they were a beacon of hope in touch with my soul, yet the words were also a reminder of pain and intense sorrow.

""People never really go away forever. Even when they die, they return to us, somehow. We remain together forever with the people that we love."

I could see Sky speaking those comforting, and now, ever so prophetic words to me as we stood on the porch at 20 John Street so long ago. The puffs of warm air leaving her mouth rose into the cold, December air, and once again, I returned there to that wonderful place, with Sky Blu, in the comfort of her presence and the comfort of her words. It was then that I realized that this too, despite the immense pain and indescribable agony, was part of God's plan for my life. Recalling the anguish of losing Sky Blu, and Father Mark solidifying the course of my life when he explained why God took Sky so early into his heavenly kingdom, provided me with some comfort now.

Father Mark had explained to me, as we stood together, watching a glorious sunset, "That is why, Paul, because God decided that Heaven needed more pieces of blue sky, so that her beauty could light up every day in both Heaven and on Earth."

The understanding of that plan and the power of God's plan eventually helped to lead me to a career in the ministry. Now, I did not agree with the plan, but I understood. Twice in my life, I felt the immense power of God's plan and now, I remain humbled in the face of the Lord, still rebellious, but cognizant of the plan when he took my glorious wife to be with him in paradise.

It was Heaven's gain.

There was little doubt that it was time to end the mourning and begin to follow the plan once again. Surely, this call from the hockey world to assist a young man during a struggle to recover from an injury was part of that plan. It was so similar to my situation many years ago when I played hockey that it was uncanny.

While I slowly crept up from the floor, rose from my knees, within the midst of unfathomable sorrow, I stood up and left the rain of tears and anguish upon the floor. Scattered tears left all around me, lost forever, tears of which I hoped would dry up and disappear.

I was now standing upon my two feet. Admittedly standing a bit wobbly, nonetheless, I was standing. Upright and standing next to the bed, where my beloved wife and I proved and honored our love more times than I could ever count or recall . . . I smiled. I smiled, because amongst the rain of tears, I needed to recall and give thanks to God for all the good things he sent to me in my life and all the joy we shared.

Despite my anguish, I needed to pause and acknowledge that as the good Lord takes from us, the Lord also gives. I knew what to do next. I needed to celebrate Binky's life. I needed to rejoice in our mutual joy. I needed to recognize all that we had been given. Bounding down the steps from the second floor, I landed with a hard "thud" upon the first-floor landing and then ran to the music center in our living room. There, I rather frantically thumbed through a catalog of compact discs. My intensity mounted as I lost patience with my inability to find what I was looking for within a few short seconds, and I felt my frustration rise and my heart race. Tossing disc after disc aside, I finally found the one of which I was seeking. I opened the jewel case, grabbed the disc, pushed the power button on the player and carefully loaded the disc into the player. The little disc happily disappeared into the throat of the CD player.

Glancing back towards the player, while standing in the center of our living room, I carefully watched and then realized my error. I dashed back to the music center when I realized that I needed to dial up the correct track from the recording.

In my mind, I clearly heard Binky's voice telling me, "Please be ready to pull over on the side of the road there, twenty-seven. My research indicated that, 'Livin' Love' is the sixth track on this recording, so you need to find a safe spot on the side of the road. You can lead of course."

I pushed the track button until the number six lit up, and I stood in the center of the room and waited for the music to begin playing. The vision of the world's most gorgeous woman stood clearly in front of me, fluffing her long blonde hair, her incredible blue eyes flickering, her laugh echoing in my mind and her love filling my soul. Her voice resounded within my heart as clear as any bell could ring upon the face of the entire Earth. The music started, and I reached out for my beloved wife.

The unique Spanish string influenced opening bars of the song began and I smiled, Binky squared off to me, smiled, fluffed her hair, and cast a sex appeal felt all the way back up the Garden State Parkway in good old Sussex County. In fact, a little earth tremor back home may have knocked over my mum's teacups.

In my mind's eye, I swept in and held her as the tempo

of the song built up; I spun her at just the right moment, and we faced each other off at the end of a spin with almost perfect timing. Soon we were whirling, twirling, and shaking, Binky followed my lead, as I was loose and feeling the flow. I was in the net making the saves and feeling the game. The old goaltender moves were serving me well! It was pure magic to a purely magical song. As the song came down to the final bars, I pulled Binky in close, held her, and then spun her for a final clasp and a dramatic, perfectly timed ending. It surely helped that I knew every beat of that song. Thank you once again, the composer of this song, wherever you were, you sure wrote a good one!

When the song ended, I once again fell upon my knees on the floor and cried my eyes out, but instead of remaining angry with God, I instead, thanked God for sending me such an amazing and perfect woman to love and to have for all the years that we did. Amidst a rain of tears and the power that I held within the intense clenching of my fists, the power and glory of Heaven shone through and remarkably, there was joy and there was aduniad.

"Dear Father, I have to say that I see the spirit restored in your eyes. Mother was correct. Your eyes always tell your story. I am so glad to see your soul restored and I know that dear Mother is too. I love you with all of my heart."

"I love you too, Heather Sarah. I love you to the moon and back." Staring at our daughter, and then our granddaughter, I realized these two precious women might just be the most gorgeous women in this world. They took my breath away.

I hugged our daughter tightly and kissed her while she held our granddaughter in her arms. The precious little girl with eyes as clear and blue as Binky's eyes reached up, grabbed a fistful of my long locks of hair, and gave them a good pull. She had done the same routine since she was just a little baby, and now that she was older, she still loved to do it.

I did not mind. Little Sarah laughed and so did I. In actuality, I deserved it for being absent for too long in their lives.

She should have pulled a lot harder.

"So, Paul, you are going to go to Boston and see your old friend and see if you can help him with this young goalie?"

I sat at the kitchen table, in the kitchen of our daughter and our son-in-law's home, with Sarah perched firmly upon my lap, looking up at me and smiling. We had all just enjoyed an outstanding dinner, prepared by Heather Sarah and instead of sipping my usual beer; I instead picked up a glass of sparkling water and slowly sipped it.

Our son-in-law, Ian, never called me Dad, or Dad Henson, or any other term of endearment, which referred to our actual in-law-son-in-law relationship. He simply used my name. I was fine with that. It bothered Binky whenever Ian used our actual names, but for some reason, it did not bother me at all. I never felt a connection with Ian. He seemed distant; therefore, I was fine with his choice of names.

Looking over the rim of the glass, while hugging Sarah, I answered our son-in-law's question, "I am going to make the trip, Ian. I am. Going to see what they have to say and how I can help. I owe my old friend, Brian McClure. He and I go back a very long time. I do think it will do me some good to get away, hang around a rink and relive some glory times. In addition, I feel this is a mission that is part of God's plan. I really do. Brian and I came up through the hockey ranks together many years ago, I am ashamed to say that time, and distance and life, caused me to lose track of him. If anything, I would enjoy sitting and speaking with him. Even if nothing comes out of the meeting, at least, I can say that I enjoyed some time with an old friend and reconnected."

Ian nodded, and I saw his eyes dart over to Heather Sarah as if he wanted his wife to interject something into the conversation, but Heather Sarah only stared at me and smiled. It seemed as if she was too overjoyed at my new plans and the recent resurrection of my soul to do anything other than smile.

Honestly, I was never quite sure about our son-in-law, it seemed as if he was a hard worker, he was a respected attorney in a law practice that specialized in real estate transactions, yet, there was something of which made my old street sense tingle whenever I studied him and spoke with him.

Binky told me that he was a womanizer. She never took to him much, nor did she like him very much. She always told me that his eyes unlocked the true personality of his soul. My wife caught him seductively checking her body out a number of times and it made her rather uncomfortable. I never witnessed such practice and when I heard of it, I wanted to confront Ian and call him out on his actions. Binky would not allow me to do so. My wife strongly renounced my plan and asked me, in the best interest of our daughter and granddaughter, to remain silent on the subject, unless Ian ever crossed the line and decided to be more than just a voyeur in his actions. Of course, I adhered to my wife's wishes. From there on in, Binky always told me that she did not trust him and that he had an eye for the ladies.

Ian came from an upper-middle class family, but he was well aware of the wealth that Binky and I accumulated. We had a large sum of money from my hockey career as well as my career in the ministry. My bishop position paid rather well, and Binky always earned a substantial salary when she worked. In addition, we had our inheritances from both sides of our families. Binky's father was a successful lawyer and a prominent politician, and she grew up wealthy and well to do. My dear mum was an investment wizard, and it was always amazing how we grew up so poor, but later in life, the old man and Mum did quite well for themselves. It was a credit to the old man and his lifetime of hard work and commitment, and to my dear mum.

We had, for the most part, until we bought our larger home, which bordered on extravagance, had lived modestly and invested very wisely. Binky claimed that Ian knew that Heather Sarah was not only a gorgeous woman, but also that she came with other attributes above her beauty. My wife did not trust him one bit.

I, too, still studied a person's eyes carefully. This unusual habit of watching the eyes of shooters in hockey, and anxious and bored church parishioners sitting in pews, served me well over the years. After a long and careful study, I agreed with Binky. Ian was always pleasant, and he was the father of our granddaughter, but I was never comfortable around him or with him.

Heather Sarah had met him when she attended university in Florida. They dated for a short time, and before we even knew it or could have the time to get to know Ian, they married. Heather Sarah was deeply in love; Ian was tall, handsome, intelligent, charismatic and successful. A year or so into the marriage, Sarah came along and their lives seemed to settle out in a quiet family life. At least, on the surface it seemed quiet. Yet, I kept a careful watch and studied everything. The experience of my many careers, growing up lean and mean on the streets of Paterson, New Jersey and learning to take some extra time to study situations and persons before making judgments served me well. There was no need to change now.

No father ever thinks a man is good enough to marry his daughter, and I certainly was no exception, but I had to be careful. Binky and I both agreed never to question our daughter's love or interfere in her life. Until Ian did something to prove our instincts correct, we both agreed to watch the situation carefully.

Of course, the world-famous Harry M. Redmond Junior never minced words or held back on anything. After meeting Ian, a number of times and reporting that he was carefully checking out, as he said, "Rose and her gorgeous ass," Harry told me, "that Ian guy, he is a weasel-faced liar. A beady-eyed asshole. He always screws his face up as if he just smelt a load of crap. He looks down at everyone else. Likes to make people feel small because he thinks he is hot shit. A pretend, want-to-be punk who thinks that he is God's gift to women. He is a jackass, and we would have kicked his ass in ten seconds if we all wuz back in the old neighborhood. Watch him carefully, twenty-seven. If he ever hurts Heather Sarah or Sarah, then there will be no place on this planet that he will be able to hide. We will track his ass down just like the old neighborhood days."

Good old, Harry tells it as he feels it and never minces words.

Ian's eyes flickered, and I watched them carefully. He seemed never to look too much at his daughter or be very interested in her. That seemed so strange to me. I was on full alert around this chap now.

As we sat there, Ian and I resumed our conversation, "That sounds as if it will be an interesting and a pleasant trip. Do you think they are serious about a consulting position, or is this just a meeting to reconnect and see how you are doing after, well, you know, after Binky passed?"

"Both. At least that is what the young fellow on the phone call told me, and I have to admit that at first, in my head, I made up a million excuses as to why I could not and should not do this. That is when God spoke to me and I knew this was part of the plan."

Looking down at the table, I became introspective in my

thoughts and I conveyed them to my family.

"Hockey is where I came from and perhaps, with all that has passed, it is as Paul William said part of the plan for me to regain my purpose and return there. Who knows?"

I then entered, plain, cold, hard facts into the situation, "That is why it is imperative that I get my old body back into shape quickly. This consulting position will entail ice time, skating and physical and athletic work."

I smiled, grabbed what had become a bit of excess flab around my waistline and laughed as I proudly reported, "Already had lost five pounds, until I came and visited with our daughter and her family and sampled too much of this amazing cooking from the world's greatest daughter!"

"Oh, I know, look at my gut," Ian commented as we compared bellies.

Heather Sarah finally stopped smiling, and she spoke, "Thank you for the compliment. You know who taught me, right? Mother was the best cook of all. I have to say that I think this is marvelous. I know that after you complete this mission, put this young goalie back on his skates, and point him toward success, then you will return to the pulpit and to the bishop's office. I know Martha will be happy to see you. She called me the other day and asked about you and inquired as if I knew of your plans yet. Martha, like everyone else, was quite concerned for your well-being. This is wonderful, your spirit is healing and a meeting with your old friend, and a visit to the ice rink and hockey world will do the trick. After all, you are still and always will be, as Uncle Harry proclaims to the entire world, the world famous, number twenty-seven."

"Yes, I will call Martha and catch up with her. I plan to return right after this mission is completed and need to call the Lutheran Governing Board too. I can only imagine how buried Martha is with paperwork. She is awesome, and I think Pastor Charles T. Braun Junior has pitched in on the pastoral duties of the office. I owe both of them a huge thank you. As far as my world-famous status, I do not know how famous old twenty-seven is these days, but I do know he is one out of shape, blob of a mess. We are improving. I plan to go for a run here in a little while after my dinner settles and that awful Florida heat subsides a bit."

I looked over at our daughter and then over at Ian. They both were studying my eyes, and I felt it. I squeezed Sarah tightly as she sat on my lap and she laughed, smiled and squeezed me hard.

"I love you, little girl," was all I could squeak out as the reality of returning full-circle to a world that I left behind hit my soul with full impact.

"I love you, Grandpa," the precious girl told me as she motioned for me to lean over so she could now hug my neck and kiss my cheek. I fought back the tears, and instead, focused on recovering and on the mission at hand. Emotions right now were not going to help me. Action will.

"I am a mess right now, physically and somewhat emotionally. Much better than I was a few days ago. A huge difference. We will get there. I have a plan and Harry, your brother, and Jim O'Malley, all told me that they all are willing to help old twenty-seven to return to topnotch form."

Heather Sarah waved her hand in the air and then held it up as a sign of a pause.

Our daughter warned me, "Look, do not go crazy out there. Get in shape, but you are not returning to play professionally, you just have to skate around and demonstrate. Right?" She leaned in for an intense stare, much as her dear mother did when she wanted to focus on an answer. Heather Sarah inherited the stare gene from Binky.

With a nod of my head, I acknowledged the plan, "Yes, no crazy stuff. I just have to skate without falling on my, you-know-what! Have to look as if I know what I am speaking of out there. First, I had to come and spend time with everyone here. Then, when I return to Jersey, it will be hit the ice time. For now, I am stealing my granddaughter and we are going to play in her room with her dollhouse. Something about a tea party, too. . .."

Dear reader, I wish that I had enough writing skills in order to convey in a grandiose and eloquent manner, with some flowing prose, how profound an experience it was for me to sit in a locker room, inside of the local ice rink, and slowly dress into my goaltending gear. However, God gave me some talents, but I missed those particular talents. Therefore, I will do the best that I can, to accurately, or somewhat accurately, convey the actual intenseness and experience of what, in reality, was such a simple practice. A practice that I had performed thousands and thousands of times before. It was just such a long time ago, in what seemed as if it were a past life. A life, which I long ago, placed upon my shelf of memories and forgot about.

A life that I never dreamt that I would someday revisit.

I sat alone in the locker room.

Since my return from Florida, I had hit the workouts hard. I was back to running two miles a day; I was in the gym on a daily basis and lifting weights, and I revisited my old flexibility exercises. I now limited my beer intakes to one or two a day with dinner, and ditched the frozen pizza for vegetables, fruits and lean poultry. Rose and Blue had whipped up some home cooking for me and in a short period of time, I had lost close to fifteen pounds and turned a ton of fat back into muscle. I was feeling well. Honestly, I was feeling superb and my mental status, as well as my physical status, had improved considerably.

My equipment bag lay opened and sprawled out in a

naked and exposed manner while it sat upon the rubber mats of the floor in front of me. I sat upon a long wooden bench inside of a locker room and stared at the open contents of the bag. My stick glove, my old catching glove, chest protector, groin protector and cup. All the requirements for suiting up in what amounts to hockey's equivalent of a knight's suit of armor. I had arrived in a full circle and returned to a hockey locker room in an old, worn ice rink, one town over from where we resided. A room, painted in a bright blue color, such a bright blue color that it almost hurt your eyes, because it was so brilliant. It seems as if all of these locker rooms all looked the same. Over my many years, frequenting countless hockey locker and ice rink locker rooms, I could testify to the fact that they all looked and smelled the same. For some reason, they always painted these locker rooms in bright colors with a durable oil paint, paint that is impervious to chipping or scuffing by errant hockey stick blades or skate blades accidentally scraped along the walls.

I had rented two hours of ice time from the ice rink and paid a pretty penny for the time, but I knew that these next few hours would not be anything of which I could put a price tag to.

It was time to dress. Harry, Jim, and Paul William would be here any minute now to meet me, and dress for our little practice skate. I did not want them to see me struggling to transform from Paul John Henson to number twenty-seven. Pastor Jim O'Malley had recently retired from a long career as a pastor for a nondenominational congregation. Jim was happy to hear of my plans and more than willing to climb back into his gear and hit the ice with us.

Funny how this life is.

My relationship with James T. O'Malley was a complex one. Many years ago, we were mortal enemies on opposing teams vying for the league championship.

Now, all these years later, and after parallel careers, we

were very close friends.

Harry, of course, remained the legendary number thirty-five. We played together on the streets, in the roller hockey leagues and then on ice skates for a long time too until the horrific injury, which Harry suffered from an errant puck to his face, forced him to hang up his skates. He still skated on a semi-regular basis, although as of late, we both let that activity slide. When Paul William was young, we taught him the game both in the driveway of our homes and on the ice here and there. Harry was still Harry, and his booming and powerful slap shot remained a skill that he retained all of these years later. Thinking about his shot hurtling at me now gave me a little pause.

Paul William was a superb ice skater; in fact, skating was his strongest attribute within his hockey skills. He played hockey on a regular basis throughout his youth, in high school and for a few years in college. He started out wanting to be a goalie like his old man, but a shift or two at center ice and the lure of finding the back of the twine with a few goals scored, lured him out of the net and into playing a center ice position. I think the stitches that he had to receive in his chin from a puck that slipped under his cage-mask one afternoon might have helped to change his mind about playing goalie too.

After all, he heard far too many of his old man's stories. He could see the scars and lines on my face, and he read a few of my books too. Paul William eventually hung up his skates, when he discovered the grind of playing hockey to be somewhat tedious and no offers from any teams, leagues, or promising positions in any of the entry drafts materialized. His true love of all sports and writing combined with his research gene that he inherited from his mother, to find him in a perfect fit of a career as a prominent sportswriter. He covered professional hockey in a syndicated column, which many news outlets and papers picked up, and he wrote about other sports for many publications and internet outlets. He was well-respected, well read, and his reputation as a young talent in the journalism world grew every day. Proud did not even describe our emotions at our children's mutual success!

I took a deep breath, reached down into my equipment bag and decided that it was time. Now stripped naked, I noticed how toned my body was now becoming, not yet where I wanted to be, but it looked a lot better than it did just a few weeks ago.

I first pulled on my jock strap, and then I grabbed my trademark thermal underwear and pulled it on over my body. The thermal was old school, but it kept me warm. It retained the heat close to my body and kept muscle tears and pulls to a minimum. The modern materials that the young man tried to sell me in the pro shop here at the ice rink, for undergarments meant for wearing under your equipment, could not lure me away from my old standby. Just because it is new, it does not always equate to better. Then, the steel groin protector went on and snapped into place. The protector covered your entire groin and part of your abdomen to prevent puck impact from damaging vital organs and muscles as well as male parts too. Then my garter belt, with dangling snaps to pull my old Long Island Rooster socks up, followed by goalie pants, shoulder pads, and my chest protector.

It all snapped into place. It fit exactly as it did so many years ago. My suit of armor was now intact and in place. Ready, once again, for battle. War on ice.

The number twenty-seven hockey sweater with the Rooster's logo went up and over my head. When I decided to return to the ice to whip this mess of a body into shape, I knew there was only one team jersey that I would select to wear from the many teams, which I played for in my career. Of all the teams that I was a part of, I always considered number twenty-seven to be forever a team member of the Long Island Rooster hockey club. Sure, there were many reasons for my feelings, such as league championships, fan clubs, MVP awards, but more than that, they were the first team ever to give me a chance, and they had special players, and coaches and fans too.

After donning my sweater, I looked over at the final pieces of the puzzle. This was going to be the sentimental part. My old skates went on, first the right foot, then the left foot. It was a superstition for me always to fit up from right to left. These skates were still solid. The boots were a little dry, but even the young man in the pro shop admired the construction, the quality, and the ruggedness of these classic skates. There was no possibility of purchasing a finer skate from any selection in the world right now, which could surpass the quality and feel of these babies.

Besides, they had stopped so many pucks, and skated too many miles for me ever to consider trading them in for something newer. My skates were in place, and now it was time to reach for the most dubious pieces of my equipment. Brand new goalie leg pads, purchased from that same persuasive young salesman in the pro shop here. My old leg pads suffered from dry rot and as painful as it was for me to admit, they had to go. I tossed them away and now strapped onto my legs the latest in high-tech fibers and materials. I had to admit; they were a lot lighter than my old leather pads were and because of the construction with modern materials; they were already quite flexible. No break-in period or rubbing with neat-foot oil to soften them up would be required.

The last piece of the puzzle, as it always will be and will forever remain, was my mask. The last line of defense. My protector and my disguise.

This was my original mask, recovered long ago from a young hockey fan, who I had donated it to, after a game. A game in which we won our league championship. That dear reader is a long and often-told story.

Suffice it to say, I now held it in my hands and the magic

of the old mask and a lifetime of memories associated with it, all returned to me once again.

I was ready. Dressed and good to go. I tucked my mask inside of my new pads, reached for a hair tie, and pulled my hair behind my head to tie it all off. I picked up my gloves and stick, and I was ready to skate and warm-up on the ice, when the door to the locker room swung open and in walked Harry, Jim, and Paul William.

After tossing their equipment bags on the floor and rushing over while warmly greeting me, Harry playfully slapped Jim on the back and pointed at me.

He then stood back and looked me up and down. "Damn. Ya look just the same as your old ass did thirty years ago, twenty-seven."

"I agree, Harry. Not only about the appearance but also about his old ass," Jim commented.

It felt wonderful to be in a locker room again with fellow hockey players, even if one was our son and the other two chaps were Harry and the infamous James T. O'Malley.

I had the one trick left in my equipment bag that I knew would cap this pregame festivity off in my mind and in Harry's mind too. Jim and our son would not understand this one, but my old pregame ritual of eating a banana, while pacing the locker room floor to ponder the upcoming mission, would be just the ticket to return Harry and me to our roots. I waited until all the greetings were complete, Jim, Harry, and Paul William were now deep into their equipment bags and dressing, and when I spotted Harry reach into his bag and pull out his skates, I knew that it was time. I took the banana out of my bag and started to peel it while I started my patented pace back and forth across the locker room floor in front of Harry. I heard Harry laugh and Jim and our son laugh along with him too, they just were not quite sure of what was so funny. I imagined that just the vision of me dressed in my goalie gear, eating a banana and pacing, was a comical enough of a scene to entice a laugh or two.

Harry waited, and after my third or fourth bite and pace across the locker room, he finally completed the memory, "Really Paul, really . . . a friggin' banana?" Harry said with the usual and replayed disdain in his voice.

I looked at him, then at the banana and said, "What? Yeah, yeah, yeah, it is my new ritual for the pregame. You know, it helps with potassium. I sweat five pounds off a game, so the potassium helps to stop the terrible cramping."

Harry shook his head and laughed, "You are a weird one, twenty-seven. Geez, man, there is no manly way for a guy to eat a damn banana! Can't ya switch to oranges or tangerines?"

We all laughed at Harry's observation and the accurate reenactment of a scene from a locker room long ago.

I walked over, and the two of us embraced.

Harry told me as we held each other, "Damn, I am so glad you are back, Paul. I thought that this time, we might have lost ya."

"Never. Harry and Paul adventures never end. They go on forever until the end of all time. I am back, thirty-five. Let's strap and buckle our asses in and get this practice going, eh?"

"Yup, let's do it, twenty-seven. Let's just do it."

About one-half hour later, after stretching, some skating drills and passing pucks around the rink, I was skating around with Harry at a pretty good pace, when he pulled up and slowly glided alongside the corner boards. I stopped, spun around and skated over to him. He was leaning on the boards, flexing his arm and huffing and puffing quite a bit. It seemed to be a bit unusual. Jim and Paul William spotted us and they, too, skated over to where we were.

"Hey you okay, Harry?" I asked as I studied him. Harry smiled and shook his arm a little and took a deep breath.

"Yeah, yeah, yeah, just got a little cramp here. Not in the best of shape myself, there, twenty-seven."

Jim and Paul William arrived and they, too, asked if Harry was feeling all right.

"Yeah, yeah, yeah, I am fine. Let's take some shots, huh?"

Paul William and Jim looked at me, I nodded and while I did not want to be a nagging pain-in-the-ass, I asked Harry one more time, "You sure? When is the last time you had a checkup at the doc?"

Harry pulled up, pushed his stick in front of him and started to skate away. He patted me on the back as he headed for the net.

"C'mon, shit . . . I am fine. Don't all of ya be old ladies now. C'mon, let's shoot a hole in twenty-seven."

Jim, Paul William and I shrugged our shoulders and followed Harry. He seemed fine; perhaps it was just a cramp. The rink was a little warm.

I skated into the net and readied myself to face the music. Death grip on the arms of the electric chair. . ..

Jim, Paul William, and Harry stood in a semicircle from the left faceoff circle to the right faceoff circle, while facing the goal net that I was standing in. Each of them had multiple pucks at their skates, and they tapped their hockey sticks on the ice hard and coaxed me to get ready to face some shots.

"You ready, twenty-seven?" Jim asked.

I pulled the mask tight over my head, tapped my goal stick on the right post, crouched down in my classic goaltender's stance and then I slowly moved on my skates, first out towards them, then I backed into the crease a little.

"Go!" I yelled.

I watched as Jim wound up and sailed a wrist shot in the air towards me. A wrist shot that cleanly beat me high on the stick side and whisked the back of the twine of the net as the puck hit the back of the net and bounced out. I had hardly even moved. In fact, I did not move at all.

Oh, oh. Not a good start.

Rather than taunt or joke with me about my inept goaltending, Jim merely yelled out, "C'mon, twenty-seven, don't get down. You are still the greatest goalie of them all. I know. I still dream of saves ya made to rob my ass. Take your time. C'mon now. Been a long time!"

All of them sensed how difficult this was going to be for me. Harry was next, a little different type of shot, but it ended with the same result. A clean goal and I barely moved, or even saw the puck sail by me. This was not going to be easy, and suddenly, my lower back cried out as a painful reminder of how long it had been since I had actually stood in front of a hockey net. Some consultant I was going to be to a young professional goalie, geez, I stink.

Harry took a few more shots, as did Jim and other than the two shooters missing the net; all the shots on goal achieved the same results. I did not stop a single shot! Still, no one taunted me, kidded me, or even said a word. They all sensed that now was not the time to poke fun at me, it was time to face reality. No doubt, it is always so hard to return to where you came from so long ago.

"Ready, Dad?" Paul William asked.

I waved my goalie stick in the air and glided out to face him. I shook my body a little and tried to get loose. I was working hard to reawaken a feeling and part of me that I had so long ago pushed aside. I needed to find the flow. It was still inside of me, somewhere. Deep inside, and when he sent a quick snapshot low on the ice on my stick side, I reacted rather well and caught the puck on the wide part of my goalie stick blade and tapped the puck easily to the side.

It was the first save that I had made in forever, and it felt magnificent. Just the feel of the weight of the puck striking the wood of the stick, and my ability to turn the shot aside and control the flight of the puck, amazingly, reawakened my senses.

Suddenly, all the old instincts returned, and I felt a warm and smooth flow come over my muscles. My eyesight was keen, my posture relaxed, and I moved in and out of my crease, my skates feeling every bump, groove and nick in the ice beneath them. Sweat started to run off my face, and it now ran off the edge of my old mask like a river. I felt the sweat run down, then drip and land on my chest underneath my protector.

Hell yeah, twenty-seven was back.

I was good to go.

"Let 'em ride, men!"

And they did. They hit me with a barrage of pucks that I knew I was sure to recall in great detail and a shower of pain when I tried to rise out of bed tomorrow morning.

Indeed, twenty-seven was back, and so it was that, together, our journey began to climb back from the anguish of despair and unfathomable grief. God's plan at work, healing for my soul.

It turned out to be a grand afternoon and after a shower, a promise to meet for dinner and a few drinks in a few hours, I found myself alone walking out of the locker room, carrying my pads and equipment bag with me. A Zamboni slowly circled the ice surface on the rink we had just utilized. The lights were now dim over the rink to keep the temperature down, and they cast a quiet glow over the ice. I stood for a long time staring at the maintenance man as he steered the machine around the hockey rink. Countless ghosts floated everywhere. They included faces and voices of my teammates and players on opposing teams, cheering fans, coaches, referees, and reenactments of games we won, and games that we lost. They haunted me wherever I looked, so I tried hard to focus on the Zamboni and ignore them. It was impossible to ignore them, because as usual, they overwhelmed me. I wondered how many times it was that I stood on the side of an ice rink like this one, in the same manner that I stood here right now, thinking, pondering, recalling.

No doubt that there is a smell to a hockey rink, a certain atmosphere that I, even to this day, know, but I just cannot describe.

It is in my mind's eye and my senses forever.

I knew that in Heaven, Binky and all the other saints were all rejoicing for me. I could hear her gentle voice encouraging me and telling me, "That not a marble can get by me now."

Tomorrow, my old body would be stiff, sore, and screaming at me in protest. It was nothing that a warm soak in a bathtub filled with bath salts would not cure.

A smile, a blink of the eyes to hold back a tear or two, and I knew that it had been another glorious reunion of my spirit.

Aduniad.

Chapter Four

The Return of Number Twenty-seven

It was now a powerful memory. A memory of some pain, and a memory, of which caused me some emotional moments while I strode down the terminal hallways of the Boston Airport.

My mind whirled with the recollection of the last time that I was here while I was still a player within the Boston Bears organization. I rode these hallways, while sitting in a wheelchair, as an airline attendant rolled me to the aircraft; three days after Doctor Dennis O'Brien reconstructed my right knee with extensive surgery. I walked up the jet-way, with a cane and a plaster leg cast from my ankle to my hip, and the attendants assisted me in sitting across the first two seats in the first row, in first class. The former hockey goalie, once able to perform wild split saves with his legs, and effortlessly skate, now reduced to a crippled shadow of his former self.

Yes, a powerful memory. I never once returned to Boston since that upsetting departure. Long ago, I came to terms with what initially, inside of my heart and soul, was a nagging pain at my failure to make it to the big league. My injury occurred a few days before the Bears were going to bring me up to their team as a backup goalie on the big-league roster. The injury caused not only a derailment of those plans and my career, but it changed the direction of my life. Yet, with the assistance of Binky, faith in God's plan, my writing, as well as a profound and a special visit to return to where my hockey roots started in the old neighborhood, I had finally put number twenty-seven to rest. I managed to chalk up the injury as just another part of God's plan for my life. It was a purposeful shift in direction, so that God could use me in the manner of which God intended for me. There were no doubts in my mind that was the intention, and many times over in my career and life as a Lutheran clergyman, God proved that to me. I agreed with that part of the plan, and now, who the hell knows? Who exactly knows why I am now riding down an escalator in the airport in Boston? Why am I heading for a meeting with my old friend, and to return to a professional rink for the first time in over twenty-five years? Yet, in my heart, I knew that this was the mission that God wanted for me. Trust and obey. I do not always agree, but I do trust and obey. My goodness, life is so full of twists and turns.

"Good afternoon, number twenty-seven. It is my great pleasure to meet you. The famous number twenty-seven. I am Tommy Hayward, special assistant to Mr. Brian McClure."

A short, young man, with very little hair, smartly dressed in a dress shirt with a tie, covered by a Boston Bears sweater vest, met me at the base of the main escalator. Mr. Hayward was quite an excitable and nervous little chap, as he hurried over to greet me with his hand extended. I was about to ask him how he recognized me when I realized how stupid a question that would have been. I was the only six-foot five or thereabouts, long-haired hippie on the escalator.

I towered over the little chap; he seemed to be about five-foot five or thereabouts.

"Nice to meet you, Mr. Hayward. It is my pleasure too. I am, Paul John Henson," I said, while I took his hand and fervently shook it.

"Oh boy, Mr. McClure warned me about the power of your handshake. Man, oh man, you are a big guy. You did not look so large in the video clips."

I watched as the little man held his hand and rubbed at it. I still had some power in my hands, and my recent return to workouts and whipping into a reasonable shape of my old body had restored some of that power. I must have been shocked at his statement about watching a video of me, and Mr. Hayward smiled as he spotted my reaction.

He quickly pointed in the direction of the front of the terminal and offered a further explanation, "Oh yes, we still have large amounts of film in the archives on number twenty-seven. I pulled it out and have studied quite a bit of it as of late. Honestly, you did not appear to be such a large man in the clips. Yes, I watched an old film of you and yes, you were, and still might be, the greatest goaltender that ever played the game. Watching films is part of my job. Everything, when you work for Brian McClure, is part of your job. No doubt, from what I saw in watching those film clips, you are the best goalie that I have ever seen. Remarkable."

I remained shocked, and the look of surprise on my face seemed as if it caused Mr. Hayward some pause.

He stopped walking and after what seemed to be some deep thought, he told me, "I mean that sincerely, twenty-seven. I am a student of the game of hockey. Love it and I tried to play, but my diminutive stature did not exactly work out in my favor. I feel that just because there are new players in the league these days, new equipment and new methods of training, does not necessarily mean that there are better players. I have great respect for all generations of hockey. I have to add that you look as if you can still play too."

He smiled at me, and recovering, I turned to the baggage claim line and offered, "Thank you for the compliments. I am not too sure that you are correct, but certainly entitled to your opinion. As far as still able to play, well, you would not have wanted to see me a few weeks or so ago. I could not see my shoes past my belly. Say, I need to get my bags from baggage claim. This bag only has some personal items and my goalie skates and my goalie mask in it. I never trust my skates and mask to anyone. Never did, always carry them with me. Nowadays, the security chaps were not too pleased with that, but we worked it out."

I walked ahead of Mr. Hayward a bit to head towards the baggage claim area, when he ran up to me and gently touched my shoulder. "No, no, no, please, Mr. Twenty-Seven. Come this way. We already have your bags and gear in the limousine in front. We are ready to go."

Once again, I must have displayed some element of surprise on my face, as Mr. Hayward shrugged his shoulders, read my mind and explained, "Yes, we were able to take your bags straight from the aircraft to the limousine. We might be in last place this year, but we are the Boston Bears and this *is* Boston. I hope you enjoyed the first-class seats and the Big Boulder beer we had brought on the aircraft, especially for you too."

Now, it was my time to smile, and I thanked him and explained a little, "Okay. However, it is just, twenty-seven. You can drop the mister part. Yes, I imagine that you do have some connections around here. That also explains the mysterious upgrade to first class, and the credit applied to my credit card for the cost of the flight. I recently, greatly reduced my beer intake in an effort to get myself in some sort of reasonable condition and allow my liver to regroup a bit, but yes, thank you for the beer. I had two glasses during the flight and it was enjoyable."

"Oh yes, I apologize, for the mister title. It is just, twenty-seven. I have it now. I promise, just a bit nervous about meeting a hockey legend. Excellent! Good, then let's move ahead. We will get you checked into the hotel and I will provide you the itinerary for this evening's dinner plans, as well as for the meeting schedule for tomorrow. The Bears have an off day today, but there is a game in Buffalo tomorrow evening. Mr. McClure and his staff, myself included, did not travel with the team so that he could meet with you. We will watch the game from our team facility tomorrow night."

An impeccably dressed, black-suited driver met us curbside in front of the airport. He nodded stoically, opened the doors for us and we both climbed into the rear seats of the limousine. A number of pedestrians passed by, stood and watched, and I am sure that their eyes caught the team logo on Mr. Hayward's sweater vest. That and the fact that we were climbing into a limousine caused some pedestrians to scurry over for a closer look at who it was from their hometown hockey club that was in front of the airport. The driver moved quickly, ushered us into the limousine and held off the small, but curious, crowds of onlookers.

Mr. Hayward, as I mentioned, was an excitable young man, and he chatted up a storm on the ride through the tunnel and into downtown Boston. As the limousine zipped along and I listened, occasionally commented, and mostly nodded to Mr. Hayward's chatting, I recalled where the main offices for the hockey club were located inside a high-rise office building located just a few blocks from the financial district of the city. While we drove along, my mind recalled a meeting in those same offices a very long time ago. I signed a contract there and had dinner with some executives of the club, but for some reason, I never met with a general manager. In fact, I could not even recall who the general manager of the Bears would have been so long ago.

It is easy in the world of sports to forget and become lost in the fact that behind the scenes, it is a major business. Before I knew it, Mr. Hayward checked me into one of the finest hotels in the old city, in a V.I.P. room fully equipped with a refrigerator full of food and snacks, ice-cold Big Boulder beer, and bottles of top-shelf booze. The room also had a full entertainment center with music, a large flat screen television with discs of taped hockey games available, movies to view, and all sorts of other top-shelf amenities. I found this very interesting. Either the Bears or Brian were concerned for my mental status or they are putting a helluva lot of faith in my abilities to assist this young man. Perhaps it was a touch of both, eh?

I sat on the edge of the bed, in the fancy penthouse room, looking out upon a remarkable view of the city and started to think deeply about where it was that I was right now in my life. Since this new adventure began, I had made a point of researching every aspect of the current state of major league hockey with a laser focus upon the current state of the Boston Bears. The last thing that I wanted was to appear to be uninterested. Even if I had disconnected myself from hockey for quite a long time. In fact, over the last month or so, I disconnected from most of life, not only from hockey. With that thought in mind, my mind wandered and I thought how it is going to be hell when I return to the office to catch up, even with the remarkable talents of Martha Wiggins holding it all down in my absence.

The Bears were struggling and right now; it was a lost season. Perhaps they were rebuilding or had no clear direction; it was not quite clear, but the team was now in last place and just playing out the last remaining five games or so of their schedule. The team had one or two stars, one player on offense and one on defense, but other than that, the team remained void of talent. As far as the goaltending situation, the hockey club had primarily used three different goalies during the season. One was a veteran of the league who played for many teams, one journeyman, who had bounced around the league for a few years, and one younger goalie, who was a high draft choice but apparently, a failed prospect. Brian fired the head coach a few weeks ago, and they now had an interim coach to finish off the schedule. The interim coach was an old name in hockey circles, a man I had heard of a number of times a long time ago when I was in Norfolk, Virginia playing in the Boston farm system. The interim head coach, a chap named William Bettermann, had been a defenseman in the farm system for many years, and while I knew his name, I could not place him, or recall if we played together at one time or another.

Brian McClure was off the hook for a year or two. Mountains of research that Paul William provided, informed me that he only recently took over as the general manager, and therefore, he had a few years of leniency to sort out the mess that the Boston Bears had become. It was very apparent that for some reason, with regard to old number twenty-seven, my old pal, Brian McClure was pulling out all the stops. He was treating me as if I was some in-demand hockey player or coach, rather than a washed-up goalie and potential "consultant." An old-time goalie, long since removed from the modern game, as well as a Lutheran clergyman, working very hard to recover from the fact that he now was a widower, and gaining, but still somewhat, lost in the world. None of this made much sense to me, even when I factored in and took account of the fact that Brian and I were old friends and he might just want to reunite and reconnect. It did not make much sense, except for the fact that despite my lack of self-confidence, I did know the sport of hockey better than what I wanted to admit. I knew that rebuilding a hockey club, started and ended with quality goaltending.

Shaking my head, I pulled the typed schedule out that Mr. Tommy Hayward had provided me and studied it. Tonight, Brian, Mr. Hayward, and a chap named Mr. Bryce Eddings, were all to meet with me for drinks at the lounge here in the hotel. After introductions and reunions, we were dining together at a restaurant that the name meant very little to me, but I was sure that it was one of the finest in the city. "The Silver Number Nine" was the name of the restaurant, and I was about to pull out my cellphone and search the internet for what it was all about, when my phone rang. Glancing over at the screen, I saw that it was Harry checking in with me.

Before I could even say hello, he was babbling, "We got the house sold already. Two days on the market and the offer is for twenty-five thousand in dough over what ya were asking for it."

Finally, I took our children's advice and put our house up for sale before I left town. Harry, as usual, stepped in with his many business connections, and recommended a topnotch realtor. The news was not surprising. I knew the housing market was in good condition, the house in pristine shape and the fact that Harry could still sell ice to an Eskimo, made a quick sale a reality. He practically marketed the house on his own. Then, of course, this too could also be part of the plan.

"I sent the contract to Heather Sarah for a look-see over and once she blesses it and you sign it, then I will turn it over to my realtor to get this deal done. Heather Sarah and Sarah are catching a flight and heading up here to close the deal. They will stay with us for a few days and I can spoil your granddaughter rotten by buying her all kinds of cool stuff. I am a thinkin' she needs a number thirty-five and a twenty-seven-hockey sweater."

He finally stopped speaking, and I managed to eke out, "She already has three of each of them."

"Really? Shit, well then I will buy her an O'Malley jersey."

"Okay, Harry, that works. She only has one of those. A home sweater. Please, buy her an away sweater. Anyway, I am sure Rose and you will be in your glory. That sounds wonderful. No need to send me any paperwork. Heather Sarah can sign it if she thinks it, is a done deal. She has my power of attorney. Thank you for everything, Harry. Please thank Rose, for me too."

"Of course. Even better, that Heather Sarah can sign it. Quicker deal, I like to move shit like this along before stuff changes. Ya got a game plan there yet or what?"

"Geez. I just got here, Harry. They put me in some fancy-schmancy hotel and we are heading for dinner to a fancy joint named, 'The Silver Number Nine.' Seems as if they have put some faith in me. I cannot really imagine why. Say, did you make a doctor's appointment?"

As usual, I was too long-winded, Harry, of course, cut me off, "What do ya expect? Ya such an old lady, I swear. It's the Boston Bears, not the Long Island Roosters, Paul. Wake ya old lady ass up. That dinner joint is the best dump in the city. Some washed up old Boston baseball player opened it up years ago and then he sold it for a fortune. I watch business all over the country. Anyway, ya have known this Brian guy for a long time. He knows you. He needs ya, he cares 'bout ya and wants to help ya, while ya can save this pussy goalie from failure. It is all right up ya old lady alley. This is the ticket ya need, to get where ya need to be right now. Don't ya see that God is still moving you around, Paul? It is part of the plan. Now, ya long-haired ass needs a joint to live in here in New Jersey. I will help. Leave it to Heather Sarah, and me. Ya would pick out some old lady community. Ya need a joint with hot chicks sunbathing naked on their decks all around ya. Rose wants ya over here for dinner when ya get back and for you to stay with us for a few weeks until you find a new joint. Better, not disappoint her cuz she misses ya. We need to go to dinner, have a long talk, and create a game plan. Don't do nuthin' for free now! Ya are too much of an old lady for making a harsh deal. Buckle ya mask straps, adjust ya crotch and I will talk to you later."

"Click!"

Typical Harry. He babbles on, never allows me to speak for too long, never says goodbye on the telephone and always hangs up with that same annoying click in my ear.

I decided against looking up the restaurant on the internet, Harry's testimony provided me with enough background information on it. Instead, I headed for the gym in the hotel, hit the treadmill and then the weights and returned to my room a sweaty mess. With a laugh at an old memory, I grabbed a cold Big Boulder beer from the cooler and sipped it for a bit. Ironic, a workout and then a beer. I was falling back into my old hockey life once again, when we would drink our beer after games and between workouts. A few beers would be all right, I just did not want to return to being pie-eyed every night. I sat and sipped the beer for a bit, took a shower and dressed for dinner and a night out on the town. Along with general attire and necessities, I brought two suits with me, as well as two sets of casual business attire. For this evening, I selected a dark blue suit and a white shirt with a dark blue tie. Binky always advised me for initial meetings; to stay away from my preferred black suits. My wife told me that the black suits made me appear even more imposing than usual. I was not quite sure what that meant, but her advice always was correct. Therefore tonight, we would go with the blue suit. If we moved from a simple meeting and reconnecting of old friends, and started negotiating something special, then I would consider pulling out the imposing factor.

Once dressed and polished, I trimmed my beard, combed out the long mop of hair and decided against the hair tie. No sense hiding what I still was. The finishing touch was my solid gold, number twenty-seven, tie clip that I had forever, and since this evening was a return of sorts of number twenty-seven, then it seemed quite appropriate to wear it.

It was now late March, and the days and nights were changing around quite a bit. The sun was starting to call it quits for the day, and the city dimmed and flickered to life below me. Mr. Hayward told me to plan on a seven o'clock meeting in the hotel lounge area, but I was, as usual, early, and with time to kill, and a touch of hunger rolling around in my stomach, I grabbed my wallet and wandered down to the hotel lobby to find the bar in the hotel lounge.

When I selected a seat on the long and half-mooned shaped bar, I watched as a tall, middle-aged woman bartender quickly looked over to me. She smiled, and she scurried over to me rather quickly.

"Good evening, number twenty-seven, or is it Pastor or Bishop Henson?" She asked with a wide smile.

The bartender was gorgeous. She was a light-skinned black woman with amazing facial features, an amazing female figure, and a friendly demeanor, impeccably dressed and kept, and as I just found out, briefed by no doubt, Brian's most capable assistant.

Mr. Tommy Hayward did not miss a trick.

"All of that works fine. I am all of those titles and I guess, perhaps, even a few more too. Not too cool about the bishop title, but Pastor Paul works out quite well. However, as far as number twenty-seven goes, it seems as if he is a cat with nine lives. Twenty-seven is on about his fifth go around now."

She laughed, smiled and extended her hand, "Good, four more to go. I like that description. Innovative. My pleasure to meet you, Pastor Paul, slash number twenty-seven, slash author, slash all the other alter egos and identities. Heard ya loud and clear on the bishop, thingy. I am Janet. Night shift barkeeper here at this same post for over twenty years."

She reached in as I gently shook her hand and admired her smile and her beauty too. Janet then leaned back and placed her slender fingers to her chin as she implied a long pondering of sorts.

"Let's see, when I started here, the hotel's name was the 'Boston Galleria in the City,' then it was sold, and the new owners changed the name to, 'The Boston Patriot,' then on and on it goes. Lost track of all the names and changes. Now, here we all are. So as far as the cat with nine lives goes, well, I can certainly relate."

I nodded and commented as well as asked, "Yes, life is full of twists and turns. Do you have a last name, Janet?"

"Chesboro. Janet Anne Chesboro."

"Gotcha. Pretty name for a beautiful woman. Now, let me guess, Mr. Hayward has brought in a keg of Big Boulder beer just for me for this visit, as well as briefed you, and the entire hotel staff, on all aspects of number twenty-seven."

Janet smiled again, waved and pointed to a tap above the bar rail.

"The man does not miss a trick. Besides, the obvious reasons that the Boston Bears are important to our business, one of the owners of the hockey club also owns this hotel. Do not even bother trying to pay for drinks or food here. He arranged all of it beforehand. Even my tips. Unless, you would like to tip me in some other manner."

All of this now made sense, and I leaned back, folded my arms across my chest and nodded. I watched as Janet took a pint glass, (my preference in beer glass selections) opened the tap and poured a Big Boulder for me.

"Here you go, Pastor Paul. Yes, all aspects. I have read most of your books and I love the story of the time bomb. Damn well, could relate to an alcohol-induced time bomb. Laughed my ass off on that one. Hayward briefed me, as well as the entire staff on all aspects of you, including one that I learned, but did not fully realize, until I met you in person just a few minutes ago. I knew when he showed me a photograph of you that damn, you are knockout handsome, but in person, you are a lot better looking. Sorry, for the language and honest opinion. I will be back. Have a pain-in-the-ass customer at the end of the bar."

With a wave and a wink, Janet Chesboro was off.

This was going to be interesting. I had been out of

circulation in the world for a very long time and forgotten how forthright some people and women could be. Everything will be well. I just needed to keep my wits about me. Remind myself to keep my head screwed on tightly. Janet was a pro. You could tell she could milk the bar patrons with her maximum bounce and sway and extract the money from their wallets for tips. In my case, since monetary tips were apparently not her desire, then I had to be careful as to exactly what she extracted from me.

I ordered a small dish of appetizers to drown with the beer, made small talk with Janet, thanked her for reading my books, and carefully sidestepped and avoided any flirting from her. Before I knew it, there was a tap upon my shoulder and turning around, I once again met the eyes of my old friend, Mr. Brian McClure.

"Some of us get older, and others, such as number twenty-seven here, just seem to get younger with age. You look great, Paulie, and please go gentle with the handshake. I think the bones in my hand just healed from a handshake that you gave me twenty-five years ago," Brian smiled and extended his hand, while I slid off the bar stool to greet him. It had been a very long time. He was, of course, humoring me as to my appearance, and he in fact, looked a little older, but certainly appeared to be in fine shape for his age. A little less hair and a bit of a belly, but he looked well. His somewhat limited hair was all gray now, but he still wore his hair neatly, with a clean part and a gentle sweep to the side. He was clean-shaven and still rugged looking, with a lantern type jaw and dark eyes. He was of medium height, about five nine or thereabouts, but Brian was a bit heavier than he was many years ago.

"Still all that hair and that beard. You make me jealous, Paulie you really do," Brian said while rubbing the top of his head.

I waved my hand at his exaggeration and said, "It is good to see you, my old friend, and my apologies for allowing so much time to pass between us. It is my fault. You invited me here more times than I want to count."

I shook his hand while being aware of my tendency to be overzealous in my handshaking. Rather quickly, Brian let go of my hand, and he instead warmly embraced me.

"No trouble, twenty-seven. You are still in the midst of a long career serving a higher mission than we do in this hockey world and have hit a bit of a gut-wrenching stretch. Knowing twenty-seven, you will not be down for long."

After letting go of me, he gently looked me up and down carefully while scanning my eyes.

In a softer voice, he asked, "You doing, okay? Once again, so sorry about your loss."

"I am, as well as to be expected, Brian. It has been difficult, but this invitation has come along at the right moment in my life. I really feel as if it did. Thank you."

Brian McClure nodded; he punched me playfully in the arm and then whistled as he commented, "I agree. It is wonderful to see you. Still, in great shape too. And I forgot how large a man you are. Man, oh, man, one big goalie. They don't cook 'em this big anymore. That is part of the trouble, Paulie."

After our rather warm and long reintroduction, Brian turned to Mr. Hayward, who was standing off to the side. It was then that I was aware of another chap standing next to Tommy Hayward. He was a middle-aged man with longish blonde hair, about the same height, weight as Brian was, and he stood smiling and observing the meeting.

"Twenty-seven, you already know my assistant, Tommy Hayward. I trust that he has taken good care of you?"

"Exceptionally so, Brian. Thank you."

"Good, good, I would like you to meet our Director of Scouting, Mr. Bryce Eddings. Bryce, the world famous, Paul John Henson, also known as Pastor Paul, number twenty-seven, and forgive me, but who the hell else knows what other titles you have had."

I extended my hand, smiled, and shook Mr. Eddings' hand.

"My pleasure to meet you, Mr. Eddings."

"Please, call me Bryce. No, the pleasure is all mine. Watched some film of your goaltending last week. Damn, the real deal. What a remarkable goalie!"

"Well, Bryce, that was a long time ago, a very long time ago. Seems as if it were a few lifetimes ago now. Thank you for the compliment. We stopped a few and let a few in too."

"Not too many got by ya," Bryce commented.

"Well, now that we are all acquainted and reacquainted, let's get Janet here to pour us a few drinks and head off for dinner. I trust that Janet has also taken good care of you, Paulie?"

Janet looked over and winked at me when she overheard the conversation, and I assured Brian that she did so. We had a few more drinks, and some general small talk as well as some conversations about old games, old times, and people we knew along the way and such.

"Whatever happened to such-and-such?"

"Do you remember that game in Bangor, Maine, and that ass-beating that what's his name took?"

The rehashing of old times went on for a long time and after downing a round or two, Brian waved at Janet to show to her that we were leaving. She quickly scooted over to me and whispered as she gathered up the empty glasses, "Good luck, Pastor Paul, number twenty-seven. I hope to see you for a nightcap. I am here until two in the morning."

I smiled and thanked her and before I knew it; we were all off to a limousine and seated in a corner table in what was without a doubt a very fine restaurant. Brian and the Boston Bears had spared no expense on this evening, and in fact, on this entire trip and the reasons behind them courting me so hard was still a bit puzzling to me. I was anxious to find out what they had in mind, and now, with a marvelous full-course dinner behind us, a few drinks rolling around in all of us; Brian loosened up and shifted from an old friend and cordial host to putting his general manager's hat on for a bit.

As far as the beer drinking went, I now resorted to sipping and nursing a Big Boulder beer, while my dinner companions were hammering down cocktails. I did so, for two reasons. One, I wanted to stick somewhat to my new program of easing up on the beer, and two, I wanted to keep my head clear, in order to understand what it was that Brian and the Boston Bears were seeking from me.

"Twenty-seven," Brian started his sales pitch as he waved the server over to order another round of drinks, "I have some time for a reprieve here. The Bears suck this year, and in fact, the last few years have been a bust. I inherited a damn mess. Old time players with iron clad contracts that my predecessors had their heads in their asses to have negotiated. Shitty drafts and scouting of players before Bryce here took over the scouting. We had insane salaries, a high payroll with poor players, and lousy coaches. . .."

His voice trailed off as he waved at me and apologized.

"Sorry about the language, always think of you as twenty-seven, the goalie and my old drinking pal and not your second career as Pastor or Bishop Paul John Henson." He studied my eyes for a reaction. Here we go now. The first test, to see if I was now thin-skinned for the somewhat rougher aspects of the hockey world.

I easily and casually dismissed the language, "It is no trouble, please continue. I have no issues with the language. Been around a few rinks, you know, as well as quite a few other situations too. The business of the church behind the scenes is often indescribable, yet I can assure you that it is a business too. Please, continue uninhibited. I am anxious to hear what is happening here and see if I might be able to help."

Brian glanced quickly at Bryce and then over to Tommy Hayward. His eyes darted around the table, studying each individual's reaction, and he quickly smiled. I had known Brian a long time and, in the past, he was always a straight shooter. Now, I could tell the many years had turned him into a seasoned businessman and an expert negotiator. I had the feeling that Brian and his staff had staged and planned parts of this conversation ahead of time. He picked the conversation back up just as the server returned with some more cocktails.

"Good, then. Yes, I imagine you have dealt with quite a bit off the ice and on it. On second thought, maybe, I cannot actually imagine what you have been through, Paulie. Regardless, we suck big time and having been in the organization forever, I will never be out of a job. Perhaps, reassigned, but never fired completely. I have some time to figure this all out. Not forever, but sometime. The team owners are not rookies. They have changed since your time within the organization, but they understand it took a few years for us to fall this far and it will take a few to bring us back to glory. After all of this . . . I want to be part of the turnaround."

I wanted to show that I was on my game and that I had performed some research ahead of time as a prelude to our meeting, so I jumped into the conversation here. "One of the owners . . . is he not Ralph Johnson's son? Ralph was majority owner years ago when you and I were in Albany together."

Tommy Hayward, being a walking and talking hockey research machine, a fact of which I am quite sure that Binky would be proud of, jumped in with the information.

"You are quite correct, twenty-seven. Ralph is now Chairman Emeritus of the Bears but his sons, and the minority owner for years, Mr. William Austin, appointed his nephew in his place. This new group are all in charge of the operation now."

I nodded my head and said, "Understood. Thank you, Tommy. Ralph is a nice guy. Must be over ninety years old by now? God bless him."

I carefully watched as Mr. Hayward took a sip of his cocktail, nodded and then pulled out a pad and pen from his suit jacket pocket and started to take notes. No doubt, his efficiency did not diminish with his alcohol intake. He must have had instructions to record the finer points of the conversation. I was sure of the strategy and the fact they felt as if I had been engaged in my interest enough to research the current events of the Boston Bears.

Brian continued, "This is a historical hockey club, one of the original six teams. A class organization and I, and in fact, we, have achieved success on all levels of this sport except for here in the big time. Twenty-seven, you and I won it all in Albany when I was doing what Bryce now does, and now, it may sound cliché or corny, but I want to win a cup. I want to win a championship in the big league."

After speaking, Brian picked up his drink and took a big gulp, while staring over the rim of the glass and carefully continuing to study me. I knew the drill here and now. They wanted to see and feel if my passion for winning remained. My passions for the sport, for what it takes to grind it out day-after-day, game-after-game.

Bryce piped up and asked, "You won with the Long Island Roosters too, right, Paulie? The Roosters are long since gone, as is the rest of that league, but Albany is thriving and we, of course, still have Norfolk. Rumor has it that Albany wants to retire your jersey number, and the EHL has you in a slot for induction into the EHL Hall of Fame. Did you know that?"

The old flow of hockey excitement came over me in waves. I felt the shiver of excitement of playing the game go up and down my spine. That feeling of competing, the feeling of winning, of leaving it all out on the ice and coming away as the champions of the game. It was a great feeling and honestly, I found it hard to suppress my smile and thoughts.

"No, I did not know that. It is the first I heard of that one, Bryce. That would be quite an honor."

Leaning back, I thought for just a second or two about those feelings and while picking up my mug, I thought, "The hell with limiting the beer." I knocked the last of the beer down in one big sip and I waved over to the server to bring a refill. I could feel all of their eyes studying me and as I pondered how good it felt to win those championships so long ago, I finally answered the question and commented, "Yes, won it all in Albany and on the island. There is no feeling like it. Brian. None. I share your feelings. I am sure that Bryce and Tommy do too. I would love to feel that way again and win it all. It is indescribable. I am sure for a player it is different, then it is for management, but still, I would love to win it."

The server brought over the fresh mug of beer and I lifted the mug in the air while my dinner partners smiled and grabbed their glasses and held them up for a toast.

"Well, now here is to the Boston Bears," Brian said, as we each took a sip. "Now, let me be honest and tell you why I brought you here. Straight up, twenty-seven. No bullshit. Our goaltending this year has been horrible. Worst in the league, by far. If we are going to rebuild—then you know where it starts. It starts at the net and works its way out. Center iceman next, but goalie first. Therefore, I want you to be our goaltending consultant for a young prospect that is in Norfolk right now. In fact, I have to say that I know what you are going to say ahead of time, I will wait for your reply. We drank too much beer together years ago, Paulie. I know you."

I laughed at what was a true statement and then said what Brian knew that I was going to say, "I have never been a hockey consultant or a coach before."

"Knew it!" My old friend slammed his hand on the table in jest. "Damn guy is fearless on the net and just as his best friend used to say, he is like an old lady out of it."

I laughed and commented, "He still says that I am an old lady."

"Bet he does! Besides, that bullshit statement, my old friend is not true, because you coached your son in peewee hockey, all the way, to when you were an assistant coach during his high school years. Bryce just told you about the plans for the EHL and the Albany Dutchman to honor you. You are still a well-known legend in goaltending and hockey circles. The long-haired hippie goalie from New Jersey. It is the basis of folklore."

Perhaps it was a bit rude on my part, but I was only being honest when I shrugged my shoulders to dismiss what Brian had just spoken. I felt as if we were dwelling upon experiences from ages ago, as well as a long-ago faded reputation that no longer counted or had merit.

Brian leaned in, as did Bryce and Mr. Hayward. The conversation was now going to head for the business end of all of this.

The General Manager of the Boston Bears grew serious and the tone of his voice reflected that seriousness, "Here is where it is at. A revolving door of shitty goalies, old vets we signed to get us through, a journeyman or two who both sucked on other teams and guess what? They sucked with us too. A prospect that did not pan out . . . but down in our farm system, we have a young goalie. A young man named Vance Howard. A young goalie that I say, and Bryce here agrees, is the best prospect the Bears have seen in the net since some long-haired, hippie, goalie named, Paul John Henson."

Brian leaned back and hammered down the rest of his drink. This was going to be one of those nights. Old-time hockey discussed and deals brokered over drinks and all-nighters. Brian's eyes were intense, and now a little bloodshot too. It had been a long day, and this was a long night too. Dinner was marvelous, but it was becoming late enough that we might need a late-night snack to suck up the alcohol and to hold us over.

Brian turned on the drama, yet I felt as if he was sincere as his voice lowered to just above a whisper, "I think you might know that name and the legend of twenty-seven."

This time, I did not react; instead, I locked eyes, followed Brian's eyes from his drink glass, and then watched as they returned to staring at me. Even after all of our years apart, I knew him well enough to know there was more to the story.

Sure enough, he rambled on a bit more with the background story of the young goalie, "The trouble is, at the beginning of last season, he got nailed big time in the throat with a slap shot. Collapsed his voice box, all kinds of surgery, time in the hospital and now he is puck shy. Physically, he is fine. Mentally, not so good. He is now a flincher, and he pulls out on low and hard shots. The kid cannot seem to shake it, and his style of goaltending is like most goalies these days. They use the leg pads as if they were cushions and slide all over the crease and stay on the ice. With that style of play, his head is always in the line of fire. We hate to give up on him, and feel as if he did not get so low on the ice all the time, then he would overcome some of his fear. I have this crazy idea to turn him from a modern-day goalie who flops and slides on the ice, into an old-time standup, angle cutting master, like number twenty-seven was, and I think still is."

While shaking my head at Brian's comments, I knew that it was time to interject my thoughts, "Brian, modern goaltending is all about flopping, sliding, staying down on the ice, and going post-to-post with your pads flat out. Only occasionally, do you find these goalies nowadays leaping out of a butterfly position. No goalies stand up and cut angles any longer. The leg pads are huge nowadays, they are like balloon cushions for them to slide and glide around on the ice on and the gloves are huge, as well as the crease is larger now too. These goalies only stand on their skates for the National Anthem, then they flop all over the place. My style and the era, of which I played, are long since gone. I am a dinosaur."

"Bullshit. Sorry, but I will say it again. Bullshit, Paulie. The old style worked for how damn long? Eighty or more years. Countless goalies in the Hall of Fame stood up, did not flop around like a bunch of drunken fools, and won countless championships. And I ain't buying the line of bullshit that the shooters are better now and that they skate faster. I know you ain't gonna agree with that either. You faced 'em, I only watched, was never good enough to play, but I damn well been watching forever. I am willing to bet that you could teach this young man. You could bring his courage back, show him the old ways. He would overcome his fear of the flight of the puck coming straight at his head on every shot because he is so low on the ice. Teach him to cut angles and stand up on his skates. Teach him old-time hockey. After all, it is basic friggin' geometry. Goaltending styles, equipment and methods changed but geometry hasn't."

Bryce and Tommy Hayward both nodded their heads in agreement. Of course, they did. I could tell that they always agreed with their boss. If I were in their place, then I would too. I picked up the mug of beer and sipped it. I was now deeply interested and as crazy as this all sounded; I found a tingle or two of excitement running up and down my body. Yet, I knew there was more than just my experience as an old-style goalie, of which the Bears were seeking.

Placing the mug down, I asked the question that my heart told me to ask, "So this young goalie. Vance. There is more to it than just his injury. What is he like?"

Brian smiled and shook his head. He softly spoke, while pointing his finger first at me and then to each of his staff individually, "See. Told ya. This is what I told you about this man. He might have been stupid enough to play the most difficult position in all of sports, but he is the smartest man you will ever meet. You nailed it, Paulie. Not just any coach, can coach or teach this kid. The kid is an asshole. A real jerk. Until he was hurt, he was cocky and arrogant. Blows all his bonus money and most of his salary on booze and sports cars and entertaining every easy woman in every city on our tour. He thinks that he is God's gift to hockey and to all women. Handsome, tall, big for a modern-day goalie. His build is similar to yours, Paulie. He might be a little shorter than you are. Has his pick of the women on the road. They fall all over the kid. Anyway, he acted as if he was a king. Not coachable. Knows everything. Now, after the injury, he is still arrogant, but mad at the world."

Brian stopped speaking, and he allowed his eyes to wander around the room. I could tell that even though he was now the General Manager of the Boston Bears and a powerful executive, he was still a man who cared deeply about the sport and about his players. Brian was a good man, and I had great respect for him.

His voice lowered a bit, and he grew less intense, as he continued to speak, "He will not admit that he is afraid. Deep down, I think he is actually a good kid. He never had a father figure in his life, so he is always out to prove to the world exactly whom Vance Howard is. The major trouble with that is the fact that Vance Howard does not yet know or realize who he is. The talent is still there, we just need to rediscover it and refine it. This plan is crazy, but I believe in Vance, and most importantly, I believe in you. Pastor Paul, you coached people, both young and old for years as a pastor and a bishop in a lot more important shit than hockey. You are a born leader. Still the best goalie that I have ever seen, and I know in my heart that you are the man for this job. This is a unique situation. It is as much about being a pastor as it is about being a goalie."

Brian turned to Tommy, nodded, and pointed. Mr. Hayward put his pad and pen down, reached into his suit jacket and pulled out a DVD in a plastic case.

He slid it across the table to me and explained, "This is a DVD with video clips of Vance Howard playing goal. Before the injury and after. The Bears, just as they did years ago, with you, have invested a ton of dough and time in Vance Howard. We need to try to salvage his talent and the investment. There is a video player in your hotel room. Please check it out."

I nodded and picked up the disc.

Brian placed his hand over my hand and commented, "Look, it is very late. This joint is closing, and it was a long day for you. Too long. Airplane flight, all that travel. Shit, you must be very tired. Let's get you back to your room. It has been an amazing discussion. We can all sober up, and you can check out the video in the morning. We can meet in my office tomorrow. Let's say, around eleven or so. Then we can have lunch. Tommy will work it out. He will call your room in the morning and have you picked up."

I placed the disc in my suit jacket and said, "Sounds like a plan. Thank you. Thank you for everything. This has been a remarkable meeting and trip."

We returned to the hotel around one o'clock in the morning, I bid my companions good evening, avoided Janet at the lounge bar while she worked her last hour or so and hustled up to my room. I could not wait to pop the disc into the player, and while I somewhat reluctantly avoided Janet's invitation for a nightcap with her, I instead chose a cold Big Boulder beer from the room refrigerator. Right for now, my plan to cut back on my beer intake had derailed. Slipping the disc into the player, I first turned the video player on and then the television. I sat on the edge of the bed with the remote control in my hand and sure enough, the video clips of Vance Howard playing goal appeared on the screen. I slowly sipped at my beer and before I knew it, I had a pad and pen in my hand and I was taking notes. I wrote down on the pad, "Fair to a weak skater. Needs to improve his balance and skating. Despite his weak skating abilities, he has exceptional lateral movement. Amazingly quick glove hand." I made a note in larger, bolder print, "Might be the fastest glove hand that I have ever seen. Reflexes are top notch and he is highly athletic in his skills. He is slow on shots about a foot off the ice on his stick side. Pulls his head out on shots above his leg pads or high on his glove side. Flinches on screen shots."

The video clips mesmerized me and I found my body swaying and darting as I returned to the net with young Vance Howard. My adrenalin captured me while I jotted down notes and other honest comments on his style of goaltending and his skills. Two or three more beers later, along with a glance in horror at the time reading on my watch, I shut the player and television off.

It was now three in the morning. I knew what I had to do.

This young man did have all the tools. Brian, Bryce, and Tommy were correct. He was an incredible talent. Standing up, I slowly undressed. It was then that exhaustion set in and I realized that I had left New Jersey at five in the morning yesterday.

Still, some words from today's conversation echoed in my head as I headed for the shower.

First, Brian's testimony hit me, "Deep down, I think he is actually a good kid. He never had a father figure in his life, so he is always out to prove to the world, exactly who he is."

Then, Paul William's words echoed in my mind, "The game is a part of you and you are a part of it. Right now, it would be what you need. It will return the parts of you that you left so long ago on the ice and allow you to regain the one thing, of which you need the most right now."

"And what is that?"

"Your purpose, Dad. Your purpose."

I finished my shower and realized that despite my exhaustion, I was smiling widely and felt as if God's plan had once more taken me for a wild twist and turn in my life. Once again, I was too blind to see and too deaf to hear. It was time to recall the one person who restored sight to the blind and hearing to the deaf.

I knelt on the floor next to my bed and prayed simply, softly, and gently, "Thank you, dear Lord. Let it be as you have led me. Amen."

I then rose to my feet, went to my luggage, found my suit carrier and unzipped it. While still smiling widely, I began pulling out the parts and pieces of my black suit.

Tomorrow, I was going to need it.

Chapter Five

Black Suits and Bar Napkin Deals

"I have told my assistant to hold all my calls and prevent all interruptions, unless one of the owners calls me. Here is the deal, after that long day and night—I can tell that number twenty-seven is still, for the lack of any other description, number twenty-seven. Ya know why?"

I sat in a guest chair, in the lush and palatial offices of Mr. Brian McClure and sipped a much-needed cup of coffee. I was bone-weary. It had been a long time since number twenty-seven did an "all-nighter."

"No, how do you know, Brian? Maybe, because, last evening, we packed away far too many beers and drinks, just as we did in Albany so long ago."

He laughed and waved at me and then leaned in close, "No, well, shit, maybe that is part of it, Paulie. Mostly because of the lick in your eyes last night when we explained about what it is that we are looking for, we all want to win the cup and the potential of young Vance Howard. I also can tell by how you are sucking down the coffee right and left. The coffee intake tells me that you did not sleep too much. I remember how you paced the floor in hotel rooms and pissed and moaned all night about cheap goals that you let in. We have not seen each other or spoken in a long time, but we did room together and I know you very well."

I nodded to agree and Brian went on to explain some more, "Mostly, because I know that after we left you back at the hotel, you disappointed poor Janet at the bar and skipped her invitation for a nightcap that was mired in amorous intentions. Janet is a goddess. She rakes in the tips in barrelfuls from guys trying to catch her eye and spend time with her. I myself have tried, and she would not give me the time of day."

I was surprised at that statement and placed the cup of coffee on the edge of his desk.

The surprise must have shown in my eyes because before I could even state my thoughts, Brian read my mind, "I am twice divorced now. Hockey life and marriages do not work out too well. They were both very good women, the fault lies with me, not with them."

I nodded and said, "I did not know that you were no longer married. I knew about your first divorce, but lost track of where you were on a personal level with your second marriage. I am sorry to hear that the marriages did not work out for you."

"It's part of the life that I chose. Anyway, let me tell you that Janet has her eye on you. I know her. She did her homework on you and knows that you are a widower. The Boston Bears sort of, kind of, own the hotel, ya know. She only teases the men for the tips, but in reality, she does not give anyone more than the drinks they order and the time of the day. But I could tell that she was gushing over number twenty-seven. The batting eyes and wiggling hips and asses of the gorgeous ladies never meant shit to you, then and now. So instead, of bathing in her perfume, and enjoying wild sex, you retreated alone to your room and watched the video clips of Vance Howard playing goal, until all hours of the night. Only you would give up a night with a hottie to check out a goalie and weigh a hockey challenge. You were, and still are, the ultimate competitor and hockey warrior. Goaltending is in your blood and I am betting part of my success in this new position on the fact that there is no one who knows the position better than you do."

"Brian, my wife has only been gone for a bit of time," I said, as I picked the coffee back up and took a long sip of it.

"Sorry, Paul. I apologize, but you are still a man."

I felt the caffeine starting to pull me out of the tailspin. I placed the cup of coffee back down on the desk and reached inside of my suit jacket. I took out the pad that I had made the notes about Vance Howard's goaltending abilities on last evening and handed the pad to Brian.

He took the pad from my hands, and with a smile on his face, he spoke gently and softly, "I knew it. Damn. Paul John Henson, will always and forever, be number twenty-seven. Passing up a chance to spend time with a gorgeous woman to study video clips of a goalie prospect. What a damn old lady you are. I love it."

"In addition, I am a clergyman, Brian."

"Forgive me, Pastor Paul. That is irrevocable bullshit, Paulie. You might be a clergyman, but as I just said, you are still a man. Time to move forward with your life, Paulie. I am sure that your wife wants you too. Not being some kind of anti-religion nutcase or being unkind here, but life goes on and you have too much to offer this world to hide away. Sorry for the lecture, but you are an old and dear friend to me. We chewed an awful lot of ice together. Anyway, you passed on them years ago, too, before you traded in your goalie mask for a Bible. You will always be a friggin' goalie and hockey nerd. You and Hayward will get along just fine. He never played but knows the game almost as well as you do."

I did not comment, but instead studied his eyes as he read my notes.

After reading the notes that I had made, Brian McClure asked, "Can I keep this?"

"I might not agree with your schedule for my return to the world of pursuing females, but thank you for caring, Brian. Yes, we are old friends, always will be, and it has been very kind of you and your team to think of me. Thank you."

He nodded, smiled and pointed at the pad because I had not answered his question.

"Yes, of course. Sorry. I have it all in my mind now," I replied.

Brian continued to smile; the notes had obviously made his day. With his big smile planted on his face, he stood up from his chair and walked over to a built-in wooden bookcase that took up one entire wall of his office. There, he poured a cup of coffee from the carafe sitting upon the shelf of the furniture. While he prepared his coffee, I looked around at his office. It was worthy of his lofty position as the executive in charge of such a historic professional hockey organization. The walls of the office were full of pictures, plaques, hockey sweaters worn by hockey stars mounted inside of elegant frames, autographed hockey sticks and pucks, and other items that signaled they were all part of a lifetime collection of hockey memorabilia. My eyes carefully scanned the walls and sure enough, I spotted a picture of Brian and me together on the ice at the rink in Albany. I was in full uniform, wearing my goaltending gear in the middle of the picture, with Brian on one side, and the coach of the Albany Flying Dutchman, Coach Davis on the other side of me. It was a wonderful picture, which invoked a tumult of golden memories.

Brian caught my eyes studying it and he commented as he walked back to his desk with the cup of coffee, "Nice picture, huh? He was a helluva guy. Coach Davis was the best."

"He was, and it is a nice photo of us. Coach Davis and I would exchange letters and Christmas cards every year. On rare occasions, we spoke on the telephone . . . you know how Coach Davis did not socialize too much outside of our small circle. My wife, Binky and I visited him a few years ago, up in Ontario Province. It was a magnificent time. We spent a week there at his place on the lake. Lots of hiking and lots of fishing, and to be honest, lots of drinking. We cried a lot, laughed a ton, and most of all remembered all those memories. I miss him. He was the best. He married that gal he knew years ago when he was a young buck coming up. A great story for them to find each other all of those years later. She is a beautiful and wonderful woman. It is a grand story of love, how they at last reconnected and had some glorious years together before he passed away. Nice memories, but that is what we have together right now. Memories."

While sitting, Brian pointed at the photograph and said, "You want a copy of that print, Paulie?"

"I would like that. Thank you. It would mean a lot to me. Lots of memories in that photo."

"Hayward will get you one. You nailed it, Paulie. Exactly. Old memories. Time to make some new ones, my old friend. Coach Davis is looking down at us now, and he is smiling and rooting us onward. So, do we have a deal, Paulie? We owe Coach Davis to get it together again. He knew you were the best too. We gonna start a new string of memories? What will it take to bring you back to the Bears to help us out?"

Leaning back, I knew what I wanted to say, but a black suit or not, I was, and I guess as Harry said, "Until they invent a pill to cure me," will always be a victim of the dreaded Old Lady Syndrome.

"It is tempting, very tempting. First off, this young man needs direction and guidance and honestly, that appeals to the pastor in me. His remarkable ability appeals to the goalie in me. He has all the tools and looking at the video clips, he could be one of the greatest. Now, I understand why you are trying hard to save him. Yet the question remains for me. Is he going to take me very seriously? I have been out of the game forever. What about your current goalie coach, Brian? Is he going to have his ass all wrapped up when you bring me in here to help this young man? Couldn't he coach and teach Vance Howard?"

Brian waved his hand in the air to dismiss what I asked and proposed while telling me, "Nah. Fired his ass when I took over. The guy was a bum! Our goalies sucked, Paulie. We are a last-place team with a revolving door of goalies. He was the clown who advised us to put our hopes on that other young prospect and leave Vance to wallow in Norfolk. The other guy was terrible and Vance ends up taking the puck in the neck." Brian calmed down a bit, but it was obvious that the goalie coach's situation was a sore subject.

I nodded and brainstormed a bit more with him, "Okay, I understand, but we would be trying to teach a style of playing goal that has long since left the game and I have no credentials. Yes, you are correct, when you say that I have coached, and obviously played professionally, but let's be honest in the fact that I never coached on a high level, never played in the big league, long hair, damn, a clergyman, a bishop in the Lutheran Church."

Brian pounded his desk and jumped up in excitement. "Hell yeah! The old lady stuff is still there too!" He shouted as he ran around to the front of the desk, sat on the edge in front of me and stared at me intently.

"Just leave the credentials to Hayward. The man is a wizard. He, along with our video team of experts, has put together a video clip disc of you playing in the net that will be all Vance Howard has to see to convince him of your credentials. He then will know what we all know, who watched you play. You were the best ever. No doubt, the best in any league, any time, any era, Paulie. I sincerely mean that. No bullshit here. Coach Davis knew it too, and I only say that with full factual honesty on my side. Not just sayin' it cuz we are buds. I mean it. The video is amazing, stop action, slow motion, high speed. An in-depth, professional training video of how to play goal according to number twenty-seven. Hayward even narrated the video."

"Really? Wow, I would like to watch that video. Mr. Hayward does love hockey. Thank you. I really appreciate the faith and testimony, but honestly, what do you think that I can do in a few weeks or so with him? Is he that non-coachable?"

"Oh, he is an asshole, Paulie. A very uptight, punk ass, but that is why I need you, your experience, and your pastoral background. I have a good plan, but I see what you mean about only having limited time."

My question caused Brian some pause to think. He stood up and walked around his office, sucking on his coffee and thinking. He stopped and asked me, "You are returning to the bishop's position when your leave and vacation time is finished?"

I nodded to indicate that would be my intention, and Brian continued to pace.

He stopped again and asked another question, "I could not lure you away with a permanent coaching position with the team, big bucks, and a penthouse apartment with all expenses paid? You could hang with Janet every night and light the world on fire."

I shook my head, smiled, and thankfully did not give his suggestion much thought. I even dismissed the lure of Janet. . ..

"Well, Paulie, do what ya can with him in a few weeks or so and we will see how he responds and come up with a plan. I know that teaching old-time hockey does not happen in a few sessions, it takes a lifetime of growing up in it."

His words immediately sent an idea rippling through my mind. I smiled, quickly stood up and surprised Brian while spouting my sudden idea rather enthusiastically, "No, but we could do it in the off-season!"

"We? Who the hell are we? You and me?"

"No, old-time hockey players and me, in New Jersey.

training the same way that I trained with some of the same people."

I grabbed Brian by the arm to force him to stop pacing and pushed all my hair away from my face. I was intense and Brian sensed it. He stopped and looked at me while still sipping his coffee. It was a rough night last night.

"It is not only old-time goaltending that Vance needs to learn. According to what I have heard about him, it is a lifestyle. A mentality, an approach to life to breed maturity. That is right up my alley."

Brian smiled and nodded while he grabbed my hand and shook it vigorously, "Easy now, Paulie. Please do not squeeze. Need the bones in my hand for another forty or so years. I love it. You mean that you want to take him home to New Jersey to train with you in the off-season?"

"Yes, not only to train but to watch, observe and learn."

"I love the plan. We can fund the ice time, expenses and training time. I guess you have people that would spend time with Vance while you work full-time."

"Oh yeah, I do. The best."

Brian downed the rest of his coffee and placed the empty cup on his desk. He then explained, "I plan to stick the kid in the net for the last games of the season. Might as well. What the hell is the difference? Yup, nothing to lose, nothing at all. The season is lost. We are in last place, only a handful of games left. The head coach is just a fill-in. He couldn't care less if we put Santa Claus in the goal. The old guy is retiring after this season. We plan to give our coach at Norfolk a shot at the big time for next season. He has paid his dues down there for long enough, Howard is his goalie now, and he has a solid coaching record. Now, we need to get you guys together and you can see what we mean. All this talk is cool, but ya have to meet this punk to understand. You two can skate together and get to know each other."

Brian looked at me to gauge my reaction, and in an

effort to let me ponder the offer and divert attention from it, he looked at his watch and announced, "It is already one in the afternoon. We had lunch reserved at the restaurant for one-thirty. We can talk some more over lunch, but as a prelude, I am going to pour us both a Scotch. Yup, top-shelf Scotch neat. You look as if you need it. The old lady shit has overtaken your ass now."

He walked over to the same bookcase and wall cabinets, where the coffee maker sat, and this time, he slid over some wooden panels and revealed a full wet bar.

Being the general manager did have some extra rewards.

I watched Brian prepare the drinks for us as I sat thinking in the chair. Having a straight Scotch right now was not what I wanted, it would break and shatter my training regimen even more than last evening's drinking episode would, but I had to admit this plan had my mentoring and pastoral juices flowing. This conversation sent me into, as my dear Mum would have said, "A bit of a tizzy." I needed to relax just a bit and the drink might do me well to do so.

He handed me the drink and looked at me as I waved in the air and toasted by saying, "Cheers. Here is to Coach Davis and to us. Old friends from old-time hockey."

We tossed back a sip or two and Brian returned to his chair behind his desk. He asked me, "You have been back in the net, haven't you?"

"I have. A month or so ago, I will be honest, that I was a bloody awful mess. Overweight, out of shape for the first time in my life, not working, not writing anything of significance, depressed and still in deep mourning, eating crappy food and drinking too much. Paul William knocked some sense into me. He convinced me to call Tommy Hayward, and I woke up to where I was in my life. Met some old friends on a local rink, rented a few hours and climbed back in the net. I knew that I would have to be in some type of condition to be able to demonstrate and consult without looking as if I am an older fool than what I actually might be right now."

Brian sipped his drink and while looking over the rim of the glass he asked, "Understandable. We did some recon on you. Your son seemed to indicate that you needed something now in your life while you took some time off. This is just what you needed, Paulie. I can see the wheels spinning. I understand why you were so down. Of course, anyone would be down. I could not even imagine what you have been through the last few months. Ever. You lost your wife in a terrible tragedy. Once again, I am so sorry. So, the plan for workouts and training includes some old friends. Anyone that I would know?"

"Thank you, it was, and still is very difficult. Unimaginable. Well, yes, as far as the workouts go, well, Paul William took some shots on his old man. He still is young and still has a solid shot. He is an excellent ice skater too. As good, a skater as anyone I have ever seen or played with. Not just saying that because he is our son. It is a shame he gave up on the game so quickly. I guarantee that he can out-skate most of the players on your team, but he did not have the heart for the grind of the game over his love for the writing. Of course, we also had my buddy Harry, who played with me for years until he took a puck to the face, took a ton of shots on me over the last month or so."

"Oh yes, Harry. The world-famous Harry M. Redmond Junior. Tough guy and built like a tank. Bet he still can shoot, huh?"

"Oh, yes indeed, especially in a shoot-around. The last player is a familiar name. Let me just say one word, O'Malley."

Brian placed his drink down upon his desk blotter and he laughed loudly as the famous name spurred a reaction, "James T. O'Malley. The legend. What a great hockey player. The king of hockey goons, who if I recall correctly, in an amazing twist of fate and I must say, the most startling career change that I ever heard of, also entered the ministry."

"Yes, and he still looks good and let me reassure you that he can play too."

"Do you know that I tried to sign him once? Tried to take him away from Toronto and he told me he would never play on the same side as number twenty-seven. It was his goal in life to defeat you just once."

I nodded, took another sip and said, "I am not surprised. That sounds like Jim. We were bitter rivals. I am surprised that he never shared that information with me. We are very close friends these days. Have been for years, ever since we both retired from hockey and we both became pastors. He is a lot calmer, but still bloody competitive. O'Malley would still cross-check and slash his own grandmother if it meant winning a hockey game."

I was only sipping the Scotch, but already the slight numbing effect trickled through my bloodstream.

Brian was far out in front of me in the drink consumption department, and he knocked down the rest of his drink, and waved to me as he asked, "Calmer, huh? Everything is relative. A calm O'Malley in comparison to the rest of the normal population is relative. I am now curious as to exactly what calm is in regard to O'Malley. Does that mean you do not have to handcuff and sedate him?" We shared a laugh over the famous antics of James T. O'Malley and Brian continued to plead his case, "You need to know that I have support on all of this from the owners already. Mentioned your name and they told me to get you here and work the deal. Just dropped your name. Even after all of these years. Amazing, right?" He waved his empty glass in the air and then he stopped waving the glass because it seemed as if he was deeply pondering something. "Might be something to do with your religion, Paulie. I think the power that you yield with God and in

Heaven is something that all of us should never take for granted. Never been much of a church person. Perhaps, I need to change my ways. So. Do ya want another? Oh no, I see you are still a slow poke on the drinking."

I did not actually answer his question, nor did I comment on his thoughts about God and Heaven's power.

While he walked over to the wet bar for a refill, he spoke again, "So let me guess, during this little workout, you were shaky as hell at first, and after a few shots and an hour or so of leaking like an old warship, you stopped a few pucks."

"I did okay. At first, I could not stop a beach ball rolling towards me. The next practice was better, and the third practice was a huge improvement. I am back in the gym, I run and skate all that I can. It is good for my soul to take care of the body. It is in the Bible to do so."

I watched a smile appear on Brian's face and after he refilled his drink, he turned to me and said rather slyly, "So perhaps, this will all work out quite well. Hopefully, you will not tumble on your ass, when you hit the ice tomorrow."

"Let's hope! Easier said than done."

A few minutes later, we found ourselves at the same fancy restaurant, at the same corner table as the previous evening. Joining us for lunch was Bryce Eddings, Tommy Hayward, and a crabby-looking chap who turned out to be an attorney from the Boston Bears, named Charles Gibbons.

"Here you go, twenty-seven, a contract. Two-month term. The money is negotiable. Road expenses are all paid and some home expenses. All of this is very typical. Not too much has changed since you were part of our organization. This can all go into your pension checks. There is bonus language in there too, as well as what is in my humble, legal opinion, an exorbitant amount of compensation for serving as a short-term consultant."

Mr. Gibbons hung his eyeglasses on the end of his nose like a cat walking a ledge, and while screwing his face up like a corkscrew, he finished his statement and "humble legal opinion" with a dubious raise of his eyebrows and a discerning glance towards Brian.

Brian waved his hands in the air and answered the stare from the attorney with a blunt and frank statement of his own, "Stick to the legal jargon, Gibby. Leave the team management to me. Tell twenty-seven what it is ya gotta tell him and get it over with. We have hockey plans to talk about here this afternoon."

Mr. Gibbons nodded. He tried to push his eyeglasses up a bit on his nose, but they slid back down again. He continued to brief me on the offer and contractual language, "I have to tell you that there is a clause in there with a waiver on injury and your right knee. If you skate out on the ice and your old ass tumbles down, you are on your own. We paid for that knee once, and we have no intention of paying once again," Mr. Gibbons stated in a rather legal-like and matter-of-fact manner, while he removed a large bundle of papers from his briefcase and dropped them on the table in front of me. He continued to explain, "For insurance reasons to step out on the ice and skate with the team, even if it is only for a few days, you need to pass a physical." He looked up again at me over his eyeglasses and asked in a somewhat blunt manner, "You can pass it . . . can you not?"

"I can. I will pass easily."

Mr. Gibbons looked back down at his papers, while simultaneously nodding and he continued his legal wrangling, "Okay, good. We shall see. So, what do you say? Do you have an attorney who can review this agreement?"

I picked up the papers and nodded my head. "Yes. Our daughter handles all of our legal matters. She is an attorney. Heather Sarah is her name, let me warn you, she takes after her mother and her grandfather, and is a bit of a pepper pot. You better make sure this agreement is all squared up and correct. She does not miss a trick and researches everything to the smallest detail."

I looked at Mr. Gibbons, but he had no discernible reaction. I continued to state my side of the deal, "She will review this, and take care of everything. I have to tell you that I do not need the money. Money at this point in my life, which I always found to be beyond a blessing from God for a poor boy from Paterson, New Jersey, is not an issue for me. I have more money than I ever imagined, and all of my family and friends are very successful. Unless they do crazy things with it, they will have money for many generations after I have joined the Lord. I assure you that I am not doing this for money."

I looked around at the table and not even one of my lunch companions reacted to my statement. I surmised that they had already performed the research required to know that was the case.

"If you do not have a permanent one, then I would like to serve as the team chaplain for the last few games. If I could have the contract language modified for the chaplain's services, then I will be happy to serve in that role. I would enjoy meeting with the young players and see if they need anything in their lives spiritually. I know what it is like playing hockey on the road, being away from your family and friends. It is difficult and lonely."

I smiled and turned to the frowning Attorney Gibbons and reading his mind, I added, "At no extra charge for serving as the team chaplain. I am a bishop. You are getting a helluva deal there, Gibby."

The stoic and somewhat crabby attorney managed a faint and slight smile, but the rest of his colleagues had a good chuckle from my humor. Time to strike once more. The black suit was serving me quite well.

I sat up in the chair to emphasize my size and

bargaining position as I explained, "I just sold my home in New Jersey and plan on finding a townhouse there when I return home. I will never leave New Jersey. It is our home. Brian and I briefly discussed this in his office this morning, but our plan is to bring the young goalie to New Jersey, work him out at a local rink, and teach him over the off-season. I have to tell you that I plan, or perhaps, warn you, that I plan to enlist our son's assistance in teaching skating, I also will call in an old-time, retired, professional hockey player who Brian is familiar with, as well as enlist my best friend's help too. Along with stand-up, old-fashioned goaltending, young Mr. Howard needs to understand old-time hockey and old-time attitude, in order to be a success. There is no better way, than learning the way that I did, and for him to learn life experiences from a collection of very special people who are my friends and my family. I have a plan and lots of backing too. Some are here and some are in Heaven, but the point is that you not only obtain number twenty-seven on this contract, but you also get an entire team."

Mr. Gibbons did not comment, and neither did any of Brian's staff.

I think that they needed time to digest our plan. A pastor and an ice hockey goaltender and now a goaltending consultant remained an unusual combination. There was no doubt, despite my brief rebellion, that I would forever remain both of them. In my heart, with the combination of new challenges evolving and the obvious involvement of all this within the plan, I felt my rebellious stance beginning to erode quite a bit.

Instead of speaking or commenting, his staff members all turned and collectively looked at their boss for his reaction and his answer.

Brian sat with his face supported in his hand, his elbow resting on the table. His drink sat on the table in front of him. He nervously tapped his fingers on the table. The taps of his fingers did not coincide with the canned music playing over the restaurant's music system; it was the beat of his thoughts.

After a long time staring at me, then at his staff, he finally nodded and proclaimed enthusiastically, "You guys might recall the old-time hockey player that Paulie mentioned. James T. O'Malley! The legendary O'Malley. King of hockey goons! Old-time piss and vinegar, combined with old-time attitude, and swagger. I love the plan. Done deal. We will keep you in the hotel in the VIP's suite for these last few weeks of the season. I roomed with you and had to eat your shitty cooking, so at least, I know the hotel will feed you. You will have decent food. No need to rework the numbers, we will make that part of the deal. You can expense the time in New Jersey, we will pay the ice time as you teach, Mr. Howard. Gibby, extend the term of the agreement to four-months and add more dough to it." He then extended his hand over the table and looked at me very intently and seriously. "This is meant to be a question, Paulie, do we say welcome back to the Bears?"

I smiled and extended my hand out and shook Brian McClure's hand while telling him, "Deal. Nice to be back."

Brian immediately grabbed a bar napkin and pulled out his pen, while explaining, "Listen to me carefully here guys. Paulie will tell you that some of my best deals many years ago, I scribbled on bar napkins and signed on them too. Until the legal eagles finish with the bullshit, here we go. Old-time hockey and old-time deals." He took the pen and wrote on the napkin, "Done deal, McClure and #27. Old-time hockey." Brian then signed it, slid the bar napkin over to me, handed me the pen and I, too, signed it. Brian smiled and handed Gibby Gibbons the bar napkin while telling him, "Here, Gibby. Put that in the legal file. Someday, you will frame that napkin for being the turning point for the Boston Bears. Mark my words. Write the off-season plan into the agreement."

Gibby took the bar napkin, opened his briefcase and placed it in there along with the other agreement. He nodded to acknowledge his boss but did not comment. Brian then took his drink glass, motioned for the rest of us to join him in a toast, and together, we lifted our glasses in a joint celebration.

"To the reunion of old friends and to old-time hockey. Maybe, this friggin' world needs to stop over thinking things and return to simpler times. My hope is that along with your skills, patience and prayers that you do bring a little power from that higher authority, Paulie. We *are* in last place, you know. Cheers!"

We all toasted, took a sip of our drinks, and Brian immediately signaled our server for another round. I waved another drink off, I needed to get back to business here and ease back on the celebrations. Brian turned to Mr. Hayward, waved with his hands in his direction and nodded towards him. Mr. Tommy Hayward knew his boss very well, as the young man instinctively grabbed his pen and pad to make a note.

He seemed to know that orders were about to be conveyed and Brian did not disappoint, "Did you work a deal with what's his name? Millhouse?"

"Done deal."

"Good, excellent. Work the deal on the clothing and the rest of our plans too."

"Yes, Brian. Done deal."

After obtaining the contact information for Heather Sarah, in order to send the contract to her and begin the signing process, Mr. Gibbons excused himself and scooted off to deal with more legalities of the Boston Bears business.

Brian returned to his general manager's role, and he explained, "The Bears are on the road tonight, but they will be back early this morning and will practice outside of Boston at our practice facility tomorrow afternoon. We have two home games remaining and then finish this wretched season with two on the road. Since we have the bar napkin deal done and the handshake out of the way, we will head out tomorrow to the practice rink and introduce you to a few of the players and staff. You have a physical scheduled out there with the team doctor, anyway. When he signs off on your old ass and tells us that you are not gonna keel over, perhaps, you can skate if you would like and watch a practice."

"You have the bar napkin and my handshake, and I think that you know that is as good as my signature on that agreement. I would enjoy that. I assure you that my old ass is not going to keel over. Too much left to do here. Once again to everyone . . . thank you."

Brian grew animated in his speech and in the waving of his hands to demonstrate a point, "I do know that your word is solid, and that is part of the reason, of why we needed you here with us so much. Men of integrity and commitment are hard to find any longer in this modern world of lunacy. Let's keep this all under wraps until we can legalize and file the papers with the league for all of this. Paulie, you can tell your family members, and once we have the formalities filed and blessed, we will prepare a pile of press releases on our new goalie consultant and the hotshot, savior goalie of the Boston Bears. I need to whip up interest, pay for some of this beer, booze and food that we all sucked down the last few days, and put some asses in the seats for the last few games." He then turned to Bryce and asked him, "When can we waive Peters and call up Howard out of Norfolk? Can you take care of that and get Howard's ass up here on a red-eye flight as soon as you can swallow that drink and shake your ass out of here?"

"I can and will. I will file the papers to make the roster moves with Tommy's help here. Do you want me to check with Coach Bettermann first?"

"What for? That old jackass is just cruising for a few

more games. He already has his luggage packed."

Coach Bettermann. The old coach slipped my mind until now. Interesting. I made a mental note of Brian's low opinion of the old coach.

With some of the business end of our dealings behind us, Brian eased back a little, and he smiled. He waved his hands at me as if to take all of me in and encompass my appearance.

While smiling, and waving towards me he said in a rather bold voice, "Did anyone ever tell you, Paulie, that the black suit you are wearing today makes you look very imposing? I mean, you are an imposing man anyhow, but it makes you somewhat, shit, I dunno, kinda overwhelmingly imposing. I was ready to pony up even more dough to get you to sign when I spotted you wearing that suit. It is as if you bring all of Heaven with you when you wear it. Anyone ever told you that before?"

For just a very brief second or two, I felt my throat close up, and I somehow managed to stop the tears from welling up in my eyes. Binky must have assisted me from her heavenly perch and I hid it well, spontaneously signaling the observant and hovering server for another drink.

The attentive server immediately dashed over and asked, "Yes, please what may I bring to you, number twenty-seven? A Big Boulder beer?"

"Please, thank you."

Recovering, and ignoring my training regimen and the pleas from my liver, I used the temporary diversion of changing my mind and ordering a beer to hide the profound impact that Brian's words had upon me. Studying my lunch companion's faces, I knew they did not detect the impact the words had upon me.

I spoke with a gentle voice just above a whisper as I took the first sip of the beer that the server magically delivered in mere seconds, "Yes, an angel told me that once, and I guess that she was correct."

Chapter Six

Old-Time Hockey

I begged out of joining my new boss and coworkers at the training facilities to watch this evening's hockey game, and instead, retreated to the hotel room for some much-needed rest and relaxation. I could catch the game on the television in my room. Sometimes, you need to be alone with your thoughts and this was one of those times. The past two days had been a whirlwind of not only activity but also of emotions. Upon my return to the room, I sat on the edge of the bed in the hotel room for quite a long time, thinking, pondering, and praying. Dear reader, most of this was, and is, as if it were a dream, and it all remains in a blur and as much of my life has been, I now conceded that this was part of God's plan and went with the flow of it all. Eventually, God would reveal the plan in its entirety to me. I knew that and prayed for that to happen, sooner rather than later.

My family and friends had been calling my cell telephone quite often, and until now, I had not had a chance or a break in the action sufficiently long enough to allow me to return those calls. I knew they were all anxiously awaiting the report of what the last few days had brought to our lives.

Heather Sarah had texted me on my cellphone numerous times, begging to speak with me about the contract sent to her, therefore, I made our daughter the first call that I returned.

"Dear Father, is this correct? Let me get this all straight

and correct. Please interrupt me if I am off base here. First, the Bears are going to pay you an incredible amount of money for this consulting adventure! Congratulations! Second, I sense the restoration of your spirit and soul. I just have a feeling that you are whole once again. Are you, dear Father? How do you feel about this?"

"I am feeling marvelous, Heather Sarah. Great. I am gaining each day and I know in my heart that all of this has very deep meanings for me, for all of us. It is part of the plan. I am sure of it. I have my faith restored."

Even over the telephone, I could sense our daughter's enthusiasm, "Everyone is thrilled for you. Rose is jumping for joy! Blue, Uncle Harry, and my brother are flipping their lids over this. Uncle Harry is jumping up and down, reliving his past and your past too. He went out celebrating last night with Pastor Jim O'Malley after I let everyone in on the news. The two of them staggered in at three in the morning as if they were drunk teenagers hiding from their parents. Apparently, it was quite the night of celebration. Uncle Harry bought out another restaurant, and they took a limousine home. O'Malley slept in their mansion and the two birdbrains are heading back out for another celebration round tonight. I swear that youse guys are reliving your glory years! Talk about a damn mid-life crisis!"

I laughed at Heather Sarah, and my family's very valid reaction to this plan.

"Youse guys wanted me back in the world . . . didn't you?"

There was a long pause on the telephone and I could tell that our daughter was thinking about what her father just told her. She was very much like her mother was; she did not answer quickly when having deep conversations.

Finally, she spoke, "Okay, yes we did. Must admit that you took it to a new level here. But, yes, we did. Honestly and remarkably, some of this makes some type of sense. All this hockey bullshit is sometimes hard for me to grasp. The way it invades your soul. I can tell by your voice that your soul is well. In addition, I know you don't really care about the money, but they *are* going to pay you a ton of money. There are some amazing bonus opportunities if the team does well, as well as if this rookie goalie succeeds. This young chap, Mr. Vance Howard. Do you understand all of this, dear Father? There are no legal gotchas here. It is all quite concise and clear."

"Yes, I understand."

"Dear Father, then, I will take care of everything."

"Thank you for everything, please sign it for me. You have my power of attorney. And that reminds me, have you had any luck in finding a townhouse?"

Heather Sarah had flown up to New Jersey with little Sarah and she closed the deal on our home, made all the arrangements to pack and then move all of our belongings out of the home and into storage. She and Harry were searching for a new townhouse for me. The two of them were currently staying with Harry and Rose for a time. I am quite sure that Rose was cooking up Italian delights and that Harry and Rose were thrilled with the prospect of playing with Sarah and spoiling her beyond comprehension.

Our daughter's voice grew excited again. She spoke quickly, and I had to listen carefully in order to follow her. At these times, her voice and mannerisms were most like her mother's voice and mannerisms were. It sent shivers down my spine.

"Yes! We have found a nice place in Wayne Township for you. I think that is where you wanted to be, or in and around there. It is brand-new and both Uncle Harry and I think it is perfect. Uncle Harry likes it because he said one of your neighbors is a hot twigeon with an amazing chest and a dynamite ass."

I sighed as not too much with Harry M. Redmond Junior will ever change too much. Now, Harry and Rose were technically not Heather Sarah's uncle and aunt, yet she addressed them as such as a term of endearment. She always had since she was a little girl, and until Blue Cloud married Paul William, Blue addressed Binky and me in the same manner. Even after our families intertwined by the marriage of Paul William and Blue Cloud, the terms of endearment did not change with Heather Sarah, but Blue Cloud now called me Dad.

Our daughter laughed and went on explaining, "He hopes, as do I, that you take notice of her too. You are too young, vibrant and handsome to hide away, dear Father. You turn the heads of women less than half of your age. Dear Mother wants you to be happy. Anyhow, aside from the hot neighbor and my hopes for an opportunity at matchmaking for you, the townhouse is still under construction. It will need a few months or so more to complete, but Rose already wants you to stay with them, so that seems as if that will not be an issue. It has five bedrooms, one magnificent master suite down and four bedrooms on the second floor, which is one more bedroom than what you had told us that you desired, but that might come in handy someday. Who knows with you? One of the bedrooms could be an office for you for your writing and work. It has three full baths and a half-bath downstairs in the entry hall. It is an open floor plan on the first floor, with a majestic stone fireplace. I love the master bedroom because it has a huge soaking tub and a huge deck with a slider leading out to it. The deck faces west, so you can sit and watch the sunsets, which you like to do so much at the end of the day. The square footage is not too large and not too small. Gated community, very prestigious, with high security, maintenance free, common grounds maintained, with the snow plowed, walks shoveled and the grass and landscape maintenance on your lot included. It has a huge three-car garage and a fantastic kitchen, with stone countertops, the best appliances, all of which, of course, you will not use, except for frozen pizza preparation. At least when Rose or I come over to cook for you, then we will have a nice kitchen."

"Sounds great. If you think it is golden, then that is good enough for me. Buy it."

"Okay, I will take care of that transaction after I take care of this hockey contract. One more thing, the accountant called and said that the taxman will hammer us with capital gains taxes even after we buy this townhouse. The house sold for a pile of money and the townhouse is not that expensive."

I thought about it for a mere second. I smiled because I knew that Heather Sarah already knew what I was going to say, "Ask him how much dough will take the pressure off, then you review it and bless it. Split the figure up amongst the usual charities. Give a little extra to Reunion Lutheran Church than the others. Please, call O'Malley and get his particulars so we can give a little to his church this go around."

"I love you, Father! I knew that you would say that. I am so glad to hear you are back in the flow. Your spirit is bright and strong. I can tell, and I know that dear Mother is cheering you on too. Let's see, first, Reunion, Uncle Harry and Grandpa Hobnobber's Paterson City Urban Fund for Needy Children, The Rabbi Goldberg Memorial Jewish Foundation, and check with O'Malley. Due to my research, I knew you would instruct me as such, although, I have to admit the O'Malley thing is a bit of a twist. If I had to guess, then I would surmise that Pastor Jim is a large part of this new plan."

"He is, and I love you too. Please, call Aunt Dottie and give her the scoop. Tell her that we love her. I will call her when I am able to free up a bit. Please, another favor. Please call Martha Wiggins and fill her in too. Tell her how sorry I am for being wayward that I love her and will be back in the office soon. I will be in touch. Thank you for everything. My love to Sarah and Rose and Blue."

"I will make the calls. I am so excited! Father, I must warn you. You had better head straight to see Auntie Rose and Blue when you return to New Jersey or they will collectively kick your skinny ass. They want plenty of number twenty-seven hugs, kisses and your time. They miss you as we all miss you. You have been away for far too long. Physically and emotionally."

"I will. I promise."

With a few closing comments and good wishes, we hung up. I proceeded to call Paul William and then Harry, and after long conversations with them both, I finally caught up with everyone. I needed to call my sister and Martha, but I was sure in the meantime that Heather Sarah's briefing would suffice for now. Right now, it was time to change out of my black suit, put on my workout gear and head for the hotel gym. There was little doubt that I needed to work off the food and drink that I was indulging in far too much of the last few days.

I worked out hard and challenged myself in a manner that I had not challenged my body in a very long time. Old number twenty-seven hit the weights, the treadmill, and some heavy resistance band training. I was a long-haired sweaty mess, but it felt great. It was time to kick it into high gear and get the lead out of my ass. My entire life, even long after I no longer was a professional athlete and while serving as a pastor and a bishop, I always took care of my body. Exercise rejuvenated my soul and healed me emotionally and physically. I now felt more than just a bit ashamed at having let my body and soul escape and go to such far extremes. It felt good to be back.

After a hot shower and a muscle-healing soak in a tub filled with as hot a temperature of water that I could stand, I realized that I was hungry. It was then that I knew that my workout had been a success. My workout had burned up a ton of calories and I needed to refill the tank.

While I dressed for dinner in a set of my casual, yet businesslike clothes, I knew beforehand that I was going to head back to the hotel bar for a few drinks and dinner. In my heart, I felt a bit guilty for ditching Janet and skipping out on her invitation for a nightcap on the previous evening. The guilty feelings were part of the motivation for my plans on making the hotel bar and lounge this evening's dinner destination, and the other part, I had to admit to, was the lure of Janet Chesboro. She was, indeed, a gorgeous woman. Since Binky passed, I had not given dating, or even looking at another woman, a second thought. Despite suggestions otherwise from Harry, our daughter, and Brian, I felt that it was much too soon for such thoughts. As I pulled on my dress shoes, I stopped and paused to ponder and determine exactly what it was that I was feeling inside of me. Was this feeling because of loneliness, companionship, sexually driven, or just the fact that after all of these years, a woman actually gave me direct attention and an in-depth glance or two?

I was not too sure.

All my years on the road in my previous hockey life, or as I would come to label it, my first hockey life (I now had to differentiate) as well as dealing with all types of women, forward, suggestive, or otherwise, had made me keenly aware of how easy it was to turn an innocent or friendly relationship into an awkward situation. Regardless, I found the attractive and intelligent barkeeper to be a person that I felt was a lot of fun to be around, and a person that I would enjoy taking some time to get to know better. No doubt that I had been depressed and sheltered and it was time to circulate in this world again. I was nowhere near venturing into a dating or intermingling adventure with a woman; it was going to take meeting a very special woman for me to go that far. The guilt that I would feel as to the betrayal of my dear wife would be overpowering.

Yet, I recalled my impassioned speech so many years

ago, to Harry when he felt the same pain over the loss of his dear first wife, Sky Blu, yet he knew that he was in love with Rose. Sometimes, it is so difficult to admit that life goes on. Often, it is impossible. Now, I had to live in the reality of my own words and my own pastoral advice. Eventually, there might be guilt or some type of strange shame, but all widowers and widows realize that their spouses are gone and it might be time to venture back into the world. If God allowed me to reverse the roles, then I have no shame in saying that I would hope Binky would seek out a companion with whom to share her life and her immense love. Not to replace what we had, or shared, or ever to compare. No, no, no. That would be an emotional mistake. The only reason would be to be happy. Above all, I would want her to be happy. I am sure that Binky desires the same thing for me. If I did venture back into the dating world, then I would do it very carefully, no ill intentions and no silly lust-driven goals. After all, I was still a clergyman.

Yet, Brian's words from earlier in the day were true, correct, and factual. I was still a man. I just needed to play it cool tonight. That would be the plan. I will play it cool.

"Well now, if it isn't handsome, and very difficult to pin down, Pastor Paul. I was wondering when you might make a guest appearance. Yes, indeed, considering the fact that you stood me up on my offer for a nightcap last evening," Janet Chesboro stood behind the bar, and she playfully, and yet, still somewhat factually, conveyed to me her inner feelings at my recent behavior.

I selected a seat towards the far end of the bar and waved my hands at her while gently commenting, "Bring it on, please, I do deserve it."

"Oh, do be careful of what you ask me to bring to you. You might not be able to handle it."

Oops! Double meaning of my words. Better be careful with this gal, Paul. She is a sharp one.

Janet folded her arms across her bulging and captivating chest in a manner to feign her anger with me, and then she smiled and hurried over to where I was sitting. I admired her warm sense of humor, even if it had flirtatious intentions. There was no doubt that it was also hard to ignore her beauty. Surely, the management of the bar and restaurant knew that Janet Chesboro brought in a terrific amount of business just because of her gorgeous appearance.

While she stood in front of me, smiling, and to be honest, she was, to a certain extent posing, I admired her shapely figure, her blemish-free and perfect light brown skin, her deep brown eyes and immaculate facial features. I was not positive, nor an expert, but there was quite a bit of mixed ethnicity in Janet's bloodline. Perhaps, some Native American, or Caucasian mixed with African or West Indian heritages, but no doubt, her ancestors had gifted Janet with perfect bone structure as well as a wonderful smile and knockout female figure.

Most middle-aged women would faint to have such curves.

"Big Boulder?"

"Yes, please, of course."

Janet nodded, pulled a frosty mug out from under the countertop of the bar and she playfully quipped with me again as she poured the beer from the tap, "I hope you know and appreciate the shock waves that you have sent throughout the entire Commonwealth of Massachusetts for importing a beer from urban New Jersey to our sacred land!" Once again, I found her humor and her ability to throw out such spontaneous quips to be appealing.

"I bet you cannot keep it in stock," I answered her in an effort to match her wit. "Have to change the keg every ten minutes or so."

"Please, only sold, a few mugs. All of them to you, but then again, in my book, as well as the young gal at the end of the bar who cannot take her eyes off of you, number twenty-seven is the only one that counts. I guarantee that despite her age, bulging breasts out of the top of her shirt and her tight pants that she is going to lose the battle for your attention."

Oh boy. Suddenly, this businesslike and casual shirt became two sizes too tight. Janet topped the brew off, sauntered over towards me, and set the mug down in front of me.

She leaned over the bar, strategically exposing just a hint of cleavage from her open blouse and looked deeply and carefully at me and spoke just above a gentle whisper, "Okay, so, did you work a deal today? Am I going to be lucky enough to see more of you around here, or what? Warning. I become grouchy when I do not know all the inside gossip."

I picked up the mug, turned my mouth up and shook my head, all while taking a deep swallow of the blessed beer.

"Sorry, dear Janet. I cannot leak a word yet. No deals are complete yet. Honest. I am *still* a pastor and bishop. You know that I have rules of honor to adhere to, both here on Earth and in Heaven. I am sorry."

"Ah, bullshit! That means, yes! I know the deal around here. Forgive my language, Pastor Paul, or maybe I should shift gears here and call you number twenty-seven from here on in."

"Still not saying. As far as becoming grouchy goes, you know, my old man had a saying that a bartender should never be grouchier than he is."

Janet leaned in and grasped my hand while laughing loudly, "I love that saying! A very wise man. True too." When her laughing stopped, she leaned in even closer to me; her blouse folded open when she leaned in, and the folds revealed even more of her glorious chest. Her voice grew softer and huskier, "I could never be grouchy with you. No, no, no, and did anyone ever tell you that your eyes are amazing. They change colors and expose your soul."

I decided a change of conversation was going to be in order and picked up one of the menus sitting upon the counter. I quickly glanced at it.

In a stupid and ill-thought-out effort to bring this conversation in a different direction, I spewed out, "Okay, well, thank you, and yes, I know my eyes do change colors. So, what is good on the menu tonight?"

Janet shook her head, and I regretted asking from the very moment that the words left my mouth. She almost laughed at my stupidity for falling into that trap. . ..

"Oh my, well, you know the answer to that." She followed that statement up with an alluring wink of her right eye, and an incredible pose, while she told me, "Are you blind? Thought you were a sharp-eyed goalie. Look closely at the menu. You have my assurance that I am the best thing on the menu. By the way, you have the only menu that has me on it." She waved and smiled as she headed off to the end of the bar to take care of another patron sitting at the bar, as she whispered to me, "This tubby, dude is such a pain in my ass."

I breathed a sigh of relief.

I was certainly not doing too well here in my entire, "playing it cool" approach to this evening's plan. Plainly, I was screwing up royally.

The young gal at the end of the bar cleared her throat in an attempt to have me look her way. Instead, I kept my head down and played with my smartphone. She was the last thing that I needed right now! Eventually, after a period of heavy thought and some soul-searching, Janet returned, and I mustered up the courage to ask once more.

This time, just as a seasoned saloon singer would do on a smokey Friday night in the barroom, I carefully enacted some exact phrasing, "So, please, let me try this once more."

I picked up the menu, pulled out the handout sheet for this evening's specials and carefully and exactly pointed to a specific item on the sheet. I asked with a smile, as Janet posed and waited for my question, "This chicken breast something or other. Honestly, I cannot pronounce it. Is this good?"

Janet smiled, sauntered over and took the sheet out of my hands.

"I will cut you a major break here. Yes. I will dial it in for you and then be right back to pester you some more for selecting a friggin' chicken's breasts over mine."

Oh my, I just needed to eat dinner and be on my way. That task would prove to be a bit more daunting than what I initially calculated. The dinner was marvelous, and the chicken was wonderful, covered in some type of sauce and layered in magnificent layers of grilled asparagus.

It was quite enjoyable and as the dinner crowd wound down, and the young gal gave up on twenty-seven and focused on another target, which was a tipsy businessman with a bit of a belly, I was able to share in some quality conversation with Janet Chesboro. The conversation ranged from my life as a clergyman, to my hockey career, to why I write the types of books that I write. Whenever my books are part of a discussion, the inevitable question always comes up, and that is, if all those wild adventures of Harry and Paul are fictional, or did they actually occur. I always leave the questioner hanging on an edge, and never actually answer the question. I admit that when the questions arose, I did the same thing with Janet.

With a coy smile, a wink of the eye, a sip of beer over the rim of the mug, I told her, "Most of them are true. Maybe. At least the ones that I have the courage to write about are true. The ones that I do not have courage for, well, you can imagine."

She proved to be more than just an extraordinary

beauty, but an intelligent and brilliant woman. When my gentle prodding successfully shifted the conversation from Paul John Henson and his various incarnations, to the subject of Janet, she explained that she not only tended the bar and lounge during the essential evening shifts, but she also was the Beverage and Lounge Manager for the hotel. She told me of her heritage, with an American father who did business on the Island of Barbados and met and fell in love with an island woman. Janet had three brothers and two sisters, and when business and life twisted and turned, they found themselves transported from an island haven of bliss to the harsh climate of Massachusetts. Her parents were not pleased with her when she abandoned her initial business aspirations, as well as an accounting degree earned in a rather prestigious university, in favor of a career in hospitality, but after these many years, she was an amazing success.

Janet's witty explanation to me of why she did so, was truthful and entertaining, "I realized that I could make more money wearing low-cut blouses and tight pants and batting my eyes at lonely, balding, beer-bellied businessmen with dreamy aspirations of some adventures that ain't gonna happen. All it takes to fill my wallet is to tease them enough to extract a few extra coins from theirs." Her beauty, frankness and engaging personality, no doubt, contributed to her resounding success.

While wiping the bar countertop, she also added, "Honestly, I do use my accounting education here to balance costs and books, as well as for budgeting purposes. I do enjoy meeting the many different people that come and go through the hotel. Not all of them are jackasses and some, such as my present company is, well, they are handsome and exceptional."

With that statement, she leaned over and whispered to me, "So, what is your plan for the rest of this evening? Am I part of it? Told you that the young gal would give up on you in favor of me. She gave up on the guy with the big belly when she realized that he was a blowhard. He probably cannot even perform. He looks like he has a limpy."

I tried very hard not to laugh at her observation and label of the poor businessman, but it was in vain. After sharing a good laugh, I pushed the dinner plate away, took my last sip of beer and looked at my watch.

There was no doubt that I was stalling.

There were very few patrons left at the bar and only a few couples left in the lounge area. It was now close to midnight. It had been a string of exceptionally long days, and I now had to tread careful waters.

Honesty was going to be the best method here.

"Janet, I enjoy your company. You have been a warm and wonderful person to speak with and great company during a few very stressful days in my life. You have been wonderful and are honest, beautiful, and intelligent. I thank you for you. Honestly, you are captivating in appearance and personality. I am just venturing back into the world, both emotionally and professionally. Right now, my plans are to retire to my room and get a good night's rest. I have to be at the Bear's training facility early tomorrow and well, I might have a new job to do."

I gave her a wink in the fact that I could not fully reveal what it was that she already knew. She smiled and carefully listened as I continued to speak.

"It seems as if I am back in this world and entering an important phase in my life too. I would like to be friends, to have someone to chat with and have a brilliant person to share some engaging conversation with while I am here."

Janet nodded. She picked up my dinner plate and smiled as she told me, "That is a deal. Honest words, from an exceptionally honest and morally solid man. I do not want to give the appearance that I ask that question often because the answer is that I never do. Men such as you are in appearance and in character, they are far and few between. You are a prize and a rare and exceptional man. I am bolder with you, because, well, I would be a fool not to try! Yet, I know that most men are pigs and they would jump at my offer. If I might be so bold as to ask, and I understand if you avoid the question, but how long has it been since your wife passed away?"

She stopped, grew serious and tilted her head, while placing my spent dinner plate into a container under the counter.

She added before I could answer, "I am so sorry. It must be beyond difficult to deal with. I have never married. Never found the right man. They are difficult to find. I have read many of your books and writings. You are an insightful and emotional man. Exceptional, and honestly, that is a large part of your appeal. The power of your soul lives in your words."

"Thank you. It has only been a short while, since she left us. Honestly, I have lost track of the exact time."

I avoided answering the question with the facts. I did not lie, just did not want to provide the exact details and dwell on time. Time meant nothing to my heart. Nothing.

At first, Janet did not speak; instead, she only nodded and then gently said, "You need to return to the world, Pastor Paul John Henson. The world needs you. You have much to do yet in your life. I can tell. Your wife rejoices in the return for your spirit. You have too much love, power and wisdom to give, for you to hide it away from this weary world. You are a rare find, and a woman, will be very lucky if she succeeds in capturing your love and companionship."

Upon hearing her words, I fought back some tears and a closing of my throat. Standing up, I motioned for her to join me on the side of the bar where I gave her a warm hug, while she kissed my cheek. I could feel the connection, Janet was a friend, and I was thankful for her presence in my life.

"Good evening, Janet. We will talk some more."

"Good night, twenty-seven, slash, Pastor Paul. Sleep well. I look forward to your future. And to our friendship and I can be honest, maybe just a bit more than just friendship."

Retiring to my room, I washed and dressed for bed. At my bedside, I performed a quick prayer specifically thanking God for the day, the continued evolution of the plan and the patience for me to wait for the plan to become clearer to me.

I slept as if a slap shot from the point had knocked me out cold.

What a quick evening! Did I even sleep at all? Before I even knew it, as I mentioned, all of this is a blur, I had a full physical examination by a team doctor, who declared me in remarkable condition for my age. The doctor lectured me on my beer intake, told me I had the body of a man half of my age and pronounced me good to go. I thought how he would not have said that if he had examined me about three weeks earlier. After the exam, I stood on the sideline of a rink that was inside the grandest hockey training facility that I had ever seen. When I walked into the locker room, an equipment man for the Bears delivered a warm-up suit for me to wear. I dressed into a full warm-up suit, equipped with the Bear's famous logo and colors emblazoned upon it, no doubt that I was in shock and awe of where I was in my life right now. On each of the sleeves of my perfectly fitted suit were diminutive, number twenty-sevens, crisply stitched in the colors of the Boston Bears. I chuckled, because I knew that Brian must have been supremely confident of my signing onboard for this crazy adventure. He must have been confident or willing to waste money, in order to have this warm-up suit ready to go for today. My old pal had a covert plan, and it evolved to perfection. I suddenly recalled Brian's questions at lunch yesterday to Tommy Hayward in regard to a deal with a player named Millhouse. I now knew what the deal worked by Hayward with Millhouse was. Millhouse must have relinquished the number twenty-seven for the last few games of the season. Nice touch.

After dressing, I began to put my goalie skates on and looking around the locker room while lacing up my old skates, I could testify to the fact that even professional locker rooms in the finest facilities had walls painted in very bright colors. This one made my eyes hurt as the bright color schemes pounded my eyes from the wall. Reaching into my pocket, I removed a hair tie, gathered up my long locks of hair and tied it all off behind my head. A short walk out of the locker room brought me to a gathering of players, coaches, and team assistants, standing and waiting on the walkways for the rink doors to open.

I met a number of players, some who looked at me and my old goalie skates rather suspiciously. Tommy Hayward introduced me to who was at first an indifferent, and very uninterested, interim Head Coach Bettermann. He glanced my way, shook my hand and then did a double take, as if he knew me, or thought we had crossed paths before. I did not have much time to dwell upon the possibility, or even to say much more than "Hello" to the coach, but I too felt as if we might have chewed some of the same ice along the way somewhere. Perhaps a long time ago. Tommy Hayward moved me on rather quickly, in a testimony that Coach Bettermann was not very important in the grand scheme of things.

As we moved on in introductions, I recalled Brian's words from the night before, when he commented, "That old jackass is just cruising for a few more games. He already has his luggage packed."

Hmm . . . interesting that my old pal so easily dismissed the future of a head coach who seemed to be an old-time hockey man. I made another mental note, as I had at the restaurant yesterday, to examine that relationship a bit more in-depth, whenever I had more time to study the situation.

After wading through introductions, through what was a myriad of players, staff and assistant coaches, I slowly and carefully wandered out onto the ice surface as the players and coaches took to the ice in a warm-up skate. Since I was still under orders to keep my actual position with the team under wraps, Tommy politely introduced me to the players, assistants and coaches, as a close friend of Brian McClure. A few glances at the number twenty-seven on my warm-up suit, as well as, I am sure the testimony of the player who gave the number up, revealed that there was much more to this than what Mr. Hayward was willing to tell the team.

Taking to the ice, I warmed up slowly and I could catch the occasional glance from players and coaches as they whirled past me at breakneck speed. My old skates cut into the ice deeply and I could tell that my teammates and fellow coaches were wondering just who in the hell was this old, long-haired hippie cruising around on a pair of ancient goalie skates at this practice.

When Tommy introduced me, some players and coaches feigned that they recognized my name, and they knew me, but I knew they had no actual idea of who I was. I had faced these types of situations more times than I could ever count, for example, whenever I would climb into the pulpit to preach to a new congregation or hit the ice in my pads to climb into the goal. I was always the outsider, the long-haired, hippie weirdo, the man who had to prove himself repeatedly. The only difference now, as opposed to all of those old adventures, was all my experience gained over the years, and on this go around, I had the power of Heaven and all the saints there behind me.

Okay, here we go. My leg muscles felt loose and warm.

The hard workouts of the past few weeks now paid off. Time to turn it up and show these young bucks how to skate. If there was one aspect of my game that I worked hard on and never lost, was my solid skating ability.

While the words of my early hockey mentor and coach, the great Gordon Gurney, echoed in my head, I leaned into the ice, slowly turned up my stride and pace.

In my head, I heard Gordon say to me with that magical Canadian burr of an accent, "Keep skating, twenty-seven. Keep skating until ya ass is draggin' on the ice. Sleep with your skates on your feet. Take 'em off only when ya have some pretty lassie in bed with ya. You would not want her to know you are an eccentric goalie, eh?"

With a smile at the words of Gordon on my face, with the memories of playing street hockey on a dead-end street named Geyer Street in Haledon, to my first skates on the rink at Ice Land Arena, all fresh in my mind. I was now ready to go. I slowly gained speed and without goalie pads on my legs or other equipment on my body, it was easy for me to wind it up and to hit a top speed and stride. Joined by other professional skaters, it was time for me to cut it loose and establish a reputation.

My mind whirled with my past. This was very emotional for me. More so than I had expected it to be. I recalled another magical time from long ago, when Binky and I renewed our spirits and after sharing a romantic dinner at a fancy nightclub, we danced to our favorite song on a dance floor. While walking out to the dance floor, after many years of not dancing, my wife voiced apprehension to me that our previously fabulous dancing skills had now eroded with time and age.

I boosted her up with a proclamation by telling my beautiful wife, "Sure, we can pull it off. It is just like ice-skating, or bicycle riding, fishing, or sex. Once ya do, it, ya never forget."

It was time to prove my words correct. As far as the ice-skating angle would go, that is.

Before I knew it, I was cutting the ice so hard that the snow spray was leaving my skate edges and landing on the boards and the glass of the rink in a snowy mist. After a few whirls, around at top speed and in top form, I stopped on a dime, spun around and skated around the rink backwards on my skates, at almost as fast a speed as I had skated forwards. A few more turns, then a hard spray stop and I walked off the ice, huffing and puffing, as an old steam locomotive would while climbing a mountainside. A short walk up the walkway of the rink brought me to a smiling meeting with Tommy Hayward and Brian McClure. While greeting them, and exchanging greetings, it was then that I heard a chorus of hockey sticks tapping against the ice. Turning around, I realized that the entire team of Boston Bears, both coaches and players, had stopped skating and were tapping their hockey sticks upon the ice in a hockey salute to my skating performance. It was very humbling to have teammates and fellow skaters acknowledge the abilities of an old hand such as I was. My old man taught me a very long time ago a very valuable lesson, and that was to win humbly and always retain poise.

Those lessons served me well for my entire life.

In this life, if you remain positive in your thoughts and actions, there are no limitations to what you can achieve if you put your mind and heart to it. The only restrictions and limitations occur when you fill your mind and heart with any self-doubt. Right now, backed by the inspiration, love and honor of my wife, and what I now knew was God's plan, I had no limitations.

Humbly, I waved back and smiled to thank them.

If only they knew how badly my ankles and hamstrings were screaming at me.

Brian McClure was ecstatic. He slapped me on my back and shouted, "Shit! Man alive, twenty-seven. I think you are superhuman. There is no other explanation. You were always an awesome skater, but really, I had no idea that you could still turn on the burners just as you did years ago."

"Well, I am not. . .."

He would not allow me to speak. His enthusiasm was now hard to contain, "Gibby called. Your daughter sent through all the papers, Hayward here, since he is an efficient machine, filed all the bullshit with the league, so we are good to go. You passed the medical exam. The team doctor said that you are in better shape than most of our players are. We sent out a press release announcing the call up of Vance Howard and the hiring of a special goalie consultant to mentor him. The media looked at your name and the emails are coming back with, ah who?" He laughed, looked at Tommy Hayward for his reaction, and when Tommy neither said a word, nor reacted in any manner Brian continued, "Anyhow, Vance Howard is in the locker room right now. He is dressing. You are about to meet your snotty-ass, smart punk of a student."

Geez, this was all moving at a rapid pace. To say the least. A few short weeks ago, I was lost in despair and depression while drinking myself silly every night. Now, I am back hanging around with Brian and working as a special part-time consultant for the Boston Bears. It was taking me a bit of time to fathom all of it. I pondered Brian's words for a few moments before answering. I dealt with many snotty-ass chaps over the years, both on the streets of the old neighborhood, on the ice and in my pastoral career. This was nothing new to me.

"I am anxious to meet him. Especially now so, after the entire prelude and warning as to his attitude."

I saw Brian's eyes glance over to the runway leading from the locker room and he tapped my shoulder while reporting, "Well, now, here is your chance, because here comes the student. Time for introductions."

A tall, goalie, with a modern cage mask tucked on the back of his head, with the mask strap dangling from it, walked up the locker room runway. He carried his goalie stick in his right hand, and his gloves, he tucked under his left arm. Ah yes, Vance Howard, the new goalie, with the uniform number of the number one. He was fully dressed in his goaltending gear and practice uniform, and he walked quickly while still making his way carefully along the rubber mats. Walking in hockey goaltending gear is not an easy task. Just before he turned his pads sideways and slipped through the open door to the ice surface, Brian McClure reached two of his fingers up to his mouth, placed them across his lips and blew a loud whistle to catch his attention.

"Howard! C'mon over here. Get ya ass over here. The least you could do is to walk over here to say hello, and to thank us for your call up to the big league. I want you to meet someone."

The young goalie looked over in the direction of where we were standing. He frowned and slipped back out of the door and made his way over to us. His goalie cage mask was still unsnapped, the gear sat perched on the back of his head, and he made no effort to remove it while he approached us. I made a note of that fact, because the usual etiquette in the hockey world, especially with goalies, called for you to remove your headgear when meeting someone or engaging in a conversation. He did not look anything like what I pictured that he would look like in my mind. He was tall, not quite as tall as I was, but he was tall. He was strikingly handsome, with jet-black hair, a close-trimmed beard and moustache, and his young face had not a blemish or detectable scar upon it. His face was a testimony to the effectiveness and blessing of modern goaltending equipment.

While studying young Vance Howard, it was then that I recalled Brian's words, "He thinks that he is God's gift to hockey and to all women. Handsome, tall, big for a modern-day goalie. His build is similar to yours, Paulie. He might be a little shorter than you are. Vance has pick of the women on the road. They fall all over the kid. Anyway, he acts as if he is a king."

"Hey, Mr. McClure. Hey, Mr. Hayward," Vance Howard said as he tossed his goalie gloves aside, took his goalie stick, and leaned it against the wall. Yet, still he kept his cage mask on. He reached his hand out and shook their hands individually, and it was then that I noticed his eyes glance towards my old goalie skates and he stared at me for a second.

Vance determined that he did not know me and said, "I *guess* I should say hello and thank you. Why, I do not know, except that you are the big boss. I earned this call up. You did not do me any favors."

Oh boy, yes. Indeed, Vance Howard did not understand who baked and buttered his bread.

Clueless.

Instantly, I spotted Brian McClure's body language change and his face displayed anger. He reached into his suit jacket, tugged at his necktie and loosened it up. Having known Brian for a long time, but admittedly, not being around him for many years; my gut feeling was that he now was a lot more ruthless in his business dealings than he was years ago. Battle-hardened might be the description to use for him now—as we all were. One aspect of his management style had not changed at all from years ago, and that was that Brian also was brilliantly smart in being able to assemble a topnotch staff around him. Tommy Hayward was the best of the best. He was there for a reason.

"Hayward! What were Howard's stats down in Norfolk?" Brian asked his walking book of hockey knowledge assistant for the information and then folded his arms across his chest and waited for the answer.

Tommy Hayward did not disappoint.

"Sixteen wins. Thirty-two losses. One tie. A very mediocre save percentage of eight, sixty-two, no shutouts and a three-point-zero-five goals against average."

Brian smiled, unfolded his arms and pointed his finger in the direction of young Vance Howard while speaking in a low growl, "Thanks, Tommy. I did you a major favor, punk-ass. Your attitude sucks and your stats suck too. Now, this is your chance for redemption. Might be your last chance. Strongly suggest an attitude adjustment or I can ship your ass back to Norfolk or even better, send you up to Albany."

Vance did not know how to be humble, and he made the classic mistake of spewing some blame shift to hockey experts who know much better than he does, "My defense sucked down there. Not my fault."

Brian waved his hand in disgust at the young goalie's excuse and then he turned towards me, waved his hand and announced, "Howard, I want you to meet your new goaltending mentor, Mr. Paul John Henson. I strongly recommend that you never call him Paul until he gives you permission to do so. Unless, you preface it with the title of pastor and call him Pastor Paul. My suggestion is simply to call him, number twenty-seven. I also will make the strong suggestion that from here on in, you listen to everything his long-haired ass tells you, that you respect him, and buckle those damn mask straps on the cage mask that you refuse to remove, even when meeting with the general manager of the team. This man is, and was, the best damn goaltender that I ever saw play, on any level, anywhere or anytime. He was playing goal when you were still little wiggles in ya daddy's sack and a lick in his eyes. As a little added twist, yes, he is a Lutheran minister. In fact, he is on a leave from his position as a bishop, doing an old pal a favor and trying hard to help us save your sorry-ass career. For a few days, he is also the team's chaplain. You might want to ask to pray with him because ya ass is gonna need all the friggin' help ya can get. Especially since you just pissed me off to an immeasurable extent with your punk-ass attitude, you just might need some divine intervention by the end of the day to stop me from marching ya sorry ass right back to the airport. One more thing, hot shit, make a note of the fact that for the last few games of this horrible and disgusting season, he is your shadow, your guide, and your teacher."

Oh boy, Brian is just a little angry and he just cut this kid up into pizza pie slices!

I reached out my hand to Vance and his eyes were wide and reflected his surprise. I had a strong handshake, and I was not going to hold back one ounce on the young buck.

It was time to knock the young man down a few pegs before we built him back up, "Hello. Nice to meet you. I am Pastor Paul John Henson. You may, as Brian just told you, call me, twenty-seven."

He took my hand, nodded, I squeezed his hand hard, and he quickly learned his first element of respect. He tried to equal my hand strength, but his hands were smaller than my giant mitts were and he did not have the hand strength.

I had to give the young man credit for holding on to his attitude, or he was just stupid, it was difficult to tell at first. He steadfastly refused to lose the huge chip on his shoulder. This was going to be a bit harder than I thought it would be. A dose of O'Malley chasing his ass around the ice seemed more and more, as if it were the way to go.

Off he went with the jaw flapping, cocky as ever, even with an aching right hand, "Okay, shit, this is weird, or some type of rookie initiation joke. Some old ass-minister of some sort, who looks like he transported from a time warp from the 1970s, pretending to be a goalie and a coach, but shit man, you are huge and strong as hell. I do not need any friggin' broken fingers there, big guy, and I most of all, I don't need any goaltending mentors. I already know how to play the position of an ice hockey goalie." He pulled his hand away and shook it in the air. He pointed at my goalie skates, and laughed, as he wryly commented, "When you came out of your time machine, did you stop off in a museum and pick up the skates?"

I did not answer him, but I almost laughed at the comment. No doubt, it might have been a smart-ass comment, but it was a good one. Vance Howard had a smart-ass sense of humor. I could take it and in a roundabout manner, I rather enjoyed his delivery and our initial meeting. It was going to be a challenge, and there was nothing that I enjoyed more than a challenge.

"One more thing," Brian McClure added before we joined the team on the ice, "Vance has homework to do tonight in the hotel room. No drinking and chasin' chicks around tonight. You will find a disc and a booklet in your locker. The disc will show you what a real goalie looks like and how he plays. Study it, and your smart-ass will not be making jokes about number twenty-seven tomorrow. If that does not humble your punk-ass, then you just might be hopeless."

Coaches were blowing their whistles out on the ice and waving for Howard to join them. Without even saying goodbye, Vance nodded to indicate that he heard Brian about the training disc, turned and almost sprinted out onto the ice surface. While he skated out to the goal, he then slipped his cage mask over his head and buckled the mask straps. The warm-up skates were over and they required a goalie for shooting drills. The backup goalies were still in the locker room, or they were victims of cuts. Who knew at this point? My old friend Brian was on a rampage!

"Good luck with this punk, Paulie. Now, you see why I needed your combined talents so much. Ya gonna have to be a pastor, a goalie, and a coach too. I am countin' on ya. Bettin' the house money. Now, I am heading to my office upstairs here to suck down some Scotch. Hayward will hang around and help you with anything that comes up. This Howard kid, he frazzles the shit outta me. To have such talent and be willing to risk it all and not realize the opportunity afforded to him. Makes my head spin. I am retreating to my office to soak my head in booze. I will watch practice from there on the video feed. Thank goodness, I have a wet-bar here too. Essential equipment for me these days. It is in my contract," Brian patted me on the back, as I nodded, bid them goodbye and took to the ice.

I asked one of the team assistants for a whistle, and it was only then that the head coach of the team called his players and staff into the center of the ice, and introduced me, as well as Vance Howard. There was a quiet silence over the team, despite my skating demonstration of earlier; it seemed as if the team had no outright or discernible reaction to my presence, or to the rookie goalie. I thought that was strange except that I had played on a few teams too, where the season was lost and the last few games were agony. You just wanted the season to end.

A few players came over, welcomed me to the staff and introduced themselves, while commenting on my skating abilities, but for the most part, we now jumped right into business. I stood on the side of the ice near the left faceoff circle along with an assistant coach and watched a shooting drill begin. The assistant coach, a chap named Andrew Hudson, was a happy chap, smiling, easy going with an upbeat and friendly demeanor. I had met him earlier, but now he made an effort to chat some more with me.

"Nice to have you here, twenty-seven. Our goaltending has been a rough spot, and I have heard that this young man has great potential, but he cannot get it together. Heard a ton about you too. I made some phone calls last night and looked you up on the internet when the news started to leak out. Long time ago, but most people, including a few around here that actually saw you play, said that until you were hurt, you might have been the best ever. The way you can skate! Wow! Old or not, there are not too many goalies nowadays who can skate as you can. Damn, skating seems to be a lost skill these days with goalies. They flop and drop all over the ice. You are just here to work with this Howard kid. Right?"

"Thank you. I am. I am here to mentor and work with this young goalie."

"Good luck with this young, smart-ass. He has a bad attitude."

We watched the drill as the head coach ran a typical shooting drill and I carefully studied young Vance Howard. He was playing by sheer instincts. Purely reactive. Now that I watched him in person, as opposed to the film, I realized that I was correct when I felt that he was an average skater, really, nothing special. He needed to be a special skater. A few million trips around cones set on the ice rink in New Jersey and he would be special. He will turn it up with Paul William, Harry, and O'Malley and with me, and by summer's end he will spray as much ice on the glass as we can. It was when he was low on the ice and faced shots into his body that I could see him flinch, and in fact, I swore he actually closed his eyes on some shots. The talent that I saw on the video was there. His upper body reflexes were beyond comparing, but he had no system, no style, and most of all, despite his cockiness, he had very little confidence. The professional shooters of the Boston Bears were now collectively eating him for breakfast. Vance was struggling to stop anything, and the drill was a mess.

When he allowed two or three long slap shots to trickle into the net, I saw the head coach, Mr. William Bettermann, nod his head and wave to me. Coach Bettermann might have his bags packed and his two feet out the door, but, despite his lame-duck status and Brian's poor opinion of him, I could tell that he still cared.

It was time to earn my money.

While nodding to acknowledge the coach's signal, I took his request and blew my whistle while waving my hands over my head to stop play.

I quickly skated out to Vance Howard, who stood up out of his stance, angrily swept pucks out of the net with his goalie stick and then looked at me and asked, "What? Don't give me any shit. I am just warming up. It was a long-ass night. Flying nowadays sucks. When they called me to rush to the airport, I was drunk and I was ready to bang a hot chick. I did not sleep much."

"Too much information and honestly, your sex life and night life are of no interest to me. Excuses and bullshit. I don't have time for either. Listen, Vance, you are going about it all wrong. All wrong. Sleep or no sleep, hot chicks mired in a haze of booze or not, a goalie leaning back on his skates that does not challenge shooters, is a goalie that is already beat on a shot. Basic geometry, Vance. We are going to get you up on your skates, make you cut down shooter's angles, and stop you from flopping all over the place like some wounded-ass duck in the middle of hunting season. You need to learn that you only drop to the ice when you have to drop. Pull up your jockstrap and get some balls to challenge shooters. Goaltending is a microcosm of life. Face it, stop retreating and most of all, you have to stop being afraid."

He glared at me and even through the cage mask; I could see the burning within his eyes, "I ain't afraid."

"Yes, you are. Standing up will get you out of the line of fire, teach you to use your stick and your gloves and recapture your confidence. Try to come out of the net, like this. Give me your gloves and stick," I took his equipment from him and glided out on my skates, while assuming my classic stand-up goaltending pose. As I worked slowly out towards the circle of shooters, I pointed my stick and asked a player in front of me, "You. Number sixteen. How much of the net do you see?"

"A little, twenty-seven."

As I glided closer to him, I asked him again, "How about now?"

"I cannot see much of the net. In fact, none. My entire shooting angle is gone, but I will skate around you and try to tuck it in the net, because you came out too far."

"Go ahead and try it," I challenged him with a smile.

"You do not even have a mask on or any leg pads. All you have is a stick and gloves."

"Exactly. I do not need them. When I first started playing, we did not even wear masks. Please, do me a favor and just try to aim for the net and not for me."

Number sixteen nodded, then he shrugged his shoulders, grabbed a puck and skated in hard towards me. I watched his eyes. My old habit never left me and sure enough, the young player gave away where he was going with the puck. He looked top shelf, left side, just under the crossbar of the net. When he ducked his shoulder in an attempt to force me to go down to the ice and he tried to flip the puck to the top of the net, I skated with him and quick as a flash, I caught the shot out of the air with the catching glove and tossed it back out on the ice.

"Damn. Nice friggin' save. Never seen any goalie stay with me that way before. You took all the net from me by standing up and skating just as fast as I can skate. You are not a joke, but a real, old-time goalie. The real deal."

Number sixteen was now a believer, and I caught just a little hint of a smile on the face of Coach Bettermann. Suddenly, the team's demeanor changed. It seemed as if they realized that at some time, somewhere, in old ice rinks and a time far away from their modern worlds of glitz, glamour, money that we only dreamed of, and hot chicks in hotel rooms that old-time hockey actually was solid hockey. We were not just a collection of old players whose names were in record books and whose play remained recorded in grainy film clips.

Damn well, we could play the game too.

I handed the equipment back to Vance.

"Nice save. Ya got lucky. I have to admit that I cannot skate that fast. I would need to flop down to cut his path to the net."

"When we are done with you, you will be able to skate just as fast as I can. This is just the beginning. I will have you skating so hard, for so long that you will want to puke your guts up."

I pointed at his skates, while he watched me very carefully as I preached the same words preached to me so long ago, "You will, from here on in, keep skating, number one. Keep skating until ya ass is draggin' on the ice. Sleep with your skates on your feet. Take 'em off only when ya have some pretty lassie in bed with ya. You would not want her to know you are an eccentric goalie, eh." I tapped his pads with my own skates and smiled.

He did not comment, but instead asked me, "Are you really a minister? You cuss a lot for a man of God."

"Yes. I am. In fact, I am a bishop, but that is there, and this is here. This is hockey and the Boston Bears. They do not pay me to mince words. We only have a short window to save you, so let's get together and do it. I know what you have been through with the injury. A long time ago, I played in Norfolk too. I tore my knee up the game before the Bears were going to call me up and I never made it here until now."

He fiddled with the ice with his goalie stick as Coach Bettermann blew the whistle for the drill to continue.

"Oh. Thought they might have been kiddin' 'bout the minister part. So ya just a long-haired, leftover hippie asshole from the 1970s? Let me tell ya that you can't teach me about God and sure as hell can't teach me to play goal. I ain't buying some old-time, hockey bullshit from an old hippie asshole, pastor, bishop or not."

Now, I had it with this punk, he had brought me to the point of no return. While the entire team watched, and heard his challenge to me, I skated up to him, and climbed right up into his face, while pushing him backwards, quite hard into the crossbar of the net.

He was tall, but I was bigger, taller, and stronger than he was, "I am a pastor. I have longhair, and when I need to, yes, I cuss a bit. God forgives me, and for what I have been through as of late, I earned the right to cuss a little too. I guess that I am a hippie. The asshole part, I will leave for you to judge. Remember that I can squeeze your neck as hard as I can squeeze your hand. Change your attitude, realize that we are here to help you, and know that I can kick your ass. This old hippie will kick your punk-ass raw. If you think you are a tough guy punk, then bring it on. I will give you a lesson from the streets of Paterson, New Jersey that you will never forget. You will crawl back to Norfolk with my fist up your ass. Now cut the bullshit, get your ass in the net, stop flinching at hard shots and you try to do what I just did. You have all the tools and can be a better goalie than I ever was. You need to stop messin' around and for once in your life, make a bloody commitment."

He stood there stunned at my reaction to his insult. After he studied the glare in my eyes and decided that I might just not be someone that he wanted to tangle with, he shook his head and skated into the net while still spouting off smart-ass comments, "I thought pastors did not cuss. By the way, I do not believe in God, Pastor Paul."

"Yeah, yeah, yeah, and Peter cut the ear off the Roman Soldier too. You will believe in God soon, Vance. You will soon. This is going to take hard work and commitment. I am going to ride your ass until you hate my guts."

"I hate your guts already, and I ain't afraid of shit."

"Yes, you are, Vance and good. I am not here to be your

best friend. I am here to make you the best ice hockey goaltender in the world."

I skated away, returned to, and stood on the side along with Andy. The two of us coached Vance and barked orders at him as the shooting drill resumed.

Coach Bettermann glided over and he smiled and patted me on the back, while saying, "Nice work, twenty-seven. Your old friend, McClure might just be on to something around here. This Howard kid, he just realized that he ain't quite as tough as what he thought he was, eh? Had his ass stood down by an old-time hockey goalie, who was chewing pucks before he was even born. I knew Coach Davis and I know who you are. You are the best goalie in the world that no one ever heard of. Even at whatever age you are, I have a feeling these players are going to be shocked by the skills and shrewdness of an old-time hockey goalie. This game has changed a ton from when you and I came up in it. In my opinion, it has all gone down the shitter . . . maybe . . . just maybe . . . this is what we all need."

Immediately, I liked Coach Bettermann.

"Coach Davis, eh? Did we play together somewhere?" I asked him.

"Yup, we passed each other along the way. Can't tell you where, but all that hair is hard to forget. Plus, you were some type of friggin' legend amongst goalies. Maybe after a few beers tonight, I will recall when and where. If Coach Davis said you were the best—then that is good enough for me."

"Coach Davis. Great man. Great coach. The best. I loved the man. I thank you for the kind words. Hang in there and believe. Sometimes, we all have to believe. Brian has a plan, but so do I and so does, God."

Vance stood in the net, buckled down and under the watchful eye of Coach Bettermann, Andy, and number twenty-seven. We yelled at him, berated him and coached him along. Occasionally, I stopped the play and took over in the net, using just his gloves and stick to demonstrate the methods that we were trying to convey. Gradually and somewhat reluctantly, Vance listened and slowly, he improved. He even started to cut angles and stand on his skates just a bit. Slight progress, but this was going to be a slow crawl, not a fast walk!

Now, the plan unfolded very clearly. This was not actually about hockey, or championships, or even about goaltending. This was about restoring an exceptional and special, young man to his place in the world and teaching an entire team of young men and some old ones too, what Harry, Jeff Porter and number twenty-seven, learned on Geyer Street Gardens so long ago. We learned that with teamwork, hard work and heartfelt desire, you could achieve almost anything that you set your mind out to do.

The plan was about combining my two careers and helping a special, young man, as well as a grieving widower, regain their faith and spirit. A young man, who had all the tools and gifts that God bestowed upon him, but for some reason that I will eventually learn about, he was too stubborn or damaged to acknowledge them. Moreover, a grieving widower who needs, once more, to shelve his anger at the details of the plan, and simply trusts and obeys. I knew that with God, all things are possible and who knows what other reason there was to all of us meeting like this. There was a ton of pain here inside of this young man; yet, I knew that deep down inside of Vance Howard, just as Brian recognized, was an exceptional talent and an outstanding young man.

Moreover, I found what our son had predicted. I found my purpose.

Coach Bettermann took the team off to teach game strategy, work on the power play, and other aspects to prepare for the upcoming game. Andy stayed with me to assist by shooting on Vance while I taught from the side of the net.

I waved over to Vance. "Now, we can go to work. I hope you do not have dinner plans, because we are going to be out here for a long, long time, young man. Your first start in goal for the Bears is tomorrow, and you have a long way to go. I need your full buy in here, Vance. A full commitment. Heart and soul. You have all the tools. You just have to trust that you might need to listen to someone other than yourself in this life. Let me teach you something that my old man taught me a very long time ago. It is the difference between making a contribution and making a commitment. You see, it was a powerful lesson that he taught to me and stuck with me, as well as my best friend for all of our lives. It has to do with bacon and eggs breakfast."

Chapter Seven

Magnificent Outpourings

When Vance, Andy, and I finally completed our practice session, a press executive for the Bears, as well as Tommy Hayward, met us at rink-side. They explained that the media was in a fervor over our news, and that we both needed to attend a press conference in the media room of the training facility.

"Looks like your old, hippie ass has caused a commotion, twenty-seven," Vance commented with his wry humor and smart-ass tendencies on full display. As each minute passed, I enjoyed the company of this young man more and more, and I sensed the hostility dying and the connection between us growing.

A blustery Tommy Hayward rushed in and his jaws were flapping a million miles per hour. This was the most excitement that the Bears had to deal with this season. Until now, it was a humdrum and lost season. Suddenly, in the last few games of the schedule, excitement surrounded the hockey club.

"Now, twenty-seven, the press has dug up your entire history. It is a sensation. Made national headlines! It will be on the national nightly news! The pastor, the author, the bishop and the hockey consultant helping his old pal out. Sorry, I tried to suppress it, but they know you are a widower." He looked at me to gauge a reaction to that statement, but I had none. It was all factual. All I could think of in my mind was that I hoped the directors on the Governing Board of the Lutheran District would understand that this was actually part of my healing process. Time would tell.

Tommy continued, "The headlines are incredible. We agreed to allow them fifteen minutes with you and five with Vance. I will need to brief you on public speaking and what to say. . .."

I placed my hand on the little man's shoulder and gripped it tightly, while trying to reassure him, "Tommy, relax, relax, you have to do what? I am quite used to being in front of crowds. It will be okay. Please, relax and breathe."

Tommy stopped and put his finger to his chin. I could tell that he forgot that I had a few previous careers to say the least.

Removing his finger, he said with a hint of a smile, "I am so sorry, twenty-seven. Please forgive me, but it is hard to keep track of all that you have done."

Vance leaned in and commented once again, as he grew more comfortable in our relationship, "I am beginning to think that you are one hundred years old, twenty-seven. How in the hell old are ya?"

I pushed Vance playfully in his back, and at first, I ignored his question.

I put my arm around Vance and then around Tommy and said, "Tommy, lead us to the media room. That question, my young friend, we can discuss over many, many beers."

We ditched the press executive. Harry and I always established our "go to guys," and the stuffy executive did not make the cut. The press conference went quite well in fact, it went fantastic. I handled the questions efficiently and quickly. The stuffy press executive had prepared a canned statement for me to read, I did so, and then the floor exploded with questions. Tommy and the stuffy press executive held them to the fifteen-minute limit, and they stepped in exactly on time to cut it all short. It was a madhouse and I could tell that Brian McClure was now sitting on top of the hockey world for pulling this off since his plan worked to absolute perfection. The old goalie returns, now a widower, a man of the world, a man of God, and now he is here to teach and steer the young, cocky, but wayward star prospect. It was pure genius on Brian's part, it really was. The reporter's questions were, for the most part, mundane, but when an older chap, a beat reporter for the largest Boston newspaper asked one particular question, it caused me some pause to answer it. This reporter claimed to have worked in Albany, New York, for a newspaper many years ago. He did look familiar, but honestly, it was difficult to tell one person from another at this point.

He told me that his memories of me playing for the Flying Dutchman were still vivid, and that he wrote of me at the time, "That I had a chance to be the greatest goalie of not only this era, but of any era." As he wrote on a little pad, he looked up and asked, "So twenty-seven, do you think that your old-time hockey style and a throwback to a different era can be successful in modern hockey? On the other hand, is this just a passing fancy and what you teach young Vance here, will cause him to be a typical flash in the pan rookie burn out? The Bears had one rookie sensation goalie in here earlier this year and he only lasted ten games."

I went to answer quickly, and then I stopped short, and thought about it. I knew that in practice today, I perplexed the shooters with my stand-up style of goaltending. They never faced a goalie of this style and did not know how to handle it. I could relate it to the first time a professional baseball player faces a knuckleball pitcher in that it takes some time to figure out.

An honest answer to the question was the best route, and I took the opportunity to boost up my young student's fragile confidence, "Modern shooters will not understand how to deal with a stand-up goalie utilizing classic form, especially so because of Vance's size. He presents an imposing target, but let's face it; shooters adapt. This style of goaltending worked for years and old-time goalies line the walls of the Hall of Fame. It is basic geometry. So, when the shooters adapt, so will Vance. He has all the tools to be the best in this league, and no, he will not be a flash in the pan."

Without revealing the entire plan, I provided enough information to intrigue the entire hockey world about the potential old-time hockey intentions of the Boston Bears. Later on, I found out that Brian and the owners, sitting together in the Bear's offices while viewing the press conference, jumped for joy at my strategic wording.

I profusely thanked the Boston Bears organization, the owners by name, Brian and Tommy by name, and because I understood where he was in his life, and rather liked an unpopular man, I personally thanked Coach Bettermann.

When I stepped off the podium and Vance took my place, I leaned in and whispered to him as a gentle and pastoral reminder, "Remember, poise makes a man a winner."

To my surprise, he nodded and seemed as if he understood. While I stood on the side of the room, next to Tommy, and together, we listened to Vance field questions from the media, I could tell that even in our short time together, we were all making an impact. Vance Howard was actually brilliantly intelligent, well spoken, and to our mutual surprise, he left his smart-ass attitude on a shelf somewhere and conducted himself professionally and cordially.

I felt a tiny ripple of pride.

When I returned to the hotel and finally caught up with all of my phone messages, it was well into the dinner hour. I spoke with everyone, and Harry told me that Jim, Paul William and he were catching a flight and heading to

Boston for Vance's first game. There was no need to scoff tickets for them; Paul William could slip O'Malley and Harry in under his press passes. As usual, my support team was intact and in place.

A short time later, my phone rang again. The display on the phone told me that it was Coach Bettermann calling in to speak with me. Tommy Hayward had borrowed my phone and the efficient assistant executive programmed all the important team numbers into my phone for me. I immediately answered the call; after all, the man was the head coach! Coach Bettermann thanked me for mentioning him in the press conference, and we had a very long and pleasant conversation.

The beleaguered coach told me, "Thank you for what you did for me today at that press conference. I can tell, even in a very short time of knowing you, that number twenty-seven is a special man. This has been a disaster of a season, and everyone has to blame someone. Even if I am only the interim head coach and just a placeholder, I sure am the subject of a ton of hockey hate in this old city. Did the best that I could with what they gave me. I am a good coach. It kinda sucks for an old-time hockey guy, such as what I am. Not the way that I want to go out, especially, after a lifetime in this sport. It might be a bittersweet thing that I am sure, with your history that you can relate to in some way."

"Do not take that hockey hatred to heart. My old man had a saying for these situations, he used to say, every, single, time the best employee in the entire company, leaves, retires, dies, or otherwise moves on, within two or three days of their departure, they suddenly become the worst employee the company ever had."

"Pastor Paul, I love that saying. Right on! I just know that you, or I guess all of us, and your team can make a difference with Vance. You work miracles."

"Easy, coach. It is not as if we have put Vance Howard

in the Hall of Fame yet."

"No, but his attitude started to change a little, and let me tell you that the mood in the locker room, changed in an instant because of today."

I gently reminded him that I have some other guidance of a much higher authority on my side. It was a meaningful and insightful conversation and deep down, I felt, as this was not yet the end of the hockey road for Coach Bettermann. Instead, I felt as if this was another part of the plan.

After handling the multitude of phone calls, it was time to relax. I enjoyed another wonderful meal at the hotel bar and shared with an ecstatic Janet Chesboro, what the news of the day meant for all of us. I planned to make it an early evening, it had been an extra exhausting day, my body had some aches and pains and I knew that a long soak in a hot tub of salts was what I required right now. Janet joked with me and she flirted with me a bit more, but we now had an understanding. She was a new friend and even if she looked for a sign from me to turn our budding friendship up a notch or two, Janet understood my position. She seemed quite content to adopt a wait and see approach. Besides, she was a fan of the Bears too! A tap on my shoulder interrupted my plan for an early evening. Turning around, there stood Vance Howard.

"Is this seat open here, twenty-seven?"

I pointed and waved while telling him, "Go ahead. Of course, it is open for you. I did not know that you were staying in this hotel, or I would have invited you to join me for dinner."

Vance took the seat and sat down while exhaling with a long sigh. "I am staying here, but they put me in a tiny and not too swift of a hotel room. Heard you are in the fancy luxury suite. Another lesson learned. Number twenty-seven is a big deal. I am not."

He looked a bit on the tired side, but he did not seem

stressed. In fact, his body language was relaxed. It was now, from a lifetime and a career of counseling people as a pastor, that I knew the young man wanted to talk. His eyes gave away his loneliness.

It was a feeling that I knew very well. Professional hockey was a grind, and when you lived on the road alone, then it was a lonely grind.

Janet looked up from our discussion. She had been leaning in close to me and she smiled at the young man. It was apparent that she recognized Vance from the press conference and the headlines in the sport sections of all the major newspapers. I am sure the handsome, young man was causing a stir amongst female fans of the Boston Bears.

"Wow! My luck is awesome today. Two handsome professional goalies in one place. I suggest that you have a mug of Big Boulder beer to impress your teacher and mentor here. Do you go waltzing around in life addressed by your uniform number and have multiple identities too? Number, number, what?"

Vance whispered and waved, "Yes. I mean no, to the uniform number and multiple identities. Yes, to the beer. I knew that it is the brand of beer that twenty-seven drinks. I never had a Big Boulder before. We do not allow rotgut beer in upstate New York, but to impress him, please pour a mug. I wear number one. My uniform number is number one."

Janet nodded; she scurried off to pour the beer.

I looked at Vance Howard and commented, "Upstate New York, eh? I did not know that. I couldn't detect any accent on you to figure out where you were from, and I have not had enough time to research much about you."

Janet delivered the beer, and she sensed that it was time to leave us alone, so she excused herself to wait on some other patrons sitting in the lounge.

I thanked Janet, asked to put all of Vance's orders for this evening on my tab, and then asked Vance, "Where in upstate? I lived there for a time too. I loved it. Honestly, out of all the places that I lived in—it was my favorite place of all."

Vance took a sip or two of the beer and between sips said, "Wish I could say that you do not have an accent. Honestly, you talk like some kind of New Jersey street thug. Never even knew they even played hockey in New Jersey. I am from a small town outside of Rochester, on the Canadian border. Hockey country. Land of bitter cold, endless winters, ice and snow. Pond hockey heaven."

When I did not comment, he took another sip of the beer and lowered his voice a bit. This was now a remarkably different young man than the man I had met on the ice rink earlier today.

"Twenty-seven, I did watch that disc of video of you when I got back to the hotel. Holy shit! You were, and probably, from what I saw this afternoon, might still be, a friggin' remarkable goalie. Some of those saves I saw in the clips were ridiculous. Unreal skills. I see what McClure meant when he said you were the best ever. I also did some reading up on you. I must say that it is a remarkable story. An internet search brings you up in a million friggin' places on the web. After practice, I spoke with Coach Bettermann, who said he knew an old-time hockey coach who knew you years ago, and said you were the greatest goalie ever. Friggin' amazing story and an amazing life."

His eyes lowered and his voice grew solemn, "By the way, I am deeply, deeply sorry about your wife. That must be beyond tough. Something that is beyond tragic, beyond description . . . and you still believe in God?"

I sensed the emotions were genuine, and I thanked him for his condolences and gently whispered, "I do still believe in God. My loss here on Earth has been Heaven's gain. It is all part of a plan that I admittedly, do not agree with. God never promises that life will be all happy, smooth and grand. In fact, it is exactly the opposite. I go along with the plan. God still is using me, despite my protests over the plan for my life."

"Protests, huh? I think I would do more than just protest. Might be an all-out war, but you are a decent and humble man. Tough and strong as hell, though. Scared the shit outta me, when you said you could squeeze my neck like that. Hey, I am sorry about the smart-ass comments about you. I can see that you care and are here to help. Besides, you are still some kinda amazing skater and goalie. Do you think this is my last chance, Pastor Paul? Was McClure blowing smoke up my ass or has the team management given up on me? You've known him for years."

I shook my head and said, "I do not know. It might be the last chance that you will have with the Bears, but I have to tell you that in this life. . .."

To emphasize the need for him to pay close attention to what I was going to tell him, I put my hand on his arm and forced him to stop taking a sip of his beer mug and look over at me.

When he did, I told him, "It is never a last chance, Vance. Never. No matter how awful a situation, there is always another chance. First, you have to believe in Vance Howard, and then admit that it is acceptable to take advice from persons, players, coaches and others, who have been down these roads before you have. Do you understand? You have to, as I told you, make a commitment to the team, to yourself, and think that this is not only all about Vance Howard. The world is not all about Vance Howard. Making other people small to elevate yourself, has limited chances at success. The world owes you nothing. It owes you jackshit. You have to earn it all. Where you are right now, well, it is about a lot more than Vance Howard."

I removed my arm, nodded at the beer, and he lifted the mug to his lips and took a long sip.

When he finished, he set the mug down and whispered,

"Bacon and eggs breakfast. The hen made a contribution and the pig, well, his ass made a serious damn commitment," Vance recited the lesson from my old man verbatim.

"Exactly."

"Your old man was a smart dude. You grew up rough and tough, yet, your parents taught you right from wrong. Are your parents gone now?"

"Yes, all of them. My in-laws and brother-in-law, too. For some reason, they were all taken from this world much too early. Our loss here was certainly Heaven's gain. I have a sister and her family and our children—a daughter and a son. Bringing our daughter and our son into this world, are our greatest accomplishments. I also have some of the greatest friends any person could ever have."

While studying Vance, it was easy to determine that this young man carried some immense burdens. Now, it was time for him to open up a bit more to me.

Vance nodded, mouthed that he understood and spoke loudly and somewhat proudly, "My old man was a heartless asshole. He took off with some young woman that he was messin' with and left my mother and me in some shitty, cold-ass dump of a house with tons of bills and no money. I was thirteen. He never even said goodbye because he just up and took off. My mother worked tons of horrible jobs, in food stores, retail stores, and shit jobs for shit pay. She died of a broken heart when I was seventeen. We moved fifty times. I swear we did. She loved my old man, for what reason, I could not tell you, but she did."

He looked over at me, but I said nothing. It was at times such as this that I knew all I had to do was to listen. Magnificent outpourings of emotions warrant listening, and often that is all that is required.

He continued while downing the last of his beer, "That is why I say there is no God. I prayed and prayed for my father to return, or for God to send me a new father. Mom always went to church, and she was an exceptionally faithful and churchgoing woman. A good woman. She cried and prayed too for the old man to return, and he never did. Why is that? Why, if there is a God, then why does God not hear the prayers of good people? Why would he allow your wife to die so tragically?"

Vance looked over at me and his eyes told of his pain, but they also told me that he longed for an answer.

"Because it does not work that way. It is not your plan, or my plan, or our wishes, or anyone's prayers. It is all according to a plan. Jesus, he prayed for the plan to be different and even his prayers were recognized, but not answered because, like it or not, it is not our plan. As I mentioned before, I do not agree with it, I went along with it for most of my life, but now the plan will become clearer, each day it does, but that does not mean that I have to agree with it or like it."

He nodded his head, mumbled something about that making sense, for not blaming me for not agreeing, and then looked at me as he fiddled with his now empty beer mug.

"Did your church come to help your mother with her sorrow?" I asked him.

"A little. I guess. The priest came to our house one day, and he told us some bullshit explanation that I thought made no sense at all. He told us that the old man was a terrible sinner and he would burn in Hell type of nonsense. How did he know that? Once they knew we were broke and poor, he told us about homeless shelters and soup kitchens and we never saw him ever again. We had no money to give, so they dumped us. The church sucked, organized religion sucks too. Sorry to say that. Each one of them, telling you that the other church down the corner is all wrong and they are right. Come over here and fill our collection plates. How the hell do they know that their way is the right way and all the others are wrong?"

When I heard his words, I leaned back and waved my hand in the air as if to signify a point that I needed to make. It was a sound observation.

"They don't know. God existed long before humanity created religion. I had a mentor, a friend, and a boss once, who was a bishop. He was the Bishop of the Northeastern Lutheran District in the area where we lived. A long time ago, when I wanted to be a Lutheran pastor, he gave me a chance when no one else took me seriously. After hockey, I worked hard, attended university, then a seminary, graduated first in my entire class, but not one single church would give me a chance. They all refused to allow me to serve as an ordination candidate and to ordain me. Everyone had the same reaction to me, very similar to the reaction that you had when we first met this afternoon. Long hair, beard, rock-and-roll tee shirts, canvas sneakers, a retired, professional hockey player. I did not fit the image of the church. This bishop, he believed in me and he gave me a chance when no one else would. He was a great man, and he told me once, mankind created religion and all the confusion that goes with it. God sends us faith and miracles to sort out all the mess that mankind makes."

Vance smiled, and I could tell that he agreed with that statement. It was not that he did not believe in God, he needed to understand the difference between God and religion.

"I like that. Smart man, to believe in you and to say something so profound."

"How did you do in school, Vance?"

"I sucked in school. Bad grades, not because I was not smart, but I was rebellious and as it usually tends to be with me, I would not make a commitment. My poor Mom. She did her best with me, and then when I found out that I could play hockey and people started telling me how wonderful I was, then it all went to my head. I could hide behind the cage mask."

I interrupted him and smiled while saying, "You could hide behind a disguise and the pain went away. No one knew who the real Vance Howard was because you became number one, the hockey goalie. Playing goalie became part of your very soul. Number one is now, Vance Howard. You two are interchangeable. You can be the bad guy and the good guy all at the same time."

He seemed surprised that I knew of his emotions and when Janet slipped another beer to him, he politely thanked her, picked the mug up and took a sip. I sensed that he was now, to a certain extent, opening up, yet he was not quite ready to reveal all of his feelings to me.

"Exactly, you make ten saves in a row, you are a hero, let one goal in and you are a clown. I love to escape there. All my troubles disappear and I hide. Love, the challenge and the intensity, playing goal is so difficult. It is amazing."

He needed to change the tone of the conversation, because he was revealing too much, too soon, "This beer is not too bad. Not sure why it is not more popular."

I dug back in, "Do you have any brothers or sisters, Vance?"

"No. Just me. Only my supposed father and one other relative that I know of out there. I have an uncle somewhere. My mom's brother. Don't know much about him. Mom died a week after I signed my first professional contract."

"I am sorry. Please, what is your mother's name? I will pray for her."

"Vivian. Vivian Howard. Her brother did not even show up at her funeral. Not a peep out of him, or my old man looking for free handouts, even when I became sorta famous playing hockey."

With a shrug of his shoulders, and sadness in his eyes, he dismissed the thought in its entirety, "Maybe they are both dead. Who knows? Hey, it makes for easy Christmas shopping. How I wish that I did not treat my mom so poorly and was such a rebellious pain-in-the ass. I regret that I never told her how much I loved her before she died. It is my deepest regret."

When I heard Vance's statement about his regret, then I jumped at that chance to teach him one of the special lessons that I had learned from one of my greatest teachers, or as someone very special in my life once described, as a rabbi, "Never have regrets for what you have done. Regrets are for fools. Regrets are only foolish doubts of decisions that we have made. They serve no purpose. They only cause us angst and worry. Make a choice, be a man, then move on. Never doubt."

Vance looked at me deeply and stared in my eyes before commenting, "Where do you keep coming up with this amazingly deep and profound shit? Is that one from your old man too?"

"No, my grandfather. He was an incredible man, and he taught me some of life's most important lessons."

"Wow, very cool. I have to tell you that after practice, while chillin' in the hotel room, I downloaded some of your books. The story about your friend, who roller-skated for a shitload of time and poured his blood and guts out for a charity cause, is a friggin' amazing story. It hit me hard. I could relate to your friend, because, I guess that I am sorta as he was. Selfish and self-centered, not willing to make a commitment to anything or anyone, except Vance Howard. Great story. Is it true? Did he really start out acting like a total jerk, sign up to impress the chick, and then make a commitment to help out the charity?"

I nodded and said, "He did. He, too, is a remarkable man. My plan is for you to meet him. Soon. Our training plans will include heading to New Jersey to work out over the off-season. My friend will be a huge part of that plan."

"I would enjoy that, and twenty-seven, I am going to make a commitment. No more, women in my hotel rooms all night and missing practice because I was bangin' them .

. . oh, err, sorry Pastor Paul, because I was making love to them all night and drinkin' myself into a blur. No more smart-ass remarks to the big boss and coaches and not listenin'. No more wasting my bonus money on fancy sports cars, instead, I am going to bank all my money and save it. You have my word. Seeing your old ass out there working hard, watchin' that video of you playin', seeing how good you are . . . even at your age, still able to stop a puck without even wearing equipment, and skate better than I can . . . it was friggin' remarkable. It changed me. I am going to work hard and make this work."

"Okay, good, in fact, great! And one more lesson in respect and etiquette, the next time that you meet with your boss and with the team's upper management, take your cage mask off."

He smiled and laughed, "I will. Since I can confess to a man of God and I ain't telling you something that you do not already know, I admit that I flinch at certain shots. I need your help with that one. Still suffer from nightmares of the impact of the puck in my throat. You know what it is like to crawl back from surgery and pain. It sucks. I need your help. I love hockey and it is my life. I cannot blow an opportunity that many young men only dream about having in their lives. I am twenty-four now. I am too old for a rookie."

I now knew the source of his pain and rebellion, and I sensed the change and my purpose within the plan beginning to evolve.

While I put my arm around him, and pulled him over to me, I told him, "You are not old. Age is just a measuring stick. The true age of a person lies deep within their soul. Look at me. Remember, Vance, I know that you miss your mom, but from what you have told me about her, how much you loved her and by the look in your eyes as you related the story, I assure you that your loss has been Heaven's gain."

Chapter Eight

The Finest Save of All

Once again, dear reader, I am not a skilled enough of a writer, to convey the remarkable range of emotions that I experienced while sitting on the Bear's bench, watching warm-ups and participating in a very roundabout way, in my first game in the big league. After the passing of so many years and dreaming so many dreams, as well as the haunting of a thousand ghosts, it was a feeling that perhaps even a skilled writer would find it difficult to capture properly. From the lowly beginnings on our street hockey rink known as "Geyer Street Gardens" to my beloved Ice Land Arena, to Albany, to countless rinks tucked in nameless corners of the world, here I landed. It was difficult to imagine, and somewhere, the pangs of sorrow ran deeply through my body and soul, as I struggled to remain focused and calm, while thinking what it would be like to have my beloved Binky here with me. I felt her spirit, her love and her presence, most of all; I knew that I needed to stick to the plan and to the mission.

I met with our son, and with Harry, and Jim O'Malley in the rear hallways of the arena and we shared a long discussion and an emotional reunion. I wished that I could have corralled Vance and introduced him to the three men who were going to be a huge part of his transformation, but he was busy dressing and preparing mentally for the game. That introduction would arrive soon enough. Somehow, all three of them were living their hockey dream through me. I could sense and feel that.

Jim's career fell about two steps short of the big league, when the hockey world changed and determined that the style of vicious play that made James T. O'Malley, the most feared hockey player in the semi-professional league circles, was part of a bygone era. I often felt that if Jim shifted his style, he would have been able to play in any league, anywhere. He actually was a gifted hockey player, and Jim felt no reason to change his style or intensity of play.

He also told me, "God made me who I am and what I am. I ain't changing God's plan for me for anyone."

Detailing the wisdom and profound aspects of Jim O'Malley's personality would fill many pages of many books.

Maybe someday.

Now, the journey was final. I had made the long climb, and it was time to go to work. During our final game prep, Coach Bettermann went on a rant. The old coach was now preaching old-time hockey such as fore-checking, blue line defense and to stop passing pucks behind our own net. After Coach Bettermann's rant, I began my own preaching to Vance while he dressed, and before we knew it, we were almost ready to hit the ice. I watched Vance stretch out his groin and stomach muscles on the floor of the locker room in his pregame stretching ritual, and I could tell that he was deep in thought over what was happening right now in his life. Coach Bettermann allowed Vance the majority of the warm-up time in the net, while his backup, a chap named Leslie Webb, took just a few shots. Webb was an older veteran of the league and while he seemed steady, he was not spectacular. Coach Bettermann informed me that Webb was a free agent after these last games. Webb seemed content to relinquish the starting net-minding duties to Vance and then hide out in the backup goalie's nook of the player's bench, while collecting his last paychecks.

The team from Detroit was in town for this game. They

were a first-place team, already in the playoffs with home-ice advantage, and they were now just cruising out the schedule and playing this game as if it were just a practice before the playoffs. A few opposing players had slick, stupid and smart-ass "old-time hockey" comments to make to me and the old coach, as they skated by the bench where I sat in the far corner just to the right of Coach Bettermann. I dressed for the game in a dress shirt, dress pants and a necktie covered by a Bear's sweater vest. Since I only brought limited clothes with me on the trip, Tommy Hayward flooded me with Bear's attire of every kind they had in stock in the equipment rooms. Coach Bettermann and I laughed off the smack-talk; we both were most likely old enough to be most of the player's fathers! I thought how if this were actually "old-time hockey" then comments such as those would have caused Jim O'Malley to erupt into one of his famous pregame brawls. Young men such as these were, had never seen the likes of a Jim O'Malley! Jim would have chased them back to the airport.

The starting goalie for Detroit did take the time to stop, and he skated over to speak with Vance and me at the side of the player's bench. He was a superstar player, a candidate for the league MVP award, and was a cordial and humble gentleman. He was pleasant, wished me as well as the rookie goalie about to start his first big league game, good luck.

Despite the pressure, the sellout crowd and the interest surrounding this game, Vance and number twenty-seven remained focused. There was no reason not to be. I might have been long since removed from the game, but I had played in thousands of hockey games at all levels of play, and as a clergyman, I had been in a few more pressure-filled situations than this one was. My nerves were not of concern to me because I felt as if I had prepped Vance well enough, it was now up to Vance. The young goalie was fragile at this point, and a poor performance would be difficult to overcome.

Before I could even take it all in, I was standing next to Coach Bettermann in the rear corner of the player's bench, in the little cutout at the end, listening to a stirring rendition of the National Anthem. Chills went up and down my spine, and I tried hard to stay focused, as the television cameraman zoomed in on me with his annoying lens closely focused on my ugly mug during the song. I stood respectfully, with a right-hand salute over my heart. I stood, as I always had stood, in respect for all this great country gave to my family and me, and when the song finished, I sat on the bench to observe the game.

A massive chorus of cheers rained down from the home crowd when the public-address announcer proclaimed the starting goaltender for the Bears to be, "Vance Howard. Number one, Vance Howard." The Bears had done an outstanding job of boosting the young goalie up to be the savior of their beloved hockey club, and the media department whipped up my role as the old-time mentor returning to teach the young prospect. Brian McClure's plan was masterfully evolving. The Bears were raking the dough in tonight. I even heard from my teammates that "Henson" number twenty-seven hockey sweaters and replica old-time goalie masks were for sale in the concession stands. The game packed the formerly empty arena full to the rafters.

Coach Bettermann and I had worked a deal with the Bear's video crew members, to focus one camera on Vance Howard in the net and never remove the camera from him for the entire game. Our plan was to study the tape and break down his every move in a marathon study period.

Coach Bettermann leaned over right before the puck dropped, tapped my shoulder with his fist and shook my hand.

He happily and enthusiastically told me, "Good luck, twenty-seven. I sure do hope that the higher power you tend to invoke has us on the God radar tonight."

I smiled, patted his arm, but I did not answer him, I already was studying Vance. The young goalie looked nervous, and I stirred uneasily as I watched him take his stick and sweep away nonexistent piles of snow from his crease in a vain effort to calm his nerves.

I cupped my hands over my mouth, yelled out to him, "In a crouch, Vance. Get in a crouch and your head in the game now."

He looked up, waved to me and immediately crouched down in a classic goaltending stance. Good, he now had a focus. He looked good, but that was about to change. Detroit had their all-star first line out there for the opening shift of the game, and I surmised since a playoff berth was already in hand for them, and we were a last-place team, then the first line, as well as their superstar goalie, might only play a limited amount of time.

I was wrong.

The Detroit hockey club came out of the gate like hurricanes. After the puck dropped in the faceoff, they immediately overwhelmed the Boston first line. They were going to use the Bears as a first course for curing their playoff hunger. They intended to warm up for the playoffs by feasting on a hapless team with a rookie goalie trying to find himself and put his career back on track. The puck slipped into the Boston defensive zone, and despite many efforts, our defense could not clear the puck. Vance tracked the play, he was staying up on his skates, looking good, cutting his angles and for the limited amount of time that we had to practice together, he was so far, an impressive student.

The first shot on goal came from just inside the high slot. It was a hard wrist shot from the center iceman and as soon as the player took the shot, Vance forgot everything we discussed. Number one dropped to his knees, pulled his head out and the shot hit him in the top of his right shoulder, bounced off at an angle, and tucked neatly inside the upper crossbar of the net for a scoring goal. Immediately, a rain of boos broadcasted down from every nook, seat, and corner of the arena and the crowd turned ugly. I looked up at the scoreboard and the clock showed that only twenty seconds had ticked off and Vance had already allowed a goal.

A heavyset blob of a fan seated behind me pounded on the glass and angrily told me, "To get off the bench and get my old, long-haired ass and this rookie goalie outta Boston! This kid sucks! He can't stop a damn beach ball."

I studied Vance, and his body language was not too good. He angrily slammed his stick on the ice and shook his head as he leaned back on the crossbar of the goal as if he was just hanging out in the crease. Suddenly, he had zero confidence. In an effort to conceal his lack of confidence, he was projecting cockiness and a carefree approach, even after allowing a poor goal. Not good.

I jumped up, looked at Coach Bettermann and asked him, "Can you call a timeout, Coach Bill? Call a timeout, please."

Coach Bettermann looked at me somewhat puzzled and replied, "Shit, twenty-seven, sure I can, but I only get one. Kinda of a waste at this point in the game."

"Trust me. Old-time hockey. We did not even have timeouts when we played."

The old coach nodded, said, "Yeah, we had to fake injuries to stop play. I trust ya, Paulie. Damn sure nice to be playing old-time hockey for a change, instead of this cupcake bullshit. Wake his ass up."

He caught the attention of the referee and called for a timeout. The referee called for the timeout and the game coverage cut to a television commercial break, which bought us a few more precious seconds. The crowd was booing so loudly now that it was hard to hear, but I waved frantically for Vance to skate as quickly as he could over to the bench. For just a fleeting second, the crowd thought that Coach Bettermann was pulling the young goalie and replacing him with the experienced backup, and a hushed silence came over the entire arena. When Vance skated over to the boards, he simply leaned over to speak to me. And when they realized that the coach was not replacing him in the game, the crowd resumed their evil chorus. Vance unbuckled his cage mask, tilted it back, and took a water bottle from a bench assistant to take a drink.

Between sips he said, "Sorry, twenty-seven. I suck. Sorry."

I angrily tore the water bottle out of his hands and tossed it onto the bench.

"You do not suck and do not need a drink of water. You will need to take a leak if you drink before you even break a sweat. You need to listen. Get your head in the game, stick your face into a shot and defy the shooters to hurt you. Stand up on your skates and believe in yourself. Mental toughness will exceed physical toughness, every time. Make this team from Detroit realize that you are the best goalie in the world. You need to do this for two people. Do you know who they are?"

He seemed stunned at my anger.

Vance shook his head and then answered sheepishly, "You and me?"

"No, you and your mother. You told me how she worked lousy jobs for lousy pay. Toiled and saved for the little that she could provide. Now, you have a chance to earn more money than you both could ever dream of and redeem her toil and efforts. Make her proud. Reward her for those endless hours so that you could have a chance to do exactly what you are doing right now. You are about to make a ton of money for playing a game. People toil their entire lives at lousy jobs and do not earn what you are going to earn in one season, hell, in one game for playing a damn game! Wake the hell up! You are on top of the hockey world in Boston. Right now, the worldwide hockey media, and every news outlet in this city and in the hockey world has their cameras pointed on you. You never told your mom how much you loved her before she died, but you sure as hell can say, thank you and I love you now. Now, get your ass back in that net and believe!"

The referee blew his whistle to signal the timeout was now over, and Vance looked at me and smiled. He did not speak a word, but buckled his cage mask straps, turned and skated briskly into the goal. He tapped the right goal post, crouched down and waved to the referee to indicate he was ready for the faceoff. Of course, the Bears lost the draw and Detroit skated like buzz saws into the Boston zone. A slap shot from the point ripped through a crowd of players and I watched, as Vance stood tall, he tracked it, stayed on his skates and easily turned it aside with a classic stick save. The puck ripped along the boards and a Detroit player beat a Boston defenseman to the puck, picked it up and fired a wrist shot towards the goal. Once more, Vance stood tall, made a save on the hard shot, and resisted the urge to drop to his knees. The puck trickled off Vance's stick glove and the same defenseman whiffed at an effort to capture it and clear the zone. The puck rolled in front of the net and on the turn of a dime, Vance skated out of the net, cut down his angles from the top of his crease and stood up on his skates. A few lazier shots made their way to the net, and Vance easily turned those shots aside. Suddenly, Detroit was having a difficult time in figuring out how to beat Vance and his stand-up style of play. He was taking away all of their angles. He easily knocked the puck aside and crouched back down while tracking the rebound. Another shot, then another, and still, the hapless Boston defense could not clear the zone! Vance made a remarkable leg pad save, and then he pounced on the rebound and held it for a faceoff.

Now, the fickle home crowd was on their feet, cheering

wildly and chanting Vance's last name loudly.

"HOW-ARD! HOW-ARD! HOW-ARD!"

The heavy-set blob of a fan seated behind me, once again, pounded on the glass. And now, he was Vance Howard's greatest fan. He screamed at me, "Good job, twenty-seven. Ya woke his ass up! Old-time hockey rules!"

I smiled at his sudden turn of loyalty. Ya gotta love hometown hockey fans.

The crowd screamed as they shifted their allegiance rather quickly. I looked high up into the upper reaches of the arena and I carefully scanned around to each of the press boxes, my eyes searching for the one where Paul William, Harry, and Jim might be sitting in. It was to no avail; I could not find them in the madness and the wide expanse of the huge arena. Ice Land Arena, this was not.

Coach Bettermann came over; he leaned in and patted me on my back as he told me, "This off-season, I have to tell you that I am going back to church."

"Good! Let's go together. Praise God! Now, can you start to pray to get the defense to clear the zone?"

"I am trying. . .."

The Bears fought back gallantly, and you could tell that Vance's play in the goal inspired the team to new heights. They listened to the coach's directions; the old coach was in his glory now, pulling out old-style plays, teaching how to forecheck and how to bottle up the Detroit team in their own zone. He pulled a speedy center aside when he sat on the bench and gave him quick lessons in back-checking, and in meeting the opposition center iceman at the red line to stop the flow of the offense. Old-time hockey had resurfaced in Coach Bettermann, and he was reliving the lessons taught to us so many years ago. This man was a great coach. I could tell. Exactly, how he knew Coach Davis, I did not know. He had not yet shared his background, but I saw an awful lot of influence from Coach Davis in his style. He just needed to reawaken his soul too.

Old-time hockey worked then, and guess what? It was working now. The Bears played carefully, did not take any risks or stupid penalties, and when the third period started, the scoreboard proudly displayed a two-to-one score in favor of the Boston Bears.

Vance was superb in the goal. He stood up on his skates, challenged shooters, and he looked as if he was a seasoned veteran and not a rookie in his first, big-league start. He was in command and displayed the qualities of a leader, directing his defense and positioning players for every faceoff in front of his net. His teammates sensed his leadership, and they took it to heart. Detroit had nothing to play for and after their initial charge, and the fact that they were a goal behind, they eased up and primarily played their third and fourth lines. When the third period started, the superstar goalie for Detroit, gave way to the backup goalie. I settled into my corner on the bench, content and at ease to enjoy this moment and study my new student.

With about eight minutes left in the final period, I watched in awe, when Vance made a classic split leg save on a shot and then he corralled the rolling rebound, before Detroit could pounce on it for a second chance. I was surprised when Vance rolled around on the ice and the referee seemed to feel as if the play had injured Vance. The referee blew the whistle, and he waved to the Bear's bench for the trainers to jump out and assist the fallen goaltender, but Vance waved them off. A quiet hush came over the crowd and I had one of those classic, "Oh shit" moments. I felt my heart pounding in my chest. Please, please, please, just let it be a cramp. It was hot in the arena tonight. It was now late May, and it was a warm day and a warm night.

Vance gallantly climbed to his skates. He seemed to be okay, and everyone breathed a sigh of relief.

Coach Bettermann leaned in and told me, "He is cramping terribly now, twenty-seven. They have beaten the livin' shit outta him tonight. Over forty shots on goal now.

It is hotter than Hell in here tonight and the kid is sucking air. This might be a make-or-break moment. See if he is a cupcake or not. I am going to leave him in and see what he does. Old-time hockey, Paulie. You stayed in the game with the blood runnin' outta ya ass and drippin' on the ice."

"Agreed, Coach Bill. He needs to suck it up now. The old Vance would have packed it in. I hope that this is the turning point for showing us that this is the new attitude, Vance Howard."

The team from Detroit sensed blood now, and playoff bound or not, they were not willing to cut the young goalie any breaks. We yelled encouragement from the bench and I waved to Vance, who lifted his stick in acknowledgement that he was hanging tough in the net. Impressive, very impressive. Detroit promptly summoned their elite first line out onto the ice. Time for the kill shot. I noticed how the sweat was running off the end of Vance's cage mask as if it were a river. I knew that feeling.

I leaned forward, said a quick prayer and whispered, "C'mon kid, suck it up. Don't quit now. Now it is time to make a commitment."

Vance bent over in a crouch and waved to the linesman to indicate that he was ready to go. Since our team had caused the stoppage in play, the faceoff was in our zone to his right. I looked up at the clock and noted the time. A little over eight minutes left on the clock. Vance had to survive for eight minutes and twenty-seven seconds. Eight lousy minutes. Eight minutes to shape a young man's life, to prove his belief in me, to prove that newer is not always better, that the separation of old and young is only in years and not an indication of skill or worth, and that faith and commitment mean more than anything in this crazy thing we call life.

I whispered, "Not a marble, number one. Not a marble," . . . and the puck dropped.

Of course, the Bears lost the draw, and the puck slid out to the right point, where a defenseman wound up for a clean slap shot, while the Detroit first line center iceman, and the only goal scorer for Detroit in this game, set the screen in front of Vance. Even from the bench, I knew that the center iceman was just a decoy; I hoped that Vance realized the play too. The actual shot was going to come from the left-winger, who was breaking in on the side of the net, and that I had hoped that Vance spotted out of the corner of his eye. The left-winger would deflect the shot, which was going to be purposely shot wide of the net. A shot, which would come in about ankle high. The Boston Bears defense remained clueless. They seemed to be stuck in sand, and now, it was up to Vance.

A million shots, plays, and players rushed through my head, and I jumped and screamed, "Fight through the screen, Vance, push his ass out of the way and only play the point shot!"

I had seen this set play a few million times before, and instinct and experience set in and took over, but I was not in the net, Vance Howard was. No doubt that Vance now needed to stop the puck before it made it to the left-winger! Goalie interference and screens did not work back in my day, and I hoped that Vance was not going to allow one now. Number one must have heard me, or he realized the play. I was not sure which one it was, but he used his huge size and he stayed up on his skates. He pushed his way to the front of the screen, caught sight of the puck hurtling through the air, went into a full-out split save and at the last second, Vance snatched the puck out of the air with his catching glove, as if he was catching a bug flying around a room. Number one spun on his skates as players rushed into him and banged him around, but Vance held the puck for a faceoff as the crowd went crazy.

The noise in the arena was deafening as they broke into a loud chorus of "HOW-ARD! HOW-ARD! HOW-ARD!"

The linesman blew the whistle and Vance casually tossed him the puck.

The Detroit center iceman sensed the moment and the emotion. He could not help but tap Vance's pads in a show of respect. A rookie's arrival moment in his first big league game.

Coach Bettermann leaned in and patted me warmly on the back and I reached over and warmly, but gently shook his hand. "Damn, twenty-seven! I think the Bears got themselves an old-time goalie!"

Vance acknowledged the crowd going crazy over his remarkable save with just the slightest lift of his stick, and I remained impressed with his humble attitude and lack of smack-talk or grandstanding. I knew the game was in the bag. Vance faced a few more shots, made a few solid saves, one dramatic stick save on a hard wrist shot that the crowd got more of a rise out of than Vance did. It was routine to Vance, at least in my opinion, it was. I was not sure if Detroit now eased up on Vance out of respect for the rookie's amazing performance in his first game, or out of not really caring any longer, but other than one or two difficult shots after the stick save, the rest of the minutes were relatively easy in the net. His remarkable glove save took all the wind out of their sails and commanded some type of respect and honor.

The home crowd counted down the last few seconds of the game, Detroit did not even pull their goalie for the last minute, and when the horn sounded to end the game, it was as if the Boston Bears had won a bloomin' championship. The crowd went crazy, the Bears jumped over the boards to mob Vance and he raised his stick and gloves in the air, in what appeared to be a salute to his mum in Heaven. I stood up, Coach Bettermann, and I warmly embraced, and the old coach fist pumped in the air with just a touch of tears in the corners of his eyes. This was not about a last-place team simply winning one game.

It was so much more than just one game. It was about recapturing all of our spirits.

The Detroit team remained on the ice and even if this was not a playoff game or a game of significance, the two teams lined up for the traditional handshake salute that is so unique to the game of ice hockey. Detroit players skated by the player's bench and warmly congratulated Coach Bettermann, his staff, and me. The Detroit coaching staff and head coach stopped by and we chatted a bit too.

The Detroit head coach told Coach Bettermann and me, "Might just look at some old-time hockey films now too. Worked then, and it worked now too. Great job. That young man just might be the new, great goalie this league sorely needs."

We genuinely appreciated their warm wishes and handshakes. When the frenzy calmed, and the bedlam ended, I found Vance Howard at the side of the player's bench and the two of us embraced. The television cameras closed in and we did not care.

I asked him, "Did you hear me yelling out the play on that shot?"

He shook his head and sweat flew off his hair in every direction, while he told me, "Nah, shit, saw you do it in the training videos. I saw the same, damn, play and thought how it was such an incredible save that you made. That Hayward guy is a friggin' genius of hockey. He dissected that play like a surgeon and said it was the greatest save in hockey history. Gotta agree that I never saw any save better than that one was. I simply remembered how ya old ass handled it!" Tears ran down the young man's face and as we held each other, he told me, "There is joy in Heaven, twenty-seven. Somehow, I know that your wife and my mom have found each other and they are rejoicing in our mutual celebration."

I smiled, hugged him tightly and asked, "So, do you believe in God yet, number one?"

"I think so. Only God could have helped your long-haired ass to make that glove save back then and me to make it here today. Yes, I think that I just might. . .. "

The aftermath of the game was another blur in my life, and I am sure in the lives of others. My cellphone voice mailbox could not accept any additional messages and I quickly scanned the texts for important ones from Heather Sarah, my sister, Blue Cloud or Rose. I decided which ones that I needed to read and return as quickly as I could.

The locker room was a madhouse and Brian, Tommy Hayward, and the team owners joined us for the post-game celebration. The owners were cordial and very pleased with our efforts, and one of them even joked with me about, "Reconsidering and signing on for a full-time coaching position."

Ah, no, not going to happen.

Coach Bettermann awarded a game puck to share between Vance and me, and he said a few words to the team before we prepared for the onslaught of the press. I begged out of the press conferences, and Tommy Hayward ran interference for me to allow me to escape any media interviews. This was about Vance Howard and not about number twenty-seven. Coach Bettermann, Brian, and Vance, all participated in the post-game interviews. I hid in the hallway next to the pressroom and watched the interviews from a safe distance. On a positive note, Paul William was able to drag along Harry and Jim to attend the press conference, and it made for a rollicking time when the happy reunion occurred.

Vance briefly met the world famous, Harry M. Redmond Junior before the press conference began and Harry shook his hand violently, and as he typically does when he meets someone new, provided him with a new nickname, and then subjected poor Vance to one of his long-winded and now famous introductions, "Nice to meet you, there fancy Vancie! Ya, a good-looking kid. Don't have all of them, there scars all ovah ya face like twenty-seven does. Helluva game in that net and I am glad to see you sucked it up and did not cave in when your hurtsy-wurtsy, winky-dinky ass started cramping. Get used to it. Old-time hockey hurts! Harry M. Redmond Jr. is the name. I am world famous, ya know! Inventor, businessman, entrepreneur, retired hockey player, champion roller-skater, kijillionaire, race car driver, hit songwriter, welder, a retired womanizer, and general, all around windbag and a loudmouth, but overall, I am not a bad guy!"

Harry pulled Vance closer to him and put his arm around Vance as the big guy's strength and his presence overwhelmed the young goalie. Harry held onto Vance's shoulder as he waved at the "team" assembled in front of the two of them.

He continued to spout some more of the famous Harry introduction and his philosophy of life, "That there, guy, there with the scar on his lip and the sneer in his eyes, is the world's most famous, now reformed hockey goon, the now retired Pastor Jim and known by his alias of Mr. James T. O'Malley. He went from ripping fellow hockey player's tongues out and feeding them back to them for breakfast and beating us over the head with his hockey stick, while calling all our living relatives' horrible names, to seeing the error of his ways and praising God. I heard about twenty-seven's plan for you in the off-season, so be nice to Jim, cuz he is going to help us to teach you what it means to be a fearless hockey player, but also what it means to be a man." He then pointed to Paul William and proclaimed him the greatest sports writer in the world and his favorite son-in-law.

"I am your only son-in-law," Paul William reminded Harry, who promptly ignored him and moved on with his blowhard speech.

"Stick with us and be part of the team there, fancy Vancie, cuz with Harry and Paul, it is one adventure after another. Let's all ride along together and see where it all takes us."

The press conference went smoothly; Vance handled all the questions and comments professionally and very maturely. He seemed quite humbled by his overnight superstardom, not ego-boosted at all.

With the press conference concluded, we said our goodbyes to Brian and team management and we huddled up with Vance, Harry, Jim and Paul William. We made plans for all of us to meet at the hotel for dinner. Paul William, Jim and Harry had an early flight tomorrow to return to New Jersey. Vance and I needed to be back at the training facility in the morning to view and break down the video from the game, so I did not want to make it too late of an evening. Since it was already past ten, that might be a very unrealistic thought.

His fellow press mates now haunted Paul William, for his reaction to his father's role in the creation of this potential superstar. We stood impatiently on the sideline and waited for him to answer some questions and look for an opening in order to escape from them. We finally escaped.

"So, fancy Vancie are you in? Are we going to see you in a few weeks down in New Jersey for a maximum dose of Harry, twenty-seven, Paul William and Jim O'Malley, off-season training?" A much under the Wallcrawler influence, Harry asked poor, overwhelmed Vance Howard. "Got me a ten-bedroom mansion that you and Paul, since he is currently homeless, will stay in while you train. Great cooking, hot women wearing skimpy clothes hanging all around, don't get no ideas or stars in ya eyes—they are all accounted for, well, maybe all of them."

I wondered what Harry meant by that statement, but quickly dismissed it as drunken ramblings. My senses then went up when I first caught Jim's eyes studying me for a reaction to Harry's statement, then Paul William's eyes too.

Hmm . . . something is going on back home.

"We would love to train your sorry ass on how to be a Geyer Street guy! Just cuz ya from upstate New York, we will not hold it against ya!

"A what?"

"Ah, we will tell ya, latah. Ya in or what? Or are you gonna stand on the sideline and let the old-time hockey bus pass you by?"

"I am in, Harry. Say, can you tell me how you managed to roller-skate for all those hours?"

"Sure, I can. It's called the eye of the tiger and you gotta learn how to get it too. First, we need more drinks." The big guy looked up, waved to Janet and bellowed, "Say, Janet baby! A'nudder round. Put it on the Bear's tab! Did anyone ever tell you that you have a great ass in those tight black pants? I bet twenty-seven here, thinks so, but he is too much of an old lady to tell you so."

Janet laughed and waved back towards us as she showed that she would bring the drinks. In a biting testimony, she commented, "And he is a hot numbah too. His ass is dynamite too and oooohhh, those muscles and hair. Bet all men at his age, wished they looked like him and women looked like me!"

She posed seductively, flipped her hair in jest, winked over to me as Vance elbowed me and put his arm around me, while he commented on Janet.

"You have a fan of more than your goaltending, twenty-seven," Vance said between laughs.

"Nah, she is just kidding," I replied.

"She ain't kidding. Believe me, I might not be as old and as wise as you are, but she ain't kidding. I know chicks."

After Vance's comments, Harry waved and bellowed out, "Hang in there, Janet. Takes him a long time to wake up, but he thinks ya hot too. When ya bring the drinks over, let's talk somewhere quiet and let me tell you how he has been a victim of the dreaded Old Lady Syndrome. . .."

We made an early evening of it, at least as early an evening as we were able to, after all the mayhem of all that happened in a very long day. It was still a bit past two in the morning by the time we hit the hay. Luckily, tomorrow we had an afternoon practice and then an off day, followed by one more home game, then two games on the road, to finish out the year.

The plan for tomorrow was to breakdown video of Vance in the morning and for us to dissect his every move in the game. We would then hit the ice in the afternoon for a light practice and hopefully, some longer rest before the next home game. Tomorrow's practice would be intense, but the morning practice on game day would be a light skate and workout. My plan for the practices would be more talking and less demonstrating, since I did not think my body could take too much of a workout where I had to stand in the front of the net and pretend to be a goaltender, old-time or not. In particular, my leg muscles were still screaming at me from the skate the other day. It was very apparent that I still had a long way to go in my conditioning, or I was just too damn old now for this bullshit. Right now, a warm bath with salts and at least, a few hours of rest would do me a world of good. I would make some phone calls in the morning; in particular, I wanted to check in with Heather Sarah. Harry's mysterious comments, our tight-lipped son, and Jim's reaction had me slightly concerned as to what was going on at home.

As usual, morning came along so quickly and before I knew it, the alarm was screaming and yelling at me to rise and shine. The rise part, I could handle, the shining part, was not looking too good.

After having some morning tea and breakfast, as well as another hot soaking bath, I called Heather Sarah, and she answered on the second ring.

"Oh, dear Father! We knew you could do it! I saw the press conference, Sarah, Blue Cloud, Rose, and I . . . we all watched it all on the internet. Congratulations."

"Thank you, Heather Sarah, but I am not sure that I did anything. Vance did all the hard work. I just gave him some pointers."

"Oh, that is not true. You showed him how to play like twenty-seven. Not that he is, or could ever be, as great as twenty-seven is, but you showed him."

"Oh, I do not know about that."

"When are you coming home now? We love you and cannot wait to see you. Remember your promise. The townhouse is still a few weeks away from completion, so you are going to stay with Rose and Harry. Your room is all set up with your clothes and the things that you will require for a few weeks. Your pastor suits and collars are all dry-cleaned, pressed and hanging up in your closet. All set for you to return to work. The rest of your things are still in storage, we have this all under control. Rose set it all up for you. She did so very lovingly. She is amazing and my goodness, she does love you, dear Father. Rose already has a huge homecoming party arranged. If you do not show up here soon, you will be toast."

"I should be home by the end of next week. Yes, I love her too and owe Rose and the gang a long visit. I understand that I will be staying there for a bit. I have to ask you, is everything okay back there? Harry, well, he had a few drinks last night, might have been some drunken ramblings, but he said something strange. Your brother and Jim reacted strangely too, but they did not elaborate or tell me. . .."

She cut me off and I could tell by the tone of her voice that something was wrong. I knew our daughter very well, there was something going on there.

"Everything is fine. We do have to discuss a situation, but not right now. Not on the telephone."

"A situation? I knew it. Please, are you okay? Sarah, Rose, Blue, Dottie, Martha?"

"They are all fine. I am fine. Please dear Father, all is well. Uncle Harry, my brother, and Pastor Jim are looking after all of us. Paul William just called Blue and reported that they have landed in New Jersey and right now, are driving from the airport to home. Please relax. We could not be in better hands while you are out of town. We will speak when you return home. I will not . . . no, I spoke incorrectly . . . we will not, allow anything to break this incredible resurrection of your spirit and of number twenty-seven. This is all God's plan. I do think that is what you and all of us believe, is it not? God's plan has us deal with the good and the bad."

"Yes, you are correct, Heather Sarah. Yes, okay, I will take your word for it. Those are three of the finest men in this world and beyond. I miss you, love you, and will be home soon."

"We miss you too. And you too, dear Father. You are in that group too, in fact, you are the leader. I am so proud of you and I know that Mother is too. It is time to move on, as it is all of us to do so too. I must say that I am so impressed with Pastor Jim. He is wonderful and while you are away, he has not only been a friend but he has provided all of us with spiritual guidance. He is quite a remarkable man. While he is not a substitute for you, Pastor Jim is brilliant. He even came over one evening and conducted Lutheran Vespers with us, despite his nondenominational background. He is an insightful man. I must say that Pastor Jim is amazing. A man who was so violent on the ice and at one time, he was your mortal enemy, yet he is such a dear and honest friend to you and to all of us. He is also a warm, intelligent, advocate for the word of God. Very impressive."

"He is a great man and an even better pastor. A man of this world and a man of God. He is a treasured friend, and he will figure greatly in our plans to transform this young goalie into a man, as well as, a superstar."

There was a little moment or two of silence on the telephone and then our daughter spoke. As I have mentioned, I know her, oh so well, and her pause was to gather some thoughts before speaking. Heather Sarah is, as was her mother, not a person to speak randomly if she was calculating her words.

"Is that the plan, dear Father? To train the student in the off-season here in New Jersey?"

"It is, why?" I found her use of the word student to be an interesting, if not in a roundabout manner, quite an accurate description. Heather Sarah also had changed her voice inflections quite a bit. Her spirit had most definitely brightened a bit.

Once again, she paused and then spoke, "I think that this is all so amazing. You made the national news. It is a story that mesmerizes everyone, even if a person is not a fan of sports—it is a human-interest story. The pride we all have in you—there are no words, dear Father. None. Here you are still teaching, still being a mentor and still a pastor. Rabboni. I hope the young man, ah, ah, what was his name? Vance?"

"Yes, Vance Howard. He is a bit angry at some terrible twists and turns in his life. He harbors regrets and is working his way back from some lingering fear of a terrible injury. Yet, he has all the tools to be a great goalie and an even better man. God has opened up his heart."

"Oh my. Wow! I hope he, I mean, Vance, I hope that he understands how fortunate he is to have you and your remarkable team to train him in much more than just being a goalie. I watched all the press conferences. And while he cannot hold a candle to you dear Father, he is a rather handsome chap. He is lean and quite tall, and he has an incredible smile and magnificent eyes."

Ah, hah! There was the reason for the pause. Young Vance Howard caught our daughter's eye! Very strange words and reactions to come from our daughter, who is a married woman. Furthermore, there has been no mention of Ian by Heather Sarah, or anyone else. Harry told me a few days ago that Heather Sarah and Sarah were coming to New Jersey to take care of the sale of our house and to shop for the townhouse. I started to put these pieces together.

Ian. The son-of-a-bitch has done something. My heart felt it. God will forgive me because God just spoke to me.

Binky and Harry were correct. He most likely was a scoundrel by doing something stupid. Jackass. I am quite sure that if he had done something physical or really stupid that he would not be alive right now. Harry, Paul William, and Jim would have been down to Florida on a fighter jet and taken care of that situation.

Hmm . . . Vance and Heather Sarah. They *were* very close in age, might be a year or two between them, and suddenly, God's plan unveiled another potential piece of the puzzle to me. Patience. Please pray for patience. It is God's plan and not yours. As flawed humans, we always strive for instant results and satisfaction, and it does not work that way.

"Are you still there, dear Father?"

"Yes, sorry. I agree that he is a handsome young chap. If I had one of those fancy cage masks back in my day, it would have saved my face from many scars. Heather Sarah, if you have a few more minutes, please, let me tell you about this new equipment they have these days. . .."

When I finished the phone call with Heather Sarah, I called my sister. After Dottie told me how proud of me that she was for pulling out of the tailspin with such a miraculous resurrection, she told me how much she loved me. I told her the same, and reassured her that I had heard her advice, as well as God's call, and would be back in the office within two weeks. Even before my approved leave expired. My sister was a firm believer and advocate for God, and she converted to Catholicism many years ago, to worship with her husband and family. She was a fine woman. There was none finer. Dottie choked up a bit when she gently told me that Mum, the old man, Gramps, and Binky were all very proud of my return to the world too. We spoke for a long time until I had to break away and get to work. I was still getting used to the fact that I now had commitments to keep. It had been a few months, where I only answered to a laptop computer and word processing programs, and honestly, my main occupation was actually in emptying beer bottles and tossing them into waste cans.

Later that same morning, Vance and I, along with a technician from the Bear's support staff, a middle-aged man named Greg Jasco, sat in a room filled with the latest in fancy large-sized video screens, computers and other electronic wizardry. Greg had filmed the video of the game and now he had set us up with the video of Vance playing goal. His plan was to load the discs, teach us how to push all the buttons, and then leave us alone to break down the film and study the science of ice hockey goaltending.

His plan had a flaw.

Both Vance and I were not too swift with modern computers and technology. Even after Greg's outstanding patience with us, and explaining the operation of the system about twenty times, we still froze the computer three times, and somehow accessed the internet and a website selling scented candles.

Greg finally conceded defeat, and he told us, "Look, twenty-seven and number one. You both just tell me whatcha need, and I will push all the buttons and control this. You two, confused goalies, just concentrate on the coaching and look up there at the big screen."

That was a better plan. Geez, how far all of this has come since my days of reviewing black and white photographs and grainy video tapes of my play in the net. This technology allowed us to view every aspect of the play of Vance. We could stop, freeze and zoom in on every motion and see where he went wrong and where he went right. It was a remarkable tool, and we studied the game, every shot, motion and even timeouts with great care. Vance was now a great student. He now had focus and listened to my teaching and coaching and he even asked, when Greg broadcasted my video clips for comparison, and we viewed my old-time performance in the net, what I was thinking, why I positioned my skates that way, and held my stick this way or that way. He was now moving to the next level. A level of honesty and maturity and a level to be coachable and respectful, and deep down, I knew our plan, although risky, gimmicky, and to be honest, somewhat strange, worked. If Tommy Hayward had never made that old-time video and forced Vance to watch it, then it might have been an even more difficult situation. Hayward was a genius and Brian was certainly a shrewd man. That video was not a project that you could create in one day; this was a plan they were working on for quite a long time. Vance knew that in my day, I could stop the puck too, and that worked in our favor.

Time passed us by quickly and an assistant coach had to venture into the film room and remind us that we had an on-ice session. He also mentioned that Coach Bettermann was hollering for us very loudly. Something about how difficult it was to have a proper hockey practice without the starting goaltender. We thanked Greg, hustled off to get into our equipment and made our way to practice. The way my body ached and squeaked, I knew that I would skate very lightly and observe from the sideline. No demonstrations today, at least none that forced me to face live shots or kick up chunks of ice. My little adventure at practice the other day, still, had some painful reminders. For this practice, I wanted to concentrate on continued teaching and coaching of the stand-up style of goaltending play for Vance and follow-up on our video studies. I stressed that this was not something he would learn in a week or two, it was going to be a long time before he grew more comfortable with the style and that ultimately, we might even refine his style into a hybrid of old and new.

Coach Bettermann watched us carefully. He skated over to the side of the rink and together, we watched the action, he warmly thanked me again, and told me how grateful he was that I was always including him in the plans, in all the press conferences, and how he now felt renewed in his spirit. He explained that he once again felt as if he was a part of the team. I really liked this old chap because he was a good guy, a great coach to lead the charge for old-time hockey and somehow, I would make sure that Brian knew that in my heart, and in my humble opinion, he might have misjudged Coach Bettermann. I might just add to the conversation, if Brian's mood was just right, I will suggest that perhaps he should give him another look before cutting ties with him.

Between coaching and speaking with Coach Bettermann, I prayed fervently that Vance would not suffer any injuries and we could cruise into the off-season training without any issues.

The practice went well, as did the next home game, which was a hard-fought battle between the Bears and the team from Winnipeg. Winnipeg, like the Detroit team, was a playoff bound team that used the game as a warm up for the opening of their playoff stretch. I happily and contently sat in my little corner on the player's bench, taking in the magic of the atmosphere, while teaching and studying Vance Howard. He played well, his confidence increased, and while he gave up two goals that I think he could have stopped, he was making great progress. We lost the game four goals to two, but the home crowd certainly received their money's worth, because it was an entertaining game. Even though Vance allowed four goals, it could easily have been a score of six to two. Vance made a number of incredible stops that stood the crowd on their feet. This crowd was a knowledgeable hockey crowd, and this was a hockey city. The hockey crowd knew that there was a bright future for the Boston Bears because of this young prospect, who was on the cusp of a superstardom. Vance just needed to learn a little more about playing goalie and about life.

A worn-out and now, beleaguered, Tommy Hayward did his best to ward off the multitude of requests for interviews with Vance and with me, while still balancing Brian McClure's thirst for publicity and attention to his hockey club.

While I refused most of the local interviews, I did agree to conduct an interview with one of the national networks. I sat and spoke with a prominent interviewer for one of those television shows, which are news reporting, combined with human interest reporting. I felt that my testimony would be of interest to not only hockey fans, but moreover, it would or could be an inspiration to other grieving spouses to hear of how I picked my life up after tragedy. The interviewer was a young, quite gorgeous woman, who was cordial and intelligent, and after we finished filming the clip, I expressed to the woman my thoughts that the interview went rather well. By all indications, it did go well, because after it had aired on the network, the positive feedback from my family, church contacts and parishioners, the hockey club and others, was a confirmation of the impact of the interview. In addition, the telephone ringing off the hook for Heather Sarah requesting more of my time, seemed to be a bit of an overwhelming response.

The last home game finished out the year in Boston and we had a well-received fan appreciation day, an autograph session and fan club breakfast, followed by our road trip with two games to finish out the entire year. From my nook on the bench, I could see the nucleus of a core of very good hockey players now taking shape out there and a team on the edge of putting all the pieces in place, led by Vance

Howard. As Brian McClure accurately stated, it all starts with solid goaltending. Vance had moments of doubt, moments of shakiness, and a multitude of mistakes that his reflexes and incredible skills covered up, but this was all coachable and most importantly, the young man now seemed eager to learn and improve.

Next year, look out, league! For now, the Bears had two more road games, one in Minnesota, and then another in Denver, Colorado that we had to work through and then a long off-season of work ahead of us. The word amazing does not even describe these moments, nor come close to summarizing, all of what happened to my family and to me during these few, short weeks of our lives. In fact, I would be hard-pressed to find a single word in any language to summarize the last few weeks. I guess when you place it all in God's hands and eventually concede your life to the plan, then this is what happens.

Vance had already agreed to train with us in New Jersey in the off-season; but first, he needed to head to his home in Virginia, break that down, and arrange to move to Massachusetts. The Bears had already narrowed an apartment selection for him to choose from; he did not want to purchase a house and deal with the maintenance that a home requires, so it would not be a long process. Harry already insisted that Vance spend the off-season in his house, and Gibby Gibbons was off the hook for some additional expenses. I agreed with Harry, and thanked him profusely, because we both knew this was about so much more than just hockey. It was going to be training for a lifestyle and a mind-set and with Vance in close quarters; we could mold him into a man as well as a world-class goaltender.

What a whirlwind few weeks in my life and in everyone's lives! The adventures of Harry and Paul included some winners, but I have to say that this one might be the most amazing one of all. I spent the last two games, in the corner of the visitor's bench in Minnesota and in Denver, just praying for this season to end on a good note and injury free. There was progress in Vance's play with each passing game, slight progress, but nonetheless there was progress. The main issues would be to allow him to develop his own style of stand-up play, intermixed with his own skills to achieve a hybrid mix of what he was comfortable utilizing. I knew, as did Vance, that he did not want to be a copy of number twenty-seven. That was not going to work because he needed to find a balance by pulling some facets of my style as well as his own. He still pulled his head out on some hard shots and although he argued with me that he did not, and that he was not, flinching on shots, when we watched the film, he could no longer dispute it. We needed to cure his fear and puck-shyness on certain shots, and I had a feeling that I knew just the hockey player to do it too. A certain player named; James T. O'Malley might have the magic cure.

We lost the game in Minnesota by a goal, but Vance played well. The winning goal was on a power play, and there was nothing that he could have done to stop it. The Bears recovered for the final game in Denver and we won the last game of the season convincingly by a score of four to one. Vance played his heart out in this match and made a number of classic, stand-up, angle cutting saves, which shocked the hockey world. He was on his way now. We just had to fine tune Vance, cure the fear and halt some of his immaturity. That was all.

When the final buzzer went off, and the season ended, I bent my head over and spoke a quick prayer of thanks for my career as a "behind the bench" consultant to have ended. As much as I loved this game, enjoyed this opportunity and gave thanks for it restoring my soul, now, it was time to do what I really wanted to do and that was, to invoke the power of Heaven, follow the rest of the plan and most of all, to be a pastor.

Chapter Nine

Warm Tea for the Soul

"For the love of Pete! This has to be the most remarkable damn road trip of all time. Talk about the adventures of Harry and Paul! This one takes the friggin' brass ring. It makes that guy that went all over the place playing polo look like a child's play."

Blue Cloud, who was sitting with her arm around Paul William on the sofa in Harry and Rose's living room looked first at her husband and then at her father.

"Who? What guy who played polo?"

"That Mark Polo guy, ya know who I mean!"

"Marco Polo. Not Mark. He was an explorer. He did not play polo, Daddy."

I laughed at Harry and his usual colorful comments. He was in rare form tonight and as usual, he never disappointed us for his waves of raw emotions and unusual humor. We were now all sitting in the living room of the Redmond's expansive mansion home in Shadow Lakes, New Jersey. I had just walked into the home, placed my luggage on the floor of the foyer, and then became overwhelmed by my family surrounding me to welcome me home and back to the world. After hugs, kisses, handshakes and greetings, we made our way to the living room where we all sat for a few minutes to catch up and recover. Heather Sarah and Sarah were upstairs. Sarah was enjoying her nightly bath and they would be down in a few minutes.

"WHATEVER! To get back to Paul here, remind me to keep better tabs on you next time. Talk 'bout a recovery from the depths of despair, geez, ya took it to new heights! I admit that ya looked pretty good on the television screen there. All that hair, the lights in the studio, some makeup artist to cover up all the hockey scars, ya looked like a movie star. Heather Sarah's phone will not stop ringing with people wanting to book ya for more interviews, and all kinds of weepy-eyed stuff. We could make a fortune on it. You get at least, ten marriage proposals per day from sex-starved whacko women."

Rose, who was sitting in the chair next to me, reached out and gently touched my arm and smiled while saying, "I don't blame them. Harry is right. You did look incredibly handsome on television."

"Well, thanks, I just thought that it might help some other people who were going through the same thing that I went through. By the way, Harry, I did not have a makeup artist."

"WHATEVER! Cut to the important stuff. Did ya ask for the phone number for that hot chickie-poo who interviewed ya?"

"No, Harry, I did not ask her for her phone number."

Harry waved his hand in the air as if to dismiss me and mumbled, "Figures. Ya such an old lady. I swear. Must be blind too."

For once, I was going to defend my position when Harry, for what had to be the millionth time in our lives together, accused me of being an old lady. It was finally time to defend my net. I reached around to the back pocket of my black dungarees, pulled my wallet out and opened it up. Then, with a coy smile and a touch of pride, I pulled out a little paper and waved it in the air.

"I did not have to ask her because she gave it to me!"

As soon as I said that and waved the paper in the air, I noticed Rose turn her head quickly and stare at the paper intently. Her eyes were intense and after staring at the paper, her eyes then worked to me and I looked at her and smiled. Rose weakly smiled, but it was not a sincere smile. She then leaned back in her chair and fingered the earrings in her ears. Rose did that quite often when she was thinking. It was a habit of hers.

I must admit that Rose looked captivating this evening. Gorgeous. Her hair was perfect and impeccable. Rose was wearing a new dress that I had never seen her wear before. A black dress, fairly low-cut in the neckline and tight fitting on her perfect figure. She looked amazing. Until I pulled out the telephone number, Rose had been laughing at her husband's usual antics and now she stopped laughing and had an intense reaction. I thought how that was an unusual reaction for Rose to have. It was as if the thought of me returning to the dating world disturbed her. Given her sister-like relationship with Binky, I could understand her response. On the other hand, was it something else that caused such a reaction? It was a bit strange.

"Well, 'bout damn time! Musta found a pill to cure ya of the Old Lady Syndrome. Been waitin' for that. . .."

The voice of little Sarah screaming at the sight of me interrupted Harry. She tore into the room, screaming, "Grandpa!" With a leap and a bound, she jumped into my arms and I hugged and kissed her. I held her so tightly that I thought we would melt into each other. It was so good to be home. So good to return to the world.

Heather Sarah leaned in; she hugged us and kissed me. "Welcome home and back, dear Father. It is so good to have you back. In every way."

"It is wonderful to be here. Now, give me some time for loving here with my granddaughter and then I think we have to have a little chat. Correct?"

"We do yes, we do, Father. It will be rather intense. We need to do so in private. Just Uncle Harry, Auntie Rose, you, and me. Blue and my brother know everything already. Now, admittedly, I need you, dear Father. I need the rock that you are."

I nodded, bent down and let Sarah down as the little girl hung around my neck and kissed me once again. I hugged her again and kissed her, then whispered to our granddaughter, "Go tell Auntie Blue and Uncle Paul William about your bath."

Blue Cloud took the prompting, and she waved for Sarah to join them on the sofa. "Yes, come over here, sit with us and tell us. I think Uncle Harry and Auntie Rose bought you a new ducky today. Did you play with it in the tub?"

Sarah scampered off happily to jump on the sofa and tell them all about her adventures. Sarah seemed very happy, and that provided me with some relief. Then again, she was always such a happy little girl.

I took Heather Sarah's hand, and we walked to the kitchen. If this was going to be as intense as I thought it would be, then we needed to sit around the old sacred kitchen table from 20 John Street that now resided in the Redmond's kitchen. The table that had been the settings for everything from a nervous groom waiting to marry, to opening impassioned letters from wayward lovers, to discussions of time bombs hidden in cupboards.

Now this.

I sat on one end of the old table, with Heather Sarah to my right, Rose to my left and Harry on the other end.

There remained no sense in prolonging my initial thoughts, therefore, I dove right in and asked, "This is about Ian. Right? It is over with you and him. Correct?"

"Yes, Daddy."

Only at certain, very emotional times in our lives, did my daughter address me as, "Daddy." Right then and there, I knew our daughter was in deep pain.

I reached over and took her hand; I reached over and took Rose's hand with my other hand.

"Okay, did he hurt you or Sarah? Did he touch you or her?"

"No, Daddy. Not physically, only emotionally."

Harry immediately piped in and told me, "In your absence, we would have taken care of that, Paul. If that were the case, Jim, Paul William, and I would have wiped the Earth clean of any trace of him."

"Thank you, Harry. I realize that, but I had to ask anyway. But of course, thank you." While studying our daughter's eyes, I asked, "So, what happened?"

Heather Sarah was a powerful woman, strong, brave and so much her mother's daughter. She took a deep breath and gripped my hand tighter. Our daughter was gathering strength. I looked at her, and then at Rose, and the tears in Rose's eyes, and her death grip on my hand, told me this was going to be ugly.

"Things have not been good between us for a long time. We put on a happy family face for you when you visited a few weeks ago, but it was forced. Ian feared you, Daddy. I could tell that he was always fearful of you and the power of Heaven and Earth that you command and invoke. He would badmouth you all the time, even in front of Sarah. His sympathy when Mother passed was so short-lived. In retrospect, he couldn't care less. I told him many times that he was jealous and would ask him what he was afraid of with you. Now, I know that he feared that you would see through him. I loved him and love is so blind sometimes. It was a huge mistake, to fall for his charisma, and his charm because he is a scoundrel. I have been speaking with Blue and Auntie Rose about the situation on and off for some time now. Ian always had an excuse for why he could not, or did not want to spend time with us. He paid little attention to Sarah. Almost none. He always worked late, played golf with important clients, you know, any excuse not to be home with us."

I nodded and continued to hold their hands. This was

difficult and painful.

"Our sex life was nonexistent, our love dying. One horrible day, I found him online, trying to access money through one of my business accounts, and when I caught him, he gave me some lame excuse that he was thinking of buying a new car or some type of other bullshit. I was enraged and told him that he needed to stop the charade and to be honest. He became wary of me, came up with a bullshit lie that he had to leave on some sham of a business trip, and promptly left for a week . . . it was then that I took action."

"Private detective?"

"Yes."

"Tried to access our accounts? You mean Harry and Rose's charities and our accounts. That is a pile of dough, my dear daughter. Did he have any success?"

Heather Sarah shook her head to indicate that Ian had no success.

"No, he cannot get into any of my business or any of the charities or our private accounts. When things started to fall apart, I divorced many of our joint accounts and the business is a stand-alone entity. Only Uncle Harry and my brother can get in. They are my backups for emergencies or if something happened to me."

"Good. I know how smart you are, Heather Sarah. Sounds as if you had been suspecting something terrible for a long time. What did the detective uncover?" When I asked, Rose let go of my hand and she started to sob. She covered her eyes with her hands and Harry jumped up and ran over to his wife to console her.

"Oh, dear Lord in Heaven, be with us all," I prayed in my mind.

"Where do I start? Let's see, three affairs, one of his girlfriends is pregnant, and she thinks it is Ian's baby. He has a cocaine habit, and he embezzled money from one of his law firm's largest clients to support his numerous love lives and his drug habit. Oh yes, he turned out to be a prize. Love is remarkably and truly blind, dear Father. I was so stupid to allow his good looks, his charisma and his charm to capture me. So, stupid. . ..''

I stopped her, stood up, went over, and hugged her from behind while she remained seated and buried her head in her hands.

"Stop! You are brilliant! Never demean yourself. You are our daughter. Please stop."

Heather Sarah was now sobbing along with Rose, and I looked over at Harry, who shook his head in disgust. I knew that he felt as I did. We both wanted to kick some ass. Harry was right, Binky was correct too. Ian was a weasel. A punk. I wanted to choke his throat with my bare hands until his eyes popped out of his head. I prayed for God to forgive me for thinking of doing that to the father of our dear Sarah. If nothing else, the bum was still Sarah's blood father. Still, I wanted to kick his ass until it was bloody raw. Thank goodness, he was half a nation away or it would be a difficult evening. My soul was on fire, and it was time to subdue the elements of the old neighborhood within me, and instead, ensure that our daughter and granddaughter had support. Justice will come later.

"I should have been here for you and am so sorry, Heather Sarah. Our precious daughter, I am so very sorry, for letting you down."

When I spoke those words, Heather Sarah quickly stood up. She wiped the tears away from her eyes, and she took me in her arms. No doubt, she inherited Binky's super strength!

"No!" Heather Sarah shouted while staring me down, "you did not, or could never let me, or anyone else down! There was nothing for anyone to do. Ian did this! I swore everyone to secrecy. I instructed them to tell you that we were here from Florida to take care of the sale of our house and to buy the townhouse. We lost my dear Mother and with you on the path to recovery, my brother and I decided that we would not allow anything to stand in the way of your resurrection. We were not going to lose our father too. We have been so worried for you, dear Father. Pastor Jim visited with us and with me. He sat with me, we read scripture, we prayed. While he is no substitute for my father, he was wonderful, he was caring and after much prayer and thought, we knew that I arrived at the correct decision in ending this marriage."

"I must say that I owe Jim so much. So very much. Hate to bring this up, have you been tested for STDS?"

She hugged me tightly, and I kissed her repeatedly.

"Yes. No issues. I love you, Daddy."

"I love you too."

"Promise me that you will never leave us in spirit again, Daddy. We thought that we lost you."

I held her as close as I could, and all I could feel was shame at being so weak and disappointing my family.

"I promise and apologize to everyone. Never again, will I be weak, no matter what the situation. Never. Please, let's sit back down here, catch our breath a bit and recover. Please, and then you can tell me the rest of this wretched story. Please, let's all sit."

Heather Sarah, and Rose nodded in agreement while they both wiped their tears away. Harry walked over to the refrigerator and he did not even ask. He grabbed red wine for both Rose and Heather Sarah, and a Big Boulder beer for me. After pouring the wine for them, and handing the beer and a beer mug to me, he went and mixed himself a Wallcrawler. It looked as if he was mixing a double.

"Ian was arrested for the embezzlement charges, Uncle Harry called to tell me that the house sold and I told him the details of what was happening. Uncle Harry told me to get the hell out of there and let Ian rot in jail, and that is what we did! We left Florida, and I left him in jail. I emailed to his parents explaining how I knew everything that their worthless son did and that I considered the marriage over. I filed the divorce papers already, and the house is up for sale. After all, I am an attorney, as is Ian, but he is a cupcake real estate attorney. I am not. When you enrage me, cross me, or my daughter or family, then I become ruthless. I am very much my father's daughter. If you piss me off, then I will tear you, limb-from-limb. I guess that I inherited the old neighborhood son-of-a-bitch gene from Grandpa Henson and my daddy."

I nodded and added, "And your, Great-Granddad Alcott. He was tougher than all of us put together."

Heather Sarah almost smiled and laughed before she continued to explain, "His parents never answered, but I know they bailed him out. Uncle Harry made some calls, he hired labor, and they cleaned the entire house out. Wiped it clean of, as you would say, the ghosts. Our clothes, our jewelry, my heirlooms and Sarah's special items such as her toys, we shipped here to New Jersey. We auctioned or donated all the rest of the worthless possessions. Ian's clothes and possessions, I told the labor to leave on the curb in boxes and asked them to call his parent's house to inform them where they were. The foreman of the crew was awesome, and he told me that Ian's father came by and picked the items up."

I took a long sip of the beer and it sure tasted cold and good. Under this type of stressful testimony, it tasted extra good. Rose and Heather Sarah took a sip or two of red wine, and Harry returned with his cocktail. He was sucking it down rather quickly. This was difficult on Rose and Harry, and they even knew the story beforehand!

"Thank you, Harry. Let me guess, you called Sal Zucchini Junior?" Harry nodded, took another sip of the Wallcrawler and gave me a smile and one thumb up.

"Yup, Sal Junior's Florida boys took care of everything for us. They guarded and escorted Heather Sarah and Sarah until she could get to the airport. They even drove them to the airport in a convoy of the famous black Galaxies. Just in case, Ian got really stupid when he was out on bail."

"I will call Sal Junior next week and thank him."

Harry nodded, downed the last of the Wallcrawler, stood up and walked over to the counter to mix another one.

"I donated a pile of dough in Sal Senior's memory to the Riverside Catholic Church there in the old neighborhood. The priest wants to speak with you and talk that bishop stuff. Sumthin' 'bout some ecomentical service."

The big guy turned and pointed at our drinks. I could tell that he was feeling the pain of this situation too.

"Youse guys good?" Harry asked.

We all ignored Harry's classic New Jersey massacre of English, I nodded to him, while the big guy added, "Yup, Sal Junior's New Jersey boys are here too. Watching our house right now. I did not ask him to do that—but he insisted. He told me anything for Pastor Paul and his family. Just in case, Ian becomes really, really stupid."

I was shocked, "Really? I did not see anyone out there."

Harry did not even turn around; he continued to chuck ice cubes into his glass while saying, "Exactly. Paul, shit man, it is Sal Junior's guys."

"Oh yes, what was I thinking? Well, Ian has chosen his course in life and Sarah and you will move on with yours. We will all move into the townhouse when it is completed."

Heather Sarah leaned over, took my hand, and asked, "Are you sure? I planned to rent a house here until I could settle things, you know, find an office for the practice and such. Good thing that, years ago, I sat for and passed the New Jersey Bar Exam. Who knew? Dear Father, you might want your privacy for your work, for your writing, maybe even for entertaining lady friends? Sarah is a little hurricane, and she makes a lot of noise and runs all over the place."

Out of the corner of my eyes, I noticed Rose fidget nervously when Heather Sarah mentioned the "lady friends." Rose picked up the red wine and downed the last remaining sips of the wine. Now, there seemed to be little doubt that the subject of me possibly dating a woman someday is bothering our lovely Rose. I could tell because I knew Rose extremely well. We remained as close as ever and I needed some more time to figure out this little twist. Right for now, I needed to settle this matter with our daughter. My anger at the situation percolated like an old teakettle and I needed to blow off a bit of steam.

'Bullshit, bullshit, and one last bullshit! It is a done deal. Not even debatable. Sarah and you will stay with me. Take your time, get it all over and done with and let's put ourselves all back together in a new place, a fresh start for all of us. That precious little girl needs her grandpa, her uncles and you, now more than ever. I am sure that Uncle Harry can arrange for an office for you in ten minutes. I will not listen to any other options. You are not going to have me worrying and wondering about you and our precious granddaughter. God will not be able to save Ian if he is stupid enough, somehow to reappear at your doorstep. I will snap him like a twig and toss what is left of him into the wind like dried leaves. This conversation is over. I need another beer and youse guys need more wine. Lots of prayers, praise, beer and wine! It is just like Jesus at the wedding! Tomorrow we will celebrate Vance's arrival, his rebirth, as well as our new directions, the new townhouse and our renewed lives. The Lord will forgive me, but I refuse even to pray for a recovery for Ian. Maybe I will someday, but not right now. No way, not right now."

I tossed the rest of the beer down, angrily picked up the empty bottle, reached over and picked up the two empty wine glasses and headed to the refrigerator for refills. My anger at Ian and this wretched situation was now manifesting in full-blown pissed off anger.

I tossed the beer bottle in the trash and opened the door to the refrigerator as Harry said, "Uncle Harry thinks that twenty-seven thinks ya idear was bullshit, my precious Heather Sarah. In fact, it earned three bullshit certifications."

'Yes, I heard, Uncle Harry. I know when to keep my mouth shut," Heather Sarah feigned closing her mouth, and she smiled at Harry's observation.

The big guy continued with his assessment of my temperament, "Yupper! Twenty-seven is back in the full twenty-seven glories. Uncle Harry thinks he is pissed. He does on occasion manage to shake the Old Lady Syndrome. I have seen this on the ice, and in life, when he reaches a point of no return. It ain't too pretty from here on in. Your father can, with a single prayer, invoke the power and the glory of Heaven and all the Lutheran saints who reside there. Some angels of war too. Believe me, cuz, Rose and I have seen it when he saved our precious Blue Cloud. I will find you an office in five minutes. Heather Sarah, please just say the word. Rent free. Let's hope and pray that your old man never sees Ian the asshole ever again or there will be very little of Ian left to place in a grave. They will have to bury one tooth, cuz that might be all that is left of 'em."

The conversation turned lighter. We joined Paul William, Blue, and Sarah in the living room, sat, and discussed some happier subjects. Rose explained how she had planned a special homecoming party as well as a meet and greet for Vance tomorrow night at their home. As usual, Rose and her amazing creativity at party planning were on full display. She was amazing!

Vance arrived tomorrow, around one in the afternoon and Harry and I were going to the airport to pick him up, have lunch and then bring him to where he was going to spend his summer, living with the legendary, thirty-five and his lovely wife, while he trained in hockey and in life. I had a plan, but right now, it had been a very long day of travel stress and horrible news. Sarah was already asleep in Blue's lap and we took our direction from her. Rest will do us all good.

After many hours of laughter, lots of alcoholic beverage consumption, wonderful home-cooked food, some more tears and much joy, we all retired for the evening.

The Redmond's mansion had many bedrooms. I think the exact number was ten, but I could not be sure. The situation with Ian caused me much distress and when I settled into the bedroom, a room, which Binky and I shared many times when we stayed here, my guilt at not praying for his forgiveness, was huge. Still, I could not bring myself to pray for him. This, in some manner, disturbed and surprised me, and instead, I got down upon my knees and prayed for the answer as to why I would not, or could not, pray for Ian. Never before was I such a judgmental pastor and never pretended to be self-righteous. I am just a man as any other man is, and I require the blood of the cross as much as any other person does. Pastor Paul John Henson always preached a true Gospel and the blood of the cross, the gore of the scene and violence was something that I never sugar coated. The words that I preached from my pulpits did not contain the happier or modern messages, "Of the polished Gospel." A Gospel, where the preachers told you how wonderful life is, and how joy, happiness, and money will come your way if you just pray for it, fill their collection plates and follow God. In particular, their Easter messages were all flowers, happy hymns, joy and hope. No, indeed, my message was about the blood of the cross, because without the blood there is no actual Gospel. There is no hope. There is no message. You need to know of the despair of life before you feel the joy.

Dear reader, if you are religious or you are not, I need to make an important point here. Let me tell you, as I did when I first began to relate my long tale that nothing great or grand can come out of the message of either the Gospel or this tale, until you first understand the pain that finally brought all of us to the promise of hope.

I knew that pain from my countless meetings with people as a pastor, as a hockey player, and even while I walked in ordinary life. Often, it is not easy to detect a person who is suffering in despair. Hiding behind many happy facades are many tortured souls. It takes some time to detect them, to help them, and to bring them back from the depths of those pits of hopelessness. I know of the pits of hopelessness because, now, I could say that I too, had returned from them. Now, our dear daughter and granddaughter knew the pain too, and that remained at the root of my anger, and why I could not, and despite my best efforts, I would not pray for Ian. Maybe someday, but not now. No one hurts my family and gets away with it.

For Paul John Henson, this was not to be my night for rest. Around two in the morning, I formally surrendered to any hopes of sleeping. I tossed the covers aside, pulled on a pair of sweatpants and an old hockey tee shirt stamped with my name and number and wandered downstairs. In my wandering mind, I thought how a nice cup of tea might just do the trick. I made my way carefully and quietly through the home, without turning on any lights. I knew the hallways, staircases, and the nooks of the home very well, therefore, wandering in the dark was without stubbed toes or those dreaded shinbone and knee knocks. My plan included a close monitor of the teakettle to make sure the whistle on the teakettle did not arouse the house. With the size of the Redmond's sprawling mansion, I felt as if I could safely pull it off.

A few minutes later, I sat once again at the faithful old kitchen table, which now possessed more than ten lifetimes of adventures around it. I sipped a warm cup of tea and thought about all that had happened in the amazing journey we had been so fortunate to take together.

Rehashing those same old memories was not what I wanted to do again, but one of the major flaws in my character was that I dwelled in the past. Despite my efforts, I knew that it was hopeless for me to change now. While running my hands over the top of the old table it felt as if it was alive with the memories, and I was easily lost in the multitudes of them as once more the ghosts of the past floated in and around me. I might have stayed lost in those same memories, if it were not for the sudden sound of the soft voice of Rose, echoing around the room and almost knocking me out of my chair.

"Can't sleep? Ghosts, huh? You do know that you can turn on a few lights, my dearest Paul." Rose stood there in the kitchen and smiled at me while she stood in the doorway leading from the dining room into the kitchen.

"Oh geez, Rose. I hope that I did not wake you. I did my best to make sure that I was quiet."

"No, you did not wake me, Paul. Sorry that I made you jump. I was coming down here to make some tea to sip too. Perhaps, it has been one of those nights for both of us. You are not the only one whom those ghosts tend to haunt." She turned towards the cooker and smiled again while waving her hands in the air as if to confirm her thoughts as not mere supposition. In the dim light of the kitchen, I caught her smile, even without makeup or a fancy dress on, Rose still looked gorgeous, and in a low whisper, Rose commented, "So, I guess that it is one of those nights for both of us."

I nodded and pointed to the teakettle while explaining, "It is one of those nights and I did jump. No need to be sorry. You caught me in the comfort of the tea and in the midst of many ghosts. There might still be enough hot water in there, Rose. Just a lick of a flame should bring the water to a boil in a minute."

In a few short minutes, Rose slid into the chair next to me, while drowning a tea bag in the steaming water. I studied her and thought how this remarkable woman was certainly just as beautiful, if not more so, than when we all met so long ago. Her dark black hair now had only just the slightest touches of gray licks here and there, and her immaculate skin remained unblemished with nary a wrinkle anywhere on her lovely face or hands. Her figure was still slim and shapely, and Harry was a lucky man to have shared the company of such a wonderful and lovely woman for all of these years. I loved Rose with all my heart and soul, and I was quite sure that the feeling was mutual. We had climbed many treacherous mountains together and walked more than our share of lonely valleys too. Yet, Rose, above all of us, remained steadfast in her faith, undaunted and unscathed. She remained solid and unwavering when Binky left us. Rose was *my* rock, we sobbed in each other's arms for days upon days. She held all of it together when all the Redmonds left us too, and when we lost Tinky and then her own mother and father. When Blue Cloud was terribly ill as a little newborn baby, Rose remained steeped in her faith. She was an amazing woman. A testimony to the love and faith that a wife, mother and a friend can have in her heart.

"Paul, all the times we have sat and spoken over the years. My goodness, all the journeys that we have taken together, both, when you were alone and then when I was too. It has been a special and astounding relationship, for the two of us. You will still often hear me say that, for me, speaking to you is as if Rose has swallowed down a magic tonic. A cure-all. You are exhilarating for a person's soul. The stories that you tell to all of us. Your experiences, your handsome appearance, your amazing voice. You are warm tea for the soul. God broke the mold with you, Paul, he really did."

Rose reached out and gently grasped my hand and I smiled at her. "Thank you, you are much too kind. No, you overreach in your opinion of me, dear Rose, but now with you, God broke the mold."

"I do not overreach. I cannot imagine what my life would have been like if not for you and your love and presence."

"Thank you for that, Rose. Yes, we have walked far in life together, and I have no doubt that we will do so forever. I could not have asked for two more dear friends than Rose and Harry, and to think that our families are now one family, well, God has blessed us greatly. I must tell you, dear Rose, studying you here in the early morning, dressed in an oversized sweatshirt, Harry's baggy sweatpants that are ten sizes too big for you, and Harry's slippers that you grow more beautiful in appearance and in your spirit every day."

Rose looked down at her garb and laughed loudly. She covered her mouth as she realized the hour of the morning and said, "Oops, I am, as you might say, a bit of a loud mouth, eh. Sexy, huh? As Binky would comment, I guess that we both do not dress to impress. Anyhow, thank you, Paul. I must tell you that I am so thrilled for you. I am heartbroken at the pain that our lovely and precious Heather Sarah has endured, but overjoyed to have you back with us. The last few months have been brutal beyond description."

I nodded, took a sip of the tea and smiled, while commenting, "Thank you, Rose. Yes, you look sexy and gorgeous. It is good to be back. Once again, I apologize from the bottom of my heart for mistreating you and being so harsh with you. I never, ever wanted to hurt you. The grief made me stupid and blind. The excess drink made me a fool."

Rose looked at me, as she never had ever before. Her eyes were dark and mysterious, almost seductive. It sent a shiver down my spine. She gently reached out and took my hand. She held it gently, and she was very warm to the touch. It was an amazing feeling.

"Paul, you are amazing and I find you listed in the dictionary under the word, sexy. You could never hurt me. No, matter what you ever did. Ever. I care too much."

Wow, this was a new feeling, and I needed to move on quickly from it. Change the subject, twenty-seven. Something is brewing here in your hearts. Dangerous feelings.

"Thank you, for the forgiveness, anyhow, I know that Harry shared his opinion of Ian with you, and Binky never trusted him either. Stupid me, Pastor Paul John Henson remained on the fence and took the high road until he proved otherwise. Well, guess, what? I was a pansy-ass and should have trusted my street instinct as Harry did. Now, Heather Sarah is in pain and Sarah has no father. Shit, I should have done a better job in this, dear Rose. A lot better to protect my family. Not my best performance."

While fiddling with my teacup, I searched for the correct words.

Finally, they arrived on my tongue and they were painfully honest, "Truly, now I have no answers, I can only follow God's guidance. Just sat next to my bed in the room there, and even after deep thought and prayer, I could not bring myself to pray for Ian. Honestly, and I can only share this with you, only with you, not even with Harry because he will take me at my word, I want to kick Ian's ass raw for hurting them. I really do. I am ashamed of my thoughts and my behavior. I cannot believe that God's plan can be so painful. It has been brutal as of late. Really brutal. Yet, this is part of it. I am sure of it. After lifting me from the pits of despair and bringing me to where I am now, what else can I do but to trust and obey? Yet, I failed miserably on this one."

Rose immediately jumped out of her chair, ran over to me and wrapped her arms around me while kissing my cheeks and hugging me tightly. I could feel her tears dripping upon my neck and her voice choked with emotion. There was never a woman that I ever met, who could cry or change emotions as quickly as Rose Redmond could. I reached over and tightly held onto her too.

She struggled to speak, but after a few starts and stops, Rose finally managed to say, "Oh, Paul. No, no, no, please do not ever think that way! You always do the best that you can do. My goodness, what you have been through in your life. Where you have come from, and to have achieved what you have, and now you take on the challenge of saving this young man's career and from what little I know, his spirit too. God will deal with Ian. Leave it to God. You did the best you could. It is not up to Pastor Paul John Henson to save everyone in this wretched world. You do what you do best, and that is take care of us, take care of your church and most of all to begin to take care of you." She kissed my cheeks, I slowly stood up, and we embraced tightly.

"Thank you, dear Rose. Thank you."

"Oh, Paul. I am sure that dear Binky intervened on your behalf in Heaven. We were all so worried for you. We never saw you like you were! You were down and out and for us that was the shocking part. None of us ever saw you ever stumble or falter. You are the rock, as Bishop Von Houten would describe you. It seemed as if, for once, the rock had cracked and split and none of us knew what to do. Therefore, I prayed endlessly for you and for your love and spirit to return, Paul. We all did, I saw Harry pray on his knees with Blue Cloud every, single, day for you. Now, I feel as if God heard all of those prayers. You have returned and let me assure you that this tired, old, world needed you to return. You still have many missions ahead of you. I can feel it as you can too."

I kissed her cheeks again and my kisses helped to wipe the salty tears from her cheeks.

"I thank you for those prayers, dear Rose. I love you."

"As I love you too, Paul. You have no idea of the depth

of how much I love you. I know, and Harry knows that our precious Blue Cloud would not be here right now if it were not for you. You saved her and forever more, I know it is true. You will never change my mind, so do not try. Don't even go there and try to minimize your role. The plan is deep, and it is complex, and we all will work through it together."

"I will not argue with you. Never won one yet."

"Good. That is correct and if I had to bet on it, you will never win one." Rose gave me a sly wink and cracked a coy smile at me while she added, "Well, you might actually have a slim chance to win one or two someday. Depends on what subject we might be discussing."

No doubt that I did not want to know right now, what that subject might be! I deeply desired to ask her about her words, as well as her reactions today, whenever someone mentioned or suggested that I should date or find a girlfriend, but this was not the time. There was too much going on right now between us, and it would not be a smart move. Instead, I just let the warm tea work at my soul and enjoyed the warmth of her touch and the emotion of her words.

This was such a special woman and honestly, it was with some shame that I admitted that Rose felt glorious in my arms.

Chapter Ten

The Rise of Number One

Vividly in my mind, I can recall the moment that Vance Howard and our daughter first met. I will never forget it. Until I close my eyes and meet the glories of Heaven, I will never forget the joy that rippled through my soul when I saw the look in each of their eyes. I can recall exactly the remarkable look in Heather Sarah's eyes when she spotted the handsome Vance Howard, as well as the lick in his eyes when he spotted those long, gorgeous red curls and that incredible smile.

I can remember looking over at Rose, who had just emerged from the kitchen, and our eyes met. It seemed as if ever since Binky left us that Rose and I were always in tune, always. The feeling was very strong that no matter where we were; we remained connected. When our eyes met, it told the story, and I knew and so did Rose. This was just another part of God's plan. Rose observed the scene, smiled and winked at me. We both knew why Vance Howard arrived in our lives.

It was as if their individual worlds stopped turning. Even little Sarah noticed the impact of the meeting. She glanced up, dropped the little stuffed dog she held in her arms and smiled as her mother reached out and shook the hand of the young goalie. Even the babble-mouth of Harry stopped cold for a second or two. He sensed the moment too.

Was it love at first sight? Who knows? Instead, I chose to believe this all happened to fulfill the plan. Suddenly, working hard to become the greatest hockey goalie in the world, took a backseat to meeting two of the most beautiful women this side of Heaven. Our daughter and granddaughter.

"My pleasure to meet you, Mr. Howard," Heather Sarah said with a gentle voice that would melt the greatest iceberg on Earth. "I'm Heather Sarah. The daughter of the world's greatest goalie and this is my daughter, Sarah. Sarah, say hello to Mr. Howard. He is a goalie as Grandpa is and plays hockey for the Boston Bears. Number one. Is that correct?"

Vance could hardly speak, but he managed to bumble and stumble out a weak, "Yes, number one. Correct."

"Sarah, Mr. Howard is the man that Grandpa is teaching hockey to. We saw him on television with Grandpa. Do you remember? He is going to stay with Uncle Harry and Auntie Rose this summer while they practice hockey."

Sarah giggled; she jumped up and gave Vance Howard a spontaneous hug around his legs. Ah yes, little children know of God's plan too.

"Oh please, call me, Vance. Please. Hi Sarah, wow, you are a pretty little gal, and what is your doggie's name?" Vance commented as he reached down to hug Sarah. He then picked up the stuffed dog and held it out to study it.

"Fritzie," Sarah squeaked out in glee at Vance's interest in her and the dog. Vance playfully made the dog dance in the air as he played with it, and Heather Sarah laughed, as did our granddaughter. It was very apparent that Vance loved and connected with children. It was then; you could see the kindness in his heart.

"Hello there, Fritzie. Nice to meet you and your pretty friend, Sarah. Let's play a little together." He looked up at Heather Sarah and smiled and with a twinkle in his eye, he commented to our daughter, "I must say that I know where your daughter obtained her astounding beauty from."

After that profound meeting, much to Vance's chagrin,

Harry grabbed Vance, put his arm around him and explained another part of the plan, "Told ya that this joint is crawling with gorgeous women! Welcome to our mansion and to our world. Cool your testosterone for just a minute or two. Now fancy Vancie, before ya go off, play with Fritzie and Sarah, flirt more with our precious Heather Sarah, and steal a few glances at her amazing backside and chest, ya got to take a time-out to listen up here. We have this big cocktail and dinner party here. It is a prelude to a fundraiser for a charity cause that I hold near and dear to my heart. No one can party like us. Read twenty-seven's books. Harry's Resort. If ya look up the word party in the dictionary, it just says, see the listing for the Redmond family."

The big guy was in rare form as Harry held poor Vance within his powerful grasp with just one arm flung over Vance's shoulders.

Harry continued his horn blowing speech, "Ya on our payroll now. Staying here with us. I might need ya handsome ass to make a volunteer, guest appearance as the famous, professional athlete at a big shindig we are planning, but right now, this party is to celebrate the return of the world famous, number twenty-seven, a homecoming for Heather Sarah and Sarah, and the arrival of number one. Ya got a long way to go before ya are in twenty-seven's class, but ya lookin' good. I have a rock-and-roll band playing here so ya can grab them pretty gals and dance up a storm. Watch out when ya dance close with Heather Sarah, cuz we got our eyes on ya. She is available but a rare and precious woman. No grabbin' and clutchin' yet. 'Member who her Daddy is and how he can grip ya throat! No out-of-order stuff. Well, not yet, at least. We catered this party with the finest foods and top shelf booze. We even have those damn Dingleberry beers. Not sure why, but who knows? Filthy rich women wearing dresses with plunging necklines and bulging breasts. Nuthin' is spared or too good. Dancin' and top-shelf booze. It loosens up the lips, hips, and a lot of other stuff! This is gonna be an all-nighter."

Poor Vance! A classic, and incredibly long, Harry M. Redmond Junior speech!

Harry turned Vance around as the big guy squeezed him in his viselike grip. Harry waved in the air with his one hand to demonstrate the vastness of Harry's power and influence and how the world is actually his oyster full of pearls.

He then continued by explaining the mission, "For Harry and Paul, Rose, Paul William and Blue Cloud and Heather Sarah and Sarah, O'Malley, hell, for you too now . . . it is one adventure after another, so come along for the ride and see where it all takes us. Are ya in or what?"

Vance leaned in and he put his arm around the big guy and smiled while he told him, "This is fantastic! It is going to be quite an off-season. I am in!"

Harry could still sell ice to an Eskimo.

Vance arrived on a Thursday and I felt relieved that we would at least have Friday to recover because this party was going to be epic! Saturday, we started training, but for now, we were going to enjoy the party.

The cocktail and dinner party, true to the word of Harry M. Redmond Junior, was a gala and grand event. Dancing, rock-and-roll, the finest food and drink, and gorgeous women with plunging necklines.

Harry and Rose turned their mansion into a glorious venue for a party. A band set up in the grand entrance foyer and the huge living room turned into a dance floor. Food, drink and fun flowed in every direction. Harry and Rose invited many of our friends from wide circles, church, business connections, and true to Harry's word, their charities and foundations. Harry was working the angles for some key fundraiser down the road. The man never stopped or relaxed. Pastor Jim O'Malley and his lovely wife worked the crowd, Jim helping Harry by planting well-spoken seeds of support for the charities with key people. It was another wild Redmond celebration of epic proportions, but over the years, there were so many that it was difficult to keep track of them all.

I shared a tearful and heartfelt reunion with Martha and then greeted and spoke for quite a long time with her husband. It was nice to see them, I thanked her for holding it all down and keeping it together, as well as thanked her husband for most likely enduring what could have been, an extra cranky, Martha. My faithful assistant must have had to work long hours at the office while covering for my waywardness. During the conversation, we drifted from work to me ensuring Martha that I was back in the world. I promised her that I would be back in the office on Monday after informing the Governing Board of my intentions to return to my position, earlier than the date we had originally agreed to.

Martha smiled, kissed my cheek and whispered to me, "About damn time! Gotta keep my voice down so Mr. Wiggins don't hear, but I missed staring at your golden locks of hair, your muscles and that tight backside of yours."

I loved Martha Wiggins! How could you not?

What a party and what a grand evening.

For Vance Howard, the evening was especially memorable. From the first moment that my "student" spotted Heather Sarah, they fell in love. Everyone could tell, and it was impossible for the two of them to hide or deny. True love is too powerful and overwhelming. It started with that wonderful interaction with Sarah and then grew while they conversed, and then he asked her to dance. From that moment on, they were inseparable. They danced alone, they danced with Sarah in their arms and they laughed the evening away. It was magical. I knew that feeling, felt it a time or two, myself. Rose grabbed me for a slow dance and she laughed at the new couple's infatuation. It reminded us of when we, too, were so young, such a long time ago. Rose seemed to be enjoying holding me close, and she felt marvelous as she nestled in closer to me than she ever did before. And we had been very close a few times before!

I was not too sure what was happening with us, but I needed to tread carefully here. For now, I chalked it up to her happiness in my return to the world and our envelopment in this glorious celebration, but I still needed to be ever watchful of this situation. It was a very different feeling from ever before in our lives together. Rose might be Rose, my glorious friend of all these years and Binky's sister in life, but she was Harry's wife.

Rose held me close, and she looked over at Heather Sarah dancing with Vance, pulled me in even tighter, while whispering to me, "Looks as if your young goalie student has his eyes on more than hockey pucks, Paul. He is checking out your daughter's chest and ass with magical stars in his eyes. Vance just stole Heather Sarah's heart. The handsome young goalie took her breath away. I know the feeling because long ago, it happened to another young woman that I know of, she too, had her heart stolen."

She winked, kissed me on the cheek and whispered, in a husky whisper, "Damn handsome hockey goalies with tight asses and lean muscles. They are a friggin' plague. They steal hearts while hiding under tricky old lady facades. As Harry warns all the time, ya gotta be careful." At first, when I heard her bold words, I was sure she spoke of Binky. Then again, when I felt the pulse of her heart in her hands that I held very tightly, and to be honest, the hardness of her glorious breasts that pressed tightly into my chest; I suddenly had some doubts as to the exact meaning of the words she spoke. Then again, the wine, beer and cocktails were flowing hard.

"My turn! You had enough dances and starry-eyed time

with this handsome hunk of man. My turn, Mommy," Blue Cloud had been dancing with Paul William and the two of them swooped in, and she stole me away from Rose. Paul William grabbed Rose, and we switched partners. Wow! Timing is everything in life.

Blue Cloud did not inherit Harry's height, rather she tended to take after her gorgeous mother and while she was a bit taller than Rose was, I towered above her, as did our son. It was fine with me; Blue Cloud was a captivatingly gorgeous woman, with lovely skin, a perfect figure and haunting, dark features. She was a very rare beauty and until Harry put the brakes on her plans in a typically, overbearing Harry move, Blue Cloud did quite a bit of professional modeling. Blue Cloud too nestled into my folds while we slow-danced. She felt just as soft as she did when she was a tiny, little, babe. She was quite an amazing dancer, very light on her feet and smooth.

While we danced, she told me, "It is so awesome to see you smiling again. Loving and having such fun, Dad Henson. I know the pain is still there as it is for all of us. But we know that Mom Henson wants you to go on with your life."

We stopped dancing for a second and I told her, "I love you to the moon, dear Blue Cloud. To the moon and then back."

She smiled and waved for me to lean over, and she kissed me on each of my cheeks.

"And I love you too! Love is not a strong enough word for how much I care for you. We have always had a special bond. Now, even more so. I would not be here if it were not for you. I am convinced of that."

Blue Cloud's eyes filled with tears and we began to dance once again.

"Oh, my dear Blue, you give me too much credit, God always has a plan and I simply. . .."

When she heard my words, Blue Cloud once again

stopped dancing, and she turned strong and forceful. She placed her fingers across my lips and stopped me from speaking.

"No, not this time, Dad. I know better. My daddy knows and so does my mommy. I know the story. All of it. Most of all, God knows. You are so much more than my father-in-law, my pastor, my daddy's brother, and my mom's special love . . . you are my special angel. In fact, you are for so many people. You just do not realize it. If not for your faith, prayers and intervention, then things might have been a lot different. We all know that I would not be here."

Blue still held her fingers gently upon my lips, and I studied her eyes as she struggled to speak and finish her words through a rain of tears and emotions.

I gently lifted her fingers off my lips and held her hands tightly while telling her, "Blue Cloud, please I love you and thank you for the kind words, but you give me too much credit. I am just a man, a man like any other man. All I do is the best that I can do. . .."

Blue Cloud interrupted me again. In so many ways, I could tell that she was Harry's daughter. She learned how to interrupt me from her father and my goodness, she could be so headstrong! It was quite apparent that she would have no part of my old lady's tendencies!

"As I love you too, Dad. I love you and Mom Henson with all of my heart! All of my soul. However, I must say, there you go, thanking people and minimizing your role. You are welcome, but do you know something, Dad?"

I shook my head to show that I did not know where the question was leading me. Blue Cloud reached up, cupped my head in her hands, and she looked straight into my eyes. She was short in stature but so much like her mother was and oh so powerful in her soul.

"It is time that you let the entire world thank you and love you as you love everyone else. It is time to enjoy your life, and all the things that you sacrificed for so many others. For once, think of Paul John Henson before you save the entire universe from the entire universe. Teach this young man, return to the world, and then find someone to love, Dad Henson. The Lord knows there are many lovely women lining up to love you in return. It is time to think of you and find another special one to share your love with."

She tugged at me, smiled and held me close as we began to dance once again. I thought how this song was so bloody awful long, but thanked God that it was.

What a party and as the hours passed on and the music played on, we found ourselves gathered in the kitchen once again. Gathered around the old kitchen table. We were all old warriors and this partying stuff was not so easy anymore. Those massive parties at 20 John Street so many years ago went on for days and we did not miss a beat. Now, age and time had caught up with us. Yet, we gathered, sat, and caught our second winds. Around the old table, it was Rose, Harry, Martha and her husband, representing the old guard, and representing the new era of partygoers, Paul William and Blue Cloud and Vance. Heather Sarah was tucking Sarah in bed. It was too late for little girls and for some of us old hippies too.

It was time for a special celebration.

"Okay guys, since this is all about the old neighborhood, then, I think that it is finally time for a special celebration that reflects back on one of the greatest legends from that sacred place." Everyone looked a little puzzled while I continued to explain, "A legend that every, single, one of us who lived there knew, from the streets, to the houses, to the backyards of John Street and beyond. Harry, what kind of beer do you have in the refrigerator? I think this might just be the time to prove what everyone has said since we were ten years old. Since forever and a day or so more, we have heard the same words and description and I think that it is finally time to try a Dingleberry beer and confirm if they really are too sweet."

"I love this! This is what I am talking 'bout!" Harry screamed while he instantly jumped up; he almost sprinted to the refrigerator and yanked the door off its hinges.

Sure enough, in what is one of the old neighborhood's greatest mysteries, Harry and Rose had a stash of Dingleberry beer in there. We always did in our house and no one ever drank one unless Ronzo wandered by to enjoy a few beers with the old man. Could that have been the reason? Ronzo did wander around a bit.

I could hear the old man's voice bellowing the question right now, "Why the hell do we even have 'em in the damn refrigerator? Worse damn, rotgut beer of all time!"

Sure, do miss the old man.

All of us kept a supply of Dingleberry beer in our refrigerators, yet Ronzo was the only person who I ever saw that actually would drink one. Not one of us knew why we even bought them or where they went. It seemed to be some type of bizarre local tradition. Just another weird aspect of our lives.

Harry took the Dingleberry beer in his hand and as he walked over to the table, he waved his hand in the air and explained, "We got to do this right. Ya got to sit on the end where Ronzo always sat, twenty-seven. Sit on the end, there. Rose and Martha, ya sit on the sides where Linny and Patty would sit and I will sit on the other end here where my old man always sat."

We all realized that this was something we needed to do to return us all to the kitchen at 20 John Street and set the spirit of the old neighborhood in our hearts and minds. We all stood up and switched seats until we were sitting in the correct positions. Vance had no idea what the hell was going on, but Paul William and Blue Cloud explained to him that they would fill him in later. The young people were enjoying watching us old hippies get our groove back on and rolling. Harry set the bottle in front of me onto the surface of the sacred kitchen table. He then walked over to what Harry called, "The Time Bomb Cupboard," reached into the cupboard, pulled a door open, and from a place of honor in the cupboard of the Redmond's kitchen, Harry grabbed Ronzo's special beer mug. A mug kept stored next to the famous Boryeungous jar in the special cupboard.

"Here ya go, Paul. Ronzo will haunt ya ass if ya didn't use his mug for the first one ya evah tried."

I nodded my head; Harry took his seat and everyone leaned in and stared at me. It seemed as if no one wanted to breathe. A quiet hush came over the entire scene. I might even have had a bead of sweat appear on my forehead.

Taking the ice-cold bottle in my hand, I twisted the cap off in one, quick, motion. I carefully took the mug by its handle, leaned it into the bottle and poured the Dingleberry beer into Ronzo's special beer mug. It poured clear and foamy, with such an amazing head of beer foam that I had to slow down on the pour, or I would have spoiled the pour and overflowed the mug edges. Immediately, I noticed a sweet aroma enhancing the air. It was a fragrance, which I could not describe. My best description of the aroma might be a combination of black jellybeans and cheap perfume. As the intensity grew to an almost uncontrollable level, I raised the mug up to my eyes, studied it carefully, and then smelled the mug again. This special celebration required the proper approach and a hallowed ritual.

Harry M. Redmond Junior was the last baby in line when God handed out patience in the baby creation factory. My old man was just before him in the line.

Predictably, Harry did not agree with my savoring of the moment, and he blew his cork with my prolonged ritual, "OH SHIT, FOR THE LOVE OF PETE! STOP BEING AN OLD LADY AND JUST DRINK THE DAMN BEER! WE HAVE BEEN WAITING FORTY FRIGGIN' YEARS FOR THIS!"

"Okay, Harry, hold on, geez. I am not too sure about

how I should. . . ."

Rose piped in and in a surprising shift of character for my greatest ally on my Harry defense team, Rose sided with the big guy, "I agree with Harry. Just drink the damn beer. I love you, Paul, with all my heart and soul, but shit, you are so damn long-winded sometimes. The suspense is ridiculous. This sniffing and testing bullshit is a little annoying. It is a mug of beer and not a friggin' work of art and we have been waiting since we were all hormone-overflowing teenagers rolling around naked in the back seats of our cars for you to take a damn sip of Dingleberry beer."

I looked over at Martha and my faithful assistant of close to twenty years was nodding her head in agreement with Rose and Harry.

She gently said, "Love ya too, but ya a pain-in-the-ass. It takes you forever to get to the point. I agree, just suck the friggin' beer down."

Here we go. I raised the mug to my lips, tilted it on back and down the throat, it went. The gang leaned in and I felt their eyes piercing right through me. I swallowed the sip of beer, smacked my lips, put the mug down on the table, folded my hands across my chest and took a deep breath.

"Well? What the hell does it taste like?" Harry asked.

I felt as if I had just officially certified the world's greatest diamond for cut, carats and clarity.

"It's confirmed. It sucks. Too damn sweet."

Harry slammed his hand on the table surface, jumped up, ran over to Rose, picked her out of her seat, leaned her over and gave her one of his famous grandstanding kisses. When he finished kissing poor Rose, he stood with his hands on his hips and laughed uproariously. We all joined him and in a group celebration, we laughed until the tears came down our cheeks. Somewhere in Heaven, Ronzo, Binky, the old man, the Big Spike and all the rest of the gang sat on a cloud and they laughed with us.

I could hear the old man say, "I told ya so!"

Our loss here on Earth is simply Heaven's gain.

Recovering, Harry screamed out once more, "I knew that rotgut beer sucked. Knew it all along. It just had to be! I love this! Now, this is what I am talking 'bout!"

Our laughter and joy reached all the way into Heaven and beyond. Dear reader, as I said, it was one helluva party!

"You know, fancy Vancie, you only know the kind, gentle, Pastor James T. O'Malley. You met him off the ice, in his gentle form, before his transformation into a wild, stick-wielding, crazy, madman. Ya see, ya met him when he was praising the Lord, holding hands around the campfire while singing hymns of salvation. In order for you to understand old-time hockey like twenty-seven and I know then ya got to meet him when he is on the ice."

"Transformation, Harry? What do you mean by a transformation?"

It was Saturday, right after the big homecoming party, and it was time to begin the formal training of number one. Party time was now over.

Harry, Vance, and I were walking a long hallway at the local ice rink, making our way to one of the practice rinks to watch a practice of the local high school team conducted by Coach James T. O'Malley. Harry stopped in his tracks, in typical dramatic Harry fashion, rolled his eyes, and waved his hands in the air in frustration that Vance Howard did not immediately follow what he was saying.

"Did you ever see those horror movies where the ordinary guy turns into a werewolf guy?"

"Well, yes, Harry, but what does that have to do with. . .."

"All youse guys gotta do is to see O'Malley now. Wait 'til ya see him and you will understand. If he touches a hockey stick, he turns into a wild man from the Island of Borneo. Charging up and down the ice, slashing and chopping, and cursing every, single relative that you have and a few that you never knew even existed. O'Malley is not prejudiced when he plays. He dislikes everyone equally. In order for you to not be a pussy in the net, ya gonna have to stand up to O'Malley trying to take ya head off with a shot."

Vance stopped in his tracks, put his hands on his hips, and shook his head in disagreement.

With a proclamation of protest, Vance reported, "I am not a pussy in the net. I flinch a little at certain shots."

"No, kid, you are a pussy. All you fancy, modern day hockey pineapples are pussies compared to old-time hockey guys like we are. When twenty-seven, O'Malley and I started playing the game, we had to clear the dinosaurs off the rink. All kinds of fancy equipment that ya wear nowadays. We had old pillows that we tied to our legs for pads. We played with damn hockey pucks that we sawed off the ends of Christmas tree trunks and practiced shootin' by bouncin' them suckers off Paul's face. Old Doctor Salami in the old neighborhood bought a new fancy car every year after hockey season, wid the proceeds of stitchin' up twenty-seven's body."

Harry stopped walking for a second, he seemed to be searching for the next phase of his inspirational thoughts, and when he captured his thoughts, he waved his hand in the air and continued leading onward to the player's benches on the side of the hockey rink. He lumbered onward while his big feet stomped on the rubber pads of the walkways.

His loud voice thundered across the ice rink, "We never did find a cure for twenty-seven's Old Lady Syndrome. Despite his affliction with the syndrome, he was never a pussy or pansy la-la in the net. Look at twenty-seven's ugly puss in the daylight. Dumb ass did not even wear a mask until they carved his ass up more than a Thanksgiving turkey. All those, there, scars on it, most of 'em comes from a certain, James T. O'Malley bouncin' shots off his noggin'. And now, these guys are the best of friends. If that don't make ya believe in God, well, then nuthin' will. C'mon. Watch and learn."

Vance laughed, shook his head, and followed the big guy. I followed them while thinking that this was now lesson number one in old-time hockey and in "life according to Harry." Vance was taking the first step to being a superstar goalie and a man. This lesson was courtesy of Professor Harry M. Redmond Junior. Next lesson, I was sure, would come from a certain James T. O'Malley.

We planned an early arrival to the rink, to observe a team scrimmage for Jim's hockey club, we promised the young players on the high school team that we would sign sticks and autographs, pose for pictures with them and allow them to meet some professional hockey players. Jim was planning to allow the players on the team to skate with us afterwards while we practiced and worked out on our own. This was going to be an afternoon to remember for a group of young hockey players.

We approached the player's bench and looked out on the ice. The team was engaged in a game scrimmage with two assistant coaches acting as referees and on-the-ice coaches. The players were skating, passing and shooting, and I had to think that was a positive sign. Currently, the players had not yet squared off with each other and were not yet rolling and brawling, so I thought that Jim must have been doing a good job in teaching hockey.

Maybe.

Jim was up on the edge of the bench, screaming at a short, stocky player who seemed to be playing the center-ice position. The center had just coughed the puck up along the boards when he pulled away from a body check from a defenseman.

"NINETEEN! SKATE YOUR SORRY ASS OVER HERE!" O'Malley screamed and waved as he pushed a player on the bench out on the ice to change up the players. Number nineteen jumped over the boards and plopped down onto the bench, and when he did so, O'Malley turned and climbed into the young player's face. The three of us watched from a few steps away. O'Malley was so intense in his focus that he had yet even to see us arrive.

"What was that goo-goo bullshit, Stevie? Do ya want a baby rattle instead of a hockey stick? You coughed that puck up like I used to puke up that rotgut, Dingleberry drain pour beer the next morning after a night on the town!"

Wow! All of these years and I never knew that Jim drank Dingleberry beer. Life is full of twists and turns, eh?

Harry leaned in and whispered to us, "Nevah knew that Jim sucked down Dingleberries. Told ya it was rotgut crap beer. Even Jim puked it up and he can drink motor oil straight outta of an engine."

We nodded, turned and listened as Jim continued with his "coaching" lesson, "You allowed Reeves to waltz in like a ballerina and steal the puck from ya. Why are you afraid of him, Stevie?"

The young center-iceman sat there on the bench and shook his head. Stevie undid his helmet straps, and he angrily tossed his stick aside, reached for a water bottle, and took a long sip.

He put his head down a little and shamefully admitted, "Reeves was always a bully. Years ago, he used to pick on my kid brother and me all the time. He butt ends us when you and the other coaches ain't looking. He is bigger than us too! He butt ends us even though we are teammates! He butt ends us all the time in the corners!"

O'Malley smiled and laughed as he eased up a little on Stevie and proudly proclaimed, "Good! I love it. That's what I taught him to do. Do you think an opponent is not going to stick a butt end up your ass when he can get away with it?"

Harry leaned in and whispered to Vance and me, "See what I mean? This is awesome, O'Malley teaching kids all 'bout old-time hockey and life lessons. He tossed his Bible and prayer guides aside today and is in full hockey goon mode."

We all nodded and listened as poor Stevie admitted that O'Malley was correct. "Sure, sure, I guess, Coach O'Malley . . . but, I am not. . .."

O'Malley cut him off, leaned in, grabbed the young player by the shoulder pads, and told Stevie, "As far as the bully bullshit goes, well, we did not have bullies when I grew up playing hockey. Do you know why? Cuz when they pushed us around unfairly, all of us took the end of our sticks, swung it upside their faces, and smashed their noses so they faced north and south at the same time. End of the bullying problem. If ya dished it out, then ya had better be able to take it back. And we didn't pin medals on our asses proclaiming us to be victims and hang our heads like little pansy-asses. We knocked the bully on their ass and then we went back to playing the game. Now, kid, quit crying, cut the bullshit and get ya ass back in the game!"

O'Malley pulled Stevie up and off the bench, tapped his shoulder pads and young Stevie fervently nodded that he understood. The young man had a little smile on his face now and confidence in his heart. Stevie hung on the boards and jumped on the ice when he could change up with a line. The puck slipped behind the goal, Stevie skated behind the defenseman named Reeves, and the two players collided hard while Stevie crunched Reeves solidly into the boards. Stevie pushed, elbowed and tangled with the big defenseman, while they battled for possession of the puck. After a big push, Stevie reached the puck and controlled it while knocking Reeves off his skates and he made a nifty pass into the front of the net, where a winger picked it up, and slipped a nice trickle shot under a hapless and fallen goaltender.

I smiled when Vance whispered to us, "Goalie needs to stand up like us old-time goalies do."

Vance still had occasional smart-ass tendencies.

O'Malley thumped the side of the boards in delight as he bellowed and thundered encouragement, "Atta boy, Stevie! Stick it to 'em! Right up his ass! Knock his damn head off if you have to! Puck possession is the name of the game!"

Coach O'Malley, now settled back to the wall of the player's bench and true to Harry's testimony, he magically transformed from a wild-eyed hockey coach to a prim and proper gentleman in mere seconds. It was then that he noticed us standing there next to him.

He smiled and reached out his hand in order to shake each of ours. "Good afternoon. Thanks for coming by, gentlemen. I greatly appreciate it, and I know that the young men here will be so grateful to meet all of you. It will certainly be the thrill of a lifetime for these fine young men and hockey players."

Vance looked at Harry and rolled his eyes as he now witnessed the "transformation" first hand.

Vance shook Jim's hand and as the young man was still inclined to do; he could not resist a smart-ass remark or two, "Kinda harsh language for a pastor to use and rough lessons to teach to young men."

Oh, oh!

Without a mere second of hesitation, Jim replied, "Just because a person chooses to follow God and identifies as a Christian or a religious person, does not mean they are cowards or pacifists. Peter cut the ear off the Roman Soldier, Vance. Jesus healed the soldier's ear and told Peter to stand down. Peter was willing to make the ultimate commitment to die for someone that he loved. Life is harsh. Hockey is harsh, and it teaches these young hockey players life lessons. Lessons such as that you need to work hard and be fearless for anything that you are willing to try, do, or attempt in this life. No one owes you jackshit in life. You have to earn it, and that is the trouble with young people these days. They all have a sense of entitlement that life should give them everything with little or no efforts on their part, and with them making zero commitment to anything."

O'Malley now grew even more wild-eyed as he turned and pointed to the corner of the ice rink.

He continued with his sermon, "Giving up pucks easily in the corners because you are lazy, or because you are afraid, is a metaphor for giving up on everything in life too easily. Hockey is a difficult game to play, and guess what? So is life. Hockey teaches valuable lessons. It is not a game for Roman Soldiers to play in. This is a game for the Peters of the world to play in and to play to win. Jesus will heal the wounds later on, but only if you are wounded and believe enough to earn the healing. Jesus never asked angry, deceitful people to follow him, he only asked for courageous and faithful believers. Believers, willing to make commitments, willing to stand up for what they believe in, proclaim their faith with courage, and live what they believe. Patsy-asses and those who hang their heads and feel sorry for their, lily-white asses because life dealt them a shitty hand of cards do not make the cut. In hockey, in Heaven, or in life."

Harry and I studied Vance Howard as he carefully listened to Pastor James T. O'Malley, and I spotted the impact of lesson number two in the eyes and tears forming in the corners of Vance's eyes. The young goalie wiped them away quickly, thinking, or perhaps hoping that we did not see them form.

It was then that I realized that Pastor Jim O'Malley had not actually retired from the ministry; he just moved his pulpit to behind a hockey bench. This sermon was simply a very small excerpt from the Gospel, according to O'Malley.

Jim's sermon connected hard and the pain of Vance's childhood and his shattered dreams with a life that included no father figures tore through him. Suddenly, Vance Howard had three fathers and all of them deeply cared, they all were teachers of different things and most of all, they all wanted him to succeed.

We met with the young players and did indeed sign autographs, take pictures and have a grand afternoon. We suited up in our uniforms and hockey gear, and Paul William joined us after he finished some work assignments. For some reason, which I too late realized, and that I would regret for a few days, I pulled all the old equipment out and suited up once more to be number twenty-seven.

We warmed up with a good skate, and my pride in the skating ability of Paul William was glowing as our son gave the young players and Vance Howard numerous skating tips and pointers. Too bad he gave up on hockey; he was a world-class ice skater! The plan included for Paul William to improve Vance's skating abilities over the next few weeks, by utilizing the same drills and techniques we used when our son began skating at five years of age. Vance could not have a better instructor.

Blue Cloud and Heather Sarah surprised us by showing up and taking in the practice. I surmised that Blue rode along with Paul William after work and Heather Sarah was there to, well, to watch Vance.

When it came time to begin a shoot around, I slipped into the goal first to face some shots. This would be the biggest thrill of all for these young hockey players to take some shots on two professional goalies—one washed up and now retired goalie and one rising, young superstar. I hoped that these young players would not make me look like an old fool. The pucks spilled out on the ice and some high school players took a few shots on me, then Harry unleashed a rocket of a slap shot, which I made a stick save on and Paul William shot a rising puck, which I gloved and turned aside.

When the puck rolled to O'Malley standing at the right point, Jim uncorked a hard, rising slap shot straight at my head!

Flashbacks!

Immediately, I went into angle cutting mode, tracked it, bent into a crouch and to the horrified cries of the young players, and Vance Howard, I snatched the puck out of the air with my glove, just seconds before it tore into my mask. I laughed, tossed the puck out of my glove and kicked it with my skates back to Jim, while skating out of the net and waving Vance in my place.

Jim picked the puck up and smiled at me. Lesson number three.

As I skated by Vance, I heard him say to me, "Damn, twenty-seven. So much for no head shots by teammates during warm-ups or practice."

I tugged at Vance's sweater to pull him close to me, lifted my mask and answered, "Just as Jim preached, Peter cut the ear off the Roman Soldier. Jesus healed it. Do you think that big league players will not have the book on you next year? You are the subject of film study by every coach in the league right now. I can hear it now. Headshots will cause the kid to fold. He is great along the ice but pulls out on headshots. Guess what, number one? Headshots will be on the menu for you. It will be a constant, steady diet, so you had better learn to handle them. Buckle your mask straps. Cut the angles, come out of the net, face the demons, and they will never haunt you again. I guarantee that James T. O'Malley has the cure for those demons that are haunting you and you are about to face them, right now."

Vance nodded, and when Jim unleashed holy hell on him, that is exactly what the young goalie did. He stood on his skates, cut the angle, stuck his head in there and followed my lead by blocking the puck with his stick glove. The only trouble was that his save gave up a horrible rebound, a rebound that Harry promptly skated in and before Vance could react, Harry had picked the puck up, passed it to Paul William, who neatly tucked it into the net.

As everyone watched and listened, I flipped my mask back down and yelled out, "No! No! No! Sometimes, you have to flop down, Vance. If you give up a poor rebound, and are caught leaning back on your skates, you have to pull a Rumber!"

Vance looked at me, lifted his cage mask and with a puzzled look on his face, shook his head. He had no idea of what I meant. Harry did, so did Jim, as did Paul William. The high school team, especially the goalies, all leaned in and listened to the lesson.

Vance knelt down on one pad and scooped the puck out of the back of the net while I skated in and explained, "Rumblehowser. He was my hero when I was growing up. He was, and is, a Hockey Hall of Fame goaltender. He played for the New York Rovers a long time ago."

Harry yelled out, "Ya got to stack the pads!"

I nodded and explained to Vance, "That was what Rumblehowser was famous for, and he did it so often, they nicknamed the move and called it a Rumber. I patented my stand-up style of play after his, but if they caught him off guard and the net was wide open, he would hit the ice, throw his legs out and stack his pads on top of each other, as if they were a wall. Like this. Harry, please shoot it."

I skated into the net, Harry picked the puck up and he skated in on me and allowed me to demonstrate as he shot the puck. I dropped down, stacked my pads and pulled a "Rumber." The players all started a hockey salute with the tradition of clapping by tapping their sticks on the ice as Vance nodded that he understood. I rolled around on the ice and tried to use the goalposts to help pull myself up and back on my skates.

Long gone were the days of being able to leap in one motion back on my skates.

As I waved Vance over to the net, number one reached down and helped pull the creaky and old number twenty-seven up on his skates.

"Here, let me pull your old, long-haired ass up, twenty-seven."

"Thanks, Vance. Now you practice the Rumber. Once you have it down pat, then I will teach you how to study shooter's eyes."

Vance took over, and I no longer was the center of attention. It was time. Now, it was time for number twenty-seven finally to fade away; you see, in a nutshell, that is what life is all about for all of us. Old goalies fade away quietly, and new ones emerge. Just as it is in life because old people fade away and newborns take their place. It is all part of the plan. Until the time comes for you to fade away, then you battle in the corners, you work hard, and you give your greatest efforts that you can give every single day. You can gain nothing, in hockey or in life, zero, zilch, squat, by giving up or being lazy. Pastor Jim O'Malley nailed it because hockey *was* a metaphor for life. As I skated off into the twilight of my career and finally hung that magical mask up for good, I transformed from a goalie to a pastor, or better yet, a rabbi. A teacher. Now, the world paid my spirit and rewarded my soul for what I know and not what I did. A new day arrived and a new player emerged to pick up where I left off. I gave him parts and pieces of number twenty-seven, just as Gordon Gurney, Jim Hikibin, Coach Davis, and hundreds of others gave to me. My friends, family, and fellow teammates will give him valuable lessons and parts of themselves too. The rest of it will be up to number one. Yes, a new player emerged and somewhere, deep inside of me, I retired from being number twenty-seven forever. This new player wore number one, not the number twenty-seven, and he will carry on the mission. Someday, number one will pass his mission off to another.

We all watched as Vance practiced the move, and right before our eyes, I knew that number one arrived. It was a day of lessons, hockey lessons, as well as life lessons. Not only for young Vance Howard and a group of very young hockey players, but for all of us. That night, after a long practice, Vance and I returned to the Redmond's mansion. We sat and talked for a bit, but the last few weeks caught up with me, not to mention how my body screamed at me, "What the hell went through your mind out on that ice today?"

We shared a few beers, some laughs, we ate a wonderful dinner prepared by Rose, and I eventually retired to my bedroom and a hot bathtub. I retired, not early enough, but I did retire to my room, but only after a few too many hours passed by, a million hockey war tales were related and too many discussions of old games were exchanged. I left Vance and Heather Sarah at the kitchen table to sow some early seeds of their love. Sarah, Harry, and Rose were the smartest of all of us because they were already in bed.

I went to my room, undressed and ran hot water in the bathtub in the bathroom. I stripped down naked, added some salts to the bath and slowly and somewhat carefully sunk into the water. My body ached, but in looking my naked body over, it now had a solid and hard tone and that grand belly that I managed to create, was now history. I sat there, soaking in the warmth, salt, and trying hard to ease my body and mind of the pain of being an old fool. As I leaned my head on the edge of the tub, my long hair dangled in the water. I closed my eyes and prayed a prayer of thanksgiving. I thanked God for this opportunity, for these amazing friends and family, and for the Gospel according to O'Malley.

It gave me quite a chuckle as I replayed Jim's remarkable sermon in my head. Jim was one of a kind, a man of God, a man that this world needs and will always need. I was quite sure that no one on the entire face of this Earth could have said it any better than Pastor Jim did today.

No one.

Chapter Eleven

The Old Man Comes Through Again

On the Monday after the homecoming and the welcoming party and our first on the ice off-season practice, I returned to the bishop's office and to my position of bishop. Over the weekend, I had called the executive in charge of the Lutheran Governing Board and informed him of my plans to return to work, a full month or thereabouts earlier than my original plans were. He was grateful for my early return as well as commenting on the hubbub of activity surrounding Pastor (Bishop) Paul John Henson and his little hockey stint as well as my new popularity with the media as a celebrity. He was quite cordial, very gracious to hear that I was improving in my mental status and that I was anxious to return to the bishop's position ahead of time. It was good to be back. After a few warm hugs and another welcome back from Martha Wiggins, also known as the greatest assistant in the history of the world, Martha proudly marched into my office and plopped what seemed as if it was a pile of papers that was at least five feet high on my desk, I sighed and went back to work.

Martha's only comment was, "Time to shake your ass, Pastor Paul. I held this together long enough. One more thing, we are quitting early and going over to 'The Elusive Lion' for a never-ending lunch. In fact, today is the day for the two of us to take a long overdue, liquid lunch on your tab."

There would be no argument from me. It felt wonderful

to be back in the office and to be working once again.

Jennifer Hollingsworth worked the afternoon bartending shift at an English pub within walking distance of the bishop's office in downtown Newark. Given my English and Welsh heritage, one would be tempted to say, how convenient, eh? I have to admit to more than just a bit of a smile on my face, when what is now almost twenty years ago, I wandered along exploring the city blocks around my new digs and found an authentic pub within walking distance of my new office. Anyhow, Jennifer had worked there for as long as I worked in Newark. We grew into kindred spirits together and shared quite a bit over the years. Both happy and sad. Jennifer was the anchor at the pub and honestly, other than boasting about the fact that they had one hundred beers on tap at "The Elusive Lion," Jennifer was the main attraction. Oh yes, the bangers and mash were pretty good too.

I found it so ironic how Jennifer shared many of the same tendencies with Janet at the hotel in Boston, she was also marvelously attractive and the two women shared the same role! Life is sure full of twists and turns.

Martha and I slid into our favorite booth for our long, liquid lunch and it took Jennifer about four seconds to spot us, smile and rush over, while screaming, "Pastor Paul! Welcome back! Oh how, I missed you. Not to mention how our Big Boulder sales have nose-dived." That statement made my liver sigh.

I heard Martha laugh as I stood up and gave Jennifer a warm hug. "Nice to be back here, my dear Jennifer. I will do my best to bring your sales back up to snuff. I missed you too."

After some warm greetings and laughs, she reached up, took my face in her hands and sincerely spoke as she told me, "In all sincerity, please, I am so sorry about your wife. Truly sorry. You are such a wonderful man. Please, know that I have prayed for you and it is so nice to have you back in the world. We all love you dearly."

I pushed back some emotions, whispered, "Thank you" and then realized that there were at least ten or more regular patrons of the lunch and dinner crowd of "The Elusive Lion" as well as the head chef, the manager, and other servers, gathered around our booth to welcome me back and to express their condolences. To say that this touched my soul would be too soft a statement. Other than Jennifer, these were, for the most part, strangers, mild acquaintances and here they were, gathering and taking the time to share their feelings over our loss. It did not touch my soul; instead, it stole my heart.

Jennifer fingered a little brass sign, screwed into the wood on the booth that read, "RESERVED."

She explained, "We put this here so that no one else sat here until you returned. In your wife's honor. In your honor. A small token. Now that you are back in the world, well, this will always be your booth."

Not all the humanity of this world is wicked, only the portions that the news media reminds you of on a daily basis. We need to start a "Good News Only" channel for some positive news instead of the dreary, bullshit news the media spouts. This was just our lunch spot, our watering hole, the local pub, and the people here cared enough to express such heartfelt expressions of their own souls.

I sat in the booth after profusely thanking everyone and Martha took a tissue out of her purse, wiped her eyes of tears, and blew her nose. She reached over the table, took my hands and I clasped hers too.

"See, all the love in this world? I know that Binky is very pleased to see you back out here, doing what you do best. That is to love the world in return. So, let's stop the teary-eyed bullshit, celebrate and drink the rest of the day away!"

Works for me.

You have to love a whole lot of Martha Wiggins.

Later that afternoon, after crawling back to the office, I did call Brian McClure and filled my old pal in on our training regimen for Vance Howard over this off-season and summer. I explained how Paul William would work on his skating with him, how our son will utilize the same training drills that we used for years, and how Jim O'Malley and Harry will work him out on a daily basis on the ice. I will work with him on intense goaltending training on Saturdays and as my time allows. In my discussions with Brian, I explained how in our training plans were some special drills that we would use to sharpen his stamina and reflexes. I told him how we would be utilizing the old goaltending drills that the old man and I used to do in our driveway at 182 Belmont Avenue in good old Haledon. There, years ago, in my off-season, the old man worked me out in the driveway on the hottest and most humid New Jersey summer days. The old man used a tennis ball and by adapting his old baseball skills, he devised an ingenious drill roughly based upon the old baseball drill known as, "Pepper." It was a brutal drill that worked up your cardio systems as well as your reflexes. The old man was not a hockey player, but in his day, he sure was one helluva baseball player.

I sure do miss the old man.

The rest of the telephone call was very pleasant and included some general discussions on Vance's living arrangements, how I was doing, Janet has been asking about you and so on and so forth. Brian seemed very pleased, and he thoroughly enjoyed hearing of the old-time hockey training methods and the assistants that I had recruited on our side to work with Vance.

I left out the part where I was fairly sure that Vance had fallen in love with our daughter. It was shaping up to be an interesting summer. I knew that Vance was in good hands.

For our son, since he was primarily a hockey beat writer for the Boston Bears, this was the off-season for Paul

William. Other than writing some regular, syndicated columns and hockey website commitments, he could devote quite a bit of time to working on the skating of Vance Howard. Improving Vance's skating was paramount to his success, and it was where I wanted to focus on the most. Just as Jim Hikibin and Gordon Gurney taught me so long ago at my first goaltending clinic, skating was the most important aspect of the goaltender's game. It was where you could separate yourself from all the others. We could teach all the rest of the game. Harry and Jim will not only turn Vance into a superb "old-time" goalie, they would make him a man. Brian McClure was quite happy with the plan and the progress. I also planted a seed and told my old friend that I thought he should take another look at retaining Coach Bettermann. A long, hard look because he was a protégé of Coach Davis.

"Look at him long and hard, Brian. Please, do not discount him, without another serious and intense look. You might just have the old-time coach that your team needs, right there, right now." He listened carefully and then promised me that he would do so.

About two weeks after my return to New Jersey, the construction company reported that the townhouse was ready to go, and after a few punch list items, and some custom decorating, Heather Sarah, Sarah, and I moved out of the Redmond's mansion and into our brand-new home. Vance was disappointed, but I had a feeling that he would be over at the new place on a daily basis. Heather Sarah, and Vance were in my opinion, deeply in love now; their relationship grew more intense every day. When we left the Redmond's mansion, I sensed some disappointment in Rose too, and that was something that I now remained keenly aware of these days.

We all loved the new townhouse. Heather Sarah, and Harry could not have picked out a more magnificent place for us to live in. It was perfect. It was a bit larger than what

I initially thought it was, but that was fine. It had an open concept floor plan on the first floor, with a gourmet, custom kitchen with granite countertops, a built-in, flush refrigerator and top-of-the-line appliances, framed by cherry cabinets. In the center island of the kitchen was a built-in downdraft cooker, which, of course, Harry proudly pronounced as he did the rest of the kitchen, a museum piece.

"Fancy-ass kitchen for the world's worst cook," Harry commented.

He was correct, but I knew that Heather Sarah would use it, while Sarah and she stayed with me, as would Rose when she came over to cook for us. It was fine for me; I was doing my best to improve my eating habits and giving up frozen pizzas in favor of salads.

Even I could prepare salads. Well, maybe I could.

The kitchen had a large eating nook, which was large enough to fit a good-sized table and other amenities. I laughed my ass off when I opened the refrigerator and there already was a six-pack of Dingleberry beer in there, with a red bow on the carton.

It also had a gift tag on it, which said, "To, twenty-seven, from thirty-five. Just in case you want to try it in another forty years."

Harry was awesome! The best housewarming gift ever!

The kitchen opened to a huge living room with an attached, formal dining space. The dining space fit our formal furniture, including Binky's heirloom china and silverware cabinet. Part of the living room had a sunken floor, which surrounded the centerpiece of the room, which was a fieldstone fireplace with a chimney that went from the floor to the ceiling. It was amazing, as were the ceilings, which towered high into a graceful arch above our heads, capped by a skylight. The master suite was on the first floor and the suite had a luxurious feel to it, all capped by a huge master bathroom complete with a soaking tub that was the size of a small swimming pool! That soaking tub would come in handy if I acted like some stupid fool again and needed a good hot soak to loosen up.

The entry hallway had a wide, two-landing oak staircase leading to the second floor, where there were four more bedrooms and two full bathrooms. All the bedrooms were large, we immediately turned one into an office, Heather Sarah took one, and Sarah had her own bedroom, as well, as a playroom. A playroom, which immediately filled with all kinds of toys and the best of everything for our granddaughter. I did not mess around with the decorating and I told Heather Sarah to hire a professional decorator, work with them and do it all up, as you would like to do it.

"Make sure that Sarah and you have all that you want and need. No budget, spend whatever it takes."

I was not surprised when I walked into my office and Heather Sarah had decorated it magnificently. Hockey memories and memorabilia surrounded me in every direction, including the photograph that Tommy Hayward recently sent me of Brian, Coach Davis and me, as well as my Long Island Rooster, number twenty-seven hockey sweater framed under glass and hanging on the wall. The walls were full of family memories, a glorious photograph of Binky and me, and a favorite sunset photograph given to me by a professional photographer who also was a parishioner at Reunion Lutheran Church. Heather Sarah even had a wet bar installed in the corner of the office. I had to have Brian over to show him this set-up! This office would turn out some glorious work, written or otherwise. I was anxious to begin writing and working here. When and if Heather Sarah and Sarah moved out, then it would be a huge place for a widower, but I would deal with that someday down the road. The townhouse even came with a three-car garage, a small garden area, and storage space. It was difficult for me to select my favorite feature of this glorious home. The office, the fireplace, the wet bar, but I had to go with the fantastic deck that was just off the living room and extended to the master suite. Two large glass sliders, one in the living room and one in the master suite, led to the deck, which overlooked a glorious sloping landscape with a heavily wooded backdrop. Our townhome was an end unit and there were no other units behind us. The best part was that the deck faced the western sky and from there, as I had my entire life, I could watch my sunsets, sit, think, and most of all, remember and dream.

Then there was the new next-door neighbor.

"Good morning, how are you?"

A soft voice startled me while I was putting my briefcase in the rear seat of my old jeep parked in the driveway of our townhouse. I had been lazy the previous evening, guilty of laziness combined with working late from still catching up on work in the office, and parked the jeep in the driveway rather than pulling it into the garage.

"Oh! Yes! Hello."

"I am so sorry that I startled you, I should have not crept up on you in such a way."

I smiled, closed the door to the jeep and recovered my heart from the atmosphere.

"No, it is fine. I just did not expect to run into anyone out here this early. I am trying to get into Newark a little early, and I am still mapping out the roads for the best routes. We just moved in."

The neighbor smiled and I have to admit, her smile was quite captivating. She was tall for a woman, lean, with a perfect figure and long brown hair that tumbled down over her shoulders in gentle curls. She was dressed immaculately in a woman's business suit, and she, too, carried a case, which might have contained a laptop computer. Her facial features were astounding and her beauty surrounded her. Wow!

I recalled Harry's comments to Heather Sarah about the

next-door neighbor and determined that this was the same woman who earned such an alluring, and I must admit, accurate, description from the big guy.

"Hi, I am, Maggie Dunlop. Nice to meet you and welcome to the community. Yes, I know that you just moved in. I saw the moving truck and all the activity. I am not being overly observant and nosey, but I see that you are a minister. In fact, another neighbor told me that you are a Lutheran bishop, television star, a professional hockey player and coach, a writer and a host of other occupations." Maggie ended her statement with a gentle smile, a bit of a chuckle, and I must admit a heavy dose of charm.

I extended my hand, looked down at my pastor's collar and tugged at it to exaggerate its presence and laughed while saying, "Well, yes, this is just one of my identities. I might be a little of all of those various occupations, but primarily, I am a Lutheran bishop. Not too sure where the television star angle came from, but anyhow, I prefer the title of, Pastor Paul. Never became used to the bishop, thingy. Hello, Maggie. Nice to meet you, I am, Pastor Paul John Henson."

"Too much, huh? Too stuffy."

"Well, I guess, I am only a pastor. That is what I do best . . . I am a pastor. Are you going to work too?"

Maggie nodded her head and I could not help but to admire how the early morning sunrise reflected some red highlights in her hair. This was a gorgeous woman, and I stole a quick glance at her hands. She did not wear a wedding ring.

"Yes, I am, I work as an executive in sales and marketing at a corporation in the city." She reached into her purse, fumbled around a bit, and then handed me her business card.

"Here is my business card. I ride to the center of town and take the train. I have only been here four months or so, it took a long time for the construction company to complete the work."

"Oh, yes, the train. I had that same commute for a few years when I went to seminary in the city with my wife . . . well . . . my wife also worked in the city." I lost it, lost my thoughts and lost it all in emotions. As a diversion to gather my thoughts and control my emotions, I reached for my wallet, pulled out one of my business cards and handed it to Maggie. She stepped in close, took my card and placed it into her purse.

It seems as though she sensed that I lost my thoughts and said to me, "Thank you for your business card. If I need any of your immense talents, then I know whom to call. The hockey part of your life, I doubt that I will ever require. I am not a fan of sports. Your wife? Oh, is that your wife that I saw here the other day, with a large man driving one of those huge Rhino vehicles. They pulled in the driveway and I waved to them."

I recovered and shook my head as I pulled my emotions together. "No, that was my best friend and his wife. They have the keys to our townhouse. We are closer than brothers are. It is a long story. I live here with my daughter and granddaughter. I am a widower. My wife passed from this world almost a year ago."

Maggie's face changed, and her mouth opened wide in a display of shock. She reached out for my hand and gently clasped it.

"Oh my. I am so sorry, Pastor Paul. Very sorry, I did not realize."

I took Maggie's hand and spoke softly because the emotions still captured me, "No, please, you would have no way to know. Say, I have to get rolling here. It has been my pleasure to meet you." Maggie seemed quite flustered at the fact that I was a widower. She forced a smile, but I do think that she was very uncomfortable at how she discovered the details of my marital status. A divorce would have been a lot easier to deal with.

She smiled and seemed very genuine in expressing her condolences for my loss. If I had to summarize Maggie Dunlop within this very brief meeting in our adjoining driveways, then it would not only highlight her astounding appearance but also that for a high-profile executive, she seemed quite genuine and well grounded.

"Yes, it has been my pleasure too. I am alone here, I too have had some recent pain, nothing compared to yours, but I am now divorced after a very short-term marriage. Anyway, I have to hit the road too and I have to catch the train. Nice to meet you and perhaps, we could share a cup of coffee or tea, or a drink someday soon."

While walking to the jeep, I waved and smiled while saying, "Yes, that would be nice. Thank you. We can do that, yes."

We parted ways; I slipped into the jeep, spun the key and took a deep breath. Wow! What a next-door neighbor. Maggie did seem very pleasant and as if she would be great company, honestly, in many ways. On my drive into Newark, I found it difficult to sort out the thoughts, the emotions, and all the various things that were all happening within my life and our lives too. All this extra attention and loving from family and friends, while I appreciated it and understood it, was overwhelming.

This was now a number of times, where attractive females seemed to be, as Gramps would say, "Peddling their wares around me."

It was a very strange feeling and right now, I tried to prevent my stomach from churning and my mind from spinning too much. Yes, my beloved wife was now gone, but now, I knew how Harry felt after Sky Blu passed away and he had strong thoughts and desires to rekindle his love and romance with Rose. It is very difficult to imagine your life with someone other than your deceased spouse. My mind whirled backwards to the counseling speech that I preached to Harry on that day so long ago when he was searching his soul for answers. To my recollection, I told him that it was normal, it was part of God's plan and that Sky would want you to move on in life and in love. Very solid advice, but it is often easier for Pastor Paul to deliver his advice to others than it is for him to implement his own advice in his own life. When I became stuck in the traffic along highway twenty-one, crawling my way with countless others on the morning commute, I decided that I would just sit back, take it slow and try to make conscious decisions rather than emotional or knee-jerk reactions. Just as I did with Janet Chesboro, I would allow God's plan to shape my life and my heart, and at first, treat as friends any women who happen to wander into my life. For now, I need to concentrate on Vance's training, catching up on my bishop's duties, settling into the new townhouse and making sure our daughter and granddaughter were stable. That is more than enough to handle!

I did share, with Maggie, a cup of tea later on in the week, when Maggie dropped off a very nice housewarming gift of an eloquent flower vase and some flowers as a welcome to the neighborhood. I introduced Maggie to Heather Sarah and Sarah and we sat and shared a cup of tea, and a quite long and very pleasant conversation. It went very well, and I was very comfortable considering her a friendly neighbor as well as a new friend. She was pleasant, engaging, and attractive, as well as a resource for questions about our new community. Heather Sarah commented on her attractiveness, her professionalism, and hinted at taking it to the next step, but I told her my plan was to ease into any relationships other than friendship. She understood.

"Paul, I must say, how wonderful this new townhouse is for you, for Heather Sarah and Sarah too. Sarah's playroom is awesome and I love the way that Heather Sarah has decorated your office. A wet bar, my goodness, it is all very cool and sophisticated too! And the fireplace and deck, this place is so Paul John Henson. Rugged is the word," the lovely Rose Redmond commented and glowed in praise as she banged pots and pans around in our kitchen.

Rose and Harry insisted on throwing us a housewarming dinner party where Rose would use our kitchen and prepare us one of her famous Italian feasts of wonder. Heather Sarah, Sarah, and I were not going to argue with that invitation.

Rose had her back to me while she spoke; I sat at the table alone, fiddling with my half-filled beer mug and thinking about this remarkable time in our lives. It was Saturday in the early evening, the summer was passing quickly and almost before I could blink my eyes, it was the middle of August. We had a hard workout with Vance today and even though I was in much better physical condition than I was during my previous adventures, I was still a little sore and tired. Now, it was not a matter of poor physical condition, but more simply a matter of my age. More salt soaks in my new soaking tub.

While the increased physical training was something that helped to tone all of our bodies and cleared our minds, I did notice how exhausted Harry appeared and I wondered how the big guy was feeling these days. He, at times, seemed so winded, and I caught him during an ordinary skate holding his chest a number of times, bent over and panting for air. It was of concern to me, as it was to Jim, Paul William, and Vance too. My questions to Harry about how he felt ended up in a typical humorous dismissal and stout proclamations that he was fine. I meant to quiz Rose when I had a chance, perhaps tonight or in a conversation within the next few days. Tonight, the plan was for us to enjoy a jovial celebration and I did not want to spoil the mood.

Vance was now a beast in the net. There was no other description for him. He was a puck-stopping and skating machine. We skated with him; he worked out with Pastor Jim and his high school hockey club in organized practices, we ran, we hit the weight rooms and we did my old flexibility exercises and workouts perfected long ago by my old man and me in our driveway at 182 Belmont Avenue. The drills might not have been pretty, nor were they in any textbooks, but I knew from experience that they worked for me and I knew they would work for Vance too. After a few hundred hours of sweating his backside off on hot and humid New Jersey summer days, I made a believer of Vance Howard.

Each day, as he worked with our old-time hockey training group, spent solo time with Pastor Paul and number twenty-seven, while he spent time with Harry and Rose in their house and skated with Jim and the team on the ice, he grew and developed. We all became the family that he never had or never knew. I could see the change in his ability as well as in his demeanor. In looking back on all of this, I am sure that as his love for our daughter and his affection for Sarah grew; he matured more. Before my eyes, a young man who came to me with a terrible attitude and no confidence in April of this same year, now as mid-August arrived and the end of the off-season crept closer, had remarkably changed into a mature man and an incredibly skilled goaltender. Jim, Paul William, and Harry rarely, if ever, could score a goal on him. I was not much of a shooter, so stopping my feeble shot was not much of a challenge; I could not dent a cream puff with my shot! Vance watched and studied Paul William skate, and our son taught him the finer points of putting the blade to the ice. Vance skated as hard as he could and improved greatly in this most important aspect of the sport. Number one mixed my old-time goaltending style with his own and each time we met, we fine-tuned the methodology and changed his approach to something that he was comfortable with and suited his unique abilities. When our team did score a goal on Vance, it was a fluke or just an error as the result of poor execution or a simple miss of his timing. His reflexes were keen, his body toned and his spirit alive. Vance was now, in my opinion, on the cusp of being the best ice hockey goalie in the world, and according to the hockey genius known as Mr. Tommy Hayward, I was the expert on that subject. All that I knew was that we had done our job and the old-time hockey team was about to deliver our promise to Brian and the Bears. My days as a consultant rapidly ended.

I knew that God's plan worked to perfection and our mission was so much more than turning Vance Howard into the best ice hockey goalie in the world, but it also was a mission to turn him into our daughter's love of her life, and I felt in my heart into Heather Sarah's eventual husband.

Heather Sarah, and Vance grew inseparable and when we were not working, if he was not over at our townhouse, or hanging with Blue Cloud and Paul William and Heather Sarah, then he was out with Heather Sarah on the town. Vance treated Sarah as the princess that she was. More importantly, he treated her as if she was his own blood daughter. On the weekends, after workouts, the three of them often went out together to the local park, to the zoo and other fun places and of course, he bought her dresses, toys and other goodies. I appreciated his love for little Sarah more than I could ever tell him, and surprisingly; we did not speak often of his relationship with our daughter and granddaughter. With the two of us for this summer, it was all business, but I knew that time would come and it was growing closer with each passing day.

Rose continued to work on the meal preparation. She excitedly spoke while she created magnificent layers of her remarkable lasagna in a pan, about how happy she felt that we were all moving on, how the townhouse was perfect, tidbits about Blue and Paul William and other general conversation. We were waiting on the rest of the gang; Harry, Vance and Paul William were at the store, picking up a few more items requested by Rose. Heather Sarah was working late on a charity project for Harry, but she would be home soon. Jim O'Malley and Mrs. O'Malley were on the way. Sarah and Blue Cloud were playing together in her playroom. We could hear them and see them on the playroom monitor that was sitting upon the kitchen counter. Blue Cloud loved children, and I hoped that day would be coming where she would experience motherhood. I knew they were trying very hard to do so.

Once more, God's plan would have the final say.

I took a long sip of the brew, awoke from my daydream and listened while I studied the remarkable Rose Redmond. She wore a tight pair of black pants, with a loose-fitting blouse, and an apron over her clothes to prevent any errant soiling, while she prepared the meal. She remained incredibly gorgeous, her perfect figure enhanced by her clothes, and I tried hard not to study her too much.

Honestly, and God forgive me, but it was a bit difficult not to focus upon her.

As of late, I still felt that same strange vibe between us, but I had been so incredibly busy, other than a few brief phone conversations, I had not spent much time with Rose. When we were together, I continued to feel those same feelings and expressions from her, where Rose seemed overly protective of me, and there was no doubt that any mention of me wandering out into any dating adventures, caused her concern and was not too popular with her. It might just be a taste of over-protectiveness. We are all guilty of that with close friends and family, and our group was guilty of that emotion, even more so than any other group that I knew of. Yet, lately, when she hugged me and touched me, it was very different. I did not and still do not know how to describe it or interpret it, but I remained keenly aware of it. I would never want any implications of something inappropriate between us, and there are in this life, some feelings, which need to stay deep within your own heart and mind and remain there. Prayer kept me strong, and it made me stronger.

Rose reached a point in her food preparation where she took a break; she turned and smiled at me while wiping her hands on a towel. I looked up, nodded to acknowledge what she had been speaking about, and hoped that she did not quiz me on the various subjects, of which she had spoken. I remained lost somewhere else with Rose, a place where I had seldom ventured.

"Would you like a glass of wine, Rose? Are you taking a break? Red or white?"

She smiled and nodded, "Sure. Thank you. Red. Of course, red. Please."

I stood up, grabbed a wine glass from the cupboard, the red wine from the refrigerator, poured the wine, and handed it off to Rose. We toasted together, gently touching the glass and my mug of beer, and she smiled over the rim of the glass, while telling me, "You look remarkable, Paul. As if, you are twenty-five years old again. Your eyes flicker again with your enlightened spirit. The workouts and return to life have been so wonderful for you. I did not think it was even possible for you to grow more handsome, but you are."

I smiled and thanked her and hoped that this conversation would not turn into an uncomfortable one for us to share. Rose walked over to the table, pulled out a chair and sat at the table.

I joined her and the conversation took an entirely different turn, "My dearest Paul, before the rest of the gang arrives and this turns into our usual bedlam, I would like to speak about some serious family matters. I must tell you that Blue Cloud and I have had long conversations with Heather Sarah, and since Ian is looking at some jail time, this divorce is rather easy. It will all go quickly. Ian will be a convicted felon for the stunts he pulled, and Heather Sarah can be a ruthless attorney with all of the proper connections. Ian has disappeared from her life and Sarah's life too. Harry calling in Sal Junior's men must have scared the shit out of him and apparently, he did not care enough anyhow."

I looked at Rose and nodded in agreement, but I was not sure where Rose was leading the conversation.

Rose sensed that, and she explained, "My chance at using my motherly instincts came into play for my family and Binky's daughter. Ah, I mean my sister's daughter and granddaughter. And your daughter and granddaughter too."

Rose took a sip of the wine and she fought back a hint of tears. It was the first time in all of our years together, dating back to forever, that I heard Rose refer to Binky as her sister. Harry and I often referred to each other as brothers, but this was a first for me to hear this reference from our dear Rose.

"I think that you know, at least, I hope you know that I love those two more than I can ever describe. Heather Sarah is like my own, as if she came from my own womb. Even more so now. I often wish that . . . well, never mind. I think you understand."

Oh boy, I needed to jump in and intercept that thought, I think that I knew where Rose was heading, "I know that, Rose, and they do too. The bonding between the two of you has always been very special to me. I know it was to Binky too. She often spoke of how close the two of you were. I understand. Binky smiles down upon your mothering care and love."

"Good, then with that in mind, I must tell you that rebounds are horrible. I know that, I made a terrible mistake on my first marriage when Harry was out of my life, you were off playing hockey, and Binky was gone. I turned to a person who was very similar to Ian. You protected me and defended my honor from that scoundrel. I know that story too. Paul, we all know that you have a special sense that God gave to you. A gift. In our hearts, we all knew that Ian was a loser. A handsome, talented, but conniving, evil loser. They are out there in droves. Heather Sarah is intelligent beyond comprehension, beautiful, in fact, gorgeous, but she could be vulnerable right now to the evil ways of men and remains susceptible to their conniving ways. Such a gorgeous young woman, wealthy, successful, a perfect figure and honestly, all these men want is to satisfy their lust. Yes, susceptible is the correct word. She was then, and she is now."

Rose paused as she swirled her glass of wine around in front of her while she gathered some additional thoughts.

"I think that I know Vance fairly well. He has lived with us for some time now. He seems to be polite, well mannered, and since he arrived here, his maturity level is remarkable. He even scrubs and cleans his own bathroom, toilet, and shower and makes his bed every day. Even does his own laundry. Now, for a man, to wash his own underwear that is as fine a catch as you can find!"

Rose laughed, took a sip of wine and I nodded while adding, "Laundry is a handy skill to have. He will have plenty of practice living his hockey life on the road."

"I imagine that he will, but on a serious note, I think he has an honest heart and Harry does too. Yet, what we think, I want to confirm. I trust Vance now, but I do need to verify my instincts. You are the ultimate in verification for me, and for us. You are our leader, and our rock. This young hockey player and to be honest, life student of yours that you are a mentor to, what is your gut feeling? Is he sincere? Because it will not be too long, he will have completely captured Heather Sarah's heart, and she will never be able to take it back or find it again."

Rose paused, sighed, and her eyes darted to my face and

to my eyes. I did not say a word. Her dark eyes deeply studied mine.

Right before she spoke again, Rose smiled ever so slightly, "I know the feeling all too well. We cannot, and will not, allow her to be hurt in any manner. I know that you would die first. In addition, you have that precious little girl playing with Blue Cloud in her room. A little girl who only knows Grandpa, Harry, Vance, and her uncle as male figures in her life now. She is almost four now, and she is confused as to why her daddy is gone. From what Heather Sarah told me, Ian never cared much for her anyhow, so the impact might be minimal. Who knows? You are the pastor or as you often call yourself in these cases, the rabbi, not me. I know you will speak to her, spend time with Sarah, and make it all well in her life. I never doubt you. I only bring this up to make sure that what we feel in our hearts is correct. That we are protecting our family."

I answered without any ounce of hesitation, "Vance is sincere. He will be, if it happens, a fine husband, he will turn into a miraculous man, a superstar, professional athlete, and his soul is honest, kind, and good. Rose, he now knows the difference between a commitment and a contribution and he will never look back. This was the final piece of this plan. I am sure of it. God has guided every step of the way. This family will always be guided and remain within the plan. Since stepping back into the world, I have spent a great amount of time pondering this, writing, thinking about it and creating notes, sermons and other works for use in a manuscript of some kind, someday. Hockey was merely a vehicle for me, for us, to ride here to the place where we all are now. It always was a vehicle for me, an incredibly important part of my life, of our lives. Yet, now this is where hockey ends for me. Number twenty-seven is no longer required. I need to put him on my dusty old shelf of memories. Now, I only need to be Grandpa, Dad, Pastor Paul, and Paul. God's plan has us all firmly within the folds, while it unfolds. Obviously, not all of it has been wonderful, nor fun, nor without intense and unfathomable pain. Trust and obey, and we go onward. It has always been that way since Harry and I first met. It will continue to be that way until we leave this world. I am sure of this."

Rose smiled widely, her dark eyes sparkling, her usual golden earrings dangling as she moved her lovely head.

She took the wineglass, downed the last of it, laughed a bit as she held it in the air indicating a request for a refill and she softly said, "Thank you, Paul. Refill, please. I will, in many ways, miss dear number twenty-seven. He is a large part of what makes you so incredibly special, but instead, I have to say that it is so nice to have you here with us as Pastor Paul, Dad, Grandpa and the most brilliant man that I have ever known and loved and his name is Paul John Henson."

"It is good to be here, Rose. I will miss him too, but I have a feeling that I am going to have to be the other versions of Henson, much more so during the rest of my life. Anyway, time to party. A refill for you and a refill for me too."

My new office was my port of a safe haven amidst the storms of life. Even more so than my work office, this office just felt right, warm, and safe. I often just randomly hugged Heather Sarah when we crossed paths in our home, and I thanked her for her loving creation of this wonderful space for me. A place to create, a place to be alone with God and my thoughts. My office was a place to allow the ghosts who haunt me continually, to journey back into time with me and write about all that happened to us, all the journeys, all the pain, humor, adventures and of course, the love.

When you are a writer, the place that you write in is very important. The surroundings are part of the process, part of the mood set and part of what generates the environment of creation. I had my old, faithful desk in there, a desk that was the foundation of countless sermons. Sermons and writing that began with one special sermon in the house, which Binky and I rented so long ago in our first house that we lived in after we married. The desk was worn, battered, nicked and dented and that is just the way I wanted it to stay. The interior designer asked Heather Sarah if we wanted the desk refinished, and our daughter wisely refused the offer. She knew not to remove the character. This office was where I retreated to, in order to write, listen to music or just contemplate some thoughts. My volume of writing had increased considerably and often at night, when I could not sleep, I wrote. Currently, between jotting down notes in creating this manuscript, a manuscript that I am not sure I will ever expand upon, fill in, or publish, I worked on a collection of short stories with autumn settings and while it was a short book in length, it was very intense and different. I was not in any type of rush; I knew that it would all wrap up in due time. Writing was currently a sideline; my primary focus was my bishop's position, which now thanks to the extraordinary efforts of Martha Wiggins, and some long hours in the office, was under control. I also had my commitment to the job that the Boston Bears and my old friend Brian McClure hired me to do.

It was late August now, a late Saturday afternoon, we were about two weeks from shipping Vance Howard out for his reporting for training camp and on my weekly wrap-up call with Brian McClure, I reported on the outstanding progress of Vance Howard. Brian also shared a bit of good news, because after the end of the season, after paying attention to my impassioned speech on the subject, some heartfelt negotiations and some radical changes of heart, Brian and the Bears decided to retain Coach William Bettermann for another year. The coach's attitude was renewed, and Brian credited me with his new spirit. I was not too sure about that fact, but I enjoyed working with the old coach, thought that he was an outstanding man, a solid, old-time hockey coach, and I looked forward to him receiving another chance at the position. He deserved a full season chance to give it his best effort, and I knew in my heart that he would do the job that Coach Davis taught him so well how to do. I felt that retaining Coach Bettermann was an outstanding idea for some stability to build upon the success we had at the end of the year. Albeit, only a few games of success, but success nonetheless. I respected the man because he was kind but hard-nosed and fair. It turns out that under some intense scrutiny, the young coach from the Norfolk team turned out to be not quite ready for the big league anyhow, and this would work out well for everyone.

Once we discussed various subjects and Brian brought me up to speed on the return of the old coach, I asked about the backup goaltending situation. Brian told me that there were two prospects that had received invitations to training camp. One was a young goalie who came up through the system, and the other was a journeyman goaltender who bounced around various leagues with different clubs. I asked if Tommy could send me some video on the two prospects so that I could make some analysis of them before camp opened and give Brian and Coach Bettermann my thoughts on them. I kidded with Brian and told Brian to let Gibby Gibbons know that I would do so, free of charge! Brian agreed and now, with the arrival of an overnight package, I had in front of me video discs of the two goalies to study. Typically, Tommy Hayward was the picture of efficiency.

I currently sat in my chair at the desk in my office and carefully studied the video of the two backup goaltenders under consideration. It only took me one or two views to decide that in my opinion, the older journeyman goalie, a chap named Chris Ridley was the superior choice for the primary backup duties. I thought that he played a solid style and while he had some rough patches, I rather liked the idea of an experienced backup to Vance, as opposed to two young goalies. After all, Vance was still a rookie, and carrying two rookies on the same hockey club in the goaltending position was a recipe for disaster.

I was taking pencil notes, watching the videos carefully, and contemplating searching my cellphone contacts for Coach Bettermann's number, to call him, congratulate him on his renewed position and to discuss the results of my study, when I heard a gentle knock at the doorway to the office. Without looking up, I knew that it was not our daughter. Heather Sarah was so much her mother's daughter and she did not knock, she just barged in, jumped on my lap and showered her father with hugs and kisses. Whom am I kidding? I loved it.

Instead, it was Vance Howard staring at me.

"Hey, twenty-seven. Heather Sarah told me that you were in here and for me just to knock. Do you have a minute or two? Whatcha doin'?"

I waved him in and reached for the mouse to shut down the video player on the computer while telling him, "Sure. Please, come in and sit down. I am watching some video clips of goalies that the Bears plan to bring to camp to serve as your backups."

While he sat, he asked, "Any good ones?" He added a smirk and commented, "Any old-time hockey stand-up type of goalies?"

Vance still had occasional smart-ass tendencies.

"No, they are quite rare these days. One chap is solid, his style is a little mixture of everything, but he is quick along the ice. I like his experience. The other goalie is a little young and very rough and awkward in his form and style. Talented but raw. Hey, good news. Brian is bringing Coach Bettermann back for another year. They had a change of heart and worked a one-year deal." Vance nodded, and I could tell by his face that he was pleased with the news. He enjoyed playing for the old coach, too.

"Nice. I like him. He is a good coach and an outstanding man. Brian listened to you. Good work."

He looked up at the wall, a wall that now held an oil portrait painted a long time ago, a painting that my sister-in-law painted under Binky's guidance. Martha suggested it was time to move it to my home office, and I agreed. It was an amazing work of art with three pictures in one on an oil canvas. The largest depiction on the portrait featured me in the net, in my Long Island Rooster uniform, as well as a faded portrait of me preaching from a pulpit. Lastly, the portrait included an even smaller depiction of me working as an electrician. All of these careers belonged to my past; it seemed so long ago that it was hard to imagine even thinking of the long journeys involved with each of them.

"Nice picture, twenty-seven. I always liked that one. It looks good there."

"Thank you. It does. Rose picked the spot."

"Heather Sarah, is reading one of your books and having some red wine in the kitchen. Sarah is napping. Do you want a beer? I will get us a few. I tried one of those Dingleberries. I think you are wrong 'bout them. They are good. A little sweet but I like them."

I almost fell out of my chair at the testimony of the first person in history, other than the immortal Ronzo Boatmann who actually enjoyed Dingleberry beer! Harry will laugh his ass off when I tell him this one.

Recovering, I skipped commenting on his opinion of the infamous Dingleberry beer and answered, "No, thank you. Maybe later. Say, what's on your mind? Are you feeling, okay?" I could tell that Vance had something on his mind. He was nervously fidgeting, and he never appeared nervous at all these days. His confidence was at an all-time high.

"I feel great. No issues. That little tightness in my shoulder is gone. Damn, Harry can shoot hard."

"Good, I am glad it is healing, and yes he can. Been on the end of a few million of them shots too. They rattle all the bones of your body."

It was time for my years as a pastor to kick in, and I leaned back in the chair and allowed Vance to gather his thoughts. The words would come to him. I needed to give him space; therefore, I pretended to fiddle with the computer to give him a bit of time. In my heart, and by studying his eyes, I knew that the subject of this visit involved our beloved daughter's heart and future.

"Twenty-seven, I have become quite fond of Heather Sarah and of Sarah. In fact, why the hell am I stalling here? I am madly in love with Heather Sarah and with that little girl too. This whole summer has been a blur. This difficult training, training that you followed years ago, when you walked this same path, it has been rough and hard but it has taught me so much. I cannot even tell you how much I have learned. Training on the streets of New Jersey combined with lessons on the rink and off them. Living with Harry and Rose, learning, and working with you and observing. Harry is one of the most amazing men that I have ever met. He is hilarious and his weird logic leads you to believe that he is this big, boisterous, bullshitter, but in fact, he is smarter and more genuine than anyone can ever imagine. He is dedicated, strong, powerful, and painfully honest. Above all, he loves his family and friends with all of his heart and soul. The man would do anything for the people that he cares for and for you. And, Pastor Jim and his religious wisdom, along with incredible hockey skills and no-bullshit ways, he has been amazing. I cannot even imagine what James T. O'Malley was like to face as a goaltender when he was twenty-five years old. Musta shot a hole right through your pads. How he did not make it to the big league is a mystery. I swear that the man could play in the big league right now."

I nodded in agreement and answered, "He was, and is indeed, the real deal. There will never be another player like him. Ever. I faced a million hockey players. I swear to you that, I faced a million of them. Jim made your body numb with pain and your soul honored to understand his endless commitment to his mission. James T. O'Malley, either as a pastor or a hockey player, is one of the special people on this side of Heaven. He taught me more about the sport, about honor, about God and life than I can ever relate. Him playing in the big league, it was not part of the plan. This was, as we have all experienced by having the amazing James T. O'Malley in our lives, part of the plan. It all interlocks. He had, as you can see, more important assignments."

Vance nodded that he understood, and he continued, "I agree and understand now. Well, you have all taught me what it is like to be a family and what true friendship is. There are no people on the face of this Earth like this group of remarkable people. And you three men, well, you are all like no other men that I have ever known in my entire life."

He put his head down for a second and then looked me straight in the eye and boldly proclaimed, "Especially you. You are like a father to me. The father that I never had. You are a rock of strength. It is so easy to understand the legend of twenty-seven now. What you have been through, where you came from, to where you arrived. Damn. Oh, sorry, for the strong word, but, your amazing courage is beyond comparison. Just as O'Malley told me, you are the ultimate warrior. He told me that you are not able to be broken. Your spirit either in the net, on the ice, or as a man, cannot be measured. He was correct. It is more than just your courage and your imposing physical presence. It is your emotional strength too. You are the rock that you often carry around with you in that vest pocket. I understand it all now. I watch how you speak only after carefully observing people. I see how you love, believe in and respect God, despite what has happened to you, but most of all, I admire how you love and protect your children, your granddaughter, family and your friends and how you lead them all."

I did not answer him, and he picked the conversation up so quickly after the pause that I am not sure I would have had the time to do so.

"Heather Sarah's divorce will be final next week and I will be packing up soon to head to training camp, so I wanted to talk to you here, in New Jersey and ask you, if you would object to, or if you would give your blessings, if I asked Heather Sarah to marry me? You see, you taught me well. The lessons of your old man are now mine to learn and accept too. I am taking the commitment lesson to the ultimate step. I sure do wish that I could have met your old man. He musta been sumthin' special."

'Yes, he was', I thought. The old man came through once again. Thanks, Dad, for that and a whole helluva lot more. My mind whirled away from the old man, to the question imposed. To guess how many thoughts rushed through my mind in mere seconds, would be an effort in futility, but the number one thought, which hit my mind first, was that I knew that Binky rejoiced in Heaven at his words. The final piece of the plan now was in place, and Rose and I were correct, when we realized that this was love at first sight.

Vance studied me for my reaction. His eyes now locked on mine and I surmised that my lessons of studying a shooter's eyes for clues of their shot intentions, now had taken hold within Vance Howard. Without additional hesitation, I knew what the question was that I had to ask him. It was a simple question.

Leaning forward, I asked him just above a whisper, "Will you die in place of them? That is the ultimate proclamation of love for a person. If you had to—would you die for them, Vance?"

His reaction would be the key here, and I leaned back and watched as the young man's eyes and face showed no surprise or reaction at all.

He answered quickly and proudly, "In less than a second. I would. Yes. In less than a second for either one of them. It would not even be in question."

I smiled and quickly stood up, and Vance did the same.

I extended my hand out to shake his hand and told him, "Then you have my blessing and please know that you have Heather Sarah's mother's blessing from Heaven too."

Number one had arrived; he had indeed arrived as a man and as a part of our family. Moreover, I knew that we would never have to worry about our daughter and granddaughter's well-being ever again.

You see, dear reader, all of us goalies, well, it is not only our nets that we protect.

Chapter Twelve

A Few Thoughts from the Father's Son

I found this manuscript in a file on a disc of material that my old man gave to me to examine, and see if there was anything here that I wanted to keep or desired to work with. It is an amazing story, and I am not quite sure why my father felt that it was something that he did not want to publish or finish. My goodness, if I had to classify it then I would say it is the final and ultimate adventure of Harry and Paul. Of course, I felt it worthwhile to keep, and more importantly, to finish. However, the old man felt it easily dismissed, and he tucked it away. It was a puzzle to me as to why.

When I asked him if he cared if I read it, finished it or edited it, he only smiled and waved in the air at me and told me, "He always needed someone to write with, please go ahead and fill it all in if you so desire to work on it or finish it."

I almost felt as if he purposely left it unfinished and made sure that I found it, in the hopes that I would pick it all up. You never know with him. His mind is still keen, and he is the most brilliant man that has ever lived. I am not just saying that because he is my old man. I sincerely mean it.

Please stick with me, dear reader. I am a writer, but not the writer that my father is. I write nonfiction. Sports, primarily covering ice hockey as a beat writer for the Boston Bears. Still, this manuscript is too important and too special not to pick it up and complete the parts that my father, for some reason, would not write about, or perhaps, wanted me to write. There remains no doubt that some of these subjects are very painful and would be tremendously difficult for my father to write about, they are for me too, but there is nothing in this world, or any other worlds that he ever shied away from or backed down from. Therefore, it is difficult to determine his motivations, but so be it, I will do the best that I can.

After our dear father renewed and rediscovered his soul, he was on a mission. Everyone around him knew it, could tell it, and encouraged it. Vance Howard, after the summer of training, was, and is, other than number twenty-seven, the greatest professional ice hockey goalie in the world. Sure, I assisted him with his skating. My father-in-law helped mold him into a man, and Pastor Jim taught him what it takes to be fearless on the ice and to stand for your honor. My father taught him the nuances of playing goal, but most of all, he taught him commitment. Commitment, to his profession, to his loved ones and most of all to his soul. Until you commit to your own soul, you cannot commit to anything or anyone in this life.

Dad was a new man, full of energy, full of love, his body toned, shaped, and his spirit reflected it too. He could have, for a companion, picked any woman from here to wherever. The next-door neighbor drooled over him, as did women half of his age. He was a tower of strength, leading his family into the battle of life. He ignored all the drooling women. Why? I did not know, but I knew he felt something in his heart. Something steered him, guided him, and above all, his anger with God's plan would not be denied, yet still, he somewhat blindly followed.

Blue Cloud and I, we often discussed it and my beloved wife often confessed how she felt as if her own mother, our dear Rose, loved my father with all her heart and soul. Not as family or the dear friends, they were, but as if they were lovers. Blue told me often, she felt it strongly and watching my dear mother-in-law after my mother passed away, I had to agree that something changed in her relationship with our father. Dad never seemed to reciprocate, but he was too honorable ever to cross any lines. Yet, I knew in my heart that he felt something too. Maybe it had been there for their entire lives. Who knows? The two of them shared everything; we all knew the stories, the two of them, went farther back in time together than my mother, and my father-in-law did. Blue Cloud emphasized how if they did love each other, it did not affect or diminish their relationships with their own individual spouses. In fact, my brilliant wife seemed to think that this, too, was part of the plan. Blue Cloud's faith was strong. Other than Rose and my father, Blue's faith was the most unshakable of all of us, maybe because the three of them remained forever connected in faith and miracles.

To steal a line from my old man, "That, dear reader, is another story."

She often told me that she felt as if our parent's connection supplemented their lives and all of their love for each other. Strange, but observant.

Then there was the subject of Harry's health. While working Vance out, we all saw it and observed it. He seemed to be losing steam, his usual zeal, losing his weight and mass. Harry was always a tower of strength, but in front of our eyes, he weakened. My wife and I begged my father-in-law to see a doctor, as did Rose, but he was too stubborn to do so. The most stubborn man on Earth. My father, and Jim, as well as Vance, all tried to convince him to see a doctor and take care of himself, but Harry, well he was Harry. He would not listen to anyone, even Rose, or Blue, or my father.

"Just gettin' older," he would say.

Well, no, there was so much more to that part of the story. . ..

As this story unfolds and slowly winds down to a

conclusion, I guess, my role will be to fill in parts and pieces where my dear father, for whatever reason, chose not to do so. I hope we can publish it someday, to tell the entire magical story of two very special men. How they cared enough not only for each other but also for so many others, to create the adventures of two special lifetimes.

The adventures of Harry and Paul.

Ordinary in the appearance on the outside, however, extraordinary on the inside. Paul William Henson the second, the father's only son, typing here at my dear father's laptop, fingers on the keyboard, doing my best to fill in the voids in this magnificent story for the man, who is impossible to fill in for in this world. All I ever wanted in life was to be like him.

I can recall sitting one day as a young boy, on the floor in front of my father as he sat in his easy chair after a long day at work. There I sat, watching my father, studying him. He took off his headphones and stopped listening to the endless music that he listens to, music that plays both in his head and through his ears, and he smiled that magical smile at me.

He asked me, "What are you thinking about, Paul William?"

I shrugged my shoulders and did not have an answer because the truth was; I was studying him in the hope that I could be like him someday. All of him. I then gathered the courage, climbed in his lap, and admitted that I wanted to be just like him.

My old man shook his head. All that hair flew around him and he told me, "No, you need to be you. No one else is as special as you are. You are rare and precious because God made only one you."

I nodded my head and then he asked me, "Do you know what my grandfather, your great-grandfather, told me one day about being yourself and taking pride in who you are?"

I shook my head, no.

The old man continued, "He gave me the advice when I was just about your age, which formed the basis for my entire life. He told me, never to allow people to judge you, Paulie boy, for how you look, or how you talk or how you walk. Make them judge you for what you do, how you treat others, and for the person whom you really are. Never change for anyone, Paulie boy, always be who you are. If they think you are different, or you do not fit in, then prove them wrong, for you will be the better man for it. God made all of us the way he decided to make us. So be who you are and always be proud of it."

And that dear reader is the magic of a man who provides priceless advice for all of us.

Chapter Thirteen

The Return of Peppermint Ice Cream

Heather Sarah's divorce finalized without any issues or delays. Ian was now in court battles that we all knew would result in plea bargains for reduced jail time. All indications were that he embezzled quite a bit of money from the law practice and needed to enter rehabilitation to shake an intense drug habit. There was no longer any contact with Ian; he did not ask for any visitation rights for his daughter; he had no demands or requests. It was as if he permanently resigned himself that he would no longer be a part of their lives. That suited me just fine. I wished the young man the best to get his life in order, but as far as ever interacting with him ever again, it was not high on my priority list.

A week after the divorce finalized, Vance proposed to Heather Sarah, and of course, Heather Sarah, accepted. The marriage proposal came two nights before he had to leave to head to Boston for training camp, and of course, we squeezed in an engagement celebration at the Redmond's house before Vance had to pack up and leave town. Heather Sarah, and Vance did not set a wedding date, they instead knew the importance of what Vance faced in the upcoming hockey season and they chose to wait and see how the future unfolded. The only item that they set in stone was a request for Pastor Paul John Henson to perform the marriage ceremony, with Pastor James T. O'Malley assisting. Jim and I both thought that we could work that one out.

The many lovely women (and all the men too) in our lives were none too happy on the day that Vance shipped out for camp. We had all worked very hard to arrive at this point and now; it was time to prove the worth of all that hard work. The entire gang brought Vance to the airport to send him on his way, with the good wishes of his support team and the loves of his life. Vance individually met with each of us while saying goodbye and thanking us. He saved Sarah and our daughter for the last goodbye. Sarah was in his arms. Poor Sarah was so sad, holding onto Vance tightly. Heather Sarah held his free hand.

"Pastor and Coach Jim, thanks for everything," Vance said when he met up with James T. O'Malley.

The two men embraced, shook hands and Jim told him, "When the first screaming puck comes from the point for the sole purpose of taking your head off, reach up, catch it, hold it for a faceoff. Then lift your cage mask and smile. All you need to do now is smile. The look in your eyes will be enough to tell the story."

Vance did not answer; he nodded his head, smiled, and patted Jim on the shoulder. Vance understood the Gospel according to O'Malley.

Vance then thanked Harry and the big guy proudly proclaimed, "Old-time hockey, fancy Vancie. Ya nevah played hockey on the street there, but you are now an honorary Geyer Street Guy. Ya just joined up. Make 'em proud and 'member, Geyer Street Guys nevah quit. Ever." Vance nodded and moved over to speaking with our son.

"Paul William, someday, I will hit that ice and out skate your speedy ass."

Our son smiled and simply said, "Do you promise? I am kind of counting on that or I did not do my job."

"I do and I will," Vance shook his hand and moved on in line to say goodbye to me. When he approached me, he handed Sarah off to her mother and he warmly embraced me, "Thanks, twenty-seven. Bacon and eggs, I will have them every day for breakfast."

"Better watch your cholesterol."

He laughed and said, "I will do my best to be like number twenty-seven."

When I heard his words, I rather forcibly cut him off, put my hand on his shoulder and commented, "No. You are, Vance Howard. Number one. The best ice hockey goaltender whoever played the game of hockey. That is who you are and what you are. God made all of us the way he decided to make us. So be who you are and always be proud of it."

We embraced again, and he looked at the four of us. Jim, Harry, Paul William, and I stood with our arms flung over each other's shoulders, joined in hockey and life brotherhood, watching our student's graduation.

Vance turned, and he specifically looked at Jim and me, while telling us, "By the way, I do believe in God."

Jim answered, "We already knew that, Vance. You always did, and God believes in you too."

We left him alone with his two loves to have a private goodbye.

For Vance, training camp was a breeze. He reported in such fine physical and mental condition that he easily impressed Coach Bettermann and Brian with his performance, as well as his dedication and commitment. When Vance called home, and he checked in with me for advice, I stressed how the hockey season was a marathon, not a sprint, and emphasized how he needed to care for his body and his mind, in order to ride it out successfully.

The Bears opened the season in mid-October on the road in Toronto and started the season with a win and a very impressive performance by Vance in the net. Of course, O'Malley's prediction of a head shot came true, and Vance followed the advice perfectly. The Bears had made a number of free-agent acquisitions in the off-season, and they acquired some veteran defenseman to stabilize the defensive corps in front of the rookie net-minder. They also had another rookie on the squad, up from Norfolk and playing the key center-iceman position. This young man could score goals in droves, and he was going to be a good one. I could tell.

The press already touted Vance Howard as a phenomenal prospect. Paul William found himself in a bit of a predicament of covering the hottest news in all of hockey of the rising superstar goalie for the Boston Bears, who also happened to be marrying his sister. Paul William had to dance around the subject of the incredible skills of Vance Howard, as he explained to his editors and syndications that Vance was going to be his brother-in-law, and writing about him would create a conflict of interest.

Vance's agent capitalized on his meteoric rise, his movie star good looks, and his now softened and calm demeanor. Young women groaned in disappointment when they found out he had a gorgeous fiancée. Vance was now the subject of endless promotion of posters, trading cards, hockey sweaters and other promotional items, all related to Vance Howard.

Sports are big business and as Harry told Vance, "Ya got to make the dough while ya a hot commodity! Even stars fade."

Before we knew it, October turned into November and the hockey season and our lives settled into a smooth flow.

It was around the middle of November, very late in the afternoon. I had worked the last hour or so away in my office in Newark trying my best to figure out how to answer one of the most absurd emails that I had ever received. I carefully studied the words of the message, which composed a bizarre request from a confused pastor, when my cellphone signaled an incoming call. I figured the call was Heather Sarah checking in. Instead, it was Paul William.

"Hey, dear Father. How is it going?"

"Good. Great, in fact. If I could straighten out some of these maniacal pastors, my life would be a little easier. Hockey players are easier to deal with. They are more honest. I see Vance had a big win last night. The Bears are two points out of first now. Looking solid."

"Yes! I am just home now from this road trip. Glad I made it in time for the weekend. Being on the road sucks. You know all too well, dear Father. Vance is awesome, might be the best goalie in the league already. He is not number twenty-seven, but he is awesome."

"Oh, I think he is much better than twenty-seven ever was. So, what's up? Everything ok?"

"Great, Father. Great. Look, Blue Cloud and I wanted to let you know now, and then we are going over to my in-laws, but I need to tell you now that I am going to be a father. Blue Cloud is pregnant!"

I almost dropped the telephone! Once I recovered, I shouted with joy and with my congratulations.

"Oh, Paul William, I cannot tell you how happy I am. This is fantastic news. I cannot wait to tell the world. Martha and I will rejoice together! Heaven is full of joy too! When is the baby due?"

"Get this. July twenty-seventh."

"Why am I not surprised?"

"Yeah, right! That magic number. Father, I just wanted to say that I am ready to be a father and if I could be half the man, and father that you are, well, then I would be proud. I love you. Blue Cloud loves you and I know that our baby loves you."

I tried not to choke up, but it was impossible. Clearing some emotions and tears, I managed to tell him, "I love them all too."

"You better hold on tight, because when we tell my father-in-law, then your telephone might explode."

"No doubt."

I hung up with Paul William, ran out of my office and

told Martha the good news. We warmly embraced, and I noticed just a hint of tears in Martha's eyes. After celebrating with Martha, we joined hands and knelt down right there in our office and we prayed for the baby's health and for the health of our precious Blue Cloud.

When the prayers were complete, I looked at my watch and tried hard to calculate when it would ring with Harry's phone call. Allowing for travel time, then a rough calculation of about an hour and ten minutes or so would be correct. It was worth sticking around the office to wait this one out.

I pictured it all in my mind.

Our children would arrive, some greetings, some small talk, Rose would offer wine, beer, cocktails and snacks. Blue Cloud would refuse and when pressed for why she would not partake, then the announcement would come. Harry would go nuts, kiss and hug their daughter, kiss and hug Paul William and then squeeze our poor son until his eyeballs almost popped out of his head. He would tilt poor Rose over and kiss her until he wore her lips out, and then he would blast off to the moon without a rocket ship. Upon his reentry into Earth's atmosphere, he would call me. Looking at my watch, I took note of the time and went back to answering ridiculous emails.

When my cell telephone rang, and I saw that it was Harry, I instinctively looked down at my watch. I was off because it was about an hour and twenty minutes later. Oh well, I had been in the ballpark.

"Hello."

"HOLY SMOKES, TWENTY-SEVEN! WE ARE GONNA BE FRIGGIN' GRANDPAS TOGETHER!"

"Well, yes, we are. It is wonderful. Congratulations."

"Wonderful? You are such an old lady. Wonderful. That is all ya got? I want to go and set the woods behind our house on fire and set off explosions! All we have been through for all of these years and now this! This is unreal.

Now, this is what I am talking 'bout! 'Bout damn time that son of yours got it together. I was startin' to worry that he did not have, ya know, a workin' thingy there. Maybe, he had a little bend in the river, or it was a shorty and it was not getting to where it needed to get to."

"Well, I guess that was not the case and that it works just fine, thirty-five."

"Yeah, yeah, yeah, I guess it does. Would have thought that he inherited his old man's genes and got him a good one. Not gonna ask, but I hope so. Blue Cloud is always smiling, so I guess that must be the case. I got so much to do! Have to buy all kinds of stuff! Damn, we are gonna have a grandkidler! Ya think it is a boy or a girl?"

"I do not have any thoughts, one way or another. I just hope and I just prayed for a healthy. . .."

Harry, of course, cut me off.

"No thoughts! Geez, ya a man of God. Don't youse guys get them promotions of these kinds of things?"

"You mean premonitions, Harry? No, it does not work like that."

"Whatever! Well, shit, ya need to go get drunk or chant, or burn them smelly ass stick thingys and meditate or whatever youse pineapples do and ask God for a vision. The suspense is killing me. When ya have a vision in the middle of the night, then give me a ring. Did you tell Marth-a-roo-ski?"

"Yes, we just prayed together."

"Good. Need the prayers. I got to go. All this talk of baby stuff has me all kinds of worked up! I have to buy baby stuff. What it is that I have to buy, I am not exactly sure, but I have to buy lots of baby stuff and hockey sticks. Going to the baby store right now. See ya!"

"Click!"

The line was dead.

Before I could even say anything else, he was gone. Nothing ever changed with Harry or with our telephone conversations.

Someday, I will hear him say goodbye.

Someday.

November turned quickly into December and the days rolled by. As usual, time passed in our lives as if it were a blur. It seemed as if the older we all grew; the quicker time flew by all of us. I can recall vividly, those lonely days on the road, playing ice hockey in strange cities and towns, then returning to my lonely apartment and going stir crazy with boredom. I would pray for practice to arrive, or another game, but they seemed to be months apart. Time moved so slowly back then; days and nights seemed to last forever. Now, my goodness, it was as if God adjusted the days to twenty hours a day and never informed any of us about the change!

Soon, Christmas and the entire holiday season loomed on the horizon. We noticed just a hint of a baby bump on Blue Cloud and if it were possible, the entire family bonded even closer during this special time. Rose, Heather Sarah, and Sarah shopped endlessly. We nicknamed them "the beautiful shopping gang." Even Paul William and Martha jumped into the shopping fray. Christmas was a special time of the year for our precious Sarah and with a baby on the horizon, let me tell you, it was no holds barred! We rented some limousines to drive around in and shop in style for the shopping gang. The shopping gang dined at fancy restaurants, sipped fancy wine and cocktails, (Blue Cloud stuck to flavored seltzer waters) and enjoyed the high life. Harry and I did not care, go ahead and spend the money! We worked hard enough for it, and we had more money than we could ever spend, anyway.

We were a long way from the old neighborhood; we sure were a long way from there. Yet, somehow, in our hearts we remained there too. For Harry and for me, we knew that we would never leave there. Ever.

For Paul John Henson, in my job as a bishop, Christmas

and the entire Advent season was quite different from when I was the pastor of Reunion Lutheran Church. For me now, it was a time of increased paperwork, more emails and more statistics, but it was also a time where I allowed myself to celebrate the season, as I never did when I was in the pulpit. I would take some time to visit different churches during the season, each year picking another group of churches to attend worship services during the season. It was actually quite social, relaxing and uplifting.

When I served as a pastor, Advent was a frenzied time of the year. It entailed long hours, endless, boring meetings, hard work for the preparations, and to be honest, I was always glad when the season was over. I often felt as if my family and our children never had their father around enough during those Christmas celebrations of their youth. Many years ago, my beloved Binky told me that I was incorrect. We always had wonderful times for the children, but in my heart, I regretted the time I spent away from them. We could never recapture those times; they passed by and were lost to time. Yet, we all do what we have to do in this life, and I could take some comfort in that, at the time, I did the best that I could. I learned in a very roundabout manner how to balance life and work and that is another story, but I learned later in my life, in my career and luckily, I learned before it greatly influenced my life, my marriage, and my health.

Now, I knew better.

It was as the old man used to say, "We stay stupid too long and become smart too late in life."

Sure, do miss the old man.

One byproduct of those times in the pulpit was that since Christmas Day was a regular workday for me, we happily borrowed from my English and Welsh heritage and revisited the Henson family tradition of celebrating Boxing Day. In retrospect, it worked out quite well, the children did not seem to mind so much, they moaned and groaned about leaving their stash of toys and fun under the tree to attend church all day, but in the end, those celebrations were memorable. We continued the tradition even now, and between the Hensons and the Redmonds, some of those celebrations, well, were more than memorable! We even snuck a few sips of the famous time bombs hidden in various cupboards here and there and everywhere. We had the religious side of Christmas, and then we unleashed the fun and celebrated Boxing Day with the grandest of times. This year would be no exception, and with a baby on the horizon and a marriage celebration creeping closer too, we all knew this year's holiday season was going to be very special.

The entire family, both on the Redmond side and the Henson side and the ones who were in between, all were members of Reunion Lutheran Church. I remained a member of the rank and roles, as did Binky right up until her passing. Her ashes remain there.

It was a very special place in our lives and in our hearts. I never felt any inclination to move my membership to another congregation. Honestly, even before my beloved wife passed, we were not that active in attendance of services there anymore. We provided our financial support and attended when we could, but for Harry and Rose, and now for me, in the new townhouse location, the church was quite a far distance from where we lived. Heather Sarah, Sarah, and now, Vance might attend services at Reunion, certainly, more than Harry, Rose and I did, but out of all of us, Paul William and Blue were very active members of Reunion.

Paul William and Blue lived in Hibernian, New Jersey, in the same town as the church, and only about four miles from the church property and the parsonage where our son spent most of his youth. He always loved the area, the natural beauty was unparalleled, and no one was surprised when he and his new bride settled down in his old hometown. They had a beautiful home, not too large a home and not too small a home either. The home was custom-built, brand-new on a secluded lot set back from the road and while Harry moaned and groaned that it was not eloquent enough, or large enough, for his beloved daughter, we all knew that the home was fabulous. In his heart, so did Harry. Harry simply required his usual bluster in order to emphasize how Blue Cloud was his little girl. The truth is that Paul William treated Blue like the princess that she was, Harry knew it and he appreciated it too!

Paul William had an outstanding job, his reputation as a notable sports writer grew each day, and the demands for him to expand his syndication and his commentary on hockey and other sports kept him very busy. Paul William gave me too much credit for his insight into hockey and the intricacy of the game, and the truth is that he was now a professor of the sport. He knew far more about the modern way of playing the game of ice hockey than I did. I was now a dinosaur because fiberglass goalie masks were now display items sitting upon museum shelves. Paul William had confided to me in private, shortly after they had announced Blue Cloud's pregnancy that he wished he could spend less time on the road and due to the heavy travel associated with it; he might give up the hockey beat writing with the Boston Bears and exchange it for syndication columns. He even hinted at following in his father's footsteps and dabbling in writing some books and sports-related fiction. Harry, Rose, and I were now partnering on a small publishing firm, so writing and publishing were part of our lives. That was something that I greatly supported and advocated for him to do. I told our son that my experience was that of a young father; you want to be home with your wife and newborn baby as often as you are able to do so.

Vance had a few precious days for a Christmas break in

the season, and he rushed home to spend the holiday with us and fall into his precious Heather Sarah's arms. We had a glorious reunion at the airport and Vance bunked in with Harry and Rose once again.

When Christmas Eve finally rolled around and Christmas Day arrived, the entire family worshiped together at Reunion Lutheran Church. Reverend Charles T. Braun Junior remained the senior pastor of Reunion Lutheran Church. He had relieved me many years ago when I received the promotion to the position of bishop. Pastor Braun Junior was an outstanding leader, and he had done a remarkable job at Reunion. I could not pride myself on many decisions that I had made in my career, but the one that I could say without reserve was the correct decision, was to appoint Reverend Charles T. Braun Junior as my replacement at Reunion. While it was always a bit strange to be sitting in the pews rather than standing behind the pulpit, I long ago accepted that this is where God wanted me to be.

It was always a huge homecoming for me whenever Pastor Paul John Henson returned to where he started his career in the ministry. All the good wishes and attention made it difficult to worship with my family. We did the best we could and I would have been happy to worship at a neutral site, but we did not want to disappoint Paul William and Blue Cloud, so we landed at Reunion. While I enjoyed the service, there remained many ghosts there and when we left the parking lot after the services, I had to admit that I turned my head, and tried hard not to look over at the parsonage that was our family's home for so many years. I drove to Christmas Eve services with Vance, Heather Sarah, and Sarah, and our daughter sat next to me in the front seat, with Sarah in the car seat in the rear, while Vance drove. Heather Sarah spotted my reaction when we passed the parsonage. She gently whispered to me that it was going to be okay, we were all still together and we always would be together. We felt the pain; we held each other's hands and remembered.

You never overcome the loss of a loved one. You only gain some type of cold acceptance of the loss.

It was a wonderful service on Christmas Eve, and Christmas Day was the same experience. Charles was a dynamic preacher and somehow, he managed to put a new spin on that well-worn, old story of the virgin birth.

Vance, Heather Sarah, and Sarah enjoyed the services at Reunion Lutheran Church and I had to admit they made a fine-looking family sitting there in the pew.

Blue Cloud looked ravishing.

She remained a goddess.

Paul William carefully followed her every move and hovered over her to a borderline level of annoyance. Once or twice, Rose and Heather Sarah assured him that everything was fine and for him to calm down, enjoy the service and ultimately to enjoy this magical time in their lives.

In pregnancy, Blue Cloud maintained her amazing figure, gorgeous looks and other features inherited (thankfully) from Rose and she was an incredibly attractive woman. I always thought how I saw a touch of Harry's mom in and around Blue's eyes and her forehead, and Harry agreed with me. But for the most part, Blue Cloud Redmond Henson was the spitting image of the lovely Rose Redmond. Now, she was even more so, with a radiant glow that expectant mothers receive from God. All of this, the new life and the old lives, remained a gift from God. Never should we forget that fact!

So far, the pregnancy was going along quite well. Blue Cloud tired easily and had some difficult bouts with morning sickness, but so far, there were no major complications. Her baby bump was quite large and Rose commented quite often at the size of it. Not knowing too much about baby bumps, I did not comment.

When one of her mother's comments at the size of the baby bump caught the ears of the entire family, I caught Blue looking over at Paul William. My habit of watching eyes from my hockey days led me to note that there might be a bit more to this than our children were choosing to share at this point.

Blue and Paul William had chosen not to reveal any details of the baby's sex or any other details to us. It was their personal choice and with Harry frantic beyond any comparisons; it was easy to see and understand their point.

We spent Boxing Day over at the Redmond's house and it was a wonderful time. Around a roaring fire in the majestic fireplace, we shared tales of old adventures and of our magnificent lives together. We all exchanged some gifts and as a prelude in the weeks before the holiday, all the men of the family, Harry, Vance, Paul William and I, plotted behind the scenes to spend an extra amount of attention and money on lavish jewelry for our wonderful women. None of us was quite sure of the motivation, but what the hell; it now sure worked in our favor! I gave our daughter and granddaughter matching diamond necklaces. Needless to say, the women admired the jewelry that all of us gave them for Christmas. Harry went overboard with lavish gifts for everyone, but he always did!

By now, the gang was accustomed to Heather Sarah, and Rose's amazing culinary skills and we all enjoyed their efforts in the kitchen. The two master chefs cooked up a Boxing Day feast for the ages. Huge servings of roast beef and Yorkshire pudding dishes mixed with Rose's magnificent Italian meals, to fill our stomachs and expand our waistlines. Heather Sarah maintained a longtime Henson family Boxing Day tradition by cooking an amazing Shepherd's Pie, based upon my dear Mum's famous recipe with Binky's modifications. Vance commented how lucky the men in these families were to have women who could cook as all of them could.

How true!

Maintaining my old playing weight from my hockey days was always going to be a challenge with talented cooks such as this in our lives. I kept my end of the bargain by serving up a Christmas Plum Pudding and now, with the meals finally ending, we were all sitting around the living room, in front of the fireplace, while enjoying some pudding and relaxing. This was a scene, which we had played many times before in our past. I ignored the ghosts of those memories, which tried very hard to interrupt my thoughts.

I focused on the present day.

The entire gang sat around the fireplace and a glorious Christmas tree, enjoying the day, trying hard to digest all the fabulous food. Since we now officially certified Dingleberry beer as "Too sweet," in a qualified taste test and sipping the dubious brew remained out of question, (except for Vance Howard) I sipped my Big Boulder beer and the rest of us enjoyed our favorite beverages.

Sarah sat on the floor watching, Dinky the Orange Teddy Bear Saves Christmas on the large screen television to Harry's rants and sad laments over the continual popularity of the famous orange bear.

"Stupid-ass cartoon been on forever. Don't that dopey bear ever grow old, keel over and croak?" He moaned when the famous theme music came on once again.

Blue Cloud scolded her father, "Daddy! Stop! Sarah will hear you. I love Dinky. He is an American icon."

I seemed to recall in one of our many past adventures, an incident of a long, long time ago. I recalled Harry suffering a scolding from an old woman in a store for berating Dinky, but that my dear reader is another story.

"I used to watch him all the time," Blue Cloud proudly proclaimed.

"Yeah, yeah, yeah, I know. My dear Blue Cloud, we raised ya, in case you forgot. So, sick of that dumb-ass bear.

You used to sit in front of the television and rock back and forth to the music and cry when the show ended. Your mother made me go to the store and buy twenty-two thousand videos of Dinky so that we could play them all day and night. I know the episodes by heart. I do like the dog, Sniffy. He is kinda cool when he takes a leak on Plugger the talkin' fire hydrant."

We focused on Dinky for a second when the show cut to a commercial. As commercials tend to do, they are always so loud in volume.

"Back again by popular demand is our famous, Big Bob's peppermint ice cream! Yes, for a limited amount of time around the holidays, I continue the tradition of my father, Big Bob Senior, and I have ordered our ice cream factories to produce my dad's favorite holiday ice cream from our secret family recipe! Hurry to your local food market and pick up a few cartons before they disappear and you have to wait until next Christmas to spoon up the minty, creamy, goodness!"

It was a commercial for another Big Bob's food product, with Big Bob Junior now taking over for his dad by yelling loudly in our ears for various foods and products from the food empire of Big Bob.

When the commercial ended, Blue Cloud leaned forward in her chair. She had a strange look on her face, and while she rubbed her baby bump, she said, "I just have to have some of that peppermint ice cream. It sounds so good." She turned to Paul William and put her arms around his neck while telling him, "I must have that ice cream. I am having cravings now!"

Harry had stood up from his chair; he was heading for the kitchen for a refill of his Wallcrawler cocktail when he heard the word "craving." He immediately spun around, handed Rose the empty drink glass and ran over to their daughter.

We all heard Rose sigh and mumble, "Oh no. This again.

Like Mother, like Daughter."

Rose must have passed the peppermint ice cream craving gene off to Blue Cloud.

Harry loudly bellowed, "Cravings! Are you having terrible cravings? Cravings are serious! Your mother had them! You popped out of her in seconds after she had 'em. Are they coming five minutes apart?"

"No, Daddy, those are contractions. We have months and months to go yet. I just want some of that ice cream. I have to have Big Bob's peppermint ice cream."

Harry stood over Blue Cloud and panted while he broke out in a cold sweat. I could see bits of plum pudding around his lips and his eyeballs rolled around in his head.

Oh, no! I have seen this a few times before too.

"Oh yeah, yeah, yeah, I got my baby babble mixed up. Well, cravings are serious too. C'mon, men! Nothing is too good or unachievable for our daughter! We are heading for Foodworld for gallons and gallons of Big Bob's peppermint ice cream! Hurry! Youse guys heard the loudmouth jerk on television there. They are gonna sell out!"

Rose put her head down and mumbled, "Two loudmouth jerks" and I tried hard not to laugh at her comparisons. Rose stood up and shook her head while trying hard to tell her husband as he dashed about the living room as if he were a madman, "One gallon is enough, dear Harry. One gallon, please. She will take one or two spoons of it and the rest will go to waste. She is just having some normal pregnancy cravings."

"Are holiday celebrations always like this, Paul?" Vance leaned in and asked me.

I knew what was coming, so I stood up and started to prepare to journey to Foodworld while answering Vance, "Usually. We have been down this road before too. It is a long story. Let me tell you the original story, it. . .."

Rose stood next to me, reached up, and put her hand over my mouth to stop me from speaking while telling me,

"Okay, not now, dear Paul. Please. I remember what happened so long ago. I was there too. All of your stories are wonderful, but so very long-winded. That is part of your magic, and one of the reasons why we all love you so much. However, it takes soooooo friggin' long for you to get to the point. No, you will not tell Vance or us the story right now. Let's all wait for the book."

Since the three of them inherited the Hobnobber head-nodding gene, Heather Sarah, Sarah, and Paul William stood in the center of the room and started a rapid head nod of confirmation. Therefore, I sighed and pretended to button my lips.

Harry stood in the center of the living room and waved his arms over his head while bellowing at us, "What are youse guys waiting for? We all know how twenty-seven goes on and on with his sermons and stories. One sermon was so long and boring that even Jesus, Moses, and Abraham fell asleep in Heaven listenin' to it! We have a mission. Fancy Vancie, you only had a few of those disgusting Dingleberries at dinner, and now have been only sipping seltzer water on ice and are the only one of us who is not half in the bag." Harry reached in his pocket, pulled out his car keys and tossed them to Vance who caught them. "You drive my Rhino. Get your coats and hats and let's roll!"

Paul William stood up, Vance kissed Heather Sarah and Sarah goodbye and I started to head for the door.

Rose gently grabbed Heather Sarah by her arm while telling her, "You had better go with them, Heather Sarah. Blue and I have Sarah. As you might recall, they tend to run into lots of trouble at food stores."

Our daughter looked at Rose with a little puzzled look on her face and she asked, "Really? They are going for ice cream at the friggin' Foodworld?"

"Heather Sarah, please, it is your father and Uncle Harry. Together . . . you know . . . the two of them at

Foodworld. We need the ice cream before the baby is in college."

Heather Sarah quickly nodded and said, "Gotcha, Auntie Rose. Let me down this wine in one shot and I will get my hat and coat."

Before we all knew it, we had parked in the local Foodworld parking lot, Harry flung the door of the Rhino open, and we tried to keep up with Harry as he sprinted across the parking lot to head for the front door of the store.

Heather Sarah commented while watching Harry sprint ahead, "I only run for my glasses of red wine and when jewelry is on sale. My chest is too huge, and it bounces too much. I am afraid of losing an eye."

I pushed Paul William ahead for our son to catch Harry, while telling him to stop Harry from picking out a shopping cart, because he always picks defective carts. Paul William nodded, and he ran to catch up with the ice cream pursuing madman.

Vance had now locked the Rhino, and he walked along with us as he asked, "Harry always picks out defective shopping carts? What the hell is with that?"

I shook my head and said, "Long story. He also has a hell of a time with zippers. Forget it. I will put it in a book."

"Way too much info, Paul. I got it."

Sure enough, by the time we arrived at the front entrance of the food store, Harry was arguing with Paul William over the cart that Harry had selected.

"Not that one. Dad Redmond, look, it has a broken wheel, see!"

"Oh well, then you pick it out! Hurry the hell up, I think I just spotted some chick with a nice ass and tight pants pushing a cart full of Big Bob's peppermint ice cream go by us. She might have bought it all up on us."

Paul William picked out a functioning cart. We rolled into the front of the store, and within about ten feet of the entrance, ran into a middle-aged man with two teenage boys with him. All three of them were wearing Boston Bears hockey sweaters.

Immediately, they spotted us. One of the teenagers pointed and shouted out, "Look! It is Vance Howard and twenty-seven! Right here in Foodworld in New Jersey!" They all smiled and rushed over to us in a wild scene as shoppers stopped and gawked at the scene.

"Oh, geez! Shit!" Harry stopped and complained, "You have got to be kidding me? I knew this would happen. Four steps into the store and some crazy nonsense happens. All of our lives it has been like this. Boston fans here in New Jersey. Youse guys are supposed to root for New Jersey and New York teams and hate all Boston teams. What the hell is wrong with youse guys?" Harry asked the fan club, which quickly surrounded us. They ignored Harry and his criticisms. The father wore a vintage twenty-seven "HENSON" sweater and his two sons both wore Vance Howard sweaters. They looked new and fresh, and I surmised that they were Christmas gifts.

"Wow! Who would have ever imagined that we would run into youse guys here in Foodworld! Wait until I tell the guys in the shop. I loved it last year when you taught old-time hockey and Vance showed 'dem bums how to play some old-time goalie! Man, you are big guys. You don't look that big on the television." The father was glowing and babbling to us as we shook their hands and thanked them for being fans.

I answered the father as the teenagers spoke with Vance and he signed autographs, "We live in New Jersey, well, Vance is from New York, but he is going to. . .."

Heather Sarah poked me and pulled at me to reach my ear to her lips and she whispered, "Long-winded bullshit, my dear father. We need the ice cream."

I nodded, stood up and said, "Well, it is a very long story."

Harry was beside himself with impatience, yet I could tell by the look in his eyes that he was a little jealous that Vance and I had the limelight and he did not. I knew the big guy, oh so well, and there was nothing that he enjoyed more than being the center of attention.

When Harry heard one teenager say to me, "It was an honor to meet youse guys," Harry dove into the conversation and introduced the world famous Harry M. Redmond Junior.

Suddenly, the ice cream could wait.

"Let me introduce myself to youse here guys. I am world famous too, ya know, as is my son-in-law here who is a famous hockey sports and news writer. I am Harry M. Redmond Junior and this here is Paul William Henson, writer par excellence."

The father, the teenagers and the crowd of gathered shoppers all looked at Harry and Paul William, shrugged their shoulders, and screwed their faces up like corkscrews. It was obvious that Harry did not ring any bells with them.

"Harry M. Redmond Jr. is the name. Inventor, businessman, entrepreneur, retired hockey player and part-time, old-time hockey coach, champion roller skater, kijillionaire, race car driver, hit songwriter, welder, a retired womanizer, and general, all around windbag and a loudmouth, but overall, I am not a bad guy!"

The father looked around and then said in less than an enthusiastic manner, "That's nice, never heard of you. Although, I do understand about the windbag part."

"What? Never heard of me! I used to run the Harry Frozen Food Empire, and I invented and marketed Harry Burgers! I sold the line off for bijillions of dollars to old man, Big Bob, who sold it to some overseas scoundrels who made the burgers thinner and the buns out of cheap flour!"

An elderly man, who was listening in, immediately reacted when Harry mentioned his line of frozen food and Harry Burgers.

"Oh, so you are the reason that I lost my job and Big Bob's Food Empire sent my job overseas!"

The elderly man rolled his cart over to us while wagging his finger at Harry. He started berating the big guy ranting and raving over his lost job, the downfall of American jobs, lost wages, evil corporations and other political drivel.

Heather Sarah shook her head, pulled both Vance and me aside, and said, "I see what Auntie Rose meant. Father, does this always happen to youse guys in food stores?"

"Usually, I must admit that this adventure is extra weird though. I must admit that the old chap is making some good points. . .."

"Sure, sure, sure, whatever. It is time to stop all this madness. Auntie Rose sent me for a reason. After all, I am my mother's daughter and inherited her amazing chest genes."

Heather Sarah unzipped her coat, tugged at her blouse to reveal a hint of her glorious cleavage, and immediately, all the men stopped speaking and their eyes focused squarely on our daughter's amazing chest. The teenagers were in their glory as their thoughts immediately ended of hockey and instead, shifted to some other types of a dream, a dream, which for them would shortly be their focus in life.

She wiggled by them, tugged at Vance's arm as she said, "Nice to meet all of you, but we have errands to run and I have better things to do tonight than linger here. Come along, my dear fancy Vancie. We need to get home for some fun."

"Holy smokes, the superstar always gets the gorgeous gal." The father said as his eyeballs bulged and he gawked.

Heather Sarah smiled and laughed as she passed the dumbfounded father and said, "Keep dreaming. Not in your lifetime, pal." She *was* her mother's daughter; all that was missing was a fluff of her hair and a dig of her foot.

This conversation and fanfare were now over.

Harry recovered and now with the fan club and crowd abandoning hockey and debating over lost jobs, in favor of dreams of lust and huge breasts, we made our way to the frozen food section.

As we approached the frozen ice cream case, Harry stopped us and he grabbed me by my shoulders while telling me, "Oh no. I know the drill here. We have been down these roads before. You, fancy Vancie, and Heather Sarah, wait here. Heather Sarah, we might need your chest, but for now, if you could zip up your coat, I would appreciate it. The heat from all the men in the store who are staring at your chest is gonna melt the ice cream. Paul William, ya follow me. We will get the ice cream."

We all nodded, stood off to the side and watched. Harry and Paul William stood in front of an ice cream freezer that stretched from one end of the aisle to the other end. There must have been fifty thousand different types of ice cream in the case. We could see them scanning the case, and Harry's limited patience tank quickly expired.

When an elderly store clerk wandered down the aisle, Harry grabbed him and nearly blew his head off by asking him, "Can you see okay, pal?"

The store clerk was a little puzzled, and he tilted his head towards Harry.

"What did you ask me?" The clerk asked. "I don't hear so well." It was then that we noticed the man wore hearing aids in both of his ears.

Harry looked over at me and shook his head while saying, "Years ago, they only hired people who were half-blind in one eye and could not see out of the other. Now, they hire guys who cannot hear! Remind me to open a hearing aid store in this town."

I shrugged my shoulders as Heather Sarah burst out laughing. Our daughter commented to Vance and me, "This is as if we are all stuck in an old vaudeville skit."

"Look, here pal. CAN YOU READ LIPS? CAN YOU

HEAR ME NOW?"

The clerk nodded his head and studied Harry's lips.

"DO YOU HAVE ANY BIG BOB'S PEPPERMINT ICE CREAM?"

"We might have some left. Been a run on it. Everyone comes in here looking for it and tells me they have pregnant wives and girlfriends craving it. Television shows must suck at night and everyone is making babies. Let's see now."

The three of them circled in and we could see the clerk scanning the frozen food case, "Let's see here, wintergreen mint, chocolate chip mint, butter mint, spearmint, peanut mint, whiz-bang Substantial Industries mint, banana mint, summer mint, spring mint, autumn mint, pumpkin mint, Christmas cookie mint. . .."

"Oh, geez! For the love of Pete! How many mints can ya have, pal?" Harry was flipping his lid.

"What did you say?"

"I SAID, FOR THE LOVE OF PETE, HOW MANY MINTS CAN YA HAVE, PAL?"

"Hey, I only stock 'em. I do not make 'em. Mr. Bluebird chirping in my ear mint, Christmas Tree Mountain mint, Big Boulder beer mint, happy mint, sad mint, Boryeungous flavored mint, Sal Zucchini Junior's famous, garlic-flavored, hitman for hire mint, Dingleberry beer flavored mint, that stuff is very sweet," on and on, he went down the line.

When Vance heard about the glorious ice cream version of his now favorite beer, he turned to Heather Sarah and asked, "I bet the Dingleberry mint is good. I might want to try some of that, honey. Can we get a gallon?" Heather Sarah only waved her hand at Vance and did not answer the question.

"Hmm . . . let's see. Next is Rabbi Fickleberg's famous kosher red wine mint ice cream. . .."

Now, Heather Sarah's taste buds were on fire, "Oh, dear

Father. We definitely have to try that for Auntie Rose and me!" I nodded as our daughter tugged at my arm when she heard of the rabbi's grand creation.

"Grouchy Bill's up your ass mint."

"Daddy, we will get two gallons of that ice cream for dear Martha."

"Nope, sorry pal, we are all out of peppermint."

The old chap stood up, blinked his eyes repeatedly and proudly announced the current status of peppermint ice cream.

Yes, we have been down this road before too.

That was the final straw. The big guy exploded.

"WHAT? ARE YOU KIDDING ME, PAL? THIS STORE IS OUT OF PEPPERMINT ICE CREAM AT CHRISTMAS TIME! WHAT KIND OF DUMP IS THIS? YOU HAVE EVERY FLAVOR OF ICE CREAM MADE ON THE FACE OF THE EARTH, BUT YOU RAN OUT OF PEPPERMINT!"

Harry calmed down a little, but not much, "CALL THE MANAGER OVER HERE. I HAVE HAD IT WITH THIS BULLSHIT!"

"Okay, I will get him on the telephone. Let me page him. Orsini the third is a pain-in-the-ass, though. Worse jerk than his old man was and let me tell you that his old man was a major jerk. We all jumped for joy when he retired and now his son is even worse."

The elderly man went to walk away and walk over to a pole where there was a paging telephone mounted. As the store's canned music system piped in a loud rendition of "Silver Bells," I knew that Harry had a flashback to the past.

Harry tugged at the clerk's arm and pulled him back to him, while asking, "SAY, PAL, THIS ORSINI GUY. DOES HE WEAR THICK GLASSES, IS STILL BLIND AS A BAT EVEN WITH THE GLASSES ON AND IS NERVOUS AS HELL?"

"Yeah, yeah, yeah. That is our big boss. Ya just described

'em, except that not only can't he see, but he cannot hear for shit too."

"DON'T BOTHER CALLING HIM. LOOK PAL, CAN'T YOU LOOK IN THE BACK FOR A FEW GALLONS? I BET YA GOT SOME STASHED BACK THERE."

The clerk shook his head and reported, "Nah. Chances are there ain't none back there. Even if there were a few gallons back there, I will get in big trouble for checking. Orsini the third tells us not to check on stuff and waste time helping stupid customers. We are just to tell 'em that we are out and get rid of youse nutcases."

Harry sighed, shook his head and waved over to Heather Sarah.

Heather Sarah nodded, sauntered and wiggled over to them, as Harry told her, "I need you and your chest, my dear niece. Sorry to keep flaunting you here, but shit, this is amazing. He can't hear, but he sure as hell will see *them*."

"No trouble, Uncle Harry. I have this covered in two ways. Say, Mistah Clerkie Guy. I MEAN, SAY MISTAH CLERKIE GUY," Heather Sarah bellowed as she unzipped her coat and we watched the clerk's eyes pop out of his head.

"CAN YOU CHECK IN THE BACK FOR *ME*?"

"I will be right back."

As the clerk scurried off to check the stockroom, Vance, and I joined up with Harry, Heather Sarah, and Paul William.

Heather Sarah grabbed Vance by his arm and made him lean down so that she could kiss his cheek as she whispered to him, "I hope that his old ass does not croak because of a heart attack before he returns."

In a flash, the older chap reappeared; he was wheeling a two-wheel hand truck, loaded with peppermint ice cream. Paul William, while pushing the shopping cart, tapped Harry on the arm and pointed to the coveted prize as it wheeled our way.

"Fantastic! Heather Sarah had to pull out the big guns, but it worked."

"GOOD WORK OLD HALF-DEAFIE MISTAH CLERKIE GUY! WE WILL TAKE 'EM ALL. THE SALE OF THE DAY!"

He looked at Harry, blinked and explained, "You were lucky. This transfer shipment just came in from Foodworld store x four dash three. They cannot sell even one gallon of the stuff. The television commercial must not be showing in that area yet.

We loaded up the ice cream. Harry whipped out fifty dollars and stuffed it in the older chap's pocket.

He bellowed in the clerk's ears, "HERE. YOU ARE ON THE PAYROLL. MERRY CHRISTMAS. PUT THE DOUGH TOWARDS NEW HEARING AIDS."

"Thanks buddy, hey don't tell, Orsini the third. Say, can I speak to the young woman again? Does she need me to look in the stockroom for anything else?"

She was our daughter and I might be a bit prejudiced, but she was her mother's daughter. Like Binky, Heather Sarah was an absolute stunner. Heather Sarah zipped her coat up, wiggled past the disappointed, but fifty dollars' wealthier clerk, as Paul William pushed the cart full of ice cream towards the checkout lanes.

While sauntering by him, and fluffing her hair in her best Binky imitation, our daughter whispered, "Sorry, pal. We are good. One view is enough. Your heart will give out."

"What did you say, young lady?"

We waved goodbye and followed Paul William to the checkout lanes.

"Are ya puttin' this adventure in a book, Paul?" Harry asked me as we followed the happy ice cream trail.

"Why, yes, of course. One long, chapter on this one."

"Figures that it would be long."

Paul William stopped short of the checkout lane and

gathered us in. He was a longtime veteran of the eternal weirdness that followed Harry and me around, and he took control of the situation and entered logic into the madness.

"Look, I can see from here that the checkout woman has hearing aids in both of her ears. This will be more madness and by the time we get back, it will be next Boxing Day. Why don't the three of you go and wait in the truck? Our father and my father-in-law have this cloud of weirdness that floats above them all the time, and as far as Vance goes, chances are that either a hockey fan will recognize him or some love-struck teenage girl will see him."

Harry nodded his head, tugged at my arm and pulled me along, as he began a typical whacky Harry speech. A speech laced with his unusual logic.

"Good thinkin,' Paul William. Glad ya got ya brains from your mother and not from twenty-seven. I can see why our beloved Blue Cloud married ya. Glad ya escaped the Old Lady Syndrome gene too and apparently, your ding-dong, dinger works okay, since Blue Cloud looks as if she is gonna float away tomorrow. That is why this ice cream is so important. C'mon men, he is right. We can wait in the Rhino."

"Okay. Good. Thank you, Dad Redmond. Not too sure all of that babble was necessary, but whatever. My sister and I will check out and meet youse guys there. That way, all the weirdness will be neutralized."

That was the best suggestion yet.

Heather Sarah, and Paul William returned, we loaded the ice cream up and just when Vance turned the key to start the Rhino, Paul William's cellphone rang. He answered it as Vance backed out of the parking space. Paul William reached over as he held the phone to his ear and touched Vance on the shoulder, held his finger up to suggest for him to stop and wait. Now we all listened.

"Okay Blue, yes, yes, yes, darling. No, we are still here. Yes, *still*. It is a long story, but Momma Rose will understand. Yes. Okay. Peach gelatin, okay . . . lots of it. Got it. Do you still want the ice cream? No, okay, we will return it."

Vance sighed, put the Rhino in forward gear and pulled back into the parking space.

Heather Sarah shook her head and moaned and groaned at the news, "Oh well. My dear brother, I will go in with you because I think I will grab some of those cool flavored ice creams for all of us."

Vance turned around and looked at Heather Sarah while asking her, "Are you gettin' a gallon of that Dingleberry mint ice cream?"

"Sure. You maniacs wait here. Paul William and I will be back in five minutes without you three pineapples."

Chapter Fourteen

The Night Always Comes

The hockey season ended and Vance Howard was the best goalie in the league, in fact, I as well as many others, felt as if he was the best goalie in the world. While the Boston Bears fell just one game short of playing for the league championship when they lost a hard-fought seventh game of the divisional series, we all knew that the Bears would win it all next year. They were close to putting all the final pieces together to assemble a championship hockey club. Vance unanimously won the Rookie of the Year award, led the league in goaltending stats to win the top goaltender award, finished second in the voting for the league's most valuable player and most importantly for him, and Heather Sarah and Sarah, he made it through the season without any serious injuries. Sure, he was bent, broken, stitched up a little here and there, and sore, but it was nothing that his young body could not heal with some time off. Vance told me that there were no truer words spoken than when I told him that the "Hockey season was a marathon and not a sprint."

Coach Bettermann won "Coach of the Year" and Brian McClure won the coveted "Executive of the Year." The Bears were on their way now!

It was now the off-season, and we anxiously waited for what was going to be a glorious summer. We all wanted Vance home so that he could spend time with his family and relax for a bit. For Vance, he could take some time off, he knew that his off-season team would be there to help him train and keep him sharp and on track. We always would be there. For me, I knew that after some workouts and hard skates, I could always get my old, worn-out ass into that wonderful soaking tub after acting like a crazy, old fool out on the ice rink.

Heather Sarah and Harry had been out and about and all over while house shopping together the last few weeks. Heather Sarah and Harry had narrowed their search down to one specific home, and I knew that Heather Sarah was eager for Vance to return home, to not only see him but also so that they could all check the home out and agree that it was the residence, where they wanted to live while they began their lives together.

I did head up to Boston for a long weekend and shared a glorious reunion with Brian and his staff. I told Brian about my new office and wet-bar and proudly showed some pictures of it, while teasing with him that the Bears paid for the wet-bar, as well as my new townhouse. Brian proudly showed me the now famous bar napkin, we scribbled on now neatly tucked in a frame, hanging on the wall of his office. We hung out with the gang at the hotel and pulled a few, "all-nighters." There, we all enjoyed the success of the hockey season, as well as our friendship, Brian, Tommy Hayward, Bryce Eddings, Coach Bettermann and Gibby Gibbons. I rather enjoyed the stuffy old lawyer with a heart of gold. When Gibby had a few drinks in him, he was a ton of fun. We hung out at the hotel bar until very late hours, all drank too much, flirted with Janet a little too much, and we had a wonderful time. Old-time hockey pals in a modern hockey world. We created wonderful memories that weekend, we really did.

Brian was very gracious for my dedication and assistance, and he remained a dear and close friend. In fact, I considered all of them to be my close and wonderful friends. I promised not to allow time, distance and life to separate all of us ever again. Brian knew that I had accomplished what I promised him that I would do, and he thanked me repeatedly for my efforts. I also kidded with Brian, Bryce, Tommy Hayward, and Gibby Gibbons over the fact that they still had my services free of charge, since Vance was marrying our daughter.

Coach Bettermann thanked me, and I assured the old coach that I would always be available for some advice if he needed me. He was an exceptional man, a great hockey coach, a good friend, and my own soul rejoiced at the renewal of his soul. Sometimes, all we need is to regain our purpose. I could testify to that fact.

It was now mid-June and Blue Cloud was nearing the end of her pregnancy. Other than a frantic Harry, the situation was under control. The women of the family commented on how large Blue Cloud's belly bump was in size. It did seem strange, but Paul William and Blue Cloud never answered those comments, nor did they reveal the details of the baby's sex. Even the obligatory baby shower, which Heather Sarah and Sarah hosted for Blue Cloud, went "old school." They exchanged only generic gifts, as was the practice years ago, before technology was around to reveal the secrets of the womb beforehand.

Rose confided to me that she felt as if Blue Cloud was having twins, but we did not mention anything to our children as to what we felt or believed.

If they chose to keep it a private matter, then so be it.

Everyone respected their wishes and did not pry with the exception being, of course, Harry, who constantly harped on the subjects and moaned and groaned over the suspense. When he reached the upper echelons of super-annoyance level, Blue Cloud or Rose shut him down very quickly. I did feel as though Blue Cloud and Paul William did not release the details on purpose, in an effort to prevent Harry from being crazier and more frantic than he was now, and knowing the big guy as well as I did, then our children might have made a very wise decision.

Blue Cloud was having a difficult time getting around these days and with hockey now in the off-season, it was easy for Paul William to work from home, write for his syndicated commitments and tend to his wife's needs.

In this off-season, Vance worked out constantly, and I helped him as much as I could, but there was not going to be the constant coaching of twenty-seven, as was the case during the previous summer. I enjoyed skating, some workouts in the gym and other activities, which kept me in good condition and feeling well. Jim O'Malley and Vance were now very close and Jim often worked out, taught, coached and skated with Vance on the ice. Jim was still coaching his high school team, and he was able to recruit his team to shoot around on Vance and keep him sharp. The young players on the team loved hanging with the famous Vance Howard! A hockey dream comes true for them!

Heather Sarah, and Vance did select that home they had their eyes upon and since it was new construction, as was the case with our townhouse, there was a bit of a delay in moving in. The home was actually in a brand-new subdivision here in Wayne, and it was only about five or six miles from our place. The home would be ready to move into by the end of the summer and until then Vance, Heather Sarah, and Sarah stayed with us in the townhouse. Rose often came over and she tended to everyone's needs, cooked for us and kept us all in line and in "smooth operating condition."

Sarah loved playing almost every day with Grandpa, and I now felt the same as Harry did when Heather Sarah and Sarah stayed at the Redmond's house. I consumed so many cups of make-believe tea that I started to believe that I had to go and pee. Sarah, as her mother and in fact, her late grandmother tended to do, would wear dresses, blouses and skirts most of the time. Heather Sarah, Rose, and when she felt up to it, Blue Cloud absolutely loved taking her shopping, buying her new clothes, combing her hair and making her gorgeous every day. Sarah was quite the little woman and someday, she will steal the hearts of many men. The dresses and blouses were beautiful and elegant attire; however, I must admit that when Rose and Heather Sarah brought Sarah shopping one day, and returned home with two hockey sweaters, one throwback, Long Island Roosters number twenty-seven and one Boston Bears number one; I jumped with joy to see them. I was even more thrilled when Sarah proudly paraded around our home, while wearing my hockey sweater with a pair of black dungarees and a pair of black canvas sneakers on her feet and dark sunglasses over her eyes. Her attire looked rather familiar! In fact, Sarah wore my sweater more often than she wore Vance's sweater.

Vance complained a bit over it, I took the opportunity to tease him, and one day when he was being a bit of a crybaby, Heather Sarah bluntly told him, "To get over it! Grandpa is Grandpa and he might have worn number twenty-seven, but he will always be number one!"

No way was Vance going to argue that one, and neither was I.

I must admit that I was curious about their wedding date, since Vance and Heather Sarah shared a common bed under our roof, with her father who is a clergyman present, but as I mentioned, I never was a judgmental pastor, just in this case, a curious one. The townhouse was large enough that we all had our privacy and it worked out well for all concerned. No father ever thinks any man is good enough for his daughter and while I thought highly of Vance and respected him, I secretly wished that Heather Sarah and Vance would tell us the actual wedding date or give us a ballpark indication of what their plans were. That date remained mired in as much mystery as the baby details were. It seemed as if they knew so much more than what they were telling anyone. My senses were tingling, and I wondered what it was that our children were plotting.

"Dear Father, it is time," Paul William told me over the telephone on a Saturday in late July. I was sitting in the kitchen of the townhouse nursing a cup of tea when the telephone call came through. I looked at my watch and I realized that the date was the twenty-seventh of July. I had inexcusably lost track of the days. The whirlwind that had become our lives caused me to lose track. It was something that I was not too proud of at the moment.

Grandpa asleep at the switch!

I started to stutter and stall, and Paul William jumped in over my thick-tongued ways.

"We are packing up and heading to the hospital. Saint Joseph's Hospital. Blue Cloud's water broke about three hours ago, and the labor is hard and steady now. I will keep you posted. If you want to let my sister, Aunt Dottie and everyone on your end know, then I appreciate it. I will make the dreaded phone call to my in-laws. I hope and pray that Rose answers and not Harry.

"Oh, wow! Okay, I am sorry, but you caught me a little off-guard here. Lost track of the days and now my heart is racing, so I am a little befuddled. Yes, of course, I will let everyone know here. I am sure that Heather Sarah, and Vance will both ride with us to the hospital. Everyone wants to come along to the hospital and I know Sarah will be very excited. As of late, all Sarah has talked about is how she wants to see the baby."

"Yes, I have heard that story. Sarah is a darling. She is already planning tea parties. Hey, how about a quick prayer for all of us, Father? Can we do that here on the telephone?"

"Sure, absolutely."

I said a quick prayer for the health and safety of everyone. A prayer for Mother, Baby, Father, and for the wisdom of the doctors, nurses and caregivers. We prayed together over the telephone.

"Amen. How is Blue Cloud feeling, Paul William?"

"Amen. Ah, geez, she is in labor, Father. How the hell well can she feel?"

"Yes. Sorry, dumb-ass question. Please drive to the hospital carefully, Paul William. Call or text me whenever you can. Good luck with Harry. I will do the best that I can with him. For sure, two seconds after you hang up with him, he will be screaming in my ear over the telephone. We all love you and Blue and the baby too."

"Two seconds? More like one. We love you too. Yes, I will keep you posted on the telephone and by texting. When we think, the birth is close, I will give you a heads up. It could be a long time. All will be well. God is with all of us. I will drive carefully. Hey, before you hang up, dear Father."

"Yes?" I asked before I hung up.

"Do you not find it interesting that today is the twenty-seventh? It is the exact date the doctors predicted."

I smiled before answering and with the smile frozen on my face I said, "Your mother would not have allowed it to be any other date."

We ended the telephone call with promises to stay in touch as the labor evolved. Heather Sarah appeared behind me and I surmised that she overheard at least enough of the conversation to know what was now happening.

I turned around and hugged her while whispering, "Your brother. It is baby time. They are off to the hospital." We did not speak for a long time; we only rocked back and forth and held onto each other.

Finally, she gently whispered, "I am sure that a million thoughts are racing through your mind, and that one of them is that you wished that dear Mother was here to see the birth of another grandchild. She is here in spirit, Daddy. I am quite sure that she is here with all of us."

"I know that she is, my dear Heather Sarah. No question that she is."

Heather Sarah held onto me and leaned her head gently on my chest while softly sighing. Such joy and such pain, too. The circle of life was amazing and agonizing.

Heather Sarah finally asked me, "How many more minutes before Uncle Harry calls screaming into the telephone that we all have to get to the hospital?"

I looked at my watch and predicted, "Well, Paul William was calling him when we hung up, so the way that I figure it, Harry will be calling in about another two minutes or so."

Three minutes later my cellphone rang, Heather Sarah laughed and she let go of me and shook her head.

"You are driving all of us, so I am going to pour a huge glass of wine for me, grab Vance a Dingleberry Beer and listen to this one. Good luck with this crazy parishioner, Pastor Paul."

I nodded and pushed the answer button.

"Hello."

"ARE YOU ON THE WAY TO THE HORSEPITAL?"

"Hi, Harry. No, I just hung up with Paul William. The labor has really just begun. We have to wait a bit more. How are you?"

"HOW AM I? HOW THE HELL DO YOU THINK THAT I AM? SHIT! WAIT! NO TIME FOR BEING AN OLD LADY, TWENTY-SEVEN. NOT NOW! OUR DAUGHTER IS HAVING A BABY! THIS IS OUR GRANDCHILD, PAUL. WE ARE GONNA BE GRANDPAS TOGETHER. WE GOTTA GET TO THE HORSEPITAL RIGHT AWAY."

"Okay, calm down, buddy, easy now. I understand, but you are blowing my ears off. Breathe. Breathe. We do not have to leave yet. Labor can take a very long time. We will all relax and wait for Paul William to call and then. . .."

"A long time! Blue Cloud popped out of Rose like a champag-na-a-roo-ski cork pops out of a bottle on New Year's Eve. Youse guys almost had to push her back in. She popped out in fifteen minutes."

"Harry, it was not fifteen minutes. It was fast, but it was not that fast. Look, why don't you come over here and we will wait together. You can have a few drinks and relax. I will drive all of us to the hospital. I have been through many births of both of our children and my church parishioners too."

"Okay, Paul, okay. I am calm and I got this. Did you pray for 'em yet?"

"Done deal."

"Okay, thanks. You got a hotline to God. Even though you go on and on, God listens to you. He don't listen to me all the time, cuz I am so loud and full of bullshit."

I did not always quite follow Harry's weird and strange logic, but on that one, he might have a valid point.

I watched as Heather Sarah carried the beer and a glass of wine and while she walked past me, she playfully bumped me with her hips and laughed as she winked at me. She was fooling around with me and at my feeble efforts to calm Harry down.

Our daughter was now enjoying my efforts at calming the mad beast, "Oh boy, this is going to be a good one. Go get him, Pastor Paul, or I mean, dear Father."

Vance sipped his beer and shook his head while he listened. He too had doubts that I would have success with number thirty-five. Heather Sarah, and Vance were both "of little faith" in my abilities to calm my best buddy down.

"Look, all is well, Harry. Just relax, grab Rose, and come on over here. I know about these things. We can all wait here together. Not all babies are born quickly."

"Okay, yes. Ya are da man. Ya always know what to do, and ya always know the best thing to do. Good idea, twenty-seven. I have it all under control now. I took a few deep breaths and I am good. See ya in a few. Thanks buddy."

"CLICK!"

The line went dead and I self-assuredly hung up and

tucked the phone in my pocket.

I puffed my chest out proudly, began praising my expert negotiating, and counseling skills with difficult people, "See, all of ye of little faith family. All I had to do was talk a little sense to him and he calmed right down. He is grabbing Rose and they will be over in a bit. He is relaxed now. I am a skilled pastor, you know. A bishop and part of my training and skills. . .. "

My cellphone ringing interrupted my speech. It was Harry.

I put my finger up to suggest a pause, as my family watched me answer the call, "Hello."

"Screw this waiting bullshit! Rose and I are heading for the horsepital. I will break every damn speed limit on the way there too. See you there!"

"CLICK!"

The line went dead.

I sighed and shook my head as I put my cellphone back into my pocket. Heather Sarah, and Vance both tried very hard not to laugh at me because my expert pastoral skills seemed to have fallen a bit short.

"Okay, gang, suck down the wine and beer, pack up little Sarah, I will grab my bag with my pastoral garments, prayer materials and Bible in it and let's all be off to the horsepital."

Vance screwed his face up and asked, "To where?"

Harry was a basket case. He paced the floors back and forth and back and forth, ranting, raving, and I almost wished that we had a bottle of whiskey with us to give him a shot or two to calm him down. Long ago, we fed Harry a few shots of hooch at his first wedding, when Father Mark could not stand his incessant talking and pacing, while waiting for the ceremony to begin. Since no one had a flask, we needed another solution to calm him down.

Rose did her best to calm him down, but it was to no avail. He listened carefully to his wife, and then continued to go crazy, two seconds after acknowledging that, she was correct and that he needed to calm down.

Countless times, Heather Sarah encouraged him to sit with her and Vance and hear about the hockey season, or better yet, to play with Sarah, but it was to no avail. The big guy continued to pace.

No luck.

When Blue Cloud was born, Harry had only about an hour or so to go bananas and to lose his mind. In addition, he had his partner in mutual calamities, Bishop Von Houten with him to go nuts with, and Harry drove us to the hospital, so he was preoccupied and concentrating on the driving. In comparison to this event, Harry had very little whacko time during that famous adventure; Blue Cloud arrived into this world in record time. This one was different, and the full Harry nervous level was unleashed. Every nurse, or person who wandered by the waiting room that remotely resembled a medical practitioner, Harry pulled him or her aside and asked if there were any updates about the birth yet. He even stopped the porter emptying a trash can and asked the porter for an update!

The poor man sheepishly looked at Harry and then at the family, shrugged his shoulders and he answered factually by saying, "Ah, sorry, but I am a porter, mister. I empty trash cans, mop floors, clean hallways and restrooms."

Harry drooled and his eyes bugged out as he realized his error and apologized.

"Oh yeah, yeah, yeah. Sorry, I saw the uniform and thought that you might be a doc. Here, please, take this here fifty bucks, pal, for doing such an outstanding job. I am the world famous, Harry M. Redmond Junior, and my grandkidler is being born right now. You are on my payroll now. I might need you later on for some diaper cleanup duty," Harry told him as he handed the now smiling porter a tip.

I saw Harry notice a maintenance mechanic walking down the hallway carrying light bulbs, tools and a ladder, and when Harry looked as if he was going to flag him down, I jumped up, grabbed his arm and stopped him.

"Harry, he is changing light bulbs, not delivering babies."

"Okay, yeah, yeah, yeah, I see that now, twenty-seven. I thought he might be an ogee-groinocologist and know something, or he might have the inside scoop of what is going on in there. Maintenance guys know everything and they got keys to all the rooms too."

Heather Sarah, and Rose shook their heads at his mispronunciation and logic but no one answered him or tried to correct him because at this point, Harry would not have paid attention, anyway. Somewhere along the line, Harry inherited the famous New Jersey tradition of chronically mispronouncing people, places, words and things.

Even little Sarah started to have her little nerves worn thin by the big guy. Sarah was under the watchful eyes of Vance and Heather Sarah. Our granddaughter played in a corner of the waiting room, within one of the typical play areas that hospitals set up and are equipped with various toys and activities.

She turned to us and bluntly stated, "Uncle Harry is talking a lot." Then she asked her mother, "Mother, can't you step on his foot really hard and make him stop talking, like you do to Grandpa when his stories take too long to tell?"

Little kiddies notice everything.

"No, Sarah. Mother cannot do that right now. Show us what you are playing with," Heather Sarah planted a diversionary tactic.

Rose then leaned in, whispered and asked our daughter, "Do you really do that to your father?"

"Sure do, so did Mother and Granddad Hobnobber. I

learned it from them. God created the universe in less time than it takes my father to tell some of his stories."

No one argued with Heather Sarah. I tried not to take these mild and constructive criticisms to heart.

My cellphone rang and everyone jumped up and gathered around me. It was now well into the labor period, and I mouthed to my family that it was Paul William calling on the phone. Immediately, Harry ran over to me, leaned on my shoulder and panted deeply as he tried to listen in on the conversation.

"Hey, Paul William. What is going on?"

Paul William carefully explained that it was not going to be much longer. The labor had progressed, but there was not enough dilation occurring, so the doctor recommended a caesarean procedure and Blue Cloud and Paul William agreed. They were now preparing Blue for the procedure and for the delivery. Paul William only had a few seconds to call before he jumped back in for the delivery. He emphasized how everything was fine, that this was the best way to go. I told him that I understood, I told him that all would be well and that we would pray. I let him go and knew that the wait would not be much longer.

"UNDERSTOOD WHAT? WHAT THE HELL WAS HE BABBLING ABOUT THERE?"

"Harry," I put my arm around him and pulled him in tightly. I waved for Rose to come over to assist me, and Rose joined us. I wrapped one arm around Rose and used my strength to hold Harry close to me and try to bring him under control. "Look, it is going to be a caesarean delivery. They are going to do a C-section to deliver the baby. This is not an unusual procedure to occur. Stay with us now. All is well."

"They are going to do a Caesar sectional? What the hell is that? Ya know that all this baby stuff is not up my alley. Paul, please just pray and invoke the power of Heaven to protect our precious Blue Cloud and the baby. Please, only you can do this. Only you, twenty-seven. Please."

"It is a type of surgical procedure. I will do all that I can, Harry. I am here. Please, please, please, all is well. I can tell you that everything is going to be fine. The spirit in my heart is very calm. Heaven is guiding all of this. This is a night of joy. Please believe me that it is. You need to trust God and trust your hearts. All is well."

Rose looked at me with pleading eyes and I knew that she was hoping that I could pull something out of my bag of tricks to settle Harry down. I nodded to her, stood up and waved my hands, while asking everyone to gather in prayer. I thought a group prayer was in order and that some divine intervention might just settle Harry down.

It was worth a shot.

"Please, let's gather in and have a family prayer here." I smiled at our daughter, held her hand as she stood up and I continued, "I promise to keep it short. My feet are sore enough."

We all held hands and formed a circle.

Vance picked up little Sarah, and he held her in his arms, while I began praying, "This is a special night, dear Lord. Our family will grow, as will your kingdom. We ask your blessings on Mother, Baby, and Father and for your wisdom to guide the doctors as they care for Blue Cloud and the precious new life entering this world. This is a special family, a family that has been through so much together over these many years. We are not only family, but we are all special friends, our lifetimes joined by special bonds and special love throughout many adventures, many days, and many years. We ask for your blessings and for your guidance from Heaven. Amen."

A few minutes after we finished the prayer, while we stood in discussion, we heard a voice behind us ask, "Are all of you all part of the Henson and Redmond families?" We turned around and there was a doctor standing there, in his surgical garb and a wide smile on his face.

We all rushed over and simultaneously answered, "YES!"

Harry rushed in and nearly blew the doctor over with his introduction, "Harry M. Redmond Junior here, Doc! *The* world-famous Harry M. Redmond Junior. Blue Cloud is our daughter!"

The doctor reached out and shook Harry's hand while smiling and he proudly said, "Nice to meet you. I am Doctor Melvin Bergstein. Well, congratulations there, world famous, Harry M. Redmond Junior. You are the proud grandfather of two, incredibly healthy, bouncing, and I must say, very handsome twin boys! Everything is well, with babies and with Momma too! Congratulations to you all. Better, start saving your pennies for college and those bills now, because you have two of them! From here on in, it is two of everything!"

I felt my heart jump in my chest and now, I could not help but rush into the fray as I heard the entire group of family members gasp at Doctor Bergstein's incredible news.

I heard Rose shout out and proclaim, "Twins! I knew it! She was so huge!"

It was a good thing that Vance and I stood next to Harry because I saw his knees buckle and he started to wobble a bit. I was holding Rose's hand, and I let go of her hand, Vance quickly handed Sarah to Heather Sarah and the two of us caught the big guy and steadied him back to his feet.

"Did you just say, two kidlers, Doc? Twins? Two . . . as in two boys in one shot?"

"I did! It is fantastic, huh?"

"HOLY SHIT! FOR THE LOVE OF PETE! I LOVE THIS! NOW, THIS IS WHAT I AM TALKING 'BOUT! PAUL WILLIAM HAD SUPER KID MAKING STUFF! WE GOT OURSELVES A WHOLE DAMN HOCKEY DEFENSE IN ONE SHOT! WE GOTTA GO OUT AND BUY TWO OF EVERY DAMN THING! TWO CRIBS, TWO STROLLERS!

TWO HOCKEY SWEATERS! TWO HOCKEY STICKS! TWO OF THOSE PLASTIC SUCKY PACIFIC THINGYS. TWO OF THOSE SWINGY THINGYS! GOOD THING, GOD GAVE BLUE CLOUD TWO, BIG, GORGEOUS BREASTS!"

Harry stopped screaming; he calmed for just a moment and shifted gears as the big guy overwhelmed Doctor Bergstein.

He put his arm around him as he commented, "She is gonna need both of 'em, right, Doc? After all, she has got two hungry boys and they could both be hungry at the same time."

"Well, I guess you do have a point, Mr. Redmond."

Harry abandoned Doctor Bergstein, grabbed Rose, bent her over, gave her one of his famous grandstanding kisses, and told Rose, "I love you to the moon, to the stars and beyond, dear Rose!"

The emotions overcame all of us and we all hugged and celebrated together.

As we followed Doctor Bergstein up the hallway to see Blue Cloud, the twins, and Paul William, Harry put his arm around the doctor, kissed the top of his baldhead (the doctor was very short) and told the doctor, "I love ya, Doc. You are on my payroll now. I am a kijillionaire ya know. Do you need a new car, a few thousand-prescription pads printed up, or a new stethoscope? Maybe a bunch of tongue depressors? Whatever it is that ya need—it is yours."

"Well, that is very kind of you. I will send my bill to you and we can negotiate."

Harry ran over the top of Doctor Bergstein and he rambled on as we continued to walk.

"Maybe, I will donate enough dough for a new wing for this here horsepital. We can name it after you and me, Doc. Of course, my name will need to be in bold letters and listed first. The World Famous, Harry M. Redmond Junior and Doc Bergstein Wing. Did you know that I am an expert on all this here baby stuff? Yup. Let me tell ya, while we were waiting, they were all going nuts. Me, nah, I was cool, calm and collective. I told 'em, to calm down. I told 'em, that this here, Doc Bergstein, he is the best in the business. How many babies ya deliver in your day?"

"Oh my, maybe a thousand."

"That is awesome. And these twins, they are the best, right?"

"Oh yes, Mr. Redmond. Very handsome boys."

"Say, the long-haired guy here following me is my best buddy. He is the other Grandpa in this mix. We have been buddies since we were ten years old. Best friend in the world. Ever. Never been a better man that ever walked this Earth. Ever. Yup, now we are Grandpas together. It is a long story. Someday, over a few Wallcrawlers, I will give you the inside scoop. Ya got to come over to our mansion and I will tell you of the adventures of Harry and Paul. Or ya can read 'bout all of 'em in the books he writes. Well, some of 'em, we can't tell a few of the stories, cuz the stattuah of limertations might not be run out on some of the stuff we did. Not only is he a writer, but he is the world famous, hockey goalie, number twenty-seven, world famous, Lutheran pastor and bishop too."

"Oh my, Mr. Redmond. I would very much enjoy that but I only drink kosher red wine."

"Yup, oh yeah, no trouble at all. We got that stuff by the gallons in our cupboards. Certified high-test, kosher go-go juice by a rabbi buddy of ours. Ya see, that beautiful chick who is a'walkin' arm-in-arm with the long-haired guy, ya know, the chickie-poo with the gorgeous chest and remarkably tight ass is my wife. What a knockout she is. The other gorgeous chick there is my niece. Well, sorta my niece, but she is the long-haired hippie's daughter. She is gonna marry the big handsome guy holding that beautiful little girl in his arms. He is fancy Vancie, superstar goalie for the Boston Bears, and the little beauty is my grandniece. Are ya a hockey fan, Doc?"

"By the way, you have a beautiful family, as far as sports, no hockey, but I do enjoy football."

Harry rolled over poor Doctor Bergstein, "Fancy Vancie is famous, not as famous as I am, but close. For two ugly mugs from the poor neighborhood, we'all got us some gorgeous women in our lives. My wife is a triple knockout, and she still keeps me up all night. Say, Doc, you must be Jewish. In fact, you are like two Jewish docs in one. Berg and stein. Ya gonna send two bills or just one?"

Yes, indeed, there was only one, Harry M. Redmond Junior.

"Everyone, I present to you, Paul William Henson, the third and Harry Michael Henson."

When Heather Sarah heard Paul William introduce the twins to the family, she whispered to a few others and to me, "Hold on world, shit, now there are four of 'em. Two of each. The Foodworld is going to lock the doors when they show up."

Between laughs at our daughter's blunt and correct observation, it brought tears to your eyes to hear our son proclaim the names and introduce us to the twins. I tried my best to be the professionally trained pastor, hold up, and not wither in my emotions, but instead, I ended up being Grandpa and Dad.

I am not ashamed to say that I did a very poor job in the withering department.

They were indeed; two handsome babies and Blue Cloud, who was doing her best to stay awake, had to be the most beautiful mother on the face of the Earth. I put my prayer shawl on, my prayer colors, my wooden cross, and then proceeded to break every rule in the religious book. First, I insisted on all the nurses and Doctor Bergstein to stay and join us in the prayers and celebration. Respecting the beliefs of the man who just brought this joy into our lives with his skill, and took such good care of Blue Cloud, I prayed a traditional Jewish blessing in Hebrew and then a Lutheran blessing over the babies, and everyone in the room.

I finished with the sign of the cross on the foreheads of the twins, and then on Blue Cloud's forehead and said another prayer, "May the words of our prayers, and the joy of our hearts reach all the way to Heaven. Glory and praise be to HaShem!"

While the gang gathered, congratulated and checked on Blue Cloud and Paul William, I wandered over to where a nurse washed and diapered the two boys. Harry joined me, he put his big arm around me, and he hugged me tightly. He had tears in his eyes, and I did too, as we stared at the two boys. A lifetime together, and this was the ultimate culmination of all the adventures of Harry and Paul. Who could have ever imagined that after all of this time, all we had been through together and here we stood? The two of us, looking down upon our two grandsons. It was the end of God's plan for Harry and Paul and the beginning of a new one for the two boys in front of us. Harry and Paul. The circle was now complete. The wonder of it all made your heart tremble, and it shook the very earth we stood upon together. Now, the two brothers will begin their own circle of life together.

"Ya, know, Paul, I think that Harry is just a little bigger than Paul is. Doc Bergstein said that Harry was born first. Of course, he was."

"Of course. Harry might be a little bigger. You are right. Not by much, but Harry is a little bigger. Yup."

"I think he is, but Paul, of course, has more hair."

"He does, and I hate to say it, but not only is his hair longer, but look down there, Harry. His well, his, well, you can see it. Paul's is a lot bigger . . . must be the genes. Yup, that is Paul all right."

On a glorious, late July day, full of golden sunshine and

beaming rays from Heaven, in a morning worship service at Reunion Lutheran Church in Hibernian, New Jersey, I baptized Harry Michael Henson and Paul William Henson the third. In the afternoon of that same glorious day, in the same church, Pastor James T. O'Malley and Pastor Paul John Henson conducted a glorious ceremony, and we presided over the marriage of Vance David Howard and Heather Sarah. In the end, it seemed as if our children did have a glorious plan for two celebrations in one day. The wedding was a magnificent service and let me tell you that to share it with my old hockey and pastoral friend was more touching than I could ever tell you in words.

O'Malley and I went back a bit in history together too.

Looking back over the years, we chewed an awful lot of ice together.

Later that evening, in an exquisite restaurant and banquet hall, we had a wonderful wedding reception and baptism party. Two amazing celebrations in one. The celebration went on well into the next day, and I have to say it one more time. Pictures were taken; many tears were shed, people laughed, people hugged, and people cried.

Vance Howard surprised us all, and he proudly announced at the end of the celebration that he had now successfully completed the adoption process, Sarah was now officially his daughter and their circle was complete.

When I had a moment to myself, I found a side door and wandered out into the cool evening air. I had danced up a storm and let me tell you that despite my age and some additional recent wear, I could still get out there and shake my parts and pieces around that dance floor. I just hoped that while I shook around like an old fool, various parts did not fall off me.

Oh yeah, yeah, yeah! What a day! Brian McClure, Tommy Hayward, Bryce Eddings, Gibby Gibbons and Coach Bettermann attended the wedding and reception to witness their superstar player's wedding ceremony, and they surprised me by bringing along Janet Chesboro. Wow! She looked gorgeous and Janet and I had a blast hanging out together and dancing up a storm together. In fact, in addition to dancing with Janet, I danced with Rose, Mrs. O'Malley, Heather Sarah, Sarah, Blue, and dear Martha. I never realized that Martha could cut up a rug like that.

It was a magnificent evening or actually, it was now early morning. A fitting end to a wondrous and memorable day. The heat and humidity of the day had long since escaped, and the stars twinkled above my head in the clear, glorious sky. God put the stars in the sky to lead us to grace and glory, so we can see all the way to Heaven, to guide us and to show us all the power and mercy of God. I knew that Binky, my dear Mum, the old man, the Hobnobbers, Sky Blu, well, all the saints in Heaven looked down upon us all and that all was well in the world. I was at peace now, because I knew in my heart that Heaven was rejoicing with us on this day, and the jubilation echoed all the way from Heaven to the inside of my heart.

I also was at peace because, you see dear reader, just as Sky Blu told me so long ago, I knew for a fact that, "People never really go away forever, even when they die, they come back to us, somehow, we are all linked forever to the people that we love."

Suddenly, from behind me, I felt our daughter grab me and wrap her arms around me. She buried her face into my back and she gently rocked me back and forth in her arms. I swayed with her grip and her love.

As we swayed together, I heard her say, "I love you, Daddy. I love you all the way to those stars twinkling above our heads and back again to where we are standing."

"I love you too, Heather Sarah. More than any words could ever tell you."

I turned, faced our daughter and kissed her cheek as she asked me, "Whatcha thinking about, Daddy? Mommy, right?"

"Oh, yes, of course. Right now, your mother is very happy. I know in my heart that your dear mother is smiling upon us right now. Today is glorious and I know your life with Vance will be wonderful. He is a great man. I know that in my heart, I am correct."

"I know you are correct too, and yes, I too, miss Mommy so much. Right now, more than any other day. So much. All is well, she is happy. Heaven's gain, isn't that what you say, Daddy?"

"It is."

We held each other and our warmth filled each other's souls. Heather Sarah piped up and said, "Say, that Janet gal is awesome and gorgeous too. She is head over heels in love with you. You do know that, right?"

"Oh, I do not know. I will take your word for it. She is a great friend. A ton of fun, I enjoy her company, but I am not ready for romance."

"Okay, I think that I understand. Janet will not understand, but so be it. Knowing you as I do, I know that you are waiting for someone special or something God driven. You will feel the love for someone very special in your heart whenever it arrives. I get it."

We held onto each other for a long time, until I looked up in the sky and had another thought, "I am also thinking of some words that Harry used to say to me all the time. Words from years ago. That for Harry and Paul, and now for, you know, for all of us, the night always comes, and that is when we are out there, running around, doing the things that we always did, and taking on the world together. Looking up at the glorious heavens above our heads tonight, yes, the night always comes. Now, instead of adventure, it brings us all great peace."

"I like that, Daddy. Uncle Harry can come up with such magical sayings. You should use that in a book someday."

And that is exactly what I did, dear reader. I used that

line in a book and I used a few more too.

Chapter Fifteen

Heaven's Gain

Once again, please stick with me here, dear reader. Paul William Henson the second here, making a sad and sorry attempt to compose a few more pages and try to tell a story. Actually, the end of this part of the adventure. The end of the story that despite myself and everyone else pleading and prodding that my father will not write.

A continued disclaimer: I am not the writer that our dear Father is. I am a writer, but I write about hockey and sports. Compared to writing about this, writing about hockey and sports is a piece of cake. It was easy to write when my brother-in-law won the hockey championship a few seasons in a row, and he won MVP awards and other honors. That was my specialty and my pride too! The main subject of the culmination of this part of the story, however, is not so easy to write. How I wish that I could convince our father to write about it, but he refuses to write any more. He claims that his writing is over and the story is finished. I beg to differ with him because in my opinion; the story is not finished unless someone tells this part of it and takes the time to write it all down. Our dear Father never published the original manuscript with the majority of this story, which surprises me, because it might just be one of his best in a long line of great material. Who knows? The man is not saying. Perhaps he wanted to leave the book open for someone to finish, but I am going to finish it and publish it too. My writing is very poor, but I will give it my best shot.

It has been a joyous five years or so. My wife and I, after much debate and thought, finally decided to sell our home in Hibernian, New Jersey and move in with our in-laws. In retrospect, it was the right choice for us. We could have bought our own fantastic home, perhaps not quite as large or elaborate, but I make a good living and we have access to lots of money. We needed to move closer to our family and while we searched for a home over in Wayne, nothing about the process felt correct in buying another home and starting anew. There were too many memories in our in-law's house, and Blue Cloud, and to be honest, the boys and I are so close to her parents. . ..

The boys have an amazing house, a huge yard to play in and run wild, and Blue Cloud had her mother and father to help us with the twins. At least we get a break here and there. Besides, they were going to sell the home, and they were always over our house, anyway. The twins have grown so quickly; they started school and at least my beleaguered wife has a few hours off from running around and keeping two twin boys in check. They are big, strong and powerful and let me tell you, they might be twins, but they are as different as night and day.

It is somewhat strange, or it might not be so strange, given all that we now have begun to understand about the intricacies of God's plan. Harry Michael is loud, bombastic, demanding and often overbearing. His brother, Paul, sits back quietly and takes it all in. He is polite and kind, but strong and powerful too. Harry knows better, because when he tweaks his brother, Paul will knock Harry Michael on his little ass quicker than Harry can blink an eye! Paul tends to speak only after carefully studying things and when, and if, he feels as if he needs to say something.

Does that sound familiar?

I will try to pretend that I am our father and write as he does. This is where he would write that life is sure full of twists and turns, eh? I have to agree with him.

I am a lucky man, two wonderful sons, and a gorgeous wife who is an awesome mother. Blue Cloud is amazing, she is a gift from God to us, to me, to the boys, and a man could ask for nothing more in life. She supports me and has pride in me. Somewhere, in the volumes of writings of our father, I recall him writing that a man often wants to hear from his woman, even more than that she loves him, is that she has pride in her man. She is proud of her man, and all that he stands for. Blue Cloud often tells me that she is proud of me, and now, I know what our father meant when he wrote those words.

Dear reader, the more I read of his work and the more that I speak to him, then, the more that I realize how lucky we are to have him not only as a father but also as a teacher, as a pastor and as a guide. I might be a bit biased, but when my father-in-law said that there has never been a finer man ever to walk this Earth, well, I feel that he was more than correct.

Vance Howard has become a first ballot Hall of Fame ice hockey player. No doubt, hands down. His career has been amazing, and Vance and my sister share a glorious life together. Vance is an amazing man, a wonderful husband to my sister and an outstanding father to their children. They have another little girl in their family now and when little Vivian Rose came into our life; we nearly fainted at her beauty. She takes after her mother and her grandmothers.

And my goodness, what a figure skater and beauty, my niece, Sarah Howard has turned out to be. Sarah has the world in her hands. The beautiful daughter of a world famous, professional ice hockey player and now, she has more trophies from winning skating competitions than I can count! Even at her young age, the young men are lining up for her hand.

Our dad, well, he is, and will always be number twenty-seven. Twenty-seven is still in amazing shape, he still runs, works out, skates with Vance and Sarah and keeps himself in fine shape. Young women, half of his age and less, turn their heads when he passes by, and sorry Vance, we love you, and you are great, but old number twenty-seven was still the best goalie of them all.

Hands down.

Not a damn marble could roll by him. I bet he could climb in the net right now and stop a few more pucks too.

Our dear father, in a grand ceremony, received an Honorary Doctorate of Theology from the seminary that he graduated from, but none of us would ever dare to call him Doctor Henson. Hell no. He would not even allow us to call him Bishop Henson! One thing about Paul John Henson is the fact that he remains humble and unassuming. I never could understand that, but he does. Our father also received an appointment for life as Pastor Emeritus of Reunion Lutheran Church. Number twenty-seven had his famous, number twenty-seven hockey jersey retired by the Albany Flying Dutchman hockey club in Albany, New York. The entire family attended the hockey ceremony, and it was a grand time. Harry bought out an entire hotel in downtown Albany, New York. Harry told us that it was the same hotel they stayed at when Blue Cloud decided to arrive on the scene around a breakfast table. Shortly thereafter that honor, number twenty-seven, received an induction invitation into the Eastern Hockey League Hall of Fame. More honors, more appreciation of a great goaltender that if God had allowed him to, would have been in the big-league Hall of Fame too. It was a touching moment and a special honor for me to write a sports column about my father's career and his achievements.

The old man still works as the Bishop of the Northeastern Lutheran District; he sits in his office every day, with Martha Wiggins, his faithful assistant by his side. Martha is as much a part of this family as anyone else is. She is amazing too. They make quite the team. I don't even know how many years now that the two of them have been together. It seems as if it is forever.

That brings me dear reader, to the final part of this chapter, in fact, the reason that I needed to write this all down and tell the final piece of this part of the adventure. In our lives, as it is in everyone's lives, it is not all joy. Mixed in with the joy, there is always some despair. It was what our father taught us to deal with. His own soul rising from the ashes of deep despair was an example for all of us, and he continued to lead us on through this chapter in our lives. I once thought the rock that was our dear father was shattered and broken forever, but it was only a dent. Through the grace of God and his faith, he recovered, and that is why he will always be as hard and strong as that rock he often carries around with him in his pocket.

Our despair came as a sudden shock and it hit all of us hard. We all could see Harry, the great thirty-five, suffering from some decline in health. We finally did convince him to see a doctor and sure enough, he was having severe heart issues. The doctors started treatment right away but my father-in-law suddenly took ill. First it was a mild heart attack, a scare, and he recovered nicely. Harry watched his health, he exercised a bit, listened to the doctors, followed a strict diet, and it seemed that he was on the road to recovery. Then about six months later, despite his changes in his diet and lifestyles, Harry suffered a massive heart attack, and he underwent an emergency bypass operation, in order to save his life.

Barely . . . save his life.

For a period, he improved, and then he grew weaker and gaunt. He lost power, lost his glory, and lost his strength. Each day, he grew weaker and older. When the doctors came to us and said that he was seriously ill and that his heart could barely pump enough blood to keep him alive, we knew it was more than serious—it was devastating. It was so much more than his heart; his other organs were shutting down due to poor blood flow. A heart transplant, even if available, was out of the question. There now were too many issues mounting. The doctors told us he would grow weaker and weaker, and that Harry required a type of special procedure. A procedure, to install some type of high technology clips on his heart valves to prevent the blood from backing into his heart chamber. It was a new and experimental procedure. A delicate operation, which required the best hospital and expert surgeons. Honestly, it looked very grim. The surgeons met with all of us and explained that in his weakened state, he only had about a 10 percent chance of undergoing the anesthesia and coming out of the operation alive. Yet, without the clips and the procedure, he would die. There was not any other choice to make but to attempt the operation, and of course, the family rallied, loved and held onto each other. It was what Pastor Paul John Henson and Harry M. Redmond Junior taught us to do in times of trouble and in times of glory. In the end, when there was nothing else left, we had our faith, and we always had each other.

After all, we were dumbfounded. This was Harry M. Redmond Junior. The immortal, world famous and legendary, Harry M. Redmond Junior, a man who you really thought would live forever.

Yet, as our father has written, we all are born and we all must die.

That brings me to the final scene of this book, of the many adventures of Harry and Paul, this final adventure was the reason that I felt so strongly that I had to record this, especially since it all ended, as it began with Harry and Paul.

I witnessed this first hand, so perhaps, in some way; I am qualified as a son and a son-in-law to record it.

Perhaps.

Right before the operation, we all gathered around

Harry's hospital bed. The entire family was present, even the twins and little Vivian Rose, Martha, and Pastor Jim. Harry held my precious mother-in-law's hand, and he smiled at all of us, while his eyes went around individually to each of us in the room. It was as if he was recording the moment, the faces, and the event in his mind, forever, just in case.

Harry had said a few words to each of us, held us and loved us all. A few minutes earlier, the doctors prepared him for the operation, with some type of relaxing medicine to calm him down. He had tubes in his arms, and monitors were set up, blinking, and beeping all over the room. Harry was awake, and somewhat alert, when our father stood up and recited a prayer for healing and guidance, as well as a blessing spoken in Hebrew or some other language. Our dear Father switched languages so often between New Jersey slang, to King's English, to Welsh, to Hebrew, to who the hell knows what that I cannot for certain say what language he used. He is a bit confusing with his linguistic abilities. In retrospect, what he spoke might have been the equivalent to Jewish last rites, if there is such a thing.

It is sometimes difficult to follow him and all of his seemingly endless talents.

After praying, Dad pulled a chair up to the bed and Harry, Rose, and our father all joined hands. Rose squeezed their hands tightly while tears poured from her eyes. In fact, other than Harry, our father, and our little, precious infant, Vivian Rose, everyone else in the room, even the great Pastor James T. O'Malley, had tears pouring from their eyes.

While Harry held on tightly to their hands, he spoke loudly and strongly to our father, "I guess this might be the end of the road for me, Paul. My last trip in the corner to dig out and to capture the puck. The last slap shot and ride in the Trans Whizzer. No eye of the tiger any longer. Even the tiger's eyes fade." Harry stopped speaking, and he smiled just the slightest hint of his famous smile. He continued to speak in a low, weak voice, "You know already. I can tell that God has already spoken to you and you know that I will be in paradise today. God tells you everything and your eyes now tell me. You can never hide your eyes from the people who know and love you. Well, Paul . . . then, ya gotta promise me things. Make sure you teach the twins everything about hockey. Everything, Paul."

Our father nodded and mouthed, "I will. I promise."

"Good. Don't leave anything out. Teach them old-time hockey and tell them all about the adventures of Harry and Paul. Better, skip some of them until they are older. Teach 'em about the old neighborhood and all the ways we knew. What my old man taught us, your old man, Ronzo, Mr. Porter . . . tell 'em all they need to know to understand it all. Teach 'em to be fearless men and stand for honor and strength and all that is good and fair in this world. Teach 'em to laugh, love, dance and cry a little too."

His eyes danced around the room a little and the smile returned again, "I gotta tell ya, it will be glorious to hold and love Sky Blu again. Glorious. Please, Paul, take care of our lovely Rose. She is so incredibly special. Please, take care of Rose. She loves you dearly, she always has, and I know that you love her too. Hold her and love her, never let her be lonely, hurt, or sad. Ever. Thanks for the prayers. Thanks for everything. When I go, then I go with joy in my heart and a smile on my face. It sure has been a helluva ride. Can't say that I would have wanted to share it with anyone else other than you. We sure did do it all. Nothing left out on the ice. Nothing. Not a damn thing. We came a long, long way from 20 John Street and 182 Belmont Avenue and good, old, Geyer Street Gardens. It has been a blast. All we did, all we shared, this glorious family we have, beautiful children, grandchildren and our gorgeous women. It has been something, Paul. I guess, in looking back, for Harry and Paul, the night always comes."

Our father smiled, and he gripped Harry's hand tightly.

Harry spoke again, this time, his voice was considerably softer in volume, "From the moment when I first met ya, when ya came running around the corner in front of my house one day, all that long hair flowing behind ya, running hard on your way to Jeff's house, we have never been apart. Even when I was miles away from you, after Sky left us, and I was miles from nowhere, I was still with you. We were always together. We always will be, I will never leave ya and you will never leave me. I guess that is what Harry and Paul are really all about—we were always together. This family can learn from us—always stay together, no matter what. In the good times and in the bad."

For the briefest of moments, Harry let go of Rose's hand. He took his one hand, patted our father's hand gently, and he said, "Ya know, twenty-seven, something that I need to admit to you. In all the years of speaking to you on the telephone, I always just hang up and never say goodbye. I guess, right now, that I need to say goodbye."

Harry once again joined hands with Rose.

Dad was silent for a long time, and after a period of silence, except for sobbing amongst the people in the room, our father finally spoke, "Yes, the night always comes, Harry. It does. It has been glorious, and I too, would not have wanted to ride this magical ride of life with anyone else either. Harry, there is no need to say goodbye, no matter what happens, just know that we are together forever and for always. As your precious mother told me so long ago around that wonderful kitchen table in 20 John Street, this life is full of mysterious things. Captivating, wonderful things, in which God has given to all of us. Friendship, love, kindness, companionship, these things never die. I have faith and I know you do too. This is not the end, not by a long shot, I know and you know too, that surely, we will all meet again."

Harry smiled at our father and they warmly embraced for a long, long time. It was only then that I saw the tears running out of our father's eyes and out of Harry's eyes too.

"I love you, Paul. You are my brother."

"And you are mine. I love you too, Harry."

When they wheeled Harry in for the operation, and we all moved to the waiting room, our father surprised us all when he took his old, familiar vest from the coat rack and carried it in his hands. He then walked over and hugged Rose for what seemed as if it were forever, he told her that he was with her always, from now until the end of all time, he kissed Rose goodbye, he gently held her face in both of his cupped hands and he told her how much he loved her. After leaving Rose, he then did the same to all of us, to his grandchildren, and as he made his way through the family, he told all of us the same, exact thing.

After he finished, he stood in front of all of us and our father told us that he loved all of us more than he could ever describe.

After he finished, he put his vest on. Apparently, he was not staying to hear the results of the operation, and I was somewhat puzzled by his behavior at such a critical moment, as I think all the family was too.

As he began to walk away, I could not help but run after him, stop him, and ask, "But, Father . . . why are you leaving? Do you not want to stay here? This could be the end . . . geez, Dad! Harry could die."

He stopped, smiled, and he warmly embraced me, kissed my cheeks, and then said, "I love you, Paul William. Yes, I am leaving. I will go home and I will pray all night, I will read both old and new scripture, light candles and incense. Together, with the ghosts that are always around me, with all the Lutheran saints of Heaven and beyond, we will pray into the morning, until I hear the news. If the news is full of sorrow, then together, we will all weep. Jesus wept when his best friend left this world, too. If the news is joyful, then we will celebrate the joy as Jesus did when he extended the celebration at the wedding. I will do all of this tonight because, no matter what happens, you need to understand that this is not the end."

He put his hands on both of my shoulders and gripped them tightly. I am this amazing man's son. I am a tall, strong, proud and powerful young man, but our father towers over me in height and strength and I must admit, he towers over me in pride. It is remarkable that he remains so straight and true, and his grip is still so powerful and strong. Age had not changed him much, if any, and age certainly had not diminished his strength. While gripping me tightly with one hand now on one of my shoulders, he pushed the long hair from his face, and I could see tears in the corners of his eyes.

While still holding me, he told me, "Our loss here on Earth would simply be Heaven's gain. It is the circle of life. Now, we pass the circle to others, for them to begin their own circles of life, circles of joy, circles of love and most of all circles of faith and of hope. We all are born into this world and we all, someday, must die. If Harry leaves this world, then I have no doubt that he will arrive in Heaven to an escort of angels blowing their golden trumpets, and to endless rejoicing. Heaven will erupt in joy! He will be riding in and amongst the clouds, in his Trans Whizzer, with his big black hat on, with Sky Blu, your dear mother and all the gang by his side and the music blaring from his sound system!"

In response to his words and the vision, I smiled and warmly embraced him again. I admired not only our father's remarkable strength but also his now restored and unshakable faith.

After we embraced, he gently told me, and in fact, all of us, "Remember, this is not the end, no matter what happens, this is not the end. Stand tall and have faith. Never despair and never doubt. I learned that the hard way. This is all part of God's plan and God is with us always."

He stopped speaking for a moment, and I saw him pat the front pocket of his vest to check for the presence of that little rock that he often carried around with him at times such as these. A rock, to remind him of the strength and power, and a rock, which I felt was so symbolic of what our father stood for and what he was.

He then continued to preach to all of us, "Do you not see? Do you not understand? Right now, at this moment, you do not need Grandpa, or number twenty-seven, or your father, your father-in-law, or most of all, you do not need, Pastor Paul John Henson here with you for this. Someday, I will leave this world too. Instead, this time, you need faith and love. More than anything in this entire world, you all need each other. You need to stand with each other, as a family, and each of you on your own. Stand in unwavering and undeniable faith. This time, each of you individually and collectively, will be the rock."

Our father emphatically shook his head side-to-side, and he told us, "This time, I am not the rock. No, not I. This time, the rock is all of you. Together."

He then looked at the precious twins and he smiled before he continued to speak, "Most of all, please, always remember that in the world of Harry and Paul, there will be another adventure right around the corner. There always will be, you see, the adventures of Harry and Paul never really end. The years may pass, but they go on forever, as long as there are memories, dreams to dream, fun-loving people who enjoy life and care for each other in special ways, stories to tell, roads to travel, music to hear, dances to dance, and love to give. They go on and on until the end of all time."

He waved to me, smiled at all of us, turned, and walked

away. I stood for a long time and watched. As he walked down the hallway, he disappeared out the door and into the evening.

There were no words to describe the pride that I felt in our father, or in the fact that his words not only taught us, but more than anything, they were words of love. Love that is not, describable. Even in the words of the greatest writers that might scribe in this humble world, there are no words to define his love.

I turned around and looked at Blue Cloud, and my wife, despite the indescribable pain, had a wide smile on her face as the endless tears streamed down her cheeks and she held the hands of little Harry and Paul.

My wife, too, knew the meaning of our father's words and my beloved wife understood. I looked at our sons as they stood on each side of the precious woman who gave them life and gave birth to them. The twins were now old enough to understand and the two of them stood there, holding on tightly to their mother, with tears streaming down their little cheeks, while they struggled with the moment and the emotions too. It was then that I knew how correct our father was and exactly what he meant. It was time for them to begin their circles. Harry and Paul.

Yes, indeed, dear reader, the adventures of Harry and Paul never end, and they do indeed go on and on until the end of all time.

Chapter Sixteen

Glory

A long time ago, I learned that life is a great, big circle. It goes around and around, and as you ride along the perimeter of the circle and travel through your life, you finally reach the end and complete the cycle.

We all are born and we all must die.

That is the beginning of the circle and the end of the circle. The ride along from start to finish, well, as far as that goes, who knows where it will lead you? As we walk through life, we experience things; we observe and we learn. For some of us, it is not an ordinary journey, and I long since gave up trying to classify what I did and whom I traveled with as ordinary. God's plan at this point, was where I obtained my marching orders from, and it surely had allowed me a full life. Now, dear reader, I will not dwell on my protest against God's plan. I have already done that here to a great extent. Slowly, as all of this evolved, I found that I was becoming more and more obedient and following what I felt was correct in my heart, rather than stomping my feet and folding my arms in protest. Part of this slow transformation in my attitude and in my actions stemmed from a realization that there actually was very little, if anything, that I could do about it. Therefore, I followed the plan, perhaps blindly, perhaps, with peace in my heart, but I followed.

Over a few short years, Harry's health declined rapidly. We knew he had some type of heart issues and by the time that he went to see the doctors; they did what they could.

Multiple heart attacks, a bypass procedure and then a furious battle ensued. Even against insurmountable odds, the great number thirty-five, with his amazing power, would not give up easily. Despite the battle, Harry was not the same man, his power and his ever-present glory slowly faded. Then there came a critical and delicate surgical operation. Harry, as well as all of us, knew the risk. It was the final hope, and the greatest doctors did the best that they could to save him. It was out of their hands. I think, dear reader, the big guy's heart was so full of joy, as well as his massive spirit, that it just wore out from pumping love and joy for so long. When the hour of the operation arrived and I stared deeply into his eyes, then I knew what the plan was going to be. Over my many years, serving as a pastor, looking into countless eyes before they leave this world, well, I knew.

When the call finally came, I wept. Just as I predicted that I would do, I wept. Wept my eyes out, yet, this time, I remained true to my word. I would not falter and I would not break or cave in. I made a vow to my beloved Rose, to our daughter, and to my family, a promise, never, ever, to repeat my worst behavior or allow grief to override my spirit ever again.

As Harry used to say, "Geyer Street Guys don't quit. Ever." He was correct.

The big guy did not quit; all he did was move his address. Our loss here on Earth simply became Heaven's gain.

I dressed for the funeral, in my black suit and collar, and slipped my old wooden cross and the urn with Binky's ashes over my neck. To remind me not to falter, I stuck the rock from my vest in my suit jacket pocket.

If someone asked me how many funerals I conducted over my years, I could not accurately answer the question, but all that I knew while I dressed, was that this one was going to be amazingly difficult. Like no other funeral that I had ever performed. Ever.

I have been with many of my parishioners, Bishop Von Houten, Rabbi Goldberg, friends, and yes; even my own loved ones as they passed from this world, and while it is never easy, it does somehow reinforce your faith. I stood by and held the hands of our beloved parents as they left this world, and our grandfather and my beloved brother-in-law and in-laws. Now, I too held Harry's hand, or rather, my brother's hand in his last few moments in this world. My only regret, of which I have now come to terms with, was that I was not there with my beloved Binky. I now believed that God had another plan for that, and he knew that would be too painful for Pastor Paul John Henson to endure. He took Binky suddenly, without pain, without any advance notice, and spared me that wretched suffering. Great suffering, of which I would most likely never recover from and that would not have fit into the plan.

I had too much work left to do.

You see, dear reader, we all are born and we all must die.

As wretched as funerals are, no matter how many I have presided over as a pastor, or attended one as a loved one while paying respects, I am always astounded at the presence of glory and to the joy of Heaven at funerals. I can feel it, sometimes even believe that I can see it, in the dancing sunlight, or golden rays of Heaven. I have seen it when witnessing the passing of both young people and old people, and it never ceases to amaze me. It is a time of such sorrow, yet in so many ways, it is a time of great joy, of redemption, of whispers of heavenly angels as they sing songs of joy and play tunes upon harps of gold.

Pastor James T. O'Malley assisted me in what was a glorious funeral service. Somehow, the two old warriors managed to muster enough strength and courage to get through the service together. Harry would not have wanted or allowed us to fold or cave in. I think the big guy sent us strength from his golden perch. Jim and I were not going to let him down.

We buried Harry M. Redmond Junior next to his beloved Sky Blu on that same hillside near that glorious tree. A tree, which was now tall and powerful, just like Harry is. I adhered to Harry's wish of so long ago to be buried with the little Christmas tree of Sky Blu's. Harry somehow knew that he would go to Heaven before I left this world.

While our faces rained tears and our hearts tore apart in sorrow, there was somewhere a touch of glory. Glory in knowing that this was a one-of-a-kind life. An extraordinary man, a special friend and the world now was such a better place because of the amazing life of Harry M. Redmond Junior. I loved him with all of my heart and soul. Loved him deeply and with the highest honor, just as I loved my own loved ones and my family, because he was my brother. I would miss him dearly, every single day, but accepted it as one more step in the plan.

One more circle of life complete.

You see, dear reader, we all are born and we all must die.

Chapter Seventeen

Dyna'i Diwedd

This is where we come to the end of the story.

Dyna'i diwedd, in Welsh. The end of the story.

As I sit here at my desk and continue to think about how to compose this story, I think that perhaps; I have chosen an incorrect word to define all of this. The word story is an incorrect word to utilize for a one-word description. Adventure works well, but perhaps the best word to use, is the word, journey. All of this has been a journey. A journey, which began so long ago, with two young boys and an extraordinary friendship, a brotherhood, a bond. Surely, a bond created by God for the service of the greater good of the kingdom, but also a journey for two souls. A journey, which began on streets known as John Street and Belmont Avenue, in an old city neighborhood in New Jersey. A neighborhood full of grit, crime, urban dust, determination and dreams. Dreams that were eventually fulfilled, because they included remarkable friends, amazing people, hard work, commitment, and most of all, endless love and proved that even ordinary people from common means and simple lives can achieve great and extraordinary things.

Perhaps, in looking back on it all, they were all not so ordinary people.

Yet, here is the part of this long story, the only one of our many adventures, where I have to say that I might just keep these thoughts in my own heart and in my own mind. Yes, I am typing them, but they might never reach the inside of two covers. It might be one of the few times where writing the actual words down, calms my soul and I am alone in my thoughts, but it might be best to keep some things private and forever in the hearts of two individuals. Thinking about it—there might be a few other times too.

It is important for me to escape there and to recall this part of the story. . ..

I was lost in email madness while sitting at my desk on a late May afternoon. The emails never stopped, and I was beginning to think that Martha was correct.

Martha would often tell me that, "Emails are a waste of time. All this nonsense of using emails of accountability bullshit. Scan them for donations, scan them for messages from your loved ones, the Governing Board and then delete the rest."

I could see her point.

I heard a gentle knock at my office door, looked up and with some surprise, I shouted out, "Rose! Wow! What a surprise. Please, please come in."

Rose stood in the doorway; she smiled and took a few steps into the office. Rose then turned and pointed out in the direction of Martha, who sat at her desk, and I could see that Martha smiled at my reaction to my visitor.

"I apologize for just popping in here without an appointment. Martha said it was fine for me to come in, she said that I was one of the few people on this side of Heaven that she allowed in to see you without an appointment."

"Of course, of course, and knowing our dear Martha, she has a very short list of those people too."

Martha leaned over and yelled out, "You bet your sweet ass it is short. Otherwise, with your endless fan club sashaying in and out here all day long, well, Pastor Paul, you would never get anything done. Then, I would have to do even more work than I do now! Just delete those stupid-ass emails and talk to Rose. I am going to lunch. I am sure that you do not want me eavesdropping on your conversation. Might go see Jennifer and have a liquid lunch. You might need to come and rescue me from the barstool. You know the drill. Jennifer and I will share small talk about my boss and what we would do with Pastor Paul if he allowed us to pursue him."

Rose started to laugh and waved her hand at Martha while telling her, "My goodness, Martha. What would we have ever done without you all of these years? You have kept us all on our toes and in stitches. Thank you for you. I and we, well, we all love you dearly. You are as much a part of our family as anyone else is."

Martha stood up, smiled and grabbed her purse. She walked over to Rose and gave her a warm and very long hug. It was one of the rarest of moments because I had only seen tears in our dear Martha Wiggin's eyes a handful of times over the many years that we worked together. And believe me; we had been through some very difficult moments together in our lives.

"No, thank you for all of you. However, who is kidding? Geez, look at the man! That is some serious hunk of man there. Seriously, all kidding aside, he is doing better, but we all try hard to get him back out into society. Maybe you will have better luck than Jennifer will and I have had. It is nice to see you out and about these days too. Will do you a world of good too, Rose. Truly, your words mean so much to me, dear Rose. I, too, love you all and you have been so special to me, in my life, in my heart. I could not see myself having spent my career with anyone else other than Pastor Paul and his amazing family. He is truly special and all of you are too. You taught me what a family is really all about in this life and beyond. You are the greatest people, kind, warm and loving. We are all a team, and I could never thank God enough for bringing me here to be part of it."

I joined the hug, kissed Martha on her cheek, and thanked her for her too.

"Well, enough of this loving and teary-eyed bullshit

stuff. Time for hard drinks and dreams of lust! Can I put this on your tab, Pastor Paul?"

"Sure, why not? Everyone else does."

"Good, thank you. I was going to do it anyhow, even if I did not ask you ahead of time. Oh, by the way, never sign your name there or at the bank on the corner, I come close to making it look like your signature, but it is not exact. You might get arrested for forgery."

Off she went, rubbing her eyes of the spent tears. Martha Wiggins was one of a kind and I, too, would not have wanted to share my working days with anyone else.

"And what brings you downtown, Newark today? This is not your usual shopping destination. Are you checking out a new restaurant or some other type of business?" I asked Rose as I kissed her cheek, walked over to my guest chairs and offered her one chair, while I took the other. It seemed unusual, but before taking a seat, Rose reached over and carefully closed the door to my office and she pushed the doorknob lock down. Rose even gave it a gentle tug to make sure that it had locked behind us.

With a smile, she walked over and took a seat in the guest chair while explaining, "No, no, no, shopping, Blue Cloud and I have done enough of that as of late." Rose finished the explanation with a nervous chuckle. I knew our dear Rose as well as I knew the back of my own hand. We had shared so much together over the years. We remained so close that it was almost indescribable. Right now, she had that, "I have to share something very important with Paul" look in her eyes. As I said, I knew our dear Rose.

"No, I met with some business persons for lunch a few blocks away from here, in order to discuss some potential other sites for expansion of our charity foundation's efforts. Efforts that include, potentially building community centers in New Jersey inner cities. We have Newark in mind for a potential site."

"Sounds wonderful. Community centers? What kind of centers, Rose?"

"I have this vision. A center in conjunction, with the charity. Not just storefronts as the foundation uses now, where we hand out food, where counseling occurs, and money donated to the needy. When I mean, a center, I mean a building. Full-services, medical, dental, perhaps a gymnasium. A nondenominational chapel. A center for the cultural arts. Teach children, music, the arts, photography, painting, and ceramics. Maybe a theatre and a stage for concerts, plays and performances. A place for all people, all races, all religions, with only one bond, which is, old, urban, New Jersey neighborhoods. Neighborhoods such as the old neighborhood of Harry and Paul . . . you know . . . your old neighborhood. It would be a hub in the center of despair."

Rose stopped speaking. Her voice choked up for a moment or two, but she recovered quickly. She was such an impressive woman, who had such a keen business mind. From her marketing skills, many years ago, in the restaurant business to now operating most of the charities on her own, this was a brilliant woman.

Rose continued to explain, "Since I was here in Newark, I thought that I would stop and see the most handsome bishop in the world, who also happens to be my favorite bishop."

Rose stopped speaking; she tucked deeply into the chair and paused. She now continued the discussion with some comments on our family, "On another subject, I must say, Vance Howard is amazing. Heather Sarah is a lucky woman, not only is Vance a huge professional success, a wonderful and kind man, but he is one good-looking man! The older he gets, the better looking he becomes. Anyhow, my goodness, she has herself some husband there."

"Yes indeed, I agree with you, Rose. Vance is amazing and we are very proud of him. More so than words can describe. He loves Heather Sarah, Sarah, and Vivian Rose, very deeply and with all of his heart and soul. It is easy to see that his love and his commitments are very deep. I am thrilled for Heather Sarah, and their children. It is all I could have dreamed of for them and what Binky would have dreamed of too."

Rose fidgeted a bit in the chair. She looked glorious as she always did, her delicate neck decorated with a thin, golden chain and diamond necklace, reflecting her sparkling eyes and enhancing her dark features. Her jet-black hair remained dark and only in the brightest of lights could you detect any gray or white hairs upon her head. Her skin was flawless, for a woman of her age she had no wrinkles, her figure remained perfect, I do not think she gained an ounce of weight over the years, and despite the recent pain and elements of despair, she kept herself impeccable. Rose was a stunning woman who seemed ageless. Her dark and enchanting eyes wandered around the office for a time before she settled back upon my face. Specifically, she studied my eyes for a few seconds. Rose leaned back and fingered her earrings, as she often did when she was deep in thought.

It was a habit of hers.

There was no doubt that Rose was deep in thought, and I felt as if this general conversation was a prelude to something intense and deep. Rose was stalling, gathering strength as well as searching for the correct emotion.

"Yes, Paul. Vance is a wonderful husband and father. I agree. He becomes better looking each day, very much as the man in my present company does. Binky is smiling down on all of this. She really is," Rose's voice drifted off, her eyes closed, and she fell silent. Oh, boy, her thoughts remained intense. When she opened her eyes, they wandered around the room once again and when they stopped wandering, her eyes locked with mine. I must say that in all of my years of knowing Rose and studying her, she never seemed more intense nor, honestly, more beautiful. She was beyond captivating today. I ignored the compliment about my appearance because here we go, I can tell. Here comes the root of the conversation.

"Paul, I guess it is confession time of sorts. After all, you *are* my pastor. We have shared so much over all of these years and yes, we have a profound connection forever. In so many ways, we have shared parts and pieces of our souls together, our lives. Bishop, pastor, friend, in-laws, my goodness, what the hell aren't you in my life?"

I shrugged my shoulders and leaned back in the chair but did not comment. Deep inside, I had a thought of where this conversation was leading us. It was a conversation that given our long past together, I knew would someday arrive on our lips. It was inevitable and to be honest, a healthy conversation to have someday with Rose. She was correct in the fact that we had shared so much together. It was time to clear the air and settle our thoughts in regard to Rose and Paul.

"I am glad that Martha left us alone for lunch, because this conversation, even for a pastor counseling session or one of our famous discussions, will be a little difficult. I need to share this and I hope and pray that it does not come across wrong or cause you or me any pain, but I need to purge this from my soul and from my heart. Especially now, with all that has happened to us and with our grandchildren in our lives. We thought that nothing would be the same with all of us when Blue and Paul William married and now, well, it sure has been quite the ride. My goodness, our connection runs so deeply. It is something that even words or an attempt at a description cannot ever capture. Ever."

"No doubt, Rose, it has been an amazing time. Rose, you could never cause me any pain. We always shared our thoughts and hearts, so please do not ever think that you could cause me pain. I hold you too dear and with such high esteem."

Rose nodded and reached out for my hands, I took them and held them tightly.

While our eyes locked, she told me what was bothering her, "Well, confession time is finally here. Luckily, or perhaps, well, anyway, forget it. I only had two glasses of wine for lunch. One or two more than that, and this would really be an interesting discussion."

Rose stopped speaking, took a gentle breath and then continued to speak, "Here goes, to carry on with my observation. You have been everything in my life . . . except we were never lovers."

I let go of her hands when I heard her words, and she seemed shocked at my reaction. I leaned back in my chair and Rose did the same in her chair.

"I am so sorry, Paul, it is apparent that I have shocked you with my words. First off, after that statement, I think you know that I loved Harry with all my heart and soul as you did Binky, and this conversation is not to dishonor them, or to forget what we shared with our spouses. We still love our spouses, and we always will. I want to clear the air and to be honest with each other. Is that the right thing to do, Paul? We have known each other for too long not to be honest."

I nodded and agreed, "Of course, it is the right thing to do. Rose, I understand. Bit of a shock. Yes, I am good now. We owe each other honesty, and I want to help you clear your soul of whatever emotion you are holding inside of your heart and mind. It seems as if this was inside of you for a very long time and the truth is always healing. You know, in this business of mine and in my life, I do my best work whenever I deal in the truth."

Rose smiled, and it seemed as if she became a little more comfortable after hearing my words. She continued to speak, "Paul, please we need to return in time for quite a bit. Because, I am not speaking of the times when we were together with our future spouses. I am speaking when it was simply Rose and Paul. Alone. Just us. I often think of the times when Harry and Binky both left our lives and except for each other, we were alone. We shared everything, Paul, but we never shared each other. Here was this amazing man, handsome beyond description, indescribably sexy, kind, brilliant, strong and powerful. I admired you and I am not ashamed to say that I love you and have always loved you, as well as desired you, but for some reason, never told you so. One night, the night when Sky Blu wrecked Harry's car, I tried to tell you how much I loved you, but you did not react in the manner that I hoped you would. I laughed it off in hopes of dismissing it, and we moved on with our lives. A few days later, I broke off my relationship with Harry, and hoped and prayed that you would show me a sign that you cared for me, but you never did. I was so young and honestly, stupid to allow that time to have slipped by me. I should have told you how I felt."

I shook my head and Rose stopped speaking when she saw me do so.

"What? Why are you shaking your head?" Rose asked.

"You were not stupid. You could never be stupid. Young yes, stupid no. Please, never call yourself stupid. You are too brilliant to demean yourself."

Rose smiled and answered, "Okay, well, thank you. That is only one reason why I love you so much because you honor people so perfectly. With Paul John Henson, it is always about honor and respect. I guess that I was young. Very young."

"We all were young, my dear Rose. This reminds me of what my old man used to tell me. He used to have a saying, by the time that I realized that I was too young to deal with things, I was too old to do anything about it."

Rose laughed that glorious laugh of hers and she smiled widely while telling me, "Perfect! I can see the old man saying that. He was amazing. He is a legend, now and forever. Remarkable, street smarts. A one-of-a-kind man who produced a one-of-a-kind son. His sayings worked so well. They were brilliant. I miss him. I bet you do too."

"Every single day, Rose. Right now, maybe more than any other time in my life. My father and my grandfather—how I wish that I could sit and speak with them just one more time."

I fell silent for a bit of time and so did Rose. It was strange. It was as if we were not sure of where the conversation was going now that Rose had exposed her feelings and most of her heart and soul.

Rose broke the silence first when she continued with her thoughts, "Anyway, to get back to my point, I do feel as if I wasted something. I always loved Harry, always will. He was a wonderful and amazing husband, friend and companion. I loved him dearly. Yet, years ago, when Binky left you and I walked away from Harry, I think I did so in hopes that we would become lovers. Honestly, I blew it. I wanted you to know that I left you alone and hurt you and I regret it. Now, all of these years later, I seek some type of peace. You were so hurt and so alone and I should have been there for you, with my heart, my love, and honestly, with my body. All I wanted was to make love to you. Back then and once again, honestly, I want to make love to you now too. I loved you then, loved you deeply, and I still do, with all of my heart and soul. Instead, I allowed you to be alone for so long. Now, you are alone again in this world and I am too. I cannot allow the same mistake twice."

Rose paused and shook her head to emphasize her point, and then she continued with even more intense feelings in her voice, "Not with the love that I feel. It bothers me greatly, but now I understand it all. That is what I just had to tell you and purge my soul of today, and I have been trying to have the courage to expose my feelings since Binky left us. That is when I wanted to tell you how much I want you and love you. I have been dropping hints at you for a long time, but you never react. The night, which is now many years ago, already . . . time passes so quickly, you might recall, the night when we had that wonderful homecoming party for you and the welcome party for Vance, we danced together in a glorious slow dance. I held you as I never held you before. You felt glorious in my arms. I told you about how I felt that Vance and Heather Sarah had fallen in love and then I told you how another young man, or specifically a goalie, stole a young woman's heart a longtime ago. You thought that I was referring to Binky and I am sure that might have been correct, but I was actually referring to *my* heart. You stole my heart so long ago and you still have it. You always will."

My mind whirled with the memory. I did recall the scene as well as Rose's words from that evening, 'I know the feeling because long ago, it happened to another young woman that I know of, she too, had her heart stolen.'

Rose explained, "I am sorry, Paul. However, I had to do it. Finally, it had to come out of my heart."

She motioned again for my hands and I reached over and clasped her hands gently while trying hard to comprehend what it was that Rose was trying to tell me. What it was that she needed to hear from me. What I could do to help her.

I still did not say a word. I looked at her lovely face, then at our hands and then back again to her face. I gently let go of her hands and eased back into my chair once again. I studied her from the chair. Rose continued to lean close to me as if she did not want me to be far away from her. This was a conversation that Rose and I both knew would surface someday, but it was so long ago.

So very long ago.

On the other hand, was it?

Time is just a measuring stick, so come on now, think,

Henson, what do you feel in your heart and in your mind? It was a long time ago, yet, I knew that we were both too close for this subject not to occur in some manner. Other than Harry, this beautiful and gorgeous woman, was the dearest and closest friend that I have and have ever had in my life. Now, perhaps she is something so much more, or she always was something more, and I just never admitted it.

Surprisingly, Rose remained solid. Usually, these types of conversations resulted in her emotions taking over, but her eyes were clear and sparkling. Rose remained intense, yet for her, it was unusual to see her remain under complete control and very confident in her words and actions. It seemed as if the words provided her some type of relief.

She spoke again, "We could have never been lovers. Not back then. I realize that now. It could never have happened because of the plan. God shaped every inch of this path, and if we had fallen in each other's arms and been lovers, then all of this would be so different. So very different. It is so remarkable, Paul. It is so wonderful to see how this all transpired, yet so horrible too. I feel as if God is leading me to purge this now and see where it leads me. Leads us. I hope that I have not embarrassed you or upset you, and I am so sorry to show up here unannounced and spring this emotional outpouring upon you. I guess you are used to it by now. Emotional Rose. I think that Harry and Binky both knew how close we were. He never asked me if we ever fell in love when he was gone and when Binky left you. He knew we spent a lot of time together, but I guess he assumed that it was as it actually was, just friends. Close, close friends. Did Binky ever ask you?"

I shook my head and said, "You have not embarrassed me and there is no need to be sorry. Please, we have been too close for so long that I knew that someday we would discuss this subject. It was inevitable and I care too much for you, not to be here for you and listen carefully to this. I need to help you. And no. Binky never asked me about us or even about my past lovers. I never asked her any details of her love life, or of her past, or any details of when she was gone from my life. It did not matter. None of my business, actually. It was before us. We either were not together or had not even met. How could it be relevant? In no manner, did it matter in our relationship."

"Yes, Paul. I understand and I feel the same way. Did Harry ever ask you about us? I think, later on in our marriage, he knew how I actually felt about you, in fact, he mentioned it on his deathbed."

"I do recall his words. Yes, I do, but it was difficult to judge the context that Harry spoke of them. But, no, Rose. We never discussed it. In fact, while we are laying our souls bare here, it will be cleansing for me to tell you that while I had a number of close girlfriends and lovers, there was only one other very special woman in my life, a woman that I met years before I knew Binky and knew you too."

Rose jumped in and said, "Maureen? You mean the older Italian gal, Maureen. Harry told me all about her."

"Well, no, not Maureen Zipperelli. I mean, Maureen and I were lovers. Yes, we were together for a long time. However, it was an on and off affair. Since we are being so honest, we were very intense lovers. Very intense. There were weekend getaways where we made love for days on end. However, she wanted to marry me and have many children. Right away. She was Italian! It was her culture. Love, babies, wine and food. Maureen was wonderful. She was gorgeous and amazing. I was not there yet and while I did love Maureen, it was not deep enough love for marriage. Once more, hockey was in the way and I was young."

"I see. Honestly, any woman married to you, I can see how love, babies, wine and food would be a rather wonderful life! Works for me and I am sure about a thousand other women, who have laid eyes on you too." Rose laughed, waved her hands in the air to dismiss the off-subject thoughts and spoke again, "Sorry, but seriously, I never heard of any other woman, who you were serious with. At least, Harry or Binky, you, or no one else in our circle of friends and families ever mentioned anyone."

"No, no, no, it was very intense and short-lived. It was a once in a lifetime romance. We were very different in our cultures and in our lives. She was wealthy, very wealthy, and she was Jewish. Very, very Jewish. Devoutly Jewish, and here I was a long-haired Lutheran man from the poor neighborhood. On the surface, it did not work out too well. Harry knew of her and he actually met her, but because of the plan, she could not be a part of my life and she left me. Binky knew nothing of her. Once again, Binky never asked about my past, therefore I never told her. This woman, her name is Renee . . . and her leaving me . . . well . . . it caused me great pain, terrible pain. Harry never asked a single word about her either. Harry was very special in that he understood when he needed to jump into your life and when a person required space. Even now, I find it hard to imagine that I never discussed details of my love for Renee with Harry. We shared everything together in our lives, especially back then, when we were so young. Women were a major topic for us! I think only my dear mum knew how much in love I was with Renee. Renee remains in a sacred place in my heart. I am a person who needs private space. I always have and will. I find it easier to share my soul in my words on paper, then to share them speaking. Harry knew me so well, and he respected that space. I am sure that is the case with you too. We are in stark contrast to Harry and to Binky, who spewed whatever it was that were on their minds."

Rose was going to quiz me, and I guess it now was healthy for me finally to speak to someone about all of this.

Truly, there was no one better to share this with then with Rose. She smiled and closed her eyes again. I knew that meant she was digging deeper and deeper into her heart and soul. This was going to be even more intense than what I had first imagined.

"I see. Paul, I have to ask, was your relationship with Renee even more magical than your relationship with Binky was?"

I did not hesitate; honesty at this point was not in short supply, "Yes. It was. Different, but my love for Renee was a very special and unique love. It was not even describable. We just could never have married. Sad but true. God's plan was not to allow it. Now, in the same regard, Binky was all I ever could wish for and desire in a wife and a mother to our children. Renee was just different, very, very different."

Rose studied me but did not say a word. I wondered what she was thinking, so I asked her, "I assume that Binky never questioned you about us?"

"Not a word, Paul. Ever. I, too, shared everything with Binky as you did with Harry. But she never asked, so I never told her," Rose said with a gentle shake of her head and her eyes drifting closed.

Once again, she was deep in thought and I respected her time to think. I found this to be a difficult, but inevitable conversation between two very close friends of the opposite sex, who were now family by marriage, who loved and respected each other entirely too much, not to have a mature and honest discussion.

Rose fell silent for a few moments.

She opened her eyes and spoke again, "Harry never asked much about my first husband either and I never asked for many details of his life with Sky Blu. Harry understood that all those years ago, we split up for a reason and he chose his path and I chose mine. I never stopped loving Harry, and he knew that fact. It was a different time and place. So long ago, dear Paul. So long ago in our journey together. A time when Harry was gone and not a part of my life. Yet, my dear Paul, I have to know your thoughts. If things were different and God's plan allowed us, could we have been lovers? Would we have been lovers?"

Rose asked, and she did so with confidence. She leaned in and studied my eyes for an answer. In my mind and in my heart, I imagined that it was a question that she wanted to ask me for a very long time. It was also a question that Rose deserved an answer to.

I did so without much hesitation and with an answer from my heart, "Of course. I think we would have been lovers. Yes, without a doubt."

Rose did not immediately react; instead, our eyes remained locked as she studied me very closely. She then smiled a little and leaned back into the chair.

Her body relaxed, and she spoke just above a whisper, "Thank you for your honesty. This is really not about Harry, Binky, or our children. This is about Rose and Paul and a time in our lives when we were so close, yet mysteriously far apart. A time that I think about now that we are older and realize that it was a special time in our lives. We were both so alone in the universe."

Rose suddenly stopped speaking, and she shook her head back and forth while exclaiming, "Wow! That was an incredible and amazing answer, Paul. You did not hesitate in the least. It sent a shudder up and down my spine and I am not ashamed to say, into my loins. Thinking about it, though, I would not expect anything less than forthright and heartfelt honesty from Paul John Henson. I have to add that I agree with you completely. We would have been lovers and should have been. And I might add, while we are being so honest and frank with each other, that it would have been amazing and passionate lovemaking. We would have lit some nights on fire. Not about lust or about sex, but it would have been about love."

Amazingly, I was very comfortable with her statement and felt as if once again, that she deserved an honest statement from me in return to her outpouring.

"Yes, I do think you are correct and I agree with that fact too. It would have been quite amazing and passionate," was my answer to her statement.

"So, are Renee and Binky the only women that you would have married?"

"No."

"Would you have married me if we were lovers so long ago?"

"Yes, I would have. It would not have even been in question. It would have been a fact."

"I would have married you too, Paul. In a friggin' half a microsecond. This Renee gal, sorry, I am probing a bit. What was her full name?"

"Renee Gorman."

My intensity was building. I answered her questions quickly and exactly.

This was no time for bullshit.

Rose nodded and continued, "Thank you. Okay, this Renee Gorman and you had an intense, yet short-lived relationship. I assume you were very passionate lovers and you would have married her in a second too?"

"Yes, we were very passionate, and to be honest, well, I took her virginity. That is a fact, of which given my beliefs and current profession, I am not proud of."

Rose only nodded and quietly answered my forthright admittance with a mumbled, "I see."

"To answer your other question, yes, I would have married her in a second. In a friggin' half a microsecond. Especially, since I was her first lover and deep inside of me, I harbored waves of guilt of being so and for not marrying Renee. No regrets, just guilt. I was madly and hopelessly in love, and I fully intended on marrying her. She was my soul mate."

Rose faintly smiled, I imagined her smile was because of my use of her own words regarding marriage, and then she motioned for my hands, I took them and we held each other's hands for a long time.

Rose asked me while still holding my hands, "Can you have more than one soul mate in this life, Pastor Paul? You just said that Renee was your soul mate. Obviously, Binky is one of your soul mates."

"Yes, and yes! No question that you can. It is a part of life that God plans for and takes great care to allow in our lives. Think of Harry and Sky Blu. Death separated them, but their love simply moved. It does not mean he loves you less, or more, or any other type of measurement of love. Love is love. Sky is his soul mate and Sky is our loss and Heaven's gain. You are Harry's soul mate too. It is part of the plan. Renee is still my soul mate. I have loved her with all my heart and soul and body, just as I did with Binky. I am not ashamed of that because it is a fact."

Rose tightly gripped my hands and asked, "I do not think there will ever be a more honest and forthright man than Paul John Henson is. You are remarkable. Have you ever heard from Renee?"

"Not a word since the day she left. A few years ago, she resurfaced in my heart and mind. It caused me great pain, Binky sensed it but never asked me or inquired as to what the trouble was. I struggled with the memory of Renee, the guilt, the mystery of our love and then after much thought, praying and a reawakening of sorts, I then came to a new understanding of our relationship. Now, Renee is where she needs to be in my life and I hope that I am where I need to be in hers."

"Wow, thank you for sharing this with me. I understand all of these feelings so much better, and understand how complex a man you actually are, Paul. I can see all of your heart and soul now."

"I need to thank you, Rose. This has actually been very

healthy for me to speak about too. Unexpected, but, nonetheless, very healing for my soul. For our souls. Thank you, for always being here. Here, in my life, here, in our lives together."

Rose let go of my one hand and she leaned in closer and with her other hand, she reached up and gently touched the side of my face.

Her voice lowered to a gentle whisper, "Oh Paul, you are wonderful in so many ways. I have said it in the past and will say it until the day I die. Speaking with you and spending time with you is like drinking some type of magic tonic." She dropped her hand from my face and once again took my other hand and we held each other tightly in our clasps.

Next in the line of incredible questions, was the one question that I knew that Rose would ask. I guess this all fell into line somehow.

While still holding my hands, Rose gently asked, "Are we soul mates?"

Yes! I was correct. This was a flood of magnificent outpourings of emotions and reasonable expectations for honest answers. Another honest question asked, and another honest answer deserved.

"Of course, we are. No question that we are and will be until the end of all time."

Now, Rose could no longer hold back the tears and I saw them starting to form in the corners of her wonderful eyes.

She spoke in a gentle whisper, "Yet, we never crossed the line of love and shared our bodies because of the plan. It would not have worked within the plan. It is sad in a roundabout sort of way, but I understand it. None of this would have happened. How amazing it all has been, and you have been in my life. I would not know what my life would have been like without you, dear Paul. I love you."

"I, too, would have been lost without you. I love you too, Rose."

Rose smiled widely. She wiped the tears away, and it seemed as if her spirit brightened quite a bit.

She leaned in and she gently cupped my face in her hands while asking me, "This will be an incredibly bold question to ask you. Sorry, if I catch you on your heels here, but what the hell, I might as well give it a shot. Sorry to ask you this . . . but will you kiss me? Just once, Paul. A real kiss, I mean a lover's kiss. Deep, long, friggin' toe curling and powerful. I need you to kiss me. Just once, it means nothing, or perhaps, it will mean everything, but just once, I have to know what it would have been like."

Her words sent a shudder down my spine and now it was my turn to ponder. It would do no harm. We have shared so much over the years and I imagined in a roundabout way, it would honor what we share and how much we care about each other.

"I am not sure, Rose. You caught me off-guard with that one."

"I guess that I did. Sorry, but truly, Paul, what would it mean? It is just a kiss. I have to know what it is like to really love you—even if it is just once."

"No, Rose, it is not just the kiss that I am thinking of, you are correct, it is simply a kiss. Now, it would honor and seal our love. This is now a very different situation."

"Different? In what way? You mean because of the conversation, which we just shared and the fact that I told you how I love you, always have, and always will and that I desired you years ago, to be my lover. Well, I still desire you. What woman would not fall into your arms and fall in love with you? Shit. You make my loins ache. Sorry, God will forgive me and Harry and Binky will too, but you always have."

I placed my hands on top of my head, pushed all my long hair back and away from my face and exhaled deeply. I needed to think about and control all these wild thoughts that were rushing around in my head.

"Rose! My goodness, you are Harry's widow. Harry! We were brothers, not in blood but in life. This is brutal. And Binky, my goodness! Why is all of this so complicated? Don't you see? If our immense love could have prevented their deaths, then our loved ones would still be with us!"

Rose nodded, she stood up and so did I. She walked over to me and held her arms out. I twisted, turned away from her and resisted.

"Stop, stop, stop!" Rose pleaded with me. She reached out and placed her hands gently upon me and turned me toward her. Her voice lowered, yet retained a command, which I had seldom heard from Rose before, "Listen to me. It is not complicated, Paul. You just told me how you felt about me and that if we were lovers years ago, everything would have changed between us. Well, we can be lovers now. It is simple. Painful, horrible and yet very simple. Binky and Harry are gone. Only because of your incredible honor, do you make it complicated."

Rose looked me straight in the eyes and in all the years of being with her, through joyful times, sad times and times of utter despair, I had never seen her eyes appear the way they did right at this moment. Her eyes filled with love, with hope, with joy, and it caused a rush of feelings to tear me apart. Feelings of conflict, yet feelings that this was so right, so powerful and wonderful. I loved her, not just as a friend, or my relation through our children's marriage, but I truly was deeply in love with her.

Maybe Rose was correct, and we always were in love.

"Doesn't the Bible say something about taking care of your brother's widow?" Rose asked with a pleading refrain.

When I heard her words, I recalled Harry's words on his deathbed.

"Hold her and love her, never let her be lonely, hurt, or sad. Ever."

I knew God spoke to me and without a moment's

hesitation, I took her in my arms, gently held her face in my hands and we shared for the first time in all of our years together, a long and amazing lover's kiss. It was passionate, loin aching and toe curling. It was real. Very, very real.

When we finished kissing, Rose leaned her head on my chest and gently said, "Please, tell me how much you love me. Tell me that I am not going to lose you ever again. That kiss was more glorious than I ever thought it would be. This is no longer about Harry, Binky, or Heaven's gain because it is now about our love here today. A love that has always been."

I smiled, grabbed her by the hand, and pulled Rose along.

"Paul, you did not answer me. Where are we going? Do you love me as I think you do?"

I still did not answer her; instead, I continued to pull her along, opened my office door, shut the lights off in my office and guided Rose out into the main office area. While letting go of her hand, I walked over to Martha's desk and took a pen and scrap pad, scribbled a note and read it aloud as I wrote it, "Hi, Martha. Gone for the rest of the day. If you come back, then I hope you had a nice lunch. I sure as hell did. I will call you tomorrow or whenever, but I will be taking a few days off. Hell, I do not care, take another long, liquid lunch and hang out with Jennifer. Put it all on my tab. Go and purchase a new dress, new shoes, and a new purse. All on me. I will explain. Thank you for you!"

I placed the note on Martha's telephone, tossed the pen down on Martha's desk, and looked up at Rose, who smiled at me and asked, "Days off? New dress? What the hell?"

"Yes, yes, and yes," I said while reaching out for her hand. Rose took it and followed me as we walked out of the office; I shut the lights off and locked the door. Rose was a bit befuddled as I put my arm around her and we started to walk down the hallway.

"Yes, yes, and yes? What the hell are you talking about, Paul?"

"Yes, I love you with all of my heart and yes, I am taking a few days off and yes, what the hell."

"Oh, okay, I think. Not sure, what the hell is going on now. Where are we going? My car is parked in the garage."

"Leave it there. Where are we going? To the place where we should have gone years ago."

Rose stopped short in the hallway, put her hands on her hips and shook her head while telling me, "You are confusing the hell outta me, Paul John Henson. Stop the riddle bullshit. What are you saying?"

I gently reached for her, put both of my hands on her glorious backside and pulled her tightly into my body, and then I once more kissed her deeply.

When we finished kissing, I took her face in my hands and gently told Rose, "First, we are going to a very exclusive and expensive jewelry store to pick out an engagement ring. Then we are going to a very fancy and expensive restaurant that I know of downtown here, where I personally know the owner, the head bartender and the maître d. They will fix me up with the best table in the joint. A table, in a quiet corner. Costs a bloody fortune. Who really cares about money, eh? Love makes you wealthy, not money. There, we will have an incredible meal and lots of red wine, Scotch and other rarities. If you do not mind a marriage proposal from a man in clerical garb, then I will, over candlelight, ask you to marry me. My hope is that you will say, yes. I will leave my jeep with the owner and call a limousine to take us back to my, ah, correction, our townhouse. There, we will have a few more drinks and we will make love like wild baboons and set tonight on fire. During time-outs, I will sit at my desk and type a very long and passionate letter to the Governing

Board of the Lutheran District, giving them three month's notice that I plan to retire. I want to marry you and travel, and we can spend every night making up for a lifetime of lost love. How does that sound?"

Rose did not immediately answer me. Instead, she put her finger to her chin and feigned that she was pondering the proposal and my plans. I smiled, gently pulled her finger away, while she laughed and smiled widely.

She kissed me and then whispered, "Works for me. In fact, we could skip all the other bullshit, the limos, the special table, you know, and just keep the drink part. Yes, it is a very romantic plan. Wonderful, but honestly, after all the years that I have waited to make love to you, we can pass on the other stuff and just skip right to the making love like wild baboons part of this plan. I assure you that even if you proposed to me wearing your hockey goalie equipment and uniform that I will say yes and I will be just fine."

We started to walk down the hallway, Rose stopped, pulled me down to her level and whispered into my ear, "Oh yes, some ground rules. This bullshit has been bugging me for a long time. As far as that hot chick that lives next door to you, I guess now to us, ah, Maggie, tight ass. No more tea, drinks, or random visits from her flirtatious and fraudulent ass. My ass is better than hers is, anyway."

I nodded and whispered back, "Absolutely, and no question that your ass is better. No contest. Way, way better."

"The same goes for Janet, what's her face, up there in Boston. Cuttin' her big-chested bullshit off right now. My boobies are better than hers are and she has a flat ass."

"Yup, I understand, dear Rose. Flat ass Janet and your amazing boobies. Got it all down, we are a'cuttin' da bullshit. . .."

When we with great apprehension and with great care announced our love and intentions to our children, they were thrilled! Surprised the hell out of Rose and me. Our children even confessed that they all realized after Harry and Binky left this world to be in Heaven that they knew that deep down; Rose and I were in love. I guess you reach a certain age in life where your children know more than you do. Oh well, part of the plan! Who knows?

Paul William even came up to me, shook my hand and used one of my own lines, as he told me, "Life is full of twists and turns, eh?"

He was his father's son.

I married the lovely Rose on a glorious October day, full of golden sunshine and captivating autumn colors. We married on this glorious day at a nondenominational service conducted by Pastor James T. O'Malley at Jim's church. Jim commented on how he actually was busier in retirement than he was when he worked! Rose and I did not want to marry at Reunion Lutheran Church; we both agreed there were too many ghosts there.

We had a marvelous honeymoon. We visited Toronto, Ontario, Canada and had a glorious time enjoying the crisp autumn days and cold evenings. Walking hand-in-hand down the main streets of the city, eating glorious meals and sipping wine and cocktails in open-air cafes while listening to live music.

Our love filled the entire world.

I am not ashamed to say that we made love for days and nights on end, some days we never left the hotel room. We enjoyed passionate and incredible lovemaking. Why the hell am I sugarcoating that statement? We had joyful and uninhibited sex for days on end. Together, we made glorious love. We absorbed into each other's bodies. There, I wrote it! It was amazing.

I guess that made up for lost time.

Who knows?

It is around two years or so, after I first started this manuscript, and while I sit here at my desk and I finish this manuscript, I am a different man than when I began this long story. I might finish this manuscript and publish it, or just place it in a file somewhere. I left out many parts, therefore, I or someone else will have to complete it and fill it in.

I do know that because of all of this I am a complete man. That is the most important fact to take from this story. Dear reader, I am renewed, restored, and at peace with it all.

The blur that has been my life, this story, as well as all the others, has slowly ground to a halt now and life has finally slowed down. The newsreel on the projectors has run out of film, and the reels continue to spin, while the film tape slaps along the now empty reels of the projector. I need to flip the switch on the projector to turn it all off in my mind.

The blur is over now.

I shut off the switch.

Yet, this story is just one part of the adventure. All of this life has been a great ride, an adventure of such magnitude that I hope my words over the many books and pages truly capture the emotions of all of it. If the good Lord takes me to Heaven tomorrow, then I have nothing to complain about at all. I have traveled many miles, danced all the dances, loved as hard as I could love, worked as hard as I could work and played the game as fair and as hard as I could play. I have the greatest family and friends that a man could ever have. In our minds, we can always remember the people we love, their faces, their voices, the smiles, the words; it is something that even time cannot diminish.

It has not been an adventure, instead; it has been a

journey.

A journey of love, joy, despair, hope, peace, and most of all, of faith. To God, all the thanks should we give. And I do.

Therefore, dear reader, I will end it here with this chapter, not because I have nothing left to say, or there will not be any more adventures, but because, it is a grand place for me to stop. Perhaps the adventures will continue in some manner, and so be it. Possibly, someone will take up the charge and write on, but for me it is time to rest. I am now a retired pastor and bishop and the only commitments that I have are to my wife, to God, and to my family. I will sit in the soaking tub with my gorgeous wife, sip Scotch and a few Big Boulder beers, (no Dingleberries and by now, you know why) work here and there on some writings if I am so inspired to do so, watch hockey games and relax. Reunion Lutheran Church appointed me Pastor Emeritus, and if they need me, or the preaching bug bites me, then I can stand in the pulpit on occasion. Rose and I will travel and visit amazing places, we will watch and observe glorious sunsets in folding chairs on our deck, and we will sit by a warm fireplace during cold evenings. Together, we will celebrate holidays, watch the children and grandchildren grow up, bless them, and enjoy it all.

It is time. If it makes some type of sense, then dear reader, I have to say that I am tired of being busy; it is time to rest and enjoy my loved ones and life.

Vance and Heather Sarah had a little baby girl, and we all rejoiced when we were blessed with the gorgeous Vivian Rose in our lives. She is our latest grandchild and Vivian Rose is around four years old now, her beauty astounds me, and I often just sit with her, absorb her energy and love into my soul. Vance is such a proud father. His love fills the entire world. The twins are around ten years old now, and they scamper about, wrestle and fight with each other as brothers often do and get into everything! It is wonderful, and amazing, and we are in our glory.

Especially when we can play all day with them and send them back to Blue Cloud and Paul William to take them home.

What a magnificent time in our lives!

Sarah has grown to be quite the young woman and quite the figure skater too. She has won many awards and finished in first place in a number of competitions. I cannot take credit for that, other than taking her to the rink for lessons, and skating with her at public skates. Vance often tags along with me, but the two of us cannot skate even two inches on figure skates! Sarah can skate circles around us and laughs at our feeble efforts to keep up with her.

Then Vance and I change into goalie skates and even the score!

When Rose and I married, we handed off the Redmond mansion to Blue, Paul William, and the twins. The townhouse is perfect for Rose and me. In our three-car garage, we presently only house two vehicles. One is a brand-new jeep with a highly polished jet-black finish, with my GOAL27 license plates for me. The other vehicle is a sports car. It is brand new, with a five-speed transmission, a turbo-charged engine, jet-black exterior with black leather bucket seats and a fold down convertible top. That car is for Rose. Rose sure turns a few heads in that car! She has men half her age flirting with her when she cruises town in that baby. Rightly, so the car is minuscule in attraction compared to the gorgeous beauty of my wife. The car makes me a bit nervous; I always tell her to be careful when she drives.

Sure, do miss my old jeep. I rode it until the floorboards rusted out and the wheels rolled off the bloody thing. Just like the old man when he finally got rid of the 1964 Putter Classic Model 200, I cried my eyes out when they towed my old jeep away to the junk heap.

Rose still ventures out with Heather Sarah, and Blue Cloud for their famous shopping excursions on Saturday mornings. The gals rent a limousine, cruise up and down main drags in the cities, visiting the various shops; they eat lunch at fancy restaurants and sip exclusive wine all day long. Vivian Rose and Sarah tag along, spend Grandpa and Grandma's money, and let me tell you, there were no more beautiful women turning heads than that gang did! The checkbook tells the story.

I couldn't care less! Let's have a grand time and spend the bloody money! I do not care. What does money actually bring to you? There are no golden sunsets to buy on the internet or joy delivered in a tidy package to rest upon your doorstep. In this thing, we call life; it is the simple things that bring you the greatest pleasures.

As the old man used to say, "Life is too short to drink cheap beer."

Oh, how true that is.

I sure do miss my old man.

Perhaps the children will add some more grandchildren to our family and we will rejoice. Who knows? The more kiddies, the merrier! Christmas and Boxing Day are as if there are wild hockey games in our house. In my greatest moments as an inadequate writer, I could never pick the words to describe what I feel when I see all these children running around amongst my feet, laughing, smiling, singing, and dancing with joy. There are no words to describe the love and joy in my heart. Thankfully, I can still move fast enough to chase them around and play with all of them. Have to keep my ass in gear, after all; there are ice skating and hockey lessons for those twin boys now.

Yes, I have to keep that promise to Harry, as well as the other promises. To take care of Rose, to hold her, to love her, to make sure that she is never lonely, hurt or sad, and to tell the stories of old.

I have them all covered my brother.

When our grandchildren are all old enough to understand these stories, if they have not yet read all the many books that I have written, then I will gather them together, maybe on a Boxing Day afternoon, in the midst of one of our grand celebrations. When we are gathered, I will then tell them of the adventures and tell them of the stories of a lifetime. Stories and tales of two special friends, brothers in life, not in blood, but nonetheless, still brothers, who formed a bond forever and the glorious places it took the two of us. I will tell them how, in our own special way, we made the entire world stand still. I will tell them of the people who touched our lives and how we touched people's lives together.

We were and are always together.

However, most of all dear reader, I think that I will gather them together and encourage all of them, the entire family and all of our friends too, to always tell stories.

Yes, indeed, always tell the stories of the old times and stories to help you dream of the new times too.

They will create new adventures of their own, and I have no doubt that they too, as Harry and I did, will travel everywhere and touch many lives. We all do and you just need to stop, laugh, smile, and realize that fact. I will remind them to always love and support each other, in the good times and in the difficult times; you need always to be there for one another.

Above all, they always need to love and to hug each other and stand together no matter what happens. You see, dear reader, love truly conquers all, and it can erase the greatest pain.

Finally, I will remind them, and I will emphatically tell them, that life is one adventure after another, so come along for the ride and see where it all takes us.

And that dear reader is the end of the story.

Dyna'i diwedd.

THE END

Epilogue

It has always been my belief that life is full of circles. There are circles of joy, circles of sorrow, circles of pain, circles of love, circles of hope, faith and peace, and circles of every other human emotion that you can imagine and feel. It does not matter too much what we do at the beginning of each circle, nor what we do at the end. What matters the most is what we do with our life as we travel around the circles, from the beginning to the end. That is what matters the most, because for each life, for each circle, there is always a beginning and an end.

As we travel each circle and trek along on life's journey, we need to live life to the fullest.

Each day, every day.

We need to smile and laugh when we need to smile and to laugh. We need to be happy and kind whenever the world requires some extra happiness and kindness. We need to be firm and powerful when we need to be firm and powerful. We need to cry when we need to cry, mourn when we need to mourn, dance when we need to dance, sing whenever there is a song in our heart that requires singing. We need to love as much as we can, play hard, work hard, touch the lives of and help our loved ones and all of our friends, and give as much of ourselves to this world, and to ourselves as we can.

Otherwise, the journey along the various circles is wasted, it is futile and we only have a beginning and an end.

Dear reader, my advice to you, is the same as my grandfather's advice was to me so long ago. Always to keep a positive attitude despite adversity and obstacles, it is the most important frame of mind that a person can have. Always recognize and then unite yourself with others who think and act the same as you do. Choose and pick people who are similar to you, and then together, you will enjoy a wonderful journey around your circles.

Once you have a circle of support, combined with the correct frame of mind, as well as loving friends and family, you will have all the power that you need to succeed at anything in life. Then you and your loved ones and friends can charge off into life's battles with your battle flags unfurled, ready to take on anything that this old world can throw at you.

Dear reader, while you make your own journeys amongst your own circles of life, always take the time to stop and admire the sunrises and sunsets, and at night, stop and look up into the stars, because the stars allow us just enough light to afford a peek at the glories of Heaven and beyond.

I stood on our deck, looked into the western sky, and admired a glorious sunset. This day was now fading and soon, the stars would appear and allow us to see all of those glories. The sky was full of gold, some yellow and long streaks of red along the horizon. It was a magnificent testimony to God's grand creation.

I heard the slider door open and without even turning around; I felt the love of my dear wife. She wrapped her arms around me and tucked her head on my back.

I heard her soft voice ask me, "What are you doing and thinking, Paul?"

"Oh, just admiring all of it."

"The sunset?"

"No, all of it. All of life. All that we have. All we shared and all that God gave to us—all it means—and how finally,

I no longer have those ghosts floating in and around me. I have memories, but those ghosts are finally gone. I no longer see them or hear the whispers of the stories of old."

"Gotcha."

"Rose, in looking back on it, I think that perhaps, for all of this time, I was wrong. They were not ghosts haunting me. They might have been the whispers of angels. Angels that guided me for all of these years. Why? I do not know why, or when, they arrived in my life, but now I feel as if their work with me is finished. The mission is complete and they no longer are present in my life. Who knows? I have come to believe most anything and doubt nothing."

"I love that theory. It is not as creepy as ghosts are and there is no doubt that Heaven guides you."

Rose turned to catch a glimpse of Heaven from the sunset, and then she smiled. It was as if the glimpse of Heaven gave her the power that she required to finish her thoughts.

"My love, my dear Paul, please, let me ask you? Did these angels cry when we cried? Did they laugh whenever we laughed? Did they love when we loved and walk with us and guide all of us, no matter what we faced? Did they stand next to us during lonely nights, when we were so lonely, afraid and helpless? Did they help us to wipe away our tears as we stood next to the graves of our loved ones? Most of all, did they dance with us at all of our joyous celebrations?"

"Of course, Rose. Of course, they did."

"Then, I wholeheartedly agree with you. They were angels. Furthermore, I think you are correct, Paul, in the fact that I think the angels are now gone, because you have now recorded all the adventures. It is so much more than just words that you have written, in many ways, it is your very being and your essence that you have shared on those pages. Yes, I think that you have written it all down, purged your soul of the words and memories, and the angels no longer need to speak to you. The stories are now all told. Perhaps, it is now time for others to tell them."

"Rose, I think you are correct."

I spun around and warmly embraced her as she buried her head into my chest and asked me, "What else?"

"Oh, just before I kiss you, I need to tell you, rwy'n dy garu di, wastad ac am byth."

Rose smiled, and just before we kissed, she whispered, "I love you too and I will love you forever, Paul John Henson, but I have to tell you that you are still such a damn old lady. An old, hopeless romantic, out here on this deck, a fantastic sunset in front of us, wooing me and still after all of these years, making my knees go weak. Please, I will have a few glasses of red wine, bring a little Scotch for you, and I promise that we will make love for all the rest of tonight. You never change and I love you with all of my heart and soul. But, damn, you are such an old lady. Yes, you are."

"I have been told that a few times before by a very special person and I was hoping that I could hear it a few times more."

Rose laughed, and I could feel her joy fill my heart and my soul. Her joy reached onward and skyward, her laugh. It reached all the way into Heaven, where a group of saints laughed along with us.

We kissed and held onto each other with that glorious sunset as a backdrop, and we held onto each other until the stars appeared above our heads in the evening sky. If you looked closely into the evening sky, you could see all the way to Heaven and just a little beyond.

In the backyard of the old house located at 20 John Street, it seemed as if this particular sunset brought with it some glorious rays of the last remnants of a sunset. As the colors glowed softly, and the night arrived, there were soft whispers in the air as the fading rays of sunlight glowed everywhere.

It seemed as if the whispers said, "The night always comes, yes it does. The night always comes."

The whispers continued to float everywhere as the rays of sunlight chased into the corners of the backyard of the old house. If you listened carefully to the whispers, as the murmurs seemed to dance in the air, you could hear that they all told stories. Stories told upon a backdrop of strumming harps while the whispers told their glorious tales in the air.

When the stories ended, if you stood in the center of the backyard, you could clearly hear laughter, loud, uproarious laughter, and then you could hear one of the whispers relate the words of the immortal Ronzo Boatmann, "Ain't this life great?"

"Yes, it is," was the answer heard.

Another voice clearly said, "It certainly is."

The sunrays left and the breeze of the early evening carried the whispers away. There is always a special wind right before and right after the sunset. It is very, very special.

The whispers gradually faded, and they disappeared into a gentle evening breeze, but tomorrow night on the sunset breeze they will return once again, because the night always comes.

Yes, indeed, in this glorious life and world, the night always comes.

ABOUT THE AUTHOR

If you ask Paul John Hausleben, he will tell you that he is not an author, he is just a storyteller. His mission is to continue to write and tell stories to warm your heart, make you laugh, and sometimes make you cry, just a little. Most of all, he deals in memories, and helps you to remember the good times of your own life, and the special people who touched you along the way. Paul was born and raised in Paterson, and then nearby Haledon, New Jersey, and began writing at an early age. He revisited a writing career later in his life, and he now is the author of a number of novels, compilations, short stories and audio and video works. Most of his work, touches upon nostalgic remembrances of simpler times, and tells the stories of heartfelt, humorous, and special human relationships. Other than writing, among many careers both paid and unpaid, he is a former semi-professional hockey goaltender, a music fan and music reviewer, an avid sports fan, photographer and amateur radio operator. He now resides in Somewhere, U.S.A., but his heart always remains along Belmont Avenue in good old Paterson, and Haledon, New Jersey.

Other Adventures of Harry and Paul and work by Mr. Hausleben that you will enjoy:

The Time Bomb in The Cupboard and Other Adventures of Harry and Paul

The Night Always Comes, Another story from the Adventures of Harry and Paul

Reunion, A sequel to the Night Always Comes and Another story from the Adventures of Harry and Paul

The Miracle Tree, Another story from the Adventures of Harry and Paul

Geyer Street Gardens
Beneath the Mask of a hockey Goaltender
Another Story from the Adventures of Harry and Paul

Where the River Bends and Curls

Crows on a High Wire

O'Malley

And there are a few others too!

Coming soon?

You may write to the author at ctte27@gmail.com

Published by God Bless the Keg Publishing
Somewhere, U.S.A.

You may write to the publisher at
Godblessthekegpublishing@gmail.com

"Life's simple pleasures are so often the best ones!"

www.ingramcontent.com/pod-product-compliance
Lightning Source LLC
LaVergne TN
LVHW020653110826
845149LV00012B/1977

9780990697954